The ATTIC

RACHEL XU

BEKAH FERGUSON

An *Original* Publication of Rock of Ages Publishing House, a division of Prodigy Digital Solutions – prodigydigital.com

Cover artwork by Rachel Xu. Used with permission.

Designed and formatted by Robbie Ferguson.

ISBN: 978-0-9782047-9-2

First self-published printing October, 2014.

Please visit the author's web site at
www.bekahferguson.com

10 9 8 7 6 5 4 3 2

ROCK OF AGES PUBLISHING HOUSE
A Division of Prodigy Digital Solutions
Barrie, Ontario Canada

Lily approached the portrait of her grandfather and stood studying it once more.

The bottom right-hand corner of the molded frame caught her eye this time. It was shinier than the rest of it, as though the dust had been rubbed off by a finger. Or was it just the way the sunlight was hitting it; a trick of the eye?

Heartbeat picking up a notch, she reached up and touched her fingertips to the shiny edge of the frame—pressing into it. A swish sounded and cold air moved over her right side. She pivoted toward the draft.

A tall opening had appeared in the wall, a twisted stairwell beyond it.

Heart beating wildly now, she stepped toward the unlit room.

Prologue

Auguste Kline struggled to turn the key in the lock, willing his gnarled fingers to cooperate.

The room was dark, save for a checkered stream of moonlight coming in from a lattice window.

He couldn't see the lock in the trunk before him—could only feel it—but a satisfying click assured him the deed was done. An exhale escaped his aching lungs and he wiped his damp brow with the back of his hand; shifting his weight off his bad leg as he straightened up from his knees to a standing position.

Noting only the vague outlines of what he knew to be stacked crates, boxes and long-forgotten furniture, Auguste tightened the grip on his cane and shuffled across the wooden floorboards—using his outstretched free hand to seek out the door. When he reached it, he paused. Listened for any sound.

Aside from his own rasping lungs, all was still and silent. Not even a mouse stirred within the walls.

But he was not alone.

With a low grunt, the old man shifted his bones into motion and reached for the doorknob. His gut churned.

There was a presence nearby.

Behind him.

The hairs on the back of his neck bristled like a startled porcupine and he spun around, nearly dropping his cane and falling. He pressed his full weight into the cane for balance and managed to still his knocking knees, straining to see through the darkness before him. "Who-who's there?" he asked.

There was neither response nor shifting shadow.

Had he imagined the presence then? It must have been the fear clouding his senses. He turned around, the sole of his cane thumping on the floor beneath him, and turned the cold knob, pushing the door forward. He squinted as he entered the dark stairwell beyond. Another lattice window above the descending stairs lit an area of the floor with more checkered moonlight.

A footfall sounded from within the room behind him.

His heart slammed against his ribs, pounding out of control. For a moment he was too terrified to move and his cane slid from his icy finger tips, hitting the floor with a thwack.

Silence screamed in his ears and chills tripped up and down his back, along with a frantic need to flee. He scrambled toward the staircase, nearly tripping over his abandoned cane in his haste, and latched onto the primitive wood railing, teetering on every step as his bad leg buckled with the movement.

He made it down a half-dozen steps, not daring to look behind him, when an upper stair creaked —suggesting a heavy weight. Lurching forward, he gasped for breath and wished he could dive down the rest of the stairwell.

Only a handful of stairs remained and with every ounce of remaining strength, he tore down them, doubling over when he reached the bottom as though he'd been punched in the gut. His heart constricted violently in his chest and a cry slipped from his lips.

Senses whirling, he stumbled toward the closed wall panel that lead to the hallway, expecting to be grabbed from behind with every step. But there came no more sound on the stairs—only his own shoes scuffing the floorboards. Smacking his fist against the wall, the door panel slid open with a swish and he dove through, falling to the floor in a wheezing heap.

Too weak and palsied to get back up on his feet, he dragged himself by his forearms down the long dark hallway, knowing his flight was futile but unwilling to surrender. His heart surged with another wave of pain and he knew his time was running out. Pausing to catch his breath, he fumbled through his jacket pocket and pulled out an elongated key. He cricked his neck and shot a glance over his shoulder at the shadowed opening in the wall.

All was still, unmoving.

He hid the key where he was sure no one would find it and collapsed on his stomach . . . arms and legs growing cold, then numb. Sucking in as much air as possible, he rolled onto his back with a grunt and tried to lean on one elbow, watching the opening in the wall. He was too weak to move any further.

A footfall sounded, ever-so-faintly, from within the black square that was the opening in the wall.

At the opposite end of the hallway, two floor-to-ceiling windows permitted twin beams of sallow moonlight, which flowed over the old man as he balanced on one elbow, clutching his heart.

A tall figure emerged from the opening but did not step into the beams of light.

"What do you want from me," Auguste cried, his voice barely a whisper.

A roaring silence.

"Your life," came the low, toneless response.

In a swift, calculated movement, the shadowed figure stepped into the moonlight and the old man's throat closed in horror. Paralyzing pain shot through his right arm and his heart gave its last beat.

With one final cry, his elbow gave out and he fell backward, head thudding against the hardwood beneath him.

Chapter 1

Lily Kline cut the ignition of her Ford sedan and pulled down the visor, tugging her fingers though her wind-tousled hair and squinting at her reflection in the mirror. Frowning, she dug through her purse and pulled out a comb, running it through her latte-brown hair. It settled about her shoulders. Satisfied with the result, she ran a mauve lipstick over her lips and flipped up the visor.

With her purse over her shoulder, she stepped out of the car and smoothed out the slight creases in her sage-green dress. It hugged her hips and tapered at the knees; sophisticated but casual all the same. It was also a warm outfit, thankfully, as the autumn air was cool.

Lily glanced at her green high-heels and flesh-toned pantyhose, checking for even the slightest run; and finding everything intact, felt presentable enough to meet her fellow joint heir for the first time.

Having been raised by a single mother, she knew of only a handful of relatives; some aunts and uncles on her birth father's side. Otherwise, she'd always been told that her mother was an orphan.

Until a week ago, that is.

A prestigious law firm had contacted Lily to

inform her that her maternal grandfather had passed away and left her half his fortune and joint-ownership of his estate.

In the frenzied, hazy week of preparations that followed, Lily had wondered time and time again why her grandfather had never sought her out while he still lived. He obviously knew she existed or he wouldn't have bequeathed his wealth to her. And if her grandfather was so wealthy, why had her birth mother lived in borderline poverty? The only conclusion she could draw was that father and daughter had been estranged. Either her mother had been banished —or had run away.

Lily fluffed her hair a little with both hands, which failed to add bounce, and lifted her chin with feigned confidence. She marched up the walkway; high heels clicking on the slabbed-stone as she went. The path lead from the gated half-circle driveway to a deep-set and sequestered Gothic mansion. She inhaled the crisp fall air deeply, admiring the various chimneys and turrets protruding above the surrounding treetops.

Before ascending the front steps to the three-story mansion, she paused to gaze upward at an azure sky, giving a sweeping glance behind her as well. An acre-sized front lawn separated the estate from the tall wrought-iron gates and a row of mature willows that lined the road. Dense forestland surrounded the back and sides of the estate. The grass was neatly trimmed, leaf-blown and well-kept, and chrysanthemums of yellow and burgundy lined the foundation of the mansion and various stone walkways. The nearest neighbor was a good four miles away and as the lawyers had explained, the property was nearly 500 acres deep and mostly forest and wet-land.

Her grandfather had clearly lived an extremely secluded life.

A hermit in a palace.

Vines covered in russet leaves crawled up and across the stone walls like a human nervous system; groups of symmetrical, leaded-glass lancet windows breaking their pathways at regular intervals.

Lily's breath caught with awe and admiration as she ascended the dozen or so stone steps leading up to the front entrance. When she reached the top, she stood warmed by the sunlight and examined a petal-shaped quatrefoil window encased in the arch-way above two heavy-duty oak doors.

On each side of the doors, a white marble creature sat on-guard atop a stone pedestal. They each had muscular bulldog bodies and fierce faces framed with the knotted curls of a lion's mane; razor-toothed mouths opened in gaping snarls. The marble was in sharp contrast to the prevalent stone work and she decided right away that they were out of place; as though added rather recently. Perhaps her grandfather had installed them. They didn't look as ancient or weathered as the rest of the medieval architecture.

Lily reached into her purse and pulled out a folded sheet of paper, re-reading the name she had written on it.

Ian Hawke.

He was to be her co-heir, and though she had

met with her grandfather's lawyers several times over the past week, she hadn't yet met Mr. Hawke. It was unknown of what relation he was to her; perhaps he would turn out to be a long lost uncle or cousin.

She took a deep breath to steady her nerves and lifted one of a pair of cast iron, lion head door pullers—thumping the door thrice. She twisted the folded paper around in her hands, waiting for a response. She hoped Ian wouldn't mind her being here, whoever he was; especially considering she'd decided to move in right away. How many times had she pinched herself over the past week wondering when she was going to wake up from this crazy dream?

Footsteps echoed in approach behind the door and Lily slipped the paper back into her purse, tucking her hair behind her ears and moistening her lips. She plastered a friendly smile on her face just as one of the giant doors swung open.

A buxom old woman stood in its frame, her face neutral and whitish hair plaited and hanging over one shoulder.

"Hi, I'm—" Lily pursed her lips, hesitating. "I'm here to see Mr. Hawke?"

A warm smile spread across the woman's features, lighting up her milky blue eyes. "Ah yes, of course—you must be Miss Kline!"

Lily smiled, nodding, relieved to be expected. "Yes. And are you Mrs. Hawke?"

"Oh, goodness, no—" She laughed. "I'm his housekeeper. Hannah Gray. You can call me Hannah." She motioned for Lily to step inside. "Please come in."

"It's nice to meet you, Hannah," she said, reaching out to shake the housekeeper's hand. She was met with a firm grip.

"Now, Ian's around here somewhere," Hannah said, breaking the hand clasp and leading Lily over the threshold like a small child, "but I can't say where for sure." She squared her shoulders and adjusted the straps of her apron as she glanced down the ribbed-vault corridor beyond them. Lily stepped over the threshold and onto a Persian rug, pulling the door closed behind her.

"It's hard to keep tabs on that man." She rubbed her hands together thoughtfully, chuckling.

"Perhaps we could search for him together?" Lily suggested, smoothing imaginary creases from her dress and glancing up at an ancient iron chandelier that was strung by a black chain. It suffused the entranceway with a yellow overture. Another matching chandelier hung some twenty feet farther down the vaulted corridor, then another, and another—each lighting the hallway in domed segments. The end of the corridor was far off and cavernous.

"Well, there's no rush, is there? I would think you'd like to unpack first and get yourself settled in, right?—before dealing with the dreary business end of things?" She pressed her lips together in a motherly smile, waiting for a response.

Lily nodded. "Yes, that might be a good idea. If you'd be so kind as to show me to my room, I'll carry my bags up myself. I haven't too much with me today."

"Oh, please don't trouble yourself. I'll get Mike to carry them up for you. Where are your things anyway—in the trunk of your car, I suppose?"

Lily nodded again, distracted. "Mike? Does he work here too?" She blushed. "Oh, I'm sorry—I shouldn't make assumptions like that. Is Mike Mr. Hawke's son?"

"Oh, heavens no! How curious. No, he's the handyman 'round here." An amused look. "And I'm sure he'll be more than happy to lend a hand to such a pretty young lady."

Lily blushed again and let her gaze return to the vaulted corridor of ornate wood work; hungrily taking in the recessed niches in the walls, each hosting porcelain vases and extravagant oil paintings. Occasional arched doorways lead into unknown rooms, and the floor was black marble with white veins and capillaries. It would take weeks, if not months, of careful study to see this place inside and out.

Excitement bubbled within her like a kindled flame. Was this spectacular place really, truly hers? It seemed too incredible to be true. She blinked to clear her thoughts. It was all so extraordinary—like standing in a royal museum and being told it was *yours*.

Hannah moved past Lily toward a hardwood staircase to the right of the entrance doors. Four steps ascended to a square landing. From there the staircase ascended along the wall to the passages above. Lily fell into step behind the housekeeper, eager to examine the hand-carved intricacies of the balustrade and baluster posts. At the base of the staircase, two four-foot-tall carved knights stood guard as newel posts, each holding a warrior's battle axe. Though the balustrades were glossy and polished, the finish was wearing thin on the steps; likely from generations of tread.

"Does Mike live here?" she asked.

Hannah stopped on the landing and glanced over her shoulder as she reached for the railing and put her foot on the next step. "Yes, but there aren't too many of us, in case you're wondering." She continued her climb up the creaky stairs. "There's Mike, myself, Angie the cook, Christopher the gardener, and of course, Ian. . . . Now Auguste, your grandfather—well, he enjoyed his privacy. Never had a lot of full-time staff. Pretty much hired contractors instead." She disappeared above and Lily hurried to catch up.

"When he died," Hannah's voice went on from above, "Ian took over the care of the estate."

Lily scaled the last handful of steps to the second floor.

"Most of us have lived here our whole lives," the housekeeper was saying, her footsteps echoing on hardwood flooring.

"Is Ian my relative?" Lily asked, breathless as she emerged onto the second floor. Hannah was standing a few feet away in a wide hallway flanked by oak doors. The walls were made of stone and draped with Gobelin tapestries. Lighted mica-bronze sconces were mounted on either side of each door, so archaic Lily figured they'd only been wired for electricity sometime in the past century; prior to which candlesticks would have sat in place of the light bulbs.

Hannah pulled a keychain from an apron pocket and unlocked the first door on the right. She removed the key from the chain and handed it to Lily. "No," she said simply. "Ian is most certainly not your blood relative."

"The lawyer's told me nothing about him—I don't even know why he's my co-heir."

Hannah paused, setting her hand on the door-knob and meeting Lily's gaze with a thoughtful expression. "Well, he *was* adopted in a way, by Auguste, though never officially. He took him in as a young child—needed a home. So, no, you're not related." She slipped out of sight into the room.

Lily hurried after her. "He took him in—like, a foster child?"

"Have a look around, Lily, get yourself com-fortable." Hannah spoke in a breezy tone, ignoring the question. Or hadn't she heard it? "I'll go fetch Michael for you."

"Was Ian Hawke a foster child? I don't fol-low."

She met Lily's eyes for a brief second and moved toward the open doorway. "We'll have to talk about it later, if that's all right. You wait here and Mike will join you shortly."

With a nod, Hannah left the room, her foot-steps fading away down the staircase.

Lily moved out into the hallway again. She still had no idea who Ian was or how old he was or what to expect. Was he a bachelor or did he have a family?

At the end of the long hallway was a set of

floor-to-ceiling lancet windows overlooking the back property and bright with sunlight. At the other end, mounted on the wall above the staircase, was an oil painting portrait. It was of a man she presumed to be her late grandfather: sombre with a hoary beard, spectacles, and receding hairline.

Deciding to examine the painting in greater detail later, she went back inside her room and let out an exclamation of wonder as she drank in the contents; contents she'd failed to notice just moments prior, having been so distracted by Hannah's vague explanation of Ian.

To her right was a mahogany chest of drawers with a pattern of unicorns inlaying its surface. Against the right-side wall was a queen bed with a mahogany headboard also hand-carved with intertwining mythical creatures; its four tapered posts nearly grazing the wood-paneled ceiling. On either side of the bed was a tall window with crimson drapery. The left side of the rectangular room was a sitting area with a marble fireplace topped by a gilded mirror. And the fireplace was surrounded by two Victorian settees upholstered with golden damask. Lily crossed the room to one of them, bending to admire the pattern carved into the crest rail. A Persian rug filled the expanse beneath an inlaid coffee table and the two settees. Above, hung a brass and iron chandelier with electric candles.

Every way she turned was a feast for the eyes, from a stuffed peacock staged on a perch, to tin-glazed ceramics filled with blossoming flowers, and Cordoba-leather walls.

"Ms. Kline?"

Fairly jumping in surprise, Lily spun around to face the owner of the smooth, masculine voice which had spoken her name.

A man with mocha hair leaned against the open door frame, his arms crossed over his chest and biceps straining against the long sleeves of his cotton shirt. She gathered he was in his late-twenties or early thirties, heartbeat picking up a notch as she took in his mild brown eyes and the grin tugging at his mouth.

Realizing she was gaping, she threw on a smile, and approached, extending her hand. "Yes, I'm Lily Kline. Are you Mike?"

He nodded, meeting her eyes keenly and straightening up. "Hannah sent me up here, said you needed my help." An easy smile spread across his handsome face.

"Yes. She said you would help me carry up my bags—though I haven't many and I can certainly carry them up myself." She smiled again.

"No problem. Happy to help. Let's say we get started."

She nodded. "Well, like I said, there isn't much—just two suitcases."

"Not planning to stay long?" He backed into the hallway, stuffing his thumbs through his belt loops as he waited for her to join him.

She blushed. "Actually, I'm—moving in. Didn't figure I'd need to bring along any furniture, you know?" She let out a nervous laugh.

A look of pleasure lit his face. "Here to stay then. Excellent! Well, all right—lead the way to your vehicle, madame. I am at your service."

Less than ten minutes later, they had returned to Lily's room and Mike set both the suitcases down at the foot of her bed.

"Do you live here too?" she asked.

He hooked his thumbs through his belt loops again, nodding. "Yeah. For about five years now."

"Then you must know so much about this place! Do you think you could take me for a tour?"

Maybe Mike could tell her all about her grandfather as well. She knew next to nothing.

He grinned. "I'd love to. Wish I could right now but I'm in the middle of a project I need to finish up before dinner. I can show you around after dinner though, if you don't mind waiting."

"That would be really nice." She smiled. "Thank you."

He made his way toward the door and Lily followed after him, blurting out the question still rolling about in her mind. "Hey, Mike—" He paused on the threshold and turned, meeting her gaze with a look of intrigue. "Hannah said something unusual about Ian Hawke," she went on. "Said he was taken in as a child but never adopted. Was he a foster child? I haven't met him yet and actually don't know a thing about him."

Mike rubbed his smooth chin and knit his brow. He seemed uncertain. "I think you'd be better to ask Ian that question . . . "

She frowned. "All I know is that he's my joint heir, yet he's not a relative."

"Well, your guess is as good as mine on that front. He's no more than a couple years older than yourself."

Only a couple years older?

A brand new image materialized in her mind's eye, vanquishing the old. Up until now, she'd been picturing a middle-aged man.

"Do you know where he is right now?" she asked. "The housekeeper, Hannah, wasn't sure."

Mike moved out into the hallway. "He might be in his workshop. It's out back in the woods. But I'd wait till dinner to meet him if I were you. I don't think you should be heading out into the woods alone, even if it is the middle of the day." The corner of his mouth dipped into a frown and he looked away—resuming his course for the staircase.

She nearly laughed aloud. What was there to be afraid of in the backyard of a gated estate? Bears? She was used to braving the lamp-lit streets of a dangerous metropolitan city night after night, year after year: a quiet country forest seemed like a walk in the park.

"I think I can take care of myself," she said with a warm chuckle as he glanced over his shoulder. "Just point me in the right direction and I'll head over there now. I'm eager to meet Mr. Hawke."

He seemed reluctant but nodded, and she followed him down the staircase to the main floor.

Chapter 2

Mike led Lily out the front entrance doors, having no time to show her some of the more direct exits just now. He decided he would simply lead her around the building to the backyard and let her be on her own from there. He didn't want to get involved.

And why had Hannah mentioned Ian's childhood anyway?

Ian wasn't going to be pleased about that. They'd never talked about it together but Mike knew a fair bit about it; at least what he'd put together as an explanation from the snatched bits and pieces of story he'd overhead Hannah and Christopher discussing from time to time over the years. What he knew for sure was that Ian refused to discuss it whenever he brought it up; and if Ian wanted his original arrival to this mansion kept a secret, then Mike wasn't about to be the one to blab the details to this Lily Kline.

She was on her own.

When they reached the backyard, Lily thanked Mike again for his help with her luggage, and they parted ways.

An elderly man was crossing the far backyard with a pair of pruning sheers in his hand. She figured he must be Christopher, the gardener. He didn't look her way and she didn't bother to call out to him. There'd be plenty of time to get to know one another in the days ahead.

The backyard and its gardens were as meticulously kept as the ones in front, and like the front, the greensward back here was at least an acre in square footage.

In the center of the back lot was a courtyard surrounded by rosebushes and hosting a beautiful fountain statue—a life-size woman carved out of marble, hair flowing in waves around her body and her garments like liquid silk. She held a jug in her hand, pouring rivulets of water into the pond submerging her feet.

Lily approached the fountain and peered into the translucent water surrounding it. Koi fish glided beneath teacup lily pads. But though the statue was fascinating, Lily was eager to find Ian Hawke, and she left the courtyard to be inspected later on, heading across the remaining expanse of greensward toward the looming forest. Behind her, the Gothic mansion was open to full view. It was going to be so fascinating to explore all those inner rooms, corridors and turrets; to be able to look up at those vine-shrouded lancet windows and actually know what lay behind their leaded glass. For now she could only guess.

Lily turned her gaze back to the forest. There was no sight of any work shed though. Beyond the trees was nothing but darkness—the foliage so thick that sunlight failed to penetrate their depths. She scanned the tree line, squinting, and stopped short at the sight of a gloomy statue dappled by sun and nearly hidden from view where it sat between two elm trees. It was too short to be human but didn't appear to be a child or an animal either. Pulse quickening in anticipation, she set across the sunny half acre of grass ahead and soon reached it.

The statue was an ebony gargoyle, dull with age. The beast—a chimera—was in mid-roar, red jewels embedded in its eye sockets. An outstretched paw held a smooth white orb.

It was then she noticed the well-worn pathway next to it, leading into the forest.

Squinting to see into the tree-shaded darkness, she realized the dirt path was lined with more gargoyle statues, of all shapes and sizes. They each encased a white orb in an outstretched hand. Like a row of unlit lamp stands.

She entered the forest.

As she passed the first gargoyle chimera, the orb in its paw lit up brightly. And like Dominoes, the rest of the globes lining the pathway switched on in quick succession, casting a pallor across the savage faces of the chimeras and lighting the dirt pathway between them. She gasped and raised a hand to her throat in delight, figuring motion detectors had set them off.

With a little laugh, she followed the pathway an additional twenty feet into the woods where it curved to the right; trees and undergrowth closing in around it. She stopped walking, considering. Despite the faintly-lit orbs, the trail ahead was dark and narrow with little sunlight penetrating the canopy above. The earth smelled damp, like wet moss and animal droppings. She vacillated between turning back or going deeper into the forest. Was this even the route to Ian's shed or was it located somewhere else?

She walked a little further and glanced behind. The greensward was no longer in sight, swallowed up by the foliage. It was like walking through the woods at dusk rather than midday. Surely it was her imagination, but the gargoyles and their glowing orbs seemed to be tightening up—the space between each one lessening. She had passed at least twenty of them by now.

Heartbeat picking up a notch, she increased her pace, rounding another sharp bend in the path; this time to the left. Straight ahead some fifty feet, beams of incandescent light permeated the gaps in the lower tree boughs and leaves, suggesting a lighted building was beyond them. She let out an exhale and smiled. It must be Ian's work shed.

Lily's pulse had just begun to slow when something grabbed her foot.

Unable to catch her balance, she let out a cry and tumbled to the ground, losing a shoe, and scuffing her palms.

She whipped onto her back, heart racing, fully expecting to see a ferocious bear.

But there was nothing.

Only a gnarled root hooked over the tip of her dress shoe.

Relief washed over her as she retrieved her shoe and stood up, frowning at a tear in her nylons. She rubbed the dirt from her palms, squared her shoulders, and started toward the shed again. Tear or no tear, she was determined to find Ian.

She stopped short and blinked.

A tall figure was standing nearby in the shadows of a pitch pine, his profile blotting out some of the light from the presumed shed.

A chill surged up her spine and she spun around, intending to run.

"Wait—" a voice called out.

She hesitated, wobbling on her high heels.

He jogged toward her, closing the gap between them.

"Who are you?" she squeaked, arms outstretched to catch her balance. Was it too late to run?

"Name's Ian," he said, reaching her.

Her legs nearly gave way beneath her and she laughed, letting out a long exhale. "Oh, for Pete's sake," she said, lifting a hand to her heart and tucking a strand of hair behind her ear, laughing some more. "You scared the daylights out of me."

"I'm sorry," he said flatly, crossing his arms over his chest. She squinted to see his facial features in the shadows but was unable to see his eyes, only the contours.

"I saw you fall a moment ago and wanted to make sure you were okay," he went on, his voice a subdued tenor. "Didn't mean to scare you. Are you all right?"

"Oh, I'm fine. Just a few little scrapes and

bruises. Nothing I can't handle." She smoothed her skirt, hoping he wouldn't think her a silly ninny. She'd worked hard to present herself as a confident, independent woman—and his first sight of her had been the face-plant over the tree root.

"What are you doing out here alone?" he asked. "There are wolves."

"Wolves?" She couldn't suppress a smirk. Was he for real? "I was looking for *you*, actually." She smiled. Best to get to the point—draw attention off herself and onto him. She disliked being scrutinized. "I was told you might be in your work shed."

"I'm sorry, but—*who* are you?"

"I'm Lily Kline."

"Oh—" He seemed surprised, though she couldn't read his expression. They might as well have been standing in a cave.

"You're here already," he said. "I thought it would be a few more weeks—" He uncrossed his arms and then crossed them again.

How could he not know she was coming? Hadn't the lawyers arranged all that? Heat prickled her cheeks. She should have contacted Ian herself; at least called ahead. Why had she assumed they'd be expecting her?

"So, when did you get here?" he asked, dropping his arms to his sides. "Are you here for a visit or —?"

"Actually, I . . . I'm here to stay. You didn't know? I thought the lawyers—!"

"Didn't know what? That we're joint-heirs?" His voice tightened. "Of course I know. But I assumed you'd want to sell and split the profits. Don't you have a house and family of your own?"

"I have no family," she said frankly. "My mother died years ago."

A handful of seconds passed, neither of them speaking.

She shifted her position, trying to think of what to say next. Standing in a dim forest with a strange man who stood at least a foot taller than she, was not the conventional meet and greet she'd envisaged.

"So . . . why was it you were looking for me?" he finally asked.

It was not the response she'd expected; she was going to have to spell it out for him.

"Oh, I don't know," she said, trying to subdue the sarcasm in her voice, "because we're going to be sharing the same house? because we've never met before?" She didn't want to sound rude but his lack of interest and curiosity in meeting her was bizarre; and downright offensive, if she was honest.

He said nothing.

Just stood there, eyes nothing more than two black patches on his shadowed face.

"I'm dying to know who you are," she said, growing jittery and cold but trying to sound friendly. She rubbed an arm. "How um, did you know my grandfather?"

"Yes, of course you'd want to know those things," he said brusquely, with resignation. "All legitimate questions. But I think we should leave the forest first. It's safer if we get you back inside. The forest gets dark . . . quickly."

She let out a laugh. "News flash, Mr. Hawke—it's already dark. Is that your work shed back there?" she asked, pointing past him.

"Yes," he said, "but you can't just come out here anytime you want looking for me." He took her elbow gently and turned her whole body, guiding her back down the gargoyle-lit trail—rather than toward the shed.

What was the deal with these men? The handyman had also suggested she shouldn't be out here by herself. It was disparaging, to say the least.

"Fine, I'll bring someone with me next time," she said, pulling her arm from his grasp. She strode ahead of him with brisk steps, eying the path for roots. He followed behind with a slower gait, footsteps crunching on twigs and dry leaves.

The greensward appeared up ahead beyond the gap in the trees and she emerged from the trail, squinting in the bright sunlight. When her eyes had adjusted, she turned around to face Ian Hawke.

Standing next to the ebony gargoyle was an athletic man wearing jeans and a dark zip-up sweater. His eyes were like black coffee, dark hair short on the sides and spiked on top. His gaze was calm but unreadable. She gaped at him for the half second it took to compose herself. There was a wild look about him that made her mouth go dry.

"How long have you lived here?" she asked, swallowing, blatantly aware of the rip in her nylons and the smudge of dirt on both palms. She shifted her weight to one foot and placed a hand on her hip to look confident.

He walked by her and started across the greensward, motioning for her to follow him with a little wave of his hand.

"I came here when I was eleven," he said as she fell into step beside him and hurried to keep up. "So that would be twenty-one years now." He glanced up at the blue sky and then down at her.

She decided to be candid. "Your housekeeper, Hannah—she said you were . . . unofficially adopted?"

He quickened his pace, frowned. "She said that? Well—there you have it then. You know my life story."

"Um, would you mind elaborating on it?"

"Yes."

An awkward silence fell between them as they made their way back to the estate and entered through a back door which happened to be at the far end of the vaulted corridor. At the front end of the long hall, sunlight streamed through the quatrefoil window above the oak doors, making a flower-shaped image on the Persian rug.

Ian's demeanor was stiff despite his agile form. He seemed angry or annoyed or self-conscious —or *something*. She couldn't decide.

He stopped beside a portal leading into a library and stuck his hands on his hips, staring down at her like a stern father. She wished she'd been more delicate in her questioning about his childhood (evidently it was a touchy subject), but it was too late now.

"So . . . " she said, burdened to make smalltalk, "that was a neat setup you had back there —the pathway with all the gargoyles. Did you build the path yourself or was it already here?"

"I guess you could say that."

"Say what—that you built the trail?"

A cold stare. "Ms. Kline, like I said, please do not go back there again by yourself—I can't stress this enough. Especially at night." His dark eyes bore into her own as though he were reading her very thoughts. Yet somehow she didn't feel threatened by the look.

"O-o-o, because that's when the monsters come out, right?" She chuckled, expecting him to join in.

He didn't.

"No—because that's when the wolves come out." He cleared his throat. "And you might get lost in the dark." There was an impatience in his voice and he glanced away from her, looking down the hall; as though eager to part ways.

It was clear now that Ian Hawke was no long-lost, kindly uncle or a fun-loving cousin delighted to make her acquaintance. They wouldn't be sitting down with tea and crumpets to discuss her grandfather and the inheritance, and each other's lives.

Who was this guy, anyway?

"So, what do you do in your work shed?" she asked, grasping at straws.

He crossed his arms again and a thin line appeared in his forehead.

"I was putting away some tools." He dropped

his hands to his sides. "So—have you met everyone around the estate yet?"

Finally, a question for *her* to answer.

"Yes, I've met Hannah and Mike so far and I suppose I'll meet the others at dinner." She smiled, regretting once again that she hadn't called ahead to let them know what date she'd be arriving; it was embarrassing. She hated to impose. "Do you eat dinner together?"

"Of course. We're a family."

She nodded, relaxing a little.

"Look, I suppose we'll have to talk about the details of the inheritance soon," he said, "but I'll tell you right now, I'm not selling."

"Oh, no-no—" she said, putting up her hands, palms out. "I wouldn't dream of doing so!" Did he not understand what she'd meant earlier when she said she was here to stay?

He lifted his chin, shifting his weight from one foot to the other. He seemed nervous. "I'm willing to buy you out instead," he said. "I'll pay you far more than your half of the estate is worth."

Perhaps a turf war was at hand.

"Mr. Hawke, Ian," she said, clasping her hands together and frowning. "I thought I explained already. *I'm here to stay.* I'm really sorry to invade on your territory like this, us being strangers and all. But I'd . . . I'd really like to live here. At least, for a little while."

A look of shock flicked across his features and he cleared his throat again. "I see," he said evenly, blinking once, eyes wide, and set off down the hall, saying over his shoulder: "I've got to run. See you at dinner, all right? Five o'clock."

He disappeared into an arched portal on the left-hand side of the corridor, leaving her all alone.

Chapter 3

After Ian took off, Lily had nothing else to do but wander upstairs to her new quarters. At first she considered taking a tour of the mansion on her own but it seemed impertinent, so she decided to wait for Mike instead. There was no hurry after all.

When she reached her room, she looked through the mahogany chest of drawers next to the door and found it to be empty and clean. Someone—she guessed Hannah—had recently dusted and polished all the furniture in this room. She decided she might as well take this time to unpack her things and get settled in.

Next to the chest of drawers was a matching dome-top wardrobe; and upon finding it empty, she hung up her clothes and stored her suitcases. Everything else she organized in the chest of drawers. There was no clock in the room so she fished through her purse to find her watch. Noting it was four-thirty now, she glanced down at her torn stockings with a sigh and kicked off her pumps. She put on a fresh pair of leggings and took the time to straighten her hair and inspect her makeup in the oval Victorian mirror above the chest of drawers. Everything was fine except for a smudge of dirt across her left cheek. With a fresh wave of embarrassment, she rubbed it off with a Kleenex and let out a huff. Great first impression she'd made on Ian; he probably thought her a scruffy squatter come to take over his personal domain.

Realizing she didn't actually know where the dining room was, she decided to go hunting for it. The last thing she wanted to do was arrive late for her first meal with the "family." She still had no clue what Ian's relation to her grandfather was.

She stepped out into the hallway and nearly collided with Hannah, who had just ascended the staircase.

"Ms. Kline," she said with a smile, "I was looking for you. May I escort you to dinner?"

Lily accepted the offer gratefully and followed the old woman down the staircase.

"Were you able to find Mr. Hawke?" Hannah asked, glancing sidelong at Lily as they walked together down the vaulted corridor.

"Yes—though it was a bit of an ordeal. He was out at his work shed."

The housekeeper slowed her step down to a pause. "So you've seen it then?"

"The shed? Um, no—not really. I didn't even reach it. I—uh—" She let out a laugh and lowered her voice: "I tripped over a tree root and fell on my face. That's when Ian showed up." She laughed again. "Not my most flattering moment."

Hannah cast a furtive glance down the corridor and resumed eye contact, speaking in a hushed tone. "Was he angry with you? I had some words with Mike about letting you wander off into the forest on your own."

"He did seem a little angry, or annoyed. I'm not sure. He wasn't very friendly but I thought it might just be his personality?" She put her hands on her hips. "Why is everyone so concerned about me going out back alone in broad daylight?"

Another furtive glance down the corridor. "Ian doesn't like anyone going near his shed, is all. He goes there to be alone and we've all learned to respect his privacy and leave him be." A pertinent look. "But anyhoo"—she started off down the hall again—"let's get you off to the dining room then. It's just here on the left, before the library."

Hannah approached a set of wooden double-doors on the left side of the corridor and turned the brass knobs, pushing the doors inward. She entered the room with a breeze of authority and Lily followed close behind.

She clasped her hands together in delight as she stepped into an elaborate room with white trim work and a stamped-tin ceiling.

"Oh, this is beautiful," she gasped, awed by the many gilt-framed paintings covering the crimson walls. A Persian rug covered the entire floor space, save for the area of raised hearth on the right side of the room where stood a two-story mantel fireplace with white columns and an intricate keystone of a chimera. Beneath the keystone was an Arras tapestry featuring a landscape and a group of nymphs near a fountain. On the far side of the room was a door leading into a kitchen and Hannah took her leave through it, urging Lily to get comfortable. There was no one else in the room yet.

Lily moved around a mahogany dining table with ball and claw foot legs—breathlessly running her fingertip along the smooth carved edging as she went. She pulled out a polished chair in front of the fireplace and sat down gingerly, wondering when the others were going to arrive. The table was already set with six place settings, though it could easily seat a dozen. There were wine glasses stuffed with cloth napkins and the silver-plated candelabra in its center was lit with five tapered candles. Across the room was an ornate China cabinet.

After a few minutes of twiddling her thumbs, she began to worry about seeing Ian again. She didn't want to impose, but she really wanted a fresh start on life. Plus, Auguste Kline *was* her grandfather, and even though she'd never met him and had only just learned of his existence, she did have a legal right to this place. Once settled in, she planned to visit the nearest town and begin seeking employment. She was in no rush for now.

As if bidden by her thoughts, approaching footsteps sounded in the corridor and Mike the handsome handyman entered the room, flashing her a grin. Behind him was the elderly man whom she recognized as the gardener. She rose from her seat to greet him, taking his rough leathery hand in her own for a quick, strong handshake. Mike introduced him as Christopher Linus. Though his sunbaked skin was in stark contrast to his snow-white hair, his smile was kindly and his face full of laughter lines. "Please call me Chris, dear," he said, a twinkle in his eye, and for a brief second she felt a pang of sorrow—wishing she could have known her grandfather while he was still living. Perhaps Chris could tell her all about him.

"Oh, there you are," Hannah said, trotting into the room with a wine bottle in each hand. "I was gearing up to go find ya'll." A petite woman with cropped graying curls was behind her, mitted hands gripping the handles of a steaming pot.

"What's on the menu tonight, Angie?" Chris asked, licking his lips and raising an eyebrow comically.

"Chicken in almond sauce with garlic and parsley *frittata*, and—an almond-praline cheesecake for dessert."

Chris rubbed his hands together in delight. "That's my gurl."

"That sounds glorious," Lily said, smiling brightly at the woman. Angie nodded an acknowledgment but didn't smile in return.

"Angie's a great cook," Mike said, dropping down into a seat across from Lily. "You're in for a treat."

Angie set down the pot on a hot plate and went back to the kitchen.

"Does anyone know where Ian is?" Hannah asked, plucking the napkins from each glass and filling them halfway with translucent burgundy. "It would be a shame to start without him." She nodded at Lily—"Especially when Auguste's granddaughter is joining us for the first time."

"You needn't worry," Ian said tonelessly, appearing from the corridor and taking an abrupt seat at the head of the table.

Lily's stomach tightened at the sight of him. She looked away and smiled politely at Christopher.

Angie returned with more food things and when everyone was settled around the table and grace said, they each served their own plates and dug in.

As expected, the food was delicious, and no one spoke during the meal; each seemingly content to enjoy their entrée in silence. Lily avoided looking at Ian but his presence was palpable, like a hovering storm cloud. When they were finished the meal, Angie and Hannah cleared the table and served coffee and dessert.

Mike took successive swigs of his coffee and inhaled his slice of cheesecake in three bites. "Still up for that tour, Lily?" He dabbed his lips with a napkin and pushed his plate away, winking at her.

She took a bite of the cheesecake, savoring its rich, creamy flavor. "Mmm," she said, closing her eyes briefly, "yes, for sure. I've been looking forward to it."

Mike grinned, soft brown eyes alight. He was doing nothing to hide his interest in her, and she sipped some coffee to avoid blushing. Though she hadn't looked at Ian even once since the beginning of the meal, she was aware now of his gaze boring into her.

She glanced in his direction.

"You're giving her a tour?" he asked Mike in a low voice.

Mike nodded, brows arched as though to say,

"Uh, yeah—duh."

"I'll come with you." Ian pushed back his chair and stood.

"Uh, you sure about that? I'm fine taking her around. It's no problem."

"I'm coming."

Mike looked at Lily, the pleasure gone from his expression. "You mind?"

"Of course not." She smiled at both men, masking her discomfort, and finished the last bite of her cheesecake.

"Thanks for dinner, Angie," Ian said politely, before heading out to the corridor.

"Do you need any help with dishes?" Lily asked the cook, rising. Typical men, she thought, not even stopping to consider that Angie had cooked dinner and was now left to clean up all the mess on her own.

"Oh, goodness, no," Hannah interjected. "You three run along. Angie and I will be just fine."

Ian trailed behind Mike and Lily as they wandered through the house from room to room and floor to floor.

He watched their interactions with a feigned air of disinterest and made no attempt to join conversation. He really needed to get back to his workshop to finish up some projects, but couldn't leave just yet. He had to make sure Mike didn't show Lily any of the rooms he wanted kept private.

He discreetly eyed her lovely form as she walked. She was going to be major trouble. He'd known it from the moment he laid eyes on her in the sunlit backyard. Even in the shadows of the woods, her feminine outline, her soft voice, had told him she was going to get under his skin. He mustn't let her get close. He had far too much to hide.

Snapping from his thoughts, he realized where they were and his pulse pounded.

Mike was reaching for one of the paintings on the wall.

"Check this out," he said, hand grazing the gilded frame.

Ian lunged forward and grabbed Mike's wrist. "Don't touch the paintings—"

"What's your problem, man?" Mike yanked his wrist free and swung around, glaring at him.

Ian met his eyes with a glare of his own.

"Oh, right, yes, sorry—how foolish of me." Mike rolled his eyes and took Lily by the elbow, leading her farther down the hall. "I wouldn't want to get any dirt on Auguste's priceless paintings."

That was close . . . too close. Thankfully Mike had taken the hint. But it was time to get rid of him. He didn't want to be mean, but he had his reasons and Mike should have known better. There were secrets he and Auguste had worked far too hard to protect to just give them away to some woman for the mere sake of manners.

"I'll take over from here," he said, stepping in front of the door Mike was about to open.

A wary look crossed Lily's face and it stung to know he was making such a bad impression. He didn't want to scare her.

Or maybe he did?

Mike stepped back, folded his arms across his chest, spread his feet, and narrowed his eyes. "Take over what, the tour? Was I doing that lame of a job?"

"I don't think it requires two of us," Ian said, taking a step forward. He was slightly taller than Mike and didn't hesitate to use that to his advantage. "So, don't trouble yourself then. Take off and I'll finish the tour." He stared him down.

For a moment Mike dallied, eyes dark with anger, but he uncrossed his arms and gave Lily a sympathetic look. "Sorry, kid. He's the boss."

Ian waited for him to vanish around a corner before he turned to face Lily.

"Look—I, um—"

She took a step back away from him. "I'm sorry," she said, "but maybe I should finish this tour another time."

His throat tightened, though he supposed it was best this way; now he wouldn't have to finish showing her around and once he'd had a private talk with Mike, Mike wouldn't be doing so either.

Yet everything within him wanted her to stay.

"No-no, I'll show you the rest," he insisted, surprising himself. He tried to smile in a friendly manner. "There isn't much more to show you, though. Most rooms are self-explanatory, right? Bedrooms and powder rooms. Sitting rooms. The usual. We might as well just get it done and over with." Never mind that there were quite a few unusual rooms and passage-ways that he had no intention of her ever seeing. It didn't matter that she was co-heir; this mansion belonged to him and him alone.

Lily studied him a moment, the guarded look fading from her eyes.

"Well, before I go anywhere else with you," she said, "you need to tell me why you're being so hostile. Why don't you want me here?"

"I never said I didn't want you here."

"You never outright said it—but it's as plain as day."

"I'm not used to having company." He scratched the side of his neck. "Please don't take it personally." That much was true, at least. The only "company" he'd ever had was the various contractors he or Auguste hired for any repairs or maintenance outside of Mike's scope of expertise.

"Okay then, so why do you want to buy my share of the estate? You seem in an awful hurry to get rid of me."

"Look, do you want me to finish the tour, or what?"

He shuffled his footing. Keep your cool, man. Don't give in to those beautiful sea-green eyes.

"Hmm, with you?" She let out a snort. "Won't that be fun."

"Fine. Have a good night." He turned to leave.

"Wait—"

He paused, giving her a sidelong glance.

A sheepish look. "I don't know how to get back to my room."

He let out a slow exhale. "Go back down this hall, take a left and—"

"Can you please take me there?"

"Fine." Just what he needed; more time for her to badger him with questions he was unprepared to answer. More time for her to work her way into his head, dismantling his resolve piece by piece. She hadn't left his mind since he'd first laid eyes on her in the forest.

He took quick strides down the hallway and she hurried after him.

"Slow down. I'm wearing heels, for Pete's sake."

Holding back a childish growl, he slowed his step so she could catch up, and avoided eye contact.

"I want us to get along somehow," she said. "I'd like to live here, so I really hope we can find a way to be friends. I realize I'm imposing on your life and I'm really sorry. My grandfather bequeathed this place to both of us, so you must have meant a lot to him. But for some reason, he thought it was a good idea to make us joint-heirs."

Ian sighed, slowing his step.

"I was hoping you could tell me about him," she said. "My grandfather."

He met her eyes briefly as she fell into step next to him.

"Were you close?" she asked.

"Auguste was . . . a complex man."

Oh, great. Here comes the barrage of questions.

"Was he nice? Did he have any friends—hobbies?" she asked. "Did he ever try to contact my mother? Do you know why he never came looking for me?"

"It was best for you that he stay away."

That much was true. He only wished the old man hadn't been foolish enough to leave half of the estate to some obscure granddaughter he'd never even met. He must have known she would come—but why risk so much? Had he lost his mind in his old age?

It had come as quite the shock to learn that a young woman named Lily Kline was to be his joint-heir. And it wasn't that he wanted the place all to himself; he just didn't want anyone to get hurt.

Ian forced himself to look at Lily again, trying not to be angry afresh with the man he'd grown to love as his own father.

"Why was it best?" she asked, looking puzzled. "Did he not know how poor my mother was? How much she struggled to put food on the table and take care of me? We had a hard life—and here all the while to find I had a rich grandfather who could have made our lives so much easier! I-just-don't-get-it."

He stopped walking and turned to face her, uncertain what to do with his hands. "Auguste was . . . he was a man with many burdens, and many —"

Oh great.

"Many . . . ?"

He sighed. "Enemies." He shook his head, inwardly kicking himself for revealing too much. Her beauty was distracting—those striking eyes. He couldn't think straight.

"Enemies!" She arched an eyebrow. "Why would he have enemies?"

"Rich men always do."

"Was he a hermit?"

"You could say that."

His chest tightened.

Just like me.

She narrowed her eyes. "Still—he should have supported his own daughter."

"I'm not trying to excuse him, Lily, but he preferred she have no contact with him in any shape or form." There was no way Ms. Kline would understand the situation in a nutshell and he wasn't at liberty to explain further. In light of all that was at stake, it was just better for her to perceive Auguste as a heartless old Scrooge.

An adorable little crease formed between her eyebrows.

"Your grandfather was an unhappy man," he said tonelessly, "and the later years of his life were not what he would've chosen." A pause. How to word this? "His greatest sorrow in life was losing his daughter and . . . and knowing he would never get to meet his granddaughter."

Her eyes darkened with emotion, perhaps compassion or regret. "How did he lose his daughter —my mother?"

Ian rubbed his forehead and crossed his arms over his chest. "You sure like to ask questions."

"I'm curious by nature."

He grinned in spite of himself, but a sudden

shyness overwhelmed him and the grin faded. Shoving his hands into his pockets so she wouldn't see them shaking, he looked down the hallway and frowned.

"What's the matter?"

He cleared his throat and forced himself to look at her. "Nothing." A fake smile. "Just tired, is all."

"You don't fool me, Ian Hawke."

Heat climbed his neck. He wanted to snap at her—to say something that would make her despise him and leave him alone.

But he couldn't. His tongue was frozen.

"It's obvious what you were thinking," she went on. " 'How do I get rid of this annoying chick who won't stop asking questions?' " Her voice was lowered to mimic him and she grinned.

Disarmed and uncertain of himself, he cracked a half smile. "Heh."

"You watch your back, mister." She poked his shoulder with her forefinger. "You won't be getting rid of me so easy. I'm one tough cookie."

"Is that so?" His tongue loosened up. "To tell you the truth, I was really just thinking how beautiful you are."

The look of blunt surprise on her face stopped him short and his cheeks burned. Oh boy. Open mouth, insert foot.

He let out an awkward laugh. "I was just joking, of course. I don't think you're beautiful." A cringe. "What I mean is, you *are* beautiful, but I wasn't thinking that." He was flustered now. "I should probably shut up."

"Good idea," she said, laughing, though a guarded look was in her eyes now.

He fidgeted, trying desperately to focus his thoughts on anything other than the woman standing only two feet in front of him. His hands were trembling again; heart pounding in his ribs. He ran a shaky hand through his hair and stuffed it back in his pant pocket, lest she notice. Of all the horrors he'd faced in life with steadfast courage and bravery, he'd never dreamed a mere woman could be so terrifying.

"Are you—shaking?" she said, looking at him like he was some kind of frightened little child.

"I'm not a people-person, okay," he snapped. "I get nervous." He took off down the hall. "Let's get you to your room already. It's late and I've got too much to do to just be standing around wasting time talking."

Chapter 4

Later that night, Lily lay wide awake in her new canopy bed, replaying the day's events in her mind.

She was certain Ian Hawke had something to hide.

And she still didn't know why he was co-heir.

At their first meeting, she was apprehensive due to his barely constrained hostility, but later he'd shown a softer side; a vulnerable one even. He also seemed to have a lot of control over Mike and Hannah. Were they afraid of him? No, she was reading too much between the lines. It was a strange new place—surreal even—and it would take time to adapt and get to know everyone.

Lily squeezed her eyes shut, trying once again to clear her mind. Sleep seemed out of reach. She'd been lying here for hours now, the glow of the moon flowing through the open drapes of the arched windows and suffusing the contours of the furniture. Though the blankets on her bed had been freshly laundered, there was an aura of dust and cobwebs and bats. The scent of polished wood and paraffin candles. Of course it was only the age of the place spooking her out. Eventually she'd get used to all the high ceilings and endless rooms.

After another ten minutes of tossing and turning, she climbed out of the bed and pulled on a housecoat and slippers.

She crossed the room toward the windows, hugging her arms around her waist for warmth. The room was chilly. She made a mental note to ask about heating and how to work the fireplace. When she reached the first window, she pulled aside the drape a little further and peered out into the night. Many of the windows in the hallways were made of leaded glass, blurring the view outside, but these windows and the windows in most of the bedrooms were clear. There was nothing much to see, other than the bronzed and dangling boughs of the willow trees.

She wanted to see the backyard.

Opening her bedroom door quietly, she stepped out into the hallway and looked in both directions. She would not be able to see anything from the floor-to-ceiling lancet windows, due to the leaded glass, but she'd learned on her tour that the bedroom at the end of the hall was unoccupied.

With soft steps, she reached the end of the hallway, relieved that the cricks in the floorboards weren't too noisy, and tried the knob of the door on the right, hoping it was unlocked. It moved inward with a creak and she froze, expecting a light to come on in Hannah's room, which was next to her own. Angie, Christopher and Mike's bedrooms were all located in this wing of the mansion as well. She hadn't finished the full tour of the estate though, and didn't know where Ian's quarters were. It dawned on her then that she also didn't know where her grandfather's room or rooms had been. What was behind the door Ian had stopped the tour at? If he'd been close to Auguste, perhaps he wasn't ready to see the elderly man's rooms again. But if that were the case, why not just say so? Why get all antagonistic and send Mike off?

Lily squinted in the darkness of the room, glad the windows were close to the door. She stepped up to the first overlooking the backyard, and opened the closed drapes.

Across the two acres of greensward, where the gargoyle path lay, the first three white orbs were aglow through the trees: like the lighted dots of a boat out to sea in the black of night.

Weren't they on a motion sensor?

A shift in the distant darkness caught her eye and she leaned in closer to the glass, bumping her nose. Was it just her imagination or did the white orb of the first gargoyle lift above the others as though floating? It was much higher than it had been a second ago. She blinked and it was low again.

Her mind must be playing tricks on her.

First chance she got, she would go out back and take a look. But not now—not in the middle of the night.

Pulse elevated, she tiptoed back to her bedroom and climbed in under the sheets, housecoat and all. She shivered and eventually drifted off to sleep— only to dream of orbs falling in the forest like snowflakes.

Lily awoke with the first rays of dawn, eyes burning from lack of sleep.

After lying awake for a full hour, drinking in her new surroundings, she climbed out of bed, donned her slippers, and padded over to the gilded mirror above the chest of drawers. Her hair hung limply and she realized that she hadn't seen any shower or bathtubs during the tour Mike had given her the night before. There must be one somewhere. She would find Hannah and ask first thing.

After gathering a change of clothes and a bag of toiletries, she stuffed them in a canvas bag, tied her hair back in a bun, and stepped out into the hallway.

Hannah was emerging from the staircase, a bundle of folded hand towels in her arms.

"Hannah—I'm so glad I found you. I have no idea where the shower is." She laughed.

"Oh, my." Hannah lowered the armload of towels and peered at Lily curiously. "Goodness. Didn't the boys take you on a tour last night?"

"They did but it was cut short."

"Oh. Well, I'm afraid this place is rather old fashioned." She shifted her weight and smiled. "Surely they showed you the master baths last night."

Master baths?

"No, I think I would have remembered that." She laughed. "I got to see the main floor rooms and the rooms in this wing, but I only saw a couple of rooms in the west wing before Ian sent Mike away. I've yet to see my grandfather's rooms."

"I don't understand though—why did Ian send Mike away?"

Lily lowered her voice to a confidential tone. "He got his nose *way* out of joint, I have no idea why, and a few minutes later took off himself. He was very awkward."

Hannah frowned but said nothing.

"So, you mentioned the master baths? Where are they located?"

"In the basement."

"There's a basement?" Despite her better judgment, a vision of dungeon chambers and cement shower stalls came to mind. "How creepy."

Hannah chuckled. "Not creepy in the slightest —Goodness me. Wait till you see! Just let me unload these towels here and I'll fetch Mike for you."

Lily blushed but realized she was being silly. If she was going to live here, she was going to have to get used to being seen in her housecoat by the staff.

Hannah excused herself and went into her room, returning a moment later, empty-handed. She then went to the third bedroom on the left side of the hallway and rapped on the door. "Mike," she shouted, "there's a damsel in distress out here."

Lily blushed again, hoping Hannah hadn't awakened him.

"Coming," a muffled voice said from within. Footsteps approached the door and it swung inward. Mike stepped out into the hallway followed by a waft of spicy cologne. He looked like he'd been up for a while already.

Hannah put her hands on her wide hips. "D'you mind showing Ms. Kline to the baths?"

"No problem." He glanced at Lily and raised

an eyebrow. "Ian didn't finish the 'tour' last night?"

She shook her head. "Unfortunately, no."

"Well, come on then," he said with a wave of the hand and a grin. "It's no trouble."

"I'll see you two kids at breakfast," Hannah said, "nine o'clock sharp." She headed back to her bedroom, leaving them alone.

Blatantly aware of her uncombed hair and cocoon-like housecoat, Lily felt like a marshmallow next to Mike who was clean-shaven and wearing designer jeans and a hoody.

"Alrighty—this way," he said, jogging down the stairs.

Lily followed him to the main floor, wondering if her furry slippers were going to get dirty in the basement. "So, what are you up to today?" she asked, walking beside him.

"Oh, the usual. Keeping this place from falling apart. Gotta work on the plumbing in the washroom next to the kitchen—that's the main thing—and some light bulbs need replacing. Angie wants me to take a look at the oven, too. There's always something to do —I keep myself busy." He gave her a sidelong glance and winked. "So-o-o," he said. "How'd you enjoy the rest of your, ahem, tour last night? Doesn't sound like Ian was all that thorough if you don't even know where the baths are." He laughed.

"He didn't finish the tour." She recounted how Ian had gotten angry and marched her back to her bedroom. She left out the part about him saying she was beautiful. Her cheeks warmed with the memory.

Mike let out a snort. "He tells me to take a hike and then just takes you back to your room? Typical. That guy has issues. Such a control freak."

They reached the opposite end of the corridor where an arched door on the left led into a stairwell. In it was a hardwood spiral staircase, identical to the one at the front entrance complete with two wood-carved knights standing guard as the newel posts. The staircase led up to the west wing rooms of the second floor.

Lily let out an exaggerated sigh. "It sure is a long journey to the bathtub."

Mike laughed. "If these baths weren't so spectacular, I would've installed modern showers years ago. But Ian doesn't want one anyway and forbids it."

She gave him a long look. "I just can't wrap my head around the idea of a bath in the basement. I didn't even know there was a basement." He grinned. "Of course I figured there might be a cellar or a storage room of sorts," she went on, "but that's about it." She shrugged, smiling. "So, how big are these 'master' baths anyway?"

He leaned an elbow against the shoulder of one of the knights, facing her. "Oh, you'll see . . . " A wink.

She glanced up the antiquated staircase which disappeared to the floor above. There was so much of the mansion she had yet to see. Hanging from the low ceiling directly above them was a small iron chandelier which cast them in a dome of light. There were no windows in the stairwell and the corners of the room were shadowed. The walls were paneled in a dark brown wood and if the light wasn't on, the room would be black.

"Why don't you and Ian get along?" she asked impulsively, hugging the wad of folded clothes tighter under her left arm and shifting her weight. She felt like a dork in her housecoat and Mike seemed in no hurry to take her to the baths; she might as well ask some questions.

He straightened, reaching up and casually gripping the pole of the knight's battle axe, one hand on his hip. "He's just weird, that's why. I do all the work around here and he's always just off in that work shed of his. He doesn't go into town and rarely speaks to anyone. Or maybe it's just me he ignores. He's chummy-chummy with Hannah, Angie and Chris—but then so was Auguste. He was a recluse, too." He dropped his hand from his hip. "It's not normal," he said, lowering his voice and speaking matter-of-factly. "I've never trusted either of them."

She frowned. "Does his behavior have anything to do with being taken in as a child?"

Mike hesitated. "It's best we not talk about that." He broke eye contact, flicking a glance up the stairs and then into the hallway as though someone might be listening.

"But why not?" she persisted, forgetting to lower her voice. So—Ian wasn't the only one keeping secrets; they all seemed to be hiding something. "What harm could it do?"

"He's very private about it, and I respect a man's privacy." Mike dropped his voice to a whisper, leaning closer. "Look, all I know is that he wasn't exactly 'taken in.' He was *found* in the mansion. In the attic."

Her eyes widened. "What!" She didn't even know there was an attic. What was a young child doing up in the attic of a house that wasn't even his home? A chill ran down her spine and her hands grew cold. She knew nothing about her grandfather. A myriad of suspicions flooded her subconscious and her pulse quickened.

"Can you show me this attic?" she asked.

"I . . . can't." He met her gaze. "It's off limits. For all of us."

"But I'm Auguste's heiress, I have the right."

"The attic is dangerous," he said in a hushed tone, body tense. He kept glancing behind her and up the stairs as though nervous. "No one ever goes up there."

"What could possibly be dangerous about it?"

"Well, for starters, it hasn't been cleaned in years and the roof has leaked, causing the floor to rot in places. You could fall through. Plus, there're plenty of spiders up there and some have a nasty bite. Check this out—" He rolled up a sleeve and showed her a round pink scar on his forearm.

"Spiders don't scare me."

He grinned at that, visibly relaxing. "I don't think there are many things that scare you," he said, cocking an eyebrow.

"What makes you say that?"

"Well, you're about to have a bath in the basement and I'm sure you've heard by now of the dead maid found floating down there a few years back."

He folded his arms across his chest. "The murderer was never found."

Lily's breath caught in her throat and she felt the blood drain from her face; realizing how vulnerable she was in this huge house full of secrets and strangers. If anything happened to her, she doubted anyone back home would even know she'd gone missing. She hadn't left a forwarding address with anyone.

Raising a shaky hand to her throat, she blinked at Mike and swallowed, trying to compose herself.

The grin faded from his lips. "Are you all right?" he said, looking concerned. "I was joking, Lily. No one was murdered here! Seriously—I was just pulling your leg."

She shoved him in the chest. "You jerk! Don't scare me like that." She let out a nervous laugh.

Mike raised both hands in mock surrender. "Hey, it's not my fault you're so gullible." He winked and reached for the battle axe.

Lily was about to retort when he tugged on the axe, bending it sideways.

A swish sounded and a sliding door opened in the paneled wall behind him. Startled, she stepped around him and peered into the opening.

Stone steps led downward into shadows.

"Here, I'll lead the way," he said, moving in front of her and starting down the steps. "Hold the wall so you don't loose your footing."

Twenty steps down they reached an arched wooden doorway, barely visible; the only light was the faint stream from the chandelier in the upper stairwell. Mike pressed down on an iron handle and pushed the door open. Warm air and yellow light spilled over them, banishing the darkness.

Chapter 5

Beyond the threshold was a deep and vibrant room redolent of chlorine.

The walls were painted with swirling, fanciful designs in rich color—aqua blue, lemon, and violet. Three large alcoves, two on one side of the room, the third on the adjacent wall, housed marble statues of angels; flecks of gold in their wings. In their out-stretched hands were gilded platters loaded with bathing supplies and towels. Narrow pillars sur-rounding the room supported a high ceiling covered with thousands of tiny white lights—like twinkling stars in a bright night sky. On the far end of the room were reclining chairs and several tropical plants in ornate pots. Lily guessed the room to be some forty meters deep and at least twenty meters wide.

It was difficult to process all she was seeing and when she sensed a shadow moving below her and away from her, she peeled her gaze from the walls and ceiling and glanced down at the floor—nearly losing her balance at the sight.

She was standing on a glass aquarium floor.

In the indigo waters beneath her feet a school of tropical fish swam by over pink coral. A couple of meters ahead of her was an empty tub built into the see-through glass; its sides and bottom as translucent as the floors.

She gasped as a small sand tiger shark moved through the waters ahead and curved around the tub —approaching her. With a yelp, she stepped backward and bumped into Mike, who laughed and gripped her shoulders. The shark turned direction and moved away from them.

"Incredible, isn't it?" he said. "I can't even begin to imagine how this thing was constructed in the first place." He didn't remove his warm hands from her shoulders and she made no attempt to nudge them off. She liked his closeness, especially after the shock of seeing a shark.

"How . . . I mean, I've never seen such a thing in my life," she stammered. "The detail and work put into this room . . . It's—I just can't believe there's an aquarium under the floor."

In slow motion, she imagined cracks forming in the glass like ice, the floor shattering beneath her feet, and both she and Mike plunging into the domain of the shark.

"Who feeds the fish and maintains the aquarium?"

Beyond the bathtub was a square swimming pool directly in the center of the room. It was filled to the brim with still water. She guessed the pool to be about fifteen feet in length and width, but because of the see-through floors, its beginnings and ends were difficult to discern.

Mike pulled his hands from her shoulders and moved away from her, folding his arms over his chest and leaning his shoulder against a pillar. "Ian takes care of all that," he said, glancing around. "Apparently there's a hired marine crew that comes in regularly, but I've never paid much mind."

A school of fish darted beneath her feet and she jumped. This was going to take some getting used to. Was she seriously expected to submerge herself in a see-through bathtub with little sharks swimming about? How thick was the glass?

"We really have nothing to do with them," Mike went on. "And they know to keep themselves out of sight. Ian likes his privacy."

She smiled distractedly. "Well, Mike, I really don't want to be late for breakfast, so I need to get a move on." She scanned the room. "There's, uh, no upright showers—?" She frowned, hugging her clothing bag to her chest.

He nodded, seeming to understand her discomfort. "You're worried about privacy."

"Yes, just slightly!" She laughed.

"No problem. Just keep the door locked till you're done and no one will be able to walk in on you."

She knit her brow. "There's only one door giving access?"

Mike unfolded his arms and looked away. "Actually no, there's another—the one the marine crew uses. It gives them direct access from outside. I'll show you." She followed him along the perimeter of the room to the other side.

Sure enough, there was another arched door between two floor-to-ceiling potted plants. She hadn't noticed it before because it was painted the same as the walls. Up close she could make out the lines of its frame quite clearly, like an outline.

"This door is always kept locked," he said, "although the marine crew does have a key. But they come at set times, so we schedule our bathing times in between."

She frowned, still not keen on the whole idea. She supposed she was going to have to bathe in a swimsuit from now on.

"You can trust us," Mike said with a charming smile. "No one's going to come in here if the doors are locked. And if no one's using the tub, the door we entered through is left unlocked, plain and simple." He paused. "I guess we could make for a more rigid security system, but we're a family here. It just doesn't seem necessary." He headed toward the door they'd come from, saying, "I'll see you at breakfast."

He reached the exit and checked his wrist-watch. "It's only eight-ten, so you're golden." With a smile and a wave, he left the room, closing the wooden door shut behind him.

When he was gone, Lily made sure both doors were indeed locked—all the while keeping an eye on the whereabouts of the shark. There were other color-ful fish moseying about, but so far she'd only spotted the one shark. It was difficult to tell what all was in the water though, as many areas were darkened with coral beds, boulders, and bright green strands of sea-weed. There could be anything in there.

Lily stood in silence for a while looking about, enchanted by the room. She stepped up to the empty bathtub and set down her canvas bag along its edge to examine it.

It was big enough for two people. Gilded pipes ran just beneath the surface of the tub floor and two taps were mounted on one end; three steps leading down into it from the other end. Water jets were placed about the tub walls as well as a raised area along the adjacent sides, which she presumed to be seating. Beneath the tub was a spread of coral. Much to her relief, it didn't look like there was enough space for a large fish to actually swim beneath it.

On second thought, Lily went back to the door, unlocked it, scooted up the stone steps, and jogged down the long corridor to the front of the mansion. She went upstairs to her room and scrounged around for her swimsuit, donning it quickly, and then returned to the far stairwell where the hidden door still stood wide open.

Reaching the tub again, she got down on her knees and leaned in to turn the knobs, adjusting the temperature as water gushed out. Deciding to indulge, she allowed the tub to fill fully. She didn't want to waste water but needed to relax. And for the time being, the shark was keeping its distance—but if it should come anywhere near, she'd be out of that tub in a flash.

When the tub had finished filling, she turned on the jets and glanced around as she removed her housecoat, still uncertain of her privacy. She wanted to trust these people but found herself presently unable. Too many unknowns.

After descending the steps, she sat down gingerly and the bubbling water swirled around her neck. She closed her eyes; not wanting to view any marine life while being submerged in it. The comforting heat began to melt away her stress and tension, and her whole body tingled. A sigh escaped her lips. She could definitely get used to this.

Something scraped against the glass wall behind her—loud enough to be heard above the water jets.

Lily's eyes snapped open and she scooted to the opposite side of the tub, looking all around the room and through the tub glass, heart pounding out of control. She shut off the jets and pulled her knees up.

The water settled and a hush fell over the room. Everything was where it should be. Even the shark was nowhere to be seen. She let out a slow exhale to steady her breathing; deciding it must have been the sound of a fish hitting or rubbing against the glass. An image of a dead maid floating in the pool filled her mind and a chill ran up her spine, despite the warmth of the water. But she rolled her eyes and let out a laugh.

Thinking back, it occurred to her that Mike might have told the story of the maid to distract her from further questions about the attic. And she'd fallen for it.

Lily reached for the shampoo and conditioner in her bag, assuming the drains would take the soap suds somewhere other than into the aquarium, and washed and rinsed her hair quickly. She was not going to let Mike off the hook so easily. Next time she saw him privately, she would ask about the attic again.

Wrapping a towel around herself as she emerged from the tub, she dressed awkwardly beneath the privacy of the towel; pulling on jeans and a thin, mauve-colored sweater. She combed her hair, and making sure she hadn't left anything behind, headed toward the exit. When she reached it, she turned the lock and stopped short, the hairs on the back of her neck prickling.

She spun around.

But there was no one there.

Only the lifeless angel statues and the gliding shadows of fish beneath the glass floors reflecting the lights above.

Lily turned back to the door and pulled it open as something very large and very black slid beneath her feet.

She yelped and jumped forward, racing up the stone steps and through the open wall panel as though being chased. Not bothering to close it, she dashed out into the corridor and ran headlong into Ian—knocking him to the floor and tumbling down on top of him.

Chapter 6

Ian searched her face, laying his head back against the marble floor and staring up at her with wide eyes. She was sprawled atop of him, palms on his chest.

"What on earth, Ms. Kline?"

She blinked at him, momentarily disoriented, and inhaled his musky aftershave.

"There was something in the baths," she sputtered, pulling herself up off him.

He sat up. "Tell me exactly what you saw."

"Well, I, I don't know. It was quite large. Black. Under my feet."

Ian stood up and dusted himself off. "You saw a shark."

The sand tiger was brown though. This thing was black, definitely black. But wait. Her cheeks burned and she felt stupid. Of course there must be more than one shark or fish species in there. Her heartbeat slowed and she broke eye contact, heat climbing her ears. How could she have been so silly?

"Right. Yes. That must've been it." She glanced up at him, afraid to find a mocking look in his eyes.

They were calm and indifferent.

"The see-through floors take some getting

used to," he said.

She ran a hand through her wet hair. "So, tell me—how did my grandfather get so rich anyway?" she asked, changing the subject.

"Uh, good investments, I suppose."

"You don't know?"

He shook his head, shrugging. "Your guess is as good as mine."

"But did he buy this place or inherit it?"

"Don't know that either. Never talked to him about it." Ian reached down and picked up her bag, handing it to her.

"Is it true he died of a heart attack?" She tucked her belongings under her arm. It was what the lawyers had told her.

Ian's countenance fell and he broke eye contact, hesitating. "Yes. I found him not far from your room. He was,"—he cleared his throat—"he was lying on his back in front of Mike's room." A sidelong glance. He seemed timid suddenly. How was it that he could be so tall and intimidating one moment, and so small and shy the next?

"We'd better get to breakfast," he said abruptly, "or Angie will wring our necks." He raised an eyebrow and smiled. "She hates it when her food gets cold."

An hour later, Lily sat on her bed and combed out the mild tangles in her air-dried hair. Exchanging her slippers for a pair of skimmers, she went out into the hallway and locked her bedroom door behind her. After glancing in both directions, she went up to the portrait of her grandfather and stood studying it.

The background was a buff-brown gradient. Auguste had blue eyes and a curly gray beard, hair thinning at the temples. He wore a tweed jacket over a white shirt with a navy tie. But other than a name plate at the bottom of the painting confirming that this was indeed Auguste Maxwell Kline, there was no new information about him to be gleaned from the painting.

As she turned away, the bottom right-hand corner of the molded frame caught her eye. It was shinier than the rest of the polished frame, as though the dust had been rubbed off by a finger. Or was it just the way the sunlight was hitting it; a trick of the eye?

Last night when Mike had reached for the corner of a picture frame in the west wing, Ian had yanked his wrist away from it.

What had Mike intended to show her?

Heartbeat picking up a notch, she reached up and touched her fingertips to the shiny edge of the frame—pressing into it gently. Would it swing open to reveal a wall safe?

Nothing happened.

She tried again, pushing harder.

A swish sounded but the painting remained still. She glanced to her left at the stairwell leading down to the front entrance as cold air moved over her right side. She pivoted toward the draft.

A tall opening had appeared in the wall, a twisted stairwell beyond it.

Heart beating wildly now, she stepped toward the unlit room and peered inside. The wooden floors and stairs were coated in a layer of dust but visible footprints made a trail up the winding steps. Someone must have been here recently.

She moved into the room and searched the wall for a light switch but found none. Above her, the stairs disappeared into blackness.

Was this the passageway to the attic?

She paused at the bottom of the stairs, feeling like Nancy Drew. The air was cold and stale. She stepped into the prints already formed on the stairs, shaking off her unease. At least this way no one would know she'd been in here—unless someone came up to the hallway and found the wall panel open—which she realized was quite likely. But oh well, what did it matter? This house was legally hers now. Correction—hers and Ian's. She had every right to climb these stairs; though she would keep in mind Mike's warning about rotting floorboards.

After climbing ten steps or so, it was too dark to see the footprints any longer. She followed the curve of the winding stairs another ten steps, holding the railing, and reached a rounded second floor lit ever-so-faintly by a lattice window—realizing now that she must be in one of the turrets. She emerged from the steps and nearly tripped over a cane lying in the dust.

Stooping, she picked it up and blew dust from the gold handle. There seemed to be text engraved in it but it was too dark to make out the words. A few feet in front of her was a red door. With a shrug she reached for the knob.

Footsteps sounded on the stairs behind her.

"Just what do you think you're doing?"

Lily spun around and came face-to-face with Hannah who was rounding the curve in the staircase. She reached the top step and put her hands on her plump hips.

"I—was just taking a look around."

It was difficult to see Hannah's features in the shadows.

"Come along then, let's get out of here. This is no place for a young woman—or an old lady like myself! It's too dangerous up here." She dropped her hands from her hips. "Say, what's that in your hand?"

"It's a cane. I found it on the floor."

Hannah stepped forward and snatched it from her. "It couldn't be—"

"What?"

"Come on—let's get out of here. We need to get into the light." She turned and hurried down the steps carelessly. Lily followed after her, worried the old woman might trip and fall.

When they reached the bottom of the stairwell, Lily noted with some regret that there were footsteps all over the place now. Oh, what did it matter? Hannah would probably tell Ian all about this anyway.

Hannah scurried out into the hallway, looking about furtively and gripping the cane in both hands. "How did you find this door?" she asked, face pale and eyes wide.

Lily stepped up to the painting and pointed, pushing on the corner. The wall panel slid shut, leaving behind no trace of the hidden door.

"Whose cane is that, Hannah?" she asked.

The housekeeper pulled a lace handkerchief from her apron and wiped the remaining dust from the handle and staff. "Look for yourself," she said, holding it up, pursing her lips.

Lily leaned forward.

Auguste Kline.

"Why was my Grandfather's cane abandoned up there in the dust?"

Hannah stuffed the hankie back in her pocket and leaned on the cane.

Her eyes were watery. "I—I don't know," she said. "He always had it with him. He couldn't walk without it, you see." She took a deep breath, frowned, composed herself. "We never found the cane after his death—I've been looking for it!" She went to the stairwell, taking the cane with her. "Excuse me, Lily. I must be going."

In a hidden equipment room next to the master baths, Ian donned his black scuba gear and zipped it up. He pulled on flippers and fastened an air tank and mask. He then climbed a short ladder and slid down into a square vat filled with water. It was used for feeding the fish and also served as the entrance into the aquarium.

He dipped underneath the cool water and swam downward and then upward through a short tunnel leading into the pool room. He swam first to the center of the aquarium, where it was deepest, and began to search through the dips and dives of the coral.

What Lily had said to him earlier that morning was curious, though most likely a false alarm. She may have only seen a sand shark—but she'd specifically said it was big and black.

He had to make sure that no one had trespassed in his aquarium.

Ian swam around some jutting coral and through a cluster of wavy seaweed. The weeds parted and he collided with the bulky side of a five foot sand tiger shark. It responded by gaping its jaw in an exaggerated yawn. Recognizing this as a warning, Ian was quick to swim away, confident the irritated shark would leave him be.

The shark didn't follow and dove down to the deepest part of the aquarium, exploring the bottom. Since sand tigers were usually docile creatures, he saw no reason to be nervous, and took his time scanning the perimeter of the aquarium; keeping his distance whenever he spotted one of the sharks. As an experienced diver, he was used to them and knew how to play it safe.

Other than coral and schools of fish, there was nothing of interest to be seen—and no sign of a fellow scuba diver having been there either. That being said, if there had been one, there may or may not be any evidence of it.

Ian decided Lily had really just seen one of the bigger sharks and he made his way back toward the exit, but stopped abruptly when he spotted a pair of sharks near the tunnel. No matter—he'd wait a minute until they moved out of the way.

He swam closer and kept out of sight behind an area of seaweed.

They seemed in no hurry to leave, so he left his hiding place and swam around the sharks, intending to duck into the tunnel behind them. But without warning, the larger of the two darted in front of him —blocking his escape.

This wasn't right.

Sand tigers weren't typically aggressive like this. He moved away from them but came face-to-face with the beady eyes of another.

Something was wrong.

Kicking upwards, he tried to swim over top the creature only to find himself stuck above three circling sharks with no access to the tunnel. His throat tightened but he willed himself to stay calm. He swam deeper into the tank, toward the middle; hoping the sharks would lose interest. They'd been fed only three hours ago—he'd specifically checked with the marine biologist to be sure.

He dove down to the bottom where a florescent-orange rock marked the spot. Flipping open a square lid next to the rock, he punched one of the dozens of panic buttons that were spread throughout the aquarium. The alarm would sound all throughout the mansion.

Ian froze, sensing a presence behind him.

He whipped around against the resistance of the water as a large male surged toward him with gaping jaws—ragged, skinny teeth exposed and bubbly water trailing through them.

With no weapon to aid him, he smashed his fist into the shark's snout, skinning his knuckles on its sandpaper flesh. The shark careened past him and disappeared deeper into the tank.

In its wake, three more sharks hovered in the shadows of seaweed and coral, watching him with cold eyes and conical snouts. The sharks had never behaved so aggressively in all his years of swimming in the tank—and he had no idea what was going on now.

Thrusting himself with all his might away from the sharks, Ian dove down and pulled himself through the mounds of coral on the aquarium floor, not daring to look back.

At a sudden yank on his flipper, he shot a glance over his shoulder.

A smaller sand tiger was only a few feet behind him—a chunk of the rubber flipper in its teeth. Ian plunged forward and swam as fast as he could toward the exit—adrenaline pumping through his veins like liquid nitrogen.

The dark circle of the exit was only five meters ahead when another shark slid out from the seaweed to his right. With a flick of its caudal fin, it tore towards him and snapped at his face—missing by inches as Ian jerked his head and body backward.

With nowhere to go but up, he pushed himself off the aquarium floor and scraped his shin on protruding coral. A trail of blood seeped from the gash, turning the surrounding waters red.

Now he'd gone and done it.

The tunnel was blocked and the surface of the aquarium was covered in thick glass. But with no other options, Ian kicked his feet and swam away swiftly, hoping the clouding of blood would confuse the sharks. Already the water was boiling behind him as they shot back and forth through the crimson streams, mouths gaping as they sought their elusive prey.

They'd be upon him in a matter of seconds.

Above him two sets of shoes appeared on the glass, running. He pressed his palms against the glass, chills tripping up and down his spine; expecting to be grabbed from below with every breath. Though he couldn't see clearly through the thickness of the floor, he knew it was Mike and Lily above him. Lily dropped down on her hands and knees and pounded on the glass, shouting his name. Her voice was muffled above the roar of the swirling waters below him.

Mike started smashing the floor with the back of a hammer or crow bar. The glass was too thick to break but maybe the vibrations would confuse the sharks.

It was his only chance.

Pivoting, Ian forced himself to look down at the frenzy beneath him. A long shadow moved through the cloudiness, less than a meter below him.

Hoping the sharks would stay where the

blood was thickest, he took off once more in the direction of the exit.

It was now or never.

Ten meters left . . . then five.

Three . . . two, one.

He dove into the tunnel, kicking wildly and frantically—and burst to the surface of the vat.

Flinging his right leg over the edge of the vat, then the other, his body flooded with relief just as a terrible pressure clamped onto his left arm.

A shark had followed him, its row of crooked teeth now clenched down on his forearm—lidless eyes dark and fierce in their intent.

There was no pain yet.

Thinking quickly, he rammed his fingers into the right eye of the creature before it could twist his arm off. The shark released him and jerked its head away. Ian pulled his mangled arm from the water and fell off the ladder, crashing to the stone floor.

The pain exploded through his body then, as though someone had skinned his whole arm and poured salt all over the exposed flesh.

He squeezed his eyes shut and clutched his bicep, momentarily unable to breathe. Forcing himself to his feet by sheer willpower, he yanked off his mask and mouthpiece and stumbled toward the wall.

Slamming his palm against the door release, the wall panel slid open and he lunged out into the pool room, losing consciousness as he hit the floor.

Chapter 7

"Over here—" Lily screamed, running toward Ian's motionless body.

They'd been pounding the floor area between the pool and the tub when an opening had appeared in the wall across the room and Ian had fallen through.

Already blood was seeping and forming a puddle around his body. He lay on his back, propped up by the oxygen tank.

"Check him for wounds—" Mike shouted from behind her.

"Why was he in the tank?" she gasped, dropping to her knees beside him. Mike reached her and followed suit.

"I don't know"—he said gruffly—"ask him later. For now, find out where all this blood is coming from. Help me take off this wetsuit and tank."

With trembling fingers, she pulled the wetsuit back off Ian's wet head and tugged the tank straps from each shoulder. She pulled his right arm through and scooted around to his other side to do the same with his left, slipping on the blood. The suit was shredded on this arm, spurting lacerations showing through.

Mike removed the tank delicately as Chris appeared and hurried toward them.

"Call an ambulance, Chris—" she shouted.

"No—" a female voice responded nearby.

Lily glanced over her shoulder. Hannah was standing a few feet away; a stern look on her face, hands on her hips.

"No?"

Hannah shook her head. "Auguste—your grandfather, told me that no doctor was *ever* to touch Ian. Even when he was found as a child . . . so ill . . . we nursed him back to health ourselves."

"What! But why? That's insane—Call a doctor now!"

"Stop wasting time," Hannah snapped, approaching them with an air of authority. "Mike—go find some scissors."

Mike took off and left the room by the east wing exit.

"But Hannah"—Lily cried—"we've got to call an ambulance!"

Hannah knelt down beside her and touched Ian's pale cheek tenderly. "No. He would have wanted it this way."

Ian's eyes were shut, hair soaked and plastered to his head.

"But—he'll die." She touched the glossy material covering his shoulder and quickly withdrew her hand. A tear slipped down her cheek, pulse pounding out of control. "He's bleeding all over the floor—" Already her hands and jeans were saturated with blood.

Ian's blood.

She could hardly breathe.

At the sound of footsteps on the nearby stone stairs, Mike burst into the room with scissors in one hand and a First Aid box in the other. Chris, who'd just been standing by like a lost puppy, joined Mike's side with a sudden look of determination and took the First Aid kit from him.

"Lily—hold the material off Ian's wounds while Mike cuts it," Hannah instructed, her white apron stained crimson.

Focusing on steadying her breathing, Lily held the sleeve as Mike sliced through it. Now that Ian's arm was free from the tightness of the suit, blood spurted violently from the ring of holes in his skin and muscle.

"Out of my way now, please." Hannah moved Lily aside. "Chris—gimme some disinfectant. And Mike—get Lily out of here."

Before she could even protest, Mike was helping Lily to her feet and hurrying her from the room, her skimmers slipping and sliding on the bloodied glass floor

Lily sat bolt upright in bed.

Visions of Ian's bloody arm and white face flooded her mind like a strobe light. But that wasn't what had awoken her.

Someone was crying softly.

In the hallway.

And the cries were growing fainter still, moving away, going down the stairs.

Several hours earlier, Hannah had come up from the basement to announce that Ian was awake and doing well. It was difficult to believe and Lily hadn't been allowed to see him either, despite her pleadings. The evening that had thus followed stretched long and lonely. She'd spent it pacing in her bedroom; skipping dinner due to anxiety.

So, who was crying in the middle of the night? Was it Hannah?

Lily climbed out of bed and went to the chest of drawers in the dark; groping around for a pair of track pants and a hoodie sweatshirt, along with her skimmers—which though thoroughly scrubbed, still bore traces of Ian's blood. She then retrieved a pocket flashlight from her purse and fastened her wristwatch, noting the time: half past one.

She slipped out into the hall and tip-toed down the stairs to the front entrance with the aid of her flashlight. She then stood in the chilly corridor with only a faint flower-shaped beam of moonlight lighting it from the quatrefoil window, and listened for any sound of crying.

A muted sound from the end of the corridor.

Indiscernible.

With the beam of her flashlight penetrating the darkness, Lily wandered down the massive hallway toward the far end stairwell. All the doors flanking the corridor were closed; and hearing no sounds, she made no attempts to open them. She didn't feel nervous really, just curious. The crying had been distinctly female and was likely Hannah. Only, where had she gone? Reaching the stairwell room, Lily stood still a moment and considered whether to go upstairs to the as yet unexplored west wing, or to venture downstairs to the pool room. Had they cleaned up Ian's blood? She shuddered and tugged on the battle axe. The wall panel slid open.

Shining her flashlight down the stone steps, which smelled now of bleach and had clearly been scrubbed clean of crimson footsteps, Lily descended and opened the wooden door. Warm, chlorinated air wafted over her.

The pool room was lit by numerous blue night lights within the aquarium—the slow-moving water reflecting off the walls and ceiling. Much to her relief, the glass floor was completely washed and polished and there was no trace of blood anywhere.

The hidden panel on the right-hand side of the room that led into the scuba room was shut and invisible from where she stood. Just how many other hidden doors might there be in this place? And more importantly, why hadn't Mike told her about the scuba room when she'd asked about privacy? Was it possible that he didn't know about the room . . . or did he lie?

Aside from the rippling reflection of the water, all was still and unmoving.

She shuddered and wandered deeper into the room, beyond the empty bathtub, taking care not to tumble into it, until she reached the center of the aquarium. A chill ran up her spine at the memory of

Ian's palms pressed up against the glass from underneath; reddish water all around him. There were several wedges in the floor where Mike had taken a crow bar to it. She got down on her knees and peered through the glass. The aquarium was deep here but there were several elongated shadows at the bottom; she wanted to see if it was the sharks.

It was—only they weren't moving.

Their bodies were sprawled over the bed of the tank, bobbing slightly in a mild current.

Dead.

Her throat clogged, back tensing. Why had they died?

A scuffling sound came from behind and she spun around as a shadow darted across the wall above the tropical plants.

"Who's there?" she said, pulse quickening. She jerked a glance around the room.

Nothing.

She took a deep breath and stood up. It must be her nerves getting to her after the trauma of that day. She left the center of the room and followed the perimeter back toward the east wing entrance; gripping her flashlight in her palm.

Another shadow darted across the far right wall. She scanned the entire room.

Nothing moved.

Were the shadows just random movements of fish swimming past the blue water lights and reflecting off the walls?

A deep, sighing breath rushed through the room—then went silent.

Lily dropped her flashlight and ducked around a marble angel, pressing her back against the wall. Inch by inch she headed toward the open door, heart hammering against her ribs. Surely she was just hearing things.

"*Run, Lily, run,*" a disembodied female voice murmured from somewhere close by.

"H-Hannah?"

As soon as the question had left her lips the blue lights of the aquarium flickered out and the room went entirely black, save for the stream of her fallen flashlight. On the verge of panic, she felt her way along the wall with wooden fingers and nearly screamed when she bumped into a statue.

All she could hear was her own rasping breath.

She held it in to mute it and moved forward again only to freeze when she realized the rasping breathing hadn't stopped.

It wasn't her at all—it was someone beside her.

A heated breath flowed down the side of her cheek and neck sending waves of terror through her body like a static charge.

She tried to run toward the door but couldn't find anything with her outstretched hands. She scratched at the walls, desperate for the door and fully expecting to be grabbed from behind.

So this is how Ian must have felt, she thought suddenly, subconsciously—*trapped in the depths of the aquarium, horror closing in—waiting to be snatched away at any moment.*

Something scraped across the floor behind her and footsteps pounded to her right, no wait—behind. No—to the right. The whole room pulsated with footsteps, making it impossible to tell which direction they came from.

Before she could react, pain shot through her back as though something sharp had sliced her skin—and a wheezing moan sounded to her right.

Lily ran blindly to the left, forgetting she might tumble into the empty bathtub and break her neck—but finding a solid wall with her hands, she scrambled forward and rejoiced to touch the edge of the door frame.

Hands grabbed her sweatshirt, pulling her backward.

Instinctively, she jabbed her elbow into something soft—but the hands didn't let go. An arm wrapped around her waist and a hand clamped down over her mouth. She wanted to scream and bite as a smooth cheek pressed against hers.

"*Hush.*" It was that female voice again.

Lily clawed at the dainty hand over her mouth and paused for a split second when she realized the sleeve of her captor was visible: a flowing white silk.

Something smacked hard against the back of her head and her body went limp.

Chapter 8

Lily's head hurt and she groaned out loud, clutching it.

At first she had no clue where she was. Then the memories of the attack in the pool room washed over her consciousness like a crashing wave. She snapped her eyes open and lifted her head. She lay in a heap in the front entranceway of the mansion, just beyond the Persian rug. Moonlight poured in through the window, reflecting off the black marble floor beneath her and accentuating the trailing white veins. Farther down the corridor, where the moonlight failed to reach, was a gaping darkness.

Far off, deep within the mansion, someone was crying again.

Faintly.

Lurching to her feet, Lily stumbled up the staircase and frantically yanked open the door leading into Mike's bedroom. Pushing it shut behind her, she turned the lock and ran to his bedside—nearly tripping over a pile of clothes in her haste.

He was already awake and turning on the lamp on his nightstand.

Mike's room was like hers but flipped, with a similar sitting area surrounding a fireplace and a hand-carved canopy bed. She climbed up on it and sat at the foot.

He struggled to sit up and rubbed his eyes with his thumb and index. "Lily?" He blinked at her. "What's going on?" The room was mostly dark but thanks to the lamp, the area around his bed was suffused in muted orange light.

She hugged her waist, heart racing. "S-someone's after me—" Her back was painfully rigid and she struggled to control her breathing. She took a deep breath. "I didn't know where else to go—"

He leaned forward and grabbed her by the shoulders. "What are you talking about?"

She gave him a frenzied look. "The baths, the murdered maid—!"

"Ahh. You're delirious then." He exhaled and let go of her shoulders. "You must have had a nightmare." He scratched his head and gave her a curious look.

Lily reached around to touch her lower back, flinching, and withdrew her hand—holding it out for Mike to see. Her fingertips were wet and red.

Mike's eyes widened and he threw back the blankets, jumping from the bed. He examined her back and helped her down. "How'd this happen?" he asked, dropping his voice to a cautious undertone and casting a glance toward the closed door. He sat her down on a ladder-back chair at his desk.

She tried to explain the attack, piecing together the fragmented memories; but the more she said, the crazier it sounded.

Mike switched on an overhead chandelier and

scrounged around in a nearby cabinet, withdrawing a First Aid kit.

"Could've been caused by anything, I guess," he said, sounding calm again. "Are you sure you didn't just scrape it against a statue while the lights were out?"

She straddled the chair and held the back of her shirt partway up. "I . . . I don't know."

He examined her back again. "It's not as bad as it seems," he said, setting down the kit on the desk and opening it. He disinfected the wound and she bit her lip to lessen the sting. "I don't think you need any stitches," he said. "It's just superficial—about two inches long."

She was beginning to feel embarrassed, but even if she had inflicted the wound herself on a statue, surely she hadn't imagined the voice or the breathing? or the white robed arm that grabbed her and knocked her out?

There was also the question of how she ended up at the front door.

Mike finished taping the wound over with gauze. She turned around in the chair to face him. "Shouldn't we call the police or check up on everyone to make sure they're okay?" she said. "What if who-ever it was is still here?"

Mike shook his head decidedly, eying her as though wary of her sanity. "I'm sure if someone was here, he or she would be long gone by now." He sat down on an upholstered settee and hooked his arm over the crest rail, facing her directly. She noticed for the first time that he was in cotton pajama pants and an undershirt.

"But someone knocked me out and dragged me to the front corridor, I'm sure of it. Why not just leave me in the pool room? It makes no sense. We really should call the police."

He shook his head again. "No, we'll check in the morning to see if anything's missing and worry about it then." He sighed. "It's been a long day for you, Lily—the accident with Ian, probably really shook you up. And the lights going out in the base-ment . . . I really just think your mind's playing tricks on you. I'm sorry you got hurt though." He gave her a look of pity and she broke eye contact, resenting his patronizing tone.

"How *is* Ian, by the way?" She met his gaze again. "I wanted to go see him—but Hannah wouldn't let me. I have no idea where his room is either."

"He's just down the hall right now, actually. Temporarily. Last room on the left. But seriously, Lily, next time you get the urge to explore in the middle of the night, come get me first, okay? As I'm sure you realize by now, it's not a safe thing to do." Again with the patronizing tone.

She leaned forward so the wound wasn't pressing against the back of the chair anymore. "I can see that now," she said flatly, cheeks prickling. He didn't believe her account; thought she'd simply hurt herself on a statue and had imagined the rest in a state of hysteria.

"Well," she said, folding her arms, "seeing as how it's the middle of the night and you don't want me wandering around alone—can you take me to see

Ian?"

Mike rubbed his knee, frowning. "Now?"

She stood up. "I need to know he's okay. It's been a, weird day, to say the least."

Mike stood too. "Fine. But let's get you a clean shirt first."

"You don't think red is my color?" She laughed, trying to lighten the mood.

"I think any color would look good on you, but a bloody shirt will send Ian off the deep end. He'd probably blame me for it, too."

She searched his face a moment, nodded. "Of course. I wouldn't want to distress him."

To ease her nerves, Mike scoped the hallway first and then her bedroom, assuring her that no one was lurking about. He waited in the hall while she changed her shirt and rinsed her hands in a ceramic basin. They went to the last door on the left, walking quietly to avoid waking Hannah. There was no sound of crying now.

"Do you want me to go in with you?" Mike asked.

"Yes, please." She gave him a weak smile. "I don't want to barge in on Ian like I just did with you." She blushed at the memory. "In retrospect, it's pretty embarrassing."

He laughed and gave her a side hug. "No worries—I got your back."

She winced at that.

They entered Ian's room, which was just a guest room, and Mike turned on a double sconce lamp next to the door. It wasn't enough light to wake

Ian but provided enough that they could find their way around the room without tripping over furniture.

The room was tiny compared to the others, with a rose-patterned settee and a dresser on the left-hand side of the room, and an iron Victorian bed in the center. On the right-hand wall was an arched lancet window with a trestle table beneath it. Atop the table were some medical supplies—gauze, tape, antiseptic, and a ceramic water basin and pitcher.

She wondered why Ian had been brought to a guest room rather than to his own bedroom, but decided to ask later. Mike motioned to her that he was going to wait by the door and she nodded distractedly. With soft steps, she went to where Ian lay sleeping. When she reached his side, she sat on the edge of the bed and stared down at his peaceful, sleeping form. He didn't look like he was in any pain—there was no visible tension in his features. His face was so serene she almost wished she could trade places with him and sleep away the nightmares of the day.

Though he was covered to the chest with a rose-patterned counterpane, he wore no shirt and both arms rested on top; his left arm heavily bandaged in gauze, and abrasions on his knuckles. Even in the dull lighting she could make out the stains saturating the layers.

Someone had taken the time to comb his dark hair, and for a second she had the urge to touch her fingertips to his cheek. But why so protective of him? After all, he was a stranger; and one that had been rather hostile at times. Nevertheless, she reached for his good hand and held it in her own as a silent gesture of care and concern.

Without warning, his left hand jerked forward and grabbed her wrist. His eyes snapped open and he stared at her in cold fury.

She gasped.

"What's wrong?" Mike asked, approaching the bedside.

"Oh—it's you," Ian said, relief draining the fury from his eyes. "I'm sorry."

"It's okay," she said, pulse dropping back down again. "I startled you, I . . . Ian—your hand." He was still gripping her wrist with a strength that shouldn't have been there.

He let go, gauzed arm falling limp against the blanket.

She rubbed her wrist. "Doesn't your arm hurt? Your muscle was . . . shredded. I saw bone—"

"Painkillers."

She clasped her hands together in her lap and nodded. "I'm sorry for waking you—I just wanted to see for myself that you're okay. I couldn't sleep."

"It's okay," he mumbled, voice thick with a slight slur. She wondered if he was under sedation. He flicked his dark gaze away from her and onto Mike.

"Don't be mad," Mike said, taking a step backward. "Lily had a fright and wanted to see you."

"Why would I be mad?" He glanced at the digital clock on his night stand and knit his brow. "Three a.m.? Why are you both up?" He looked from Mike to Lily with narrowed eyes.

"We weren't together," she blurted out, surprised at herself for needing to clarify that. She opened her mouth to explain further but weakness washed over her and she closed it again. She had no energy to recount for a second time all that had happened to her in the pool room. Besides, Ian didn't need any more burdens on his plate.

"There's something you're not telling me," he said.

"Oh, Lily hurt herself," said Mike flippantly, as though he'd been holding his breath. "She says she was attacked by someone in the pool room."

"What—" Ian scooted up to a sitting position, eyes wide. "By whom?"

Instantly averting her gaze from his bare chest, Lily debated how to explain. "Well, it was actually . . . a woman, I think." She met his eyes, bracing herself for a rebuff.

His eyes smoldered in response. "Did you see who she was?" The slurred thickness was gone from his voice.

She shook her head. "No, the lights were out."

"What were you doing down there in the middle of the night, Lily? Are you nuts?" He was angry now.

Her lower lip began to tremble and she blinked back tears.

"Ian, just chill man," Mike cut in. "We'll talk about it in the morning. Let's go, Lily."

Ian leaned back against the headboard and shut his eyes in what appeared to be resignation. "Fine, you're right," he said without tone. "She should go and get some sleep."

"Would you both stop it already?" Lily snapped, tears drying. "Since the moment I got here everyone has been treating me like a child." She crossed her arms over her chest and spoke in a level voice: "I *own* half this place now, buddy, and if I choose to go wandering around in the middle of the night, it's none of your business. Got it?" She let out a snort. "Mind you, after tonight, I don't know if I should stay here even one more day . . . "

Both men stared at her but neither spoke.

"Oh, and one more thing," she went on. "I will decide myself when to go to sleep, thank you very much."

Ian exchanged a glance with Mike. "There's only one thing to do in a situation like this," he said.

"What's that?" Mike raised an eyebrow.

"Back away, slowly."

A smile tugged at her lips but she forced herself to scowl at Ian instead.

"Fine, fine," he acquiesced, "go to sleep whenever you want—but I'll be keeping an eye on you."

"What?"

He grimaced. "That came out wrong."

Something niggled at her then and the smile died on her lips. "What were you doing in the pool yesterday?" she said. "Were you in there while I was using the bathtub?" The question had troubled her all afternoon and evening but she hadn't allowed herself to face it fully—until now. True, he'd been in the hallway when she ran straight into him after the bath, but in the time it took her to dress, he could have changed quickly enough and waited for her to come up.

He blinked once but his expression was unreadable.

Butterflies picked up in her stomach.

"No, I never go in the tank before the sharks are fed," he said, maintaining steady eye contact. "And I would never . . . spy on you like that," his voice trailed off and fatigue filled his features. He looked away.

Mike cleared his throat but she ignored him. She had to know if Ian was telling the truth. "But why were you in the tank?" she pressed. "Is that something you do often?"

It occurred to her then that the large black form that had slid under the aquarium glass prompting her flight up the stairs, may have in fact been a scuba diver. But if that were true, it couldn't have been Ian.

Mike's presence prickled in her peripheral then and she shuddered inwardly.

Was there not anyone in this house she could trust?

Ian focused his gaze on the lancet window and didn't answer.

She stood up. "We'll talk about it later, Ian. Glad you're okay . . . " She turned and started for the open door. Mike followed.

"No—wait."

She pivoted.

Ian was struggling to get out of the bed, his bandaged arm making it awkward. "It's not safe—" he said, "not until we can be sure your attacker is gone." He winced when he tried to stand, and sat back down. "I'm going to—stay with you. On the couch." He tried to stand again, holding the bed for support with his good hand.

"Don't be silly," she said. "I'll lock my door."

He caught her gaze then. "That's—that's not good enough."

"For Pete's sake," she said, "get back in bed." She crossed the room to his side and gently pushed him back against the pillows.

"Mike," he said over her shoulder, raising his voice, "go warn the others—make sure their doors are locked."

Lily pulled the sheets and counterpane up over his pajama-clad legs, holding up his bandaged arm so it could rest on top.

As she pulled the blankets the rest of the way over his bare chest, she stopped short, breath catching in her throat.

Jagged scars ran criss-cross over his toned pectoral muscles as though he'd once been attacked by a bear.

She blinked, pretending not to notice, and tugged the blankets up to his underarms. He laid his head against the propped pillows and shut his eyes.

"I'll watch over her," Mike said from beside her. "I'll just grab a blanket and sleep on the couch."

"No. It's best she stay here with me." Ian opened his eyes and locked gaze with Mike. "I'm better trained to handle a situation like this."

"You can't even get out of bed." Mike moved closer, arms folded over his broad chest, looking Ian up and down. "Better trained are you? Were you a ninja in another life?" He let out a sharp laugh. "Look man, you were nearly eaten by sharks today. Do you seriously think you could do a better job watching Lily tonight than I could?"

"Guys—come on," she said, "let's not make a big deal of this. I'll just sleep on the sofa over there if that'll make him happy. All right?" She went to the dresser and searched the drawers for blankets. There was a quilt in the bottom drawer. It smelled fresh enough so she unfolded it and plunked down on the stiff settee, trying not to yelp when her back pressed against the wooden arm.

Mike stared at her in stunned silence and she waited with interest to see what would happen next.

"Well, I'll see you in the morning, I guess," he said, unfolding his arms. He crossed the room without another glance and closed the door behind him as he went out into the hall.

Lily kicked off her shoes and pulled her knees up to her chest, tucking the quilt about herself and trying to get comfortable. Not too likely with a cut on her back and no pillow. The settee wasn't long enough to stretch out her legs either. She glanced at Ian but couldn't make out his shadowed facial expression from this distance. The dim streams from the wall sconces just weren't bright enough.

He wasn't looking at her either but rather at the door.

Oh, right—she hadn't locked it.

"I'll lock it," she said, throwing back the quilt and going to the door. The hardwood floor was slick beneath her socks.

"Please take the bed," he said gruffly, pulling the covers back again and sitting up straight. "I'll take the couch."

"Oh, don't be ridiculous." She started toward him, intending to lay him back down, but he was already standing to his feet. "Ian, come on—what are you doing? You're impossible." She avoided looking at his scars as he went to the dresser. He crouched down and tugged open the middle drawer with his gauzed arm. He pulled out another folded blanket with his good hand and brought it to the settee, arranging it as a pillow. He laid back against it, long legs draping over the side of the couch.

"You gonna sleep like that?" she asked. "Half hanging to the floor?" She walked up to him and pulled the quilt from his lap. "What was that, anyway?"

"What was what?"

"You tugged the drawer open with your injured arm. You shouldn't be able to—" She dropped the quilt to the floor and grabbed his bandaged forearm.

He winced and yanked it from her, cradling it to his chest. "Ga-a-ah—it hurts like heck when you do *that*."

She let go and softened her tone, earlobes burning. She hadn't meant to hurt him. "May I change those bandages for you?"

He raised an eyebrow, considering for a moment. "Oh, fine," he said with a half smile. "Let's see what kind of hack job Hannah did on me. . . . Can you turn on the overhead light?"

Lily switched on the light and carried the trestle table across the room to the settee, taking care not to slosh the water. She squinted at Ian in the incandescent lighting and on second thought, went back to the window to grab the waste basket.

Ian moved stiffly to the end of the settee and she sat down next to him.

She reached for him with a tentative hand and unraveled the gauze, tossing bloodied sections of it into the waste basket one layer at a time. "I need to tell you something," she said suddenly, heartbeat racing as a memory came to her like a slap across the face. He met her eyes and she noticed they were brown, not black like she'd originally thought. She resumed the unwrapping. "The sharks, I saw them, and . . . I think they might be dead."

"Mmhm."

" 'Mmhm'? That's it?"

"Yes—I had them put down."

"What!"

"Why would I want to keep a tank full of man-eaters? Something was wrong with them—sand sharks don't behave like that. I've swam with them for *years* now and they've never been a threat to me before. They were also injured and would have required medical attention. I don't know what happened to them." He shrugged his right shoulder. "What choice did I have?"

She stopped unwrapping the gauze and dropped her hands to her knees. "So—instead of figuring out what was wrong with them, you killed them. Just like that." Her pulse pounded, heat coursing through her body. He could have at least acquired a professional opinion from a marine biologist before doing something so rash—and so cruel.

Then again, maybe she'd feel differently if she was the one who'd nearly been eaten for lunch.

"I had my reasons," he said. "I know a lot more about the situation than you do."

"Yeah? So, why don't you enlighten me for a change? I've been kept in the dark about everything else, it seems."

He looked away.

The silence grew awkward and she lifted his arm again and unraveled more of the gauze, tempering her frustration. When she reached the final layer, she peeled it off gingerly, grimacing on his behalf.

"You sure you wanna see this?"

She smiled with sympathy. "If you can handle it, I can handle it."

"Well, if you throw up, aim away from me."

With a nervous laugh, she tossed the final piece of gauze into the bin and examined his arm.

It was swollen and red with uneven purple lacerations in a semi circle on either side of his forearm. Hannah had done a decent job of stitching up each cut, but the wounds were gruesome; though not nearly as severe as she'd recalled.

Her stomach clenched and she had to turn away to collect her bearings and swallow down the nausea.

"Think they'll scar?" he said.

She met his gaze and found him grinning.

"How can you joke about it?" She gaped at

him. "What if you never regain full control of your arm or hand? What if it gets infected? You could lose your arm, you know. I highly doubt Hannah is trained in nursing—or is she? You should be in the hospital. You should also be in horrible pain, but you seem—well—rather fine to me. Just what meds are you taking anyway?"

He rubbed the bridge of his nose with his good hand. "Would you rather I rolled around on the floor groaning? I can do that if it'll make you feel better."

"Maybe you're still in shock."

"You seem to know a lot about this, is there a book on how to react to a shark bite? I must not have read it."

"Oh, you're hopeless—" She flung her hands upward. "So, what now—any treatment or just fresh bandaging?"

"A quick rinse with water and new bandaging will be fine."

Ian focused on the red digits of the alarm clock by his bed while Lily dabbed a damp cloth on his arm. Her touch was soft and gentle and caring. He flinched a little each time she applied pressure. It was 4:19 a.m. and Hannah would be around within the hour to check on him. He was going to be in for a verbal beating when she found Lily lying in his bed instead of him—that is, if he could actually convince

Lily to sleep there while he took the settee. Hannah would go on and on about his need for bed rest and he'd have to assure her he felt fine.

He'd been through it all before.

Many a time.

Lily dried his arm with a clean hand towel and wrapped gauze around it, one layer at a time, taping it as needed. She was so focused on what she was doing that he allowed his gaze to linger. She was very pretty; those long lashes brushing against her cheeks, latte-brown hair mussed up and half tucked behind her ears. She smelled like flowers. He felt silly even just to think it.

"There," she said, patting his arm lightly when she was done. "Now, where's the pain killers? You in for another dose?"

"Hannah will bring them." He was exhausted and did not need a sedative.

"Now, back to bed," she insisted, standing and rinsing her hands in the water basin, drying them on a towel. She reached for his good hand.

He pulled it from her grasp. "No-no, I'll sleep here."

"I'm not taking the bed, that would be absurd."

Ian leaned back against the blanket pillow he'd arranged earlier and pulled the quilt up to his chin and shut his eyes.

At the sound of her leaving his side, he peeked through the slit of one eye in time to see her switch off the overhead light. She left the sconce lights on and to his relief, went to his bed. Pulling the blankets up, she plopped down on top of them and turned onto her side, facing him. It was too dark to see if her eyes were open but when she tucked her hands under her chin, he presumed she was going to try and sleep.

He tried to relax, mentally cursing Auguste for his taste in Victorian furniture. It was nice enough to look at but rigid to lounge on, let alone nap. But at least his arm wasn't throbbing anymore.

He should have been more careful. Lily was too savvy to keep making careless mistakes around her. What had he been thinking using his injured arm to grab her wrist like that? Instinct, he supposed. This was the very reason he'd always instructed Hannah not to disturb him while he was sleeping. He didn't trust himself to be woken that way. He'd been jumpy since childhood. Everything was a threat and for good reason. And why had he gone and opened the drawer with his bad arm as well? Such an obvious and thoughtless mistake. He'd have to be much more conscious of what he was doing from now on.

Now that Lily was here.

And what should he do with her anyway? It was too dangerous to let her stay, especially now that she'd been attacked by something.

A very bad sign.

He shuddered involuntarily.

Several minutes later the door burst open with a lingering creak and he opened his eyes. A disheveled Hannah stood in its frame, suffused by the sconce light; the hallway cavernous behind her. She had sunken eyes and a haunted expression; long hair all a-toss.

Without noticing Lily, her gaze went straight to Ian and she crossed the room to him, thrusting her hand out from behind her back.

She was holding Auguste's cane.

"I've been wanting to tell you—"

Ian motioned toward the bed and she followed his gaze with a jerk. Surprise visibly replacing the look of distress, she asked no questions but gave him a look of stern warning and left the room, closing the door behind her.

No one else had found that cane since Auguste's death, though Ian had known where it was all along. Hannah must have been in the attic recently, despite him forbidding her to do so. She'd barely spoken two words to him while tending his wounds and putting him to bed earlier, but each time she'd checked on him there'd been a look of grief and fear in her eyes and in the lines of her face. Several times she'd started to say something but had bit her lip instead. Had the discovery of the cane been troubling her all this time?

He would have to talk to her about it in the morning.

Chapter 9

The next morning, breakfast out of the way, Hannah stood next to the carved-knight newel post in the front entrance with her hands clasped together at her waist.

She watched Ms. Kline who stood conversing with the uniformed police officer at the door. He had thoroughly searched the basement and the outside grounds over the past hour and was now ready to take his leave.

"Sally lives with the Conners at the end of the road," he explained to Lily in a baritone voice, " 'bout five miles north of here. She has some kind of dementia and every once in a while she gets it in her head to run away, and when she does, she usually finds a way to break into a neighbor's home." He scratched his cheek with his index finger. "Don't know where she gets the energy to do that, but this isn't the first time. As soon as you called I figured it was her." He chuckled, perusing the open notepad in his hand. "She must have thought you were a threat somehow." He looked up. "Explains why she nicked you with a knife. I wouldn't worry about it happening again though—the Conners are making arrangements for her to move to a nursing home next month."

Lily was nodding but her expression was difficult to read.

Was she buying the story?

"I'll be giving 'em a call this afternoon," he was saying, "and making sure they keep Sally under lock and key till moving day." He crooked a grin and tugged on the rim of his peaked cap. "You just be sure to keep your doors locked this time 'round." He winked and flipped the notebook shut, stuffing it into his jacket pocket. "You take care now," he said to Lily, nodding a good-bye to Hannah.

Lily shut the heavy oak doors behind him and gave a half-hearted smile to Hannah before heading to the dining room where she had plans to spend the greater part of the day baking with Angie. It was Hannah's idea; she was determined to keep Lily away from Ian all day if possible.

She had not been amused to learn of Lily's plight in the master baths the night before. The whole thing was a figment of the girl's imagination, of course, but she must be kept quiet for Ian's sake.

Hannah pulled a cell phone from the pocket of her apron and hit redial.

"Hello," a male voice answered on the second ring.

"Andrew—" she spoke in an undertone, glancing down the corridor. "It's me. Hannah."

"How'd I do? She buy it?"

"I'm not sure. I think so. You did well—excellent costume, by the way. Almost fooled *me*." She stepped to the base of the stairs and looked upward. No one seemed to be in ear shot but she spoke in a hushed tone. "If she has any further concerns, I'll be sure to verify your story about Sally. And if I need your help again, I'll pay cash, as usual."

"That all for today?"

"Yes. Thank you. Bye for now."

She slid the phone back into her apron and went upstairs.

Early in the evening, having washed her hair with great awkwardness in a ceramic basin and dry-shaved her legs, Lily changed into jeans and a ruby red sweater. She dried her hair and combed it out, as pin-straight as ever, and pulled on her skimmers.

It was time to go check out Ian's work shed while he was sleeping in the guest room. That is, she assumed he was sleeping or at least resting, since he hadn't joined them for any of the meals that day. Hannah had assured her he was fine but didn't want any visitors.

Lily left the mansion from the exit at the far end of the corridor and waved at Chris as she passed by the rose bushes that encircled the maiden fountain. Chris paused his yard work to give her a friendly wave and returned to his wheelbarrow. He appeared to be wrapping up for the day and would probably be heading home shortly. There was no sign of Mike from back here but she quickened her pace nonetheless, eager to reach the forest without being caught. The window in Ian's room was leaded glass and she doubted he could see through it well enough to notice her. Dusk was approaching and she wanted to get this over and done with quickly.

When she reached the ebony gargoyle, she stopped to stare at it, remembering what she'd seen the other night in the dark. She'd expected to find the white orb lying on the grass next to the base but it was clutched firmly in the gargoyle's paw as it had been the first day she'd come back here. Had she just been seeing things that night?

No—the white light had definitely fallen to the ground in that split-second before the lights had gone out. But how? The gargoyle's paw wasn't even cracked.

She hesitated a moment longer, thinking about Ian's repeated warnings to stay out of the forest.

He must have something to hide—and now was the perfect opportunity to find out what.

Lifting her chin with determination, she took a deep breath and followed the dirt trail into the forest, not even blinking when the orb lights flicked on and lit the path.

The forest was dull due to the overcast sky and descending dusk, but not yet dark. When she reached the jutting root that she'd previously tripped over in her high heels, she peered into the tree-shrouded area where she'd seen lights shining from Ian's work shed. She pushed aside the heavy boughs of two spruce trees and stepped through into a clearing.

Ahead of her was a massive tree, like an

African baobab, some twelve feet wide in diameter, and endless intertwining limbs stretching up and out of sight above it. The gray sky seemed miles above.

In the center of the trunk was a hinged door cut from the bark itself, and above it were three ocular windows, one atop the other with two meters of space between each. The upper two were dark but the lowest one was yellow, casting her in a dome of light. Was Ian here? She inhaled slowly and stepped up to the door to examine the tree, breath catching in her throat. Intricate, mythical creatures had been carved into the wood all the way up the trunk; unicorns on haunches leaped out at her around the base and angels curved their bodies and wings around the windows.

Had Ian done all this? Was he an artist?

Overcome with a fierce curiosity, she tapped on the door and waited. Receiving no answer, she tried the handle and found it unlocked. Glancing once over her shoulder, she pulled the door open, gasping at the sight inside.

The walls of the hollowed-out tree were covered from floor-to-ceiling with precious gems and trinkets, sparkling in the light emanating from a dozen stained-glass lanterns which hung from the ceiling. Ancient scholarly tomes were stacked in a tall pile on the left-hand side of the room and the dirt floor was spread with a geometric Turkish rug, blue and red. Against the far wall, which was at least as deep as the room was wide, was an upholstered wingback chair.

With a hand over her pounding heart, she

entered the room and did a slow circle, inhaling the scent of bark and soil. The lanterns hovered about a foot and a half above her head. How were they receiving electricity? Beside the door was a polished wooden ladder disappearing through a round opening in the ceiling to the floor above, just wide enough for a man's shoulders, though an overweight individual would not make it through. Lily climbed the ladder and emerged into a bedroom of sorts, the furniture contours outlined by the dim light coming through the round window. She felt around for some kind of light switch and finding a button, pressed it.

The walls of the room lit up instantly: they were covered in shards of multicolored glass, artfully arranged into a panoramic picture of mountainous landscapes, and suffused from behind like sunshine on stained-glass.

Completely out of place from the tranquility and beauty of the walls was a wooden cot with purple velvety blankets in a scattered heap on the mattress. On the adjacent side of the room was a walnut table with detailed carvings curling up the thick legs. There was no way such a table could've been brought up the ladder; someone must have built it within this very room, piece-by-piece. Across its heavy-duty, glossy surface was an assortment of carving tools and a four-foot long block of wood; half-formed into a unicorn. It lay on its side, staring out at her with unseeing, sapphire eyes.

Between the bed and the table was another wooden ladder disappearing to a third floor. She crossed the surprisingly sturdy hardwood flooring and climbed the ladder to the final floor. She figured she must be twenty-five feet above ground by now.

Surprised that she could be shocked yet again after all she'd already seen, she sucked in her breath to realize these walls were entirely covered with rows and rows of what looked like marble-sized diamonds. She emerged from the ladder onto the hardwood floor, found a light source, pressed it, and stood gaping at the twinkling walls. Perhaps they weren't real diamonds though—glass maybe. They couldn't possibly be real—could they? And no security either: why, anyone could wander into the forest and find this tree, come back later and strip it bare of its jewels. Even the front door had been left unlocked. No, it must all be an illusion: carefully molded glass that had been colored and shaped to look like precious jewels.

She was so distracted by the diamond-studded walls that it took her a moment to notice the golden cage filling the center of the room. It was the size of a standard refrigerator. Inside sat a turquoise bird with fiery tail feathers cascading from the perch to the floor in a slew of orange, red and yellow. It tilted its head to one side and studied her curiously with an emerald eye; letting out a cluck with its tongue.

She'd never seen any bird like this before. Was it some kind of rare exotic species from deep within the Congo? How strange that Ian would keep such a valuable pet hidden away from everyone. With only an ocular window, she didn't expect the poor creature to be getting enough sunlight—especially in the summertime when the full leaves of the trees probably blocked out every last ray.

A gold key hung from a string around one of the bird's pinkish ankles.

How bizarre.

She stepped up to the bars of the cage to examine the key when a door slammed below, sending a jolt up her back.

Ian!

Lily scrambled down the ladder—hoping to hide under the cot—a silly, childish reaction—but it was too late. By the time she reached the base of the ladder, he was already climbing up into the room on the other side.

He stood to his full height, the ceiling nearly grazing his head, and glared at her; bandaged arm hanging at his side. "I thought I told you never to come here alone."

She ran a shaky hand through her hair.

"I—just wanted to talk to you and, well"—she shrugged, trying to appear casual—"I thought maybe I'd find you out here."

"You obviously didn't look too hard. I've been lying on the bed in that blasted guest room all day bored out of my mind. Just where you left me."

She smiled sheepishly. "Okay, I lied . . . I wanted to see what your workshop looked like. Is that so bad?"

"Yes—*it is*." His brow tightened in apparent anger. "What if some hungry wolves had spotted you?"

"Oh, stop being so paranoid." She laughed

and leaned her shoulder against the ladder rail.

"I'm not paranoid." He sat down on the low cot, draping his arms over his knees and hanging his head, looking up at her sidelong. "I just don't want you to get hurt."

She sat down beside him gingerly. Was he furious or just annoyed?

His brown eyes were almost black in the cozy lighting. "You could have just asked me to take you here and I would have," he said.

On impulse, she put an arm around his shoulder gave him a side squeeze. "I'm sorry. I was sure you'd refuse. And you were bed-ridden, too." He stiffened at her touch and she withdrew her arm. "Did you . . . make all this?"

He nodded, staring across the room at the unfinished unicorn. "Took about ten years to build. I'm still not finished."

"No kidding? You actually hollowed out the tree, made the walls, the jewels, and all the carvings?"

He smiled bashfully. "Yeah."

A thought came to her. "Did you sculpt all those gargoyles lining the pathway, too?"

"Huh? No." He met her eyes and straightened his back, blinking once. "Oh, yes, I mean. Yes, I made those, too." He looked down and fiddled with the edging of the tape that held the gauze in place on his arm.

"Ian . . . This might seem silly, but—please indulge me."

He glanced at her and one of his dark eyebrows twitched. "Okay?"

"The first gargoyle at the entrance to the forest —he is holding an orb . . . "

"Yes. They light up when they detect motion."

"Yes, of course. I realize that. It's just that, two nights ago, I could've sworn I saw the first light fall to the ground. But when I came out here this morning, it was back in place."

"That's not possible. It's attached to a wire which runs through the arm and into the base. You'd have to break off the fingers to remove the bulb."

"So . . . you didn't repair it?"

"Nope. Wasn't broken. You must've been seeing things." He went back to picking at the gauze on his arm, looking like a sulky little boy. He glanced at her sidelong. "Is that all you wanted to ask?"

"Well . . . " She gathered her hair in one hand and let go again. "If you're open to questions, answer me this one: Why did my grandfather make us co-heirs? Surely you know. Hannah says we aren't related."

A long pause.

"No, we aren't related, that's for sure. I was an orphan, the old man took me in. Guess he wanted some company in that ancient mansion of his."

"So, you're adopted."

"Not exactly."

"But you can't keep a child that isn't your own without first going through some kind of legal process—can you?" She turned toward him, pulling a knee up on the bed and gripping her shin.

He didn't make eye contact—just sat there hunched over, fiddling with his bandages. A white scar ran along his jawline to his chin, about an inch long.

"No one ever came looking for me, so there was no need." His dark hair was black in contrast to the bright multicolored walls. She wondered if this was actually his bedroom.

"Did you ever know your parents?"

A slight nod. "Yes. My mother was . . . " He cleared his throat. "She was killed. And my father . . . well, I guess you could say he's dead, too."

This was opening up way too many new questions and she'd barely begun to ask about the bejeweled tree fort they were sitting in. As much as she wanted to learn more, she needed to get things back on track or they'd be here all night.

"I know I've asked before, but how did my grandfather get to be so rich?"

He sighed and rubbed his eyes with his thumb and forefinger, showing exaggerated patience. "Like I said the last time you asked—I don't know!"

"So, he never told you."

"No—and I never asked."

She huffed. It was like pulling teeth to get any information from him. "Why didn't he ever contact my mother? He left us to live in near poverty."

"Lily—" He twisted to face her head on. "In all honestly, until he died, I had no idea you even existed."

She searched his eyes, trying to read them. They were beautiful eyes, intense and provocative. But there was a certain coldness to them as well. She hoped it wasn't violence.

"Frankly, I was shocked when his will was read to me," he went on, sounding truthful. "But now I must admit, I'm glad to have . . . met you." He broke eye contact and she sensed that come-and-go awkwardness again. One minute he was relaxed and confident, the next reticent and bumbling. It was endearing somehow.

"Why?" she asked softly, hoping he'd tell her that he was as captivated by her as she was with him. He was so close she could smell his cologne: overwhelmingly masculine, but also faint. It suited him.

"Because now Hannah has someone else to fuss over—" he said, "making more breathing space for me." He laughed and winked at her, no longer shy. The smile lingered on his face.

She smiled pleasantly to hide her disappointment. "And here I was expecting some kind of romantic, poetic lines about your undying love."

"Poetry? The day I start spouting poetry, put me out of my misery."

She let out a belt of laughter, swatting his shoulder. "You crack me up."

The smile faded. "So, what's up with you and Mike?" He spoke in a lower tone now, dropping his gaze. The awkwardness was back.

"What do you mean?"

"When you had that scare in the pool room . . . he was the one you went to for help."

"That's because I didn't know where your room was—and for that matter, I didn't even know if you were okay! The last time I saw you, you were unconscious in a puddle of your own blood." She glanced at his hands and startled.

The abrasions on his knuckles were gone.

How could they possibly have vanished in only two days?

"Why are—" She hesitated. "What happened to the scuffs on your hand?"

He jumped to his feet, nearly hitting his head on the ceiling, and crossed the room in two strides, folding his arms. "Why can't you just mind your own business? Why must you continually badger me with endless questions? I have things to do."

She left the cot and stepped in front of him, forcing him to look down at her. "Like what, Ian? Let me guess: You want me to leave so that you can just sit here and sulk like a child."

"I think you should go now," he said quite evenly, though his gaze was fierce.

She sighed. His unpredictable mood swings confused her; made her uneasy.

"Look—" he said, "you want to know everything about me, but you haven't told me a single thing about yourself."

She tucked a strand of hair behind her ear and blushed. "That's because you've never asked me anything."

He studied her face a moment, the angry look in his eyes fading and filling up with something else.

Her pulse picked up a notch.

Without warning, he wrapped his good arm around her waist and pulled her against him, pressing his warm lips into hers.

She kissed him back, wrapping her arms

around his neck and closing her eyes, heart pounding wildly.

He broke the kiss but didn't let go of her.

She was speechless and could only blink.

Ian's dark gaze bore into her own, eyes sharpening with passion. He leaned in to kiss her again, but stopped. Letting go of her waist, he stepped around her and leaned into the work table with his palms, his back to her.

Bewildered, she moved toward him and touched his shoulder blade with her fingertips. His back stiffened.

"What's wrong, Ian?"

He let out an exhale. "It's just that . . . "

She pressed her hand against his upper back in a comforting manner. "It's just what?"

He sidestepped her hand and turned around, scowling. Something not unlike hatred flashed in his eyes, making her suddenly afraid. "This is no good," he spoke in an undertone.

"What are you talking about?" She gripped her forearm in a self-conscious manner.

The passion was gone, like a snuffed-out flame.

He glanced toward the darkened window and swallowed, Adam's apple bobbing up and down. A look of fear filled his eyes. "What time is it?" He grabbed her wrist and tugged back the sleeve, exposing her watch. "Nightfall is coming—we need to go."

She pulled her arm away and rubbed her wrist. "Or what—you'll turn into a werewolf?"

"Funny. Let's go." He scooted her toward the

ladder and she shucked him off.

"I have my own two legs."

With the way he was acting, she couldn't wait to get away from him.

As soon as they were out of the tree, Ian grabbed Lily's wrist again and fairly dragged her down the path, ignoring her protests. He hated to be so hands on but there was no time to explain.

It was twilight.

How had he lost track of time like that? Night was falling fast and he must get her out of the forest—now.

A faint tune of a bird's song filled his ears.

No—it couldn't be this late already.

Scooping her up into his arms, he pounded down the uneven path, struggling to see where he was going as she fought to break free from his grasp.

"Put me down—" she yelped, unable to move within the strength of his arms.

It was too dark to see her face clearly but he knew she was afraid of him. Nevertheless, he gripped her body tighter to his chest and ran. It killed him to be rough with her like this but she would just have to despise him—he wasn't about to slow down, and he wasn't going to let go of her either.

He strained to see the yard up ahead as he rounded the bend in the pathway. The white streams of light from the gargoyle orbs had the path lit up in zig-zags like Zebra stripes. He reached the ebony gargoyle and tore out across the grass.

The sky above hung low, pewter clouds blotting out the moon and stars.

He reached the mansion and yanked open the back door, barging inside. Setting Lily down on her feet, he whipped around and bolted the door.

It was over.

She was safe.

"Ian!" She stood glaring at him with feet wide apart and hair windblown, hands on her hips. "You're acting like a crazy person. What was that!" A pink flush mantled her cheeks, lips red, and green eyes wide and bright.

"I told you . . . there are, there are wolves out there," he said lamely, rubbing the back of his neck. "They come out at night." Ouch.

"You acted like a monster was at your heels."

"Hey—you might not care about your life, but I'd rather not get eaten just yet." Argh, this was impossible.

"So, you're deathly afraid of wolves—I get it. Yet, funny thing, no one's ever been attacked by one here. Yes—I've inquired."

He stared at her wide-eyed, knowing she could see his desperation; there was nothing he could say to appease her now.

"I'm sorry, Ian," she said, "but I think you've lived alone for far too long. When someone is kept away in a secluded house without getting out or seeing new people, it starts to affect them . . . "

"You think I'm mentally ill."

"I think you need help." She dropped her hands to her sides.

That hurt. More than he cared to admit.

All he wanted to do was go straight back to his workshop and be alone—like the crazy person she thought he was. But he couldn't do that right now, not after the whole wolf story. He'd have to sleep in the mansion another night.

He narrowed his eyes and said nothing.

With a look of exasperation, Lily took off down the hall; he let her go without following.

Chapter 10

Lily sat on the gold damask fabric of one of the two matching settees in her room, her slippered feet crossed at the ankles and perched on the coffee table, her hands clasped behind her head. It was four in the morning and she hadn't had any success at sleeping. There was too much on her mind—too much uncertainty.

Though her room was heated by a cast iron radiator, she'd lit a fire in the marble fireplace, and had been prodding it now and again for the past three hours, adding more wood as needed. The night sky was cloudy and no moonlight shone through the windows. They were nothing but draped black wedges in the wall. A milk-glass lamp on the fireplace mantel provided an orange glow to the sitting area, as did a matching one on the end table next to the canopy bed. Otherwise, the rest of the room—the corners, the nooks, the ceiling—were dark and shadowed.

She didn't know what to make of Ian Hawke.

He seemed so normal half the time and then he'd say or do such bizarre things—really frightening things. How could a man who was so afraid of wolves, have the guts and daring to swim around in a tank full of sharks? She'd gladly face a wolf over a shark any day. And how had he carried her all that way with a mangled arm?

Earlier, she'd spent some time examining the carvings on her bed's headboard and the surface of the chest of drawers. The images were so similar to what she'd seen on the front of Ian's tree shed, she was almost certain he'd done this work as well. The carvings were remarkable and exquisite, carefully polished. He could make a fortune selling them. But then, he had no need of income. She wondered again if the jewels lining the walls of his work shed were real or just glass look-a-likes.

Hungry, she briefly considered investigating the kitchen pantry for a snack, but after her experience in the pool room the night before, she didn't have the nerve to wander around. It was also difficult to believe the police officer's deductions; they didn't add up. And with the way Ian had bolted the door that evening, she doubted the front door of the mansion had been left unlocked for anyone to just stroll on in. Then again, he did leave his work shed unlocked. Ugh. It was all so maddening. Perhaps he wasn't as cautious during moments of paranoia, if he was suffering from such a thing. But even then, if the door had been left unbolted, how could an elderly woman with dementia possibly have had the strength to drag Lily up the stairs and all the way down the corridor to the front entrance? And even more unsettling—how had the woman known her name?

A muffled cry sounded from out in the hall-way.

Lily bolted to her feet and rushed to the door,

straining to hear through the heavy wood. Someone was indeed crying again—just like the other night. But the cries were fading and moving away . . . downward.

She opened the door a crack and peeked out into the hallway. All the rooms were dark—no crack of light beneath any of the doors—and none of the wall sconces were lit. The hallway was tar black without moonlight.

Moving slowly, she reached out and felt for the staircase newel post. Finding it, she held the rail and followed the stairs downward, attempting to avoid any creaky spots.

The cries continued faintly below. Had Sally returned and broken in again, or was it Hannah crying, as she'd originally suspected?

A chill ran up her spine at the thought.

Was it possible that it was actually Hannah who had attacked her in the pool room?

She considered retreating, locking herself in her room and hiding under the blankets till morning. Pausing on the landing, she took a deep breath and tried to steady her nerves. The cries were only a few feet away.

"Hello?" she squeaked, gripping the railing like a life line.

The cries stopped and a figure, blacker than the darkness, leaped out from behind the staircase and started down the corridor.

"Wait—!" Lily hurried down the last four steps and went after it. The hunching figure was only a meter ahead of her now, shuffling as though tired.

"Stop—" she said, overtaking it.

"Get away from me," a woman gasped as Lily grabbed her shoulder and spun her around.

"Oh, Hannah—what's the matter?"

Tears glistened on the housekeeper's face, her white hair all awry.

"I told you to leave me alone," she cried, collapsing to her knees.

"Please talk to me, Hannah. What is it?" She knelt down next to the housekeeper and wrapped her arm around her shoulders for support. "You can tell me."

Hannah lifted a soggy tissue and dabbed it at her eyes. "It's just . . . Auguste." She moaned and put her head in her hands. "I miss him so much. I . . . loved him."

Lily's heartbeat slowed with sudden understanding. The housekeeper was still in mourning. "Were you together?"

Hannah shook her head and sniffed. "No. I never told him my true feelings . . . " She let out a sob and stared up at the vaulted ceiling; indiscernible in the darkness. "My poor poor, Auguste. What happened to you?"

Lily didn't know what to say, so she gave the housekeeper's shoulder another squeeze.

Hannah looked at Lily. "He didn't die of a heart attack, you know."

"What do you mean?"

"You found his cane up in the attic—remember? He never went anywhere without his cane."

"Maybe that's where he had the heart attack?

Tried to hurry to get help and lost his cane?"

"No—it was that cursed attic! Whenever he went up there, he was never quite the same when he came back down again. Eventually he had the door removed and completely sealed up the entrance. I have no idea what he used to do up there, but it seemed to eat away at him."

"Wouldn't the police have investigated if any foul play was suspected?"

"The police are fools," she said bitterly, dabbing her eyes again.

Lily swallowed a lump in her throat, butterflies tingling in her stomach. She lowered her voice to a whisper. "Do you—do you think he was murdered?"

"I *know* he was."

"Does anyone else think so? . . . Does Ian?"

"We discussed it yesterday afternoon. He said the cane being there didn't mean anything."

Lily pursed her lips. Perhaps the poor woman's grief was taking a toll. Surely the police would have investigated if there were any question.

"I raised that boy and I can tell when he's lying," she said pointedly, locking gaze with Lily. She was no longer crying.

"Yes, I've noticed it's difficult to get a straight answer from him."

"Mhm. He's like your grandfather in that way." Hannah continued to speak in an undertone. "So secretive—shutting out anyone who tries to care for him. He really hit rock bottom after Auguste died. Spent his days locked up in that tree fort of his, not even joining us for meals. Until now." She took Lily's hand in her own. They were soft and wrinkled. "Until you arrived."

"What do you mean?"

"He likes you. But I doubt he'd ever admit it. He's a fool when it comes to emotions—just like Auguste was. Acts like he doesn't need anyone in the world. But when I look at him—at Ian—all I see is that poor little orphan boy. . . . A boy starved for love. You know, when he was young, he followed me around just like a shadow. Always needed someone to be nearby." She sighed and let go of Lily's hand, looking over her shoulder at the cavernous corridor beyond them. "But as he got older," she went on, "Auguste tainted him, I guess—turned him into a young version of his own, twisted self."

"I thought you loved my grandfather."

"I did! But that doesn't mean he didn't put me through the wringer." She struggled up to a standing position and smoothed the folds of her gown. Lily followed suit. Her eyes had adjusted to the dark enough that she could see Hannah's facial expressions more clearly. "No one could ever measure up to your late grandmother, you see," she said. "Believe me, I tried."

"You knew her?"

"No. She died twenty years before I came to work here."

"She must have been so young then! How did she die?"

"Childbirth."

They made their way up the corridor toward the front staircase, taking a slow pace.

Endless questions swirled through Lily's mind, her cheeks hot and palms damp. Why had Auguste sent his infant daughter—her *mother* it would seem—away? Was it because he didn't want to be reminded of his wife, or did he perhaps blame her for the death of his wife?

They stopped at the foot of the staircase.

"Hannah . . . Why did my grandfather abandon his daughter?"

A long sigh. "I don't know, Lily, I'm sorry. I've always wondered about that myself. I have my theories of course, but I suppose it's just one of the many questions that went to the grave with him."

"Unless Ian knows. Whenever I've asked though, he seems to beat around the bush. Says he never knew I existed."

"Well, it's possible Auguste told him about your mother at least. He treated Ian like a son, after all. He was so depressed and gloomy all the time, but after we found Ian, it was like he'd taken a drink from the fountain of youth. He was a changed man in so many ways. I suppose Ian filled a void in his heart."

"But I just don't get why he'd be so quick to treat Ian like a son while he had a flesh and blood daughter—*and* a grand-daughter." She was angry now. What kind of man was he anyway? Things just didn't add up.

"If I knew Auguste as well as I think I did, he must have a had a very good reason. He was a good man, Lily. You have to believe that."

Lily sat down on the steps and Hannah sat next to her.

"Can you tell me more about Ian being found as a child?" She kept her voice at a whisper.

Hannah rubbed her pudgy knees and clasped her hands together in her lap. She seemed to be considering and took a deep breath. "Well, going on about twenty-one years ago now, I was doing my last rounds of the night—making sure all the lights had been turned off—when I heard a loud thump." She looked Lily in the eyes. "I was positive it came from the attic, but I was too afraid to go up there alone. So I woke up Auguste and we headed up there together. He brought his rifle just in case it was an intruder and when we—when we reached the door to the attic, there was this terrible growling noise inside. Like a rabid dog."

The hairs prickled on the back of Lily's neck and she hugged her waist, the shadows in the corridor seeming to come to life all at once. For the first time she noticed the cold, vault-like air surrounding them.

"Auguste went in alone with his gun and shut the door behind him. I waited in the stairwell. I would've run screaming down the stairs I was so frightened, but I didn't want to leave Auguste alone in case he needed my help."

"Was it an animal?"

"Yes. He shot three times and the growling stopped. For a moment, I feared the worst, but Auguste opened the door and told me it was safe."

"What kind of animal was it?"

"I didn't get a close look. It was lying dead in the far corner. All big and furry-like. I'm pretty sure it was a wolf. Though heaven knows how it ever got up there." Hannah took another deep breath and stared into the darkness ahead. "I forgot all about the animal as soon as I looked to my right and saw a little boy huddled against the wall. I was downright flabbergasted. He was just ten or eleven! And what a pitiful sight." She shook her head. "Clothes torn, covered in terrible wounds. It was horrible."

Lily's stomach turned and nausea rose in her throat. No wonder the poor thing was deathly afraid of wolves. And here she'd chastised him like he was some kind of delusional shut-in.

"He was terrified of us at first," Hannah went on. "Shivering and crying, begging us not to hurt him. My heart instantly melted—I tell you, from that moment on, he was *my* son. I wrapped my housecoat around him to keep him warm, and Auguste carried him downstairs to the spare bedroom at the end of the hall. He then went back up to get rid of the dead animal while I treated Ian's wounds."

"Did you call an ambulance?"

"Ah, no. No. Auguste liked his privacy. And . . . and I didn't want anyone to come and take Ian away. It was so foolish of me, I know—so very wrong. But I just—I felt like he was my child somehow. I was self-ish." A long pause. She seemed lost in thought. "It's my fault Ian is who he is today," she said suddenly. "If he'd been adopted by a regular family, he'd proba-bly have a wife and children by now. *Friends* for that matter. A social life! He certainly wouldn't be locking himself up in some fantastical tree house day after day." She shivered.

"But weren't you afraid he might die of his injuries?"

"I was—yes, at first. But Auguste—well—he forbid me to and he was a very persuasive man. Strangest thing was though, within a week Ian was running 'round the place like nothing had even happened—skin as pink and healthy as a rosebud." She put her hand on Lily's forearm, leaned in closer. "I've never seen someone heal so fast in my life. Mind you, he did end up with some nasty-looking scars. But you should have seen his wounds, Lily. I tried to stitch him all up but some of those bites and cuts were straight through to the bone. Just like, well, just like the shark bite. You must believe me though, if there'd been any sign of infection, I would have called the hospital."

"What you're telling me is impossible, Hannah," she said gently, struggling to think straight. It was too much to process all at once.

The housekeeper withdrew her hand, straightened her back. "If you don't believe me, ask to see his arm then. The only reason he's still wearing that silly bandage is to fool you."

Hannah reached for a balustrade and pulled herself up with a humph. "We should get some sleep, goodness me," she said, starting up the stairs. "Must be nearly sunrise by now."

Sure enough, the faintest bit of light was beginning to show through the flower-shaped window above the doors.

It was dawn when Lily went to bed and she slept fitfully for two hours before giving up and getting dressed for the day in jeans and a long-sleeved v-neck. She pulled her hair up into a twist and went downstairs to the dining room for breakfast.

She felt awful for what she'd said to Ian last night. To think she'd told him he "needed help." How insulting. If only she'd known more of his background she would have been much more understanding of his behavior. Whatever his actual thoughts had been, he honestly believed she was in danger out in the woods, and no harm had been done. Except, perhaps, to his dignity.

Somehow she needed to set things right. Apologize.

Mike, Chris, Hannah and Angie were already sitting at the dining table when she entered the room, but Ian was nowhere to be found. She didn't ask where he was though, figuring he'd either be out in his work shed or still asleep in the guest room. She would go and find him presently. In the meantime, she wanted to take a look at the attic again.

She politely took her leave after some coffee and toast; and making sure no one was following, she went up the stairs and pressed the bottom right-hand corner of Auguste's portrait.

The secret door to her right slid open with a swish and she went into the stairwell.

Before heading up the dusty stairs, she examined the shadowy wood-paneled walls to see if it was possible to close the door from inside. Sure enough, a small button was located to one side, about waist-height. She pressed it and the wall panel slid shut, leaving her in darkness. At least now no one would know she was in here.

She felt for the rough railing and ascended the twisted stairs, reached the next level where the lattice window provided checkered light across the floorboards.

Lily stood staring at the closed red door before her, thinking about what Hannah had said only a few hours prior. Was it possible there was something sinister behind her grandfather's death? It did seem strange that he'd leave his cane at the top of the stairs. Though, if he was having a heart attack, perhaps he just couldn't hold on to it any longer because of the pain.

She tried the cold iron knob and the attic door opened easily with a faint creaking of the hinges. The room beyond was in shadow where sunlight failed to penetrate from two arched windows. She felt along the inside wall, found a light switch and flicked it on. A deep narrow room came to life full of junk and cobwebs. She shut the door behind her and took a good look at the contents of the room.

Lily wasn't sure exactly what she'd expected, but this wasn't it.

The ceiling angled upward on one side to a loft with a ladder. It was filled with boxes and ancient Christmas decorations; clumps of pine garland, piles of corded teardrop bulbs, a giant wreath, and tarnished candelabras filled with tapered candles, half burned. Below the loft were more stacked boxes, a cracked sink, a rolled up rug, a child's bookcase, ancient toys, an old bicycle, a set of lamps; and endless other items of discard. A threadbare armchair and ottoman filled the adjacent corner, along with several unmarked crates. A nice trip to the dump was what this stuff needed, though perhaps some of the antiques were worth something.

Why go to all the trouble to design a secret door that lead up to a whole lot of nothing? And why all this "stay out of the attic" business? The floorboards didn't look rotten either.

With a sigh, she turned to leave and noticed the edge of something protruding beside the door, otherwise hidden from sight behind cardboard boxes. She pushed one of the stacks out of the way, exposing a long wooden trunk with a rounded top and a warded lock. Her mouth went dry.

It looked like a coffin.

She dropped onto her knees to examine it more closely. It appeared to be made of pine or oak, but being covered with a layer of dust, it was difficult to tell. Designs of interacting creatures were carved into the sides and the lid—unicorns, beasts, angels, gnomes—strikingly similar to the images in her bedroom and all over Ian's tree shed.

She tried to lift the lid but the trunk was locked.

Letting out another sigh, she thought about where she might possibly find its key. The key she'd seen tied around the ankle of that strange bird up in Ian's tree came to mind immediately; but it seemed a long shot. Then again, maybe not.

A creak in the floorboards outside the attic

door made her back go rigid. Someone was coming up the stairs. If they caught her in here after all the ominous warnings, she'd never hear the end of it.

She flicked off the light—knowing it was pointless since whoever was coming would have already seen the light beneath the door—and dove in behind the loft ladder. She huddled beside a crate, hoping she was out of sight.

It was futile to hide, she knew, but somehow she couldn't bear the thought of being caught like a deer in the headlights.

The door swung open and a man's form filled the frame.

Chapter 11

From where Lily huddled, a thin gap between the crate and a box provided her with a partial view of the doorway.

The man stood still, listening.

She held her breath. Why was she being so silly? This whole situation was ridiculous; what was the worst that could happen? A finger-waggling lecture? She should have just opened the door all nonchalant, and greeted whoever it was.

A whiff of mild cologne filled her senses.

Ian.

He flicked on the light and stared at the stack of boxes that had been pushed away from the trunk. He looked down at the floor and then toward her.

Could he see her within the shadows of the boxes?

Oh, for Pete sake—what an idiot she was—her footprints in the dust led a trail straight to her. Prickly heat climbed her neck and she swallowed hard. How embarrassing this was panning out to be.

He stepped toward her and she squeezed her eyes shut like a child, waiting for the inevitable. A second later a hand clamped down on her arm and gently pulled her from the hiding place.

She stood in the center of the cluttered room and looked up at him with a sheepish expression. Her pants were coated in dust, and a stringy cobweb hung from her sleeve.

He stood only two feet away, glowering, hands on his lean hips. "What are you doing up here."

She peeled the spiderweb from her arm and tried to flick it away. It clung to her fingertips. "I wanted to see the forbidden attic."

He narrowed his eyes and spoke in a low tone: "You have no idea how much danger you keep putting yourself into."

She glanced at the trunk and shivered involuntarily. What if it *was* a coffin? What if Ian was some sort of psycho serial killer? She was such a fool. If he tried to kill her right now, no one could possibly come to her rescue in time.

"All right, all right," she said, trying to sound casual though her pulse was pounding in her ears. "I'll get going. I've seen all there is to see."

She sidestepped him, heading for the open door, but he reached out and gripped her forearm. "Don't ever come up here again."

She said she wouldn't, shaking her head, all the while knowing she'd be returning later with the key from his pet bird. If she was going to live here indefinitely, she had to be sure it was safe.

He stepped closer, so close she could feel his warm, minty breath on her cheek. "'Cause you know," he said, "if I ever do find you up here again, I'll have to kill you."

She stiffened, heart stopping.

"I"m kidding, Lily," he said, unrestrained annoyance in his tone, letting go of her arm and moving away from her.

"I know," she squeaked, letting out a blip of laughter. She had the strangest feeling that he *could* kill, maybe already had. All she wanted to do was get away from him, like before, in the tree.

She forced herself to look at him.

He was frowning now. "You went dead white just there."

She nodded. "Yes, I'm just . . . hungry, I think. Didn't eat much breakfast." She tried to laugh. "And it's kind of stuffy in here, too."

"I didn't mean to freak you out or anything."

It seemed a true statement somehow and she calmed a bit. If she'd been in any real danger, the moment had passed. He was acting normal again.

"Ian . . . can I, uh, see your arm?"

"Why?"

She moved toward him and reached for his bandaged arm, gripping his wrist. It was time to do some intimidating of her own.

She hated being bullied.

"Maybe later," he said, prying her fingers from his wrist.

"When?" she snapped, overcome with anger. "You never give me a straight answer about anything."

"I'm crazy, remember? Haven't gotten around to getting help just yet, so until then, you'll have to put up with me." He moved past her and went to the door.

"I'm so sorry, Ian. I wish I hadn't said that."

He shrugged. "It's no big deal. You aren't the first person to think that." With a sweep of his arm, he motioned for her to leave, and she went out into the stairwell. He shut off the light, closed the door, and followed her down the stairs.

Mid-morning, Lily was in the kitchen helping Angie make pies when Mike appeared and asked if he could steal her away for a little while. He had some free time, he said, and thought it would be fun to show her the rest of the mansion since he knew Ian hadn't finished the tour.

Angie shooed her off with a smile, and Lily spent the next hour with Mike exploring the rooms of the west wing; most of which had not been used in decades. Much of the furnishings were draped in sheets, the walls bare. Behind one door was Auguste's bedroom.

"No one but Ian has been in here since he died," Mike explained. "Eventually someone's gonna have to take the time to sort through his belongings. I know Hannah wants to but she's not ready yet."

Lily decided to talk to Hannah about that. She would love the chance to look through her grandfa-ther's possessions; perhaps get to know him a little bit through the things that had meant something to him.

"Why did Auguste isolate himself to this side

of the mansion when there's plenty of space in the east wing with everyone else?" she asked.

Mike shrugged and she followed him back out into the hallway. "I guess he just liked his privacy."

At the far end of the hallway, next to an opaque lancet window overlooking the back yard, Mike opened the last door. Inside was a flight of wooden stairs heading up. They took the stairs straight to the third story which consisted of a narrow hallway and six empty servant rooms. The air was cool and stagnant. She decided this floor must run directly parallel to the attic. Sunlight streamed through naked windows in each room: arched wedges of light across dull wood floors.

"We keep these rooms closed off," he said. "No sense wasting money to heat rooms that no one uses anymore. This place is just too darned big."

After that, Mike led her back down to the main corridor and took her into the library which had also been Auguste's study.

He pulled open the heavy crimson drapes covering the two lancet windows behind the desk, and the room flooded with sunshine. Dust floated in the beams.

Enchanted, Lily took the time to peruse some of the endless volumes of books on the shelves, most of which were antique hardcover or leather-bound editions. The shelves thoroughly lined the walls of the high-ceilinged room, and a quaint roll-ladder rested in one corner. Deciding to come back later when she actually had the time to read a book, Lily sat down in the tall-backed leather chair behind Auguste's tiger-oak desk, placing her palms on the desktop—and gasped in delight to spot an inkwell on its surface with a feather pen perched beside it. Like the furniture in many of the other rooms, the three sides of the desk featured hand-carved scenes of mythical beings. Every nook and cranny of it had been dusted and polished, and she gathered Hannah had taken loving care of it over the years.

Directly across the hall from Auguste's study was a large parlor. They left the study then and entered it. Lily had peeked into this room a few times already over the past couple of days but hadn't yet had the chance to spend any time it. Next to a cozy fireplace was an LCD TV on a stand and two modern couches faced it. A credenza along one wall held a computer and printer. It was a comfortable, lived-in room with lots of books, magazines, boardgames, and DVDs scattered about. A pool table filled half the room and she figured this must be where everyone liked to gather for recreation. It was the most modern-looking room in the entire mansion.

Mike plunked down on a couch as Ms. Kline sat on the other. He hiked his booted feet up onto the coffee table in front of him and studied her face, noting the delicate cheekbones and pouty lips.

"So, what's the deal with the attic?" she said, interrupting his thoughts. "I went up there this morning—found this really weird trunk. Have you seen it?"

He frowned. "You were in the attic?"

A nod. "Ian caught me though—cut my visit short. I felt like a naughty little child."

He let out a laugh. "Yeah, before Auguste hid the entrance, Ian wouldn't allow me within ten feet of the place, not even to repair the rain damage. He'd rather let the roof rot than allow anyone in there."

"He told me to never go up there again."

Mike dropped his feet back down to the floor with a thump and sat up straight, rubbing his palms together. "You got it easy then." He crooked an eyebrow. "Last time he caught me poking around in there, he said I was fired." A laugh. "Hannah talked him out of it, fortunately." He rolled his eyes and leaned back.

Truth be told, his motives for being in the attic at that time had been less than pure. He wasn't about to tell Lily that though.

"Good thing," she said, smiling. "I don't know what I'd do without you here."

Heat trekked up his neck and into his cheeks. "Why d'you say that?"

She smiled again. "I feel safe around you."

That got him going. He stood up and went to her, reaching for her hand. "Come—I want to show you something."

To his pleasure, she didn't pull her hand away, so he kept on holding it as he led her out into the corridor.

No one was around but he lowered his voice nonetheless. "If you ever did find yourself in trouble,

I think it would help if you knew about some good hiding spots."

Her eyes lit with obvious delight. "Hiding spots? How exciting! Somewhere the wolves can't get me—or where I can hide from escapee mental patients." She let out a musical laugh, and he grinned. She was so pretty.

"I was actually going to show you some the other night," he whispered into her ear, folding her arm over his own and leading her down the hallway, "but Ian stopped me, as you know. It's why he cut the tour short. But—as you've already discovered on your own—there are many hidden passageways in this place. You can gain entrance to most of them from the paintings."

When they reached the front entrance stair-case, he reluctantly let go of her arm and they went upstairs single-file. He took her into his own room and stood in front of a landscape painting. It hung on the wall separating his bedroom from the one adjacent to it.

"Check this out." He pressed his thumb to the bottom right-hand corner of the frame and a vertical opening appeared in the wall next to it. Unlike the entrance to the attic or the pool room, however, this opening was no more than a foot wide.

A waft of cold air flitted over them.

She stared at him wide-eyed, lips parted.

"Wait a sec," he said. Heading to his desk, he fished a flashlight from the drawer, and returned to her side. "All right, let's go." He slid sideways through the gap and she followed. Once inside, he pressed a waist-height button, closing the panel, and aimed the flashlight beam down the narrow tunnel in front of him. They could go either direction.

"These passageways run between the walls of most of the rooms on each floor," he explained in a hushed tone as he began walking along the dusty floorboards. Lily followed closely behind. Electrical wires and outlets ran up the walls at various conjunctions.

"Is there anything stashed in these tunnels?" she asked, a thrill in her voice.

"Nope, I've been through them all. Just a bunch of empty tunnels; a few peep holes here and there though. But no worries, nothing in the washrooms or pool room or anything creepy like that." He lowered his voice even more. "Hey, Lily—we should probably keep our voices low from now on. Don't want anyone to overhear. Ian would freak if he knew we were doing this."

"Can you get lost in these passages?" she whispered.

"Not a chance. There're exits everywhere. As long as you know your way around the mansion, you shouldn't have any trouble getting out. Just look for the panel buttons."

"Do the others know about them, too?"

"No idea. Ian sure does, but as far as Hannah and them goes—who knows. They've never talked to me about it."

Mike had been through these tunnels dozens upon dozens of times over the past five years, searching in vain, wondering what their purpose was, yet never finding anything even remotely interesting.

They spent the next half hour or so exploring the narrow passageways, most of which were no more than two feet in diameter, whispering back and forth. Wooden ladders along the perimeters of the mansion enabled travel to upper and lower levels. On the basement level, there were no floorboards, just flat slabs of stone. When he'd first discovered the tunnels, he'd hoped to find hidden rooms in the basement, but other than the scuba equipment room, there'd been nothing to see besides the aquarium.

A bitter disappointment for him.

He took the time to show Lily how to access the scuba room, but they didn't go inside. Instead, they continued around the perimeter of the pool room, heading toward the east wing entrance. Down here, the stuffy air was damp with an occasional whiff of mildew, and the tunnels were wider than they were on the upper floors.

Behind him, Lily let out a yelp and fell forward into his back. He turned around, taking her into his arms, and straightened her up. "What happened?"

"I think I tripped over a rock or something."

She leaned back against the rock-cut wall, and he shone the flashlight beam at her feet; squatting down to get a closer look.

A slab of stone was raised an inch above the others along one edge. He set the flashlight on the ground beside him and tugged on the slab. To his surprise, it lifted up toward him. It was heavy and round, about three feet long and two inches thick. He leaned it up against the wall beside him and picked up the flashlight again, aiming it at the ground where the slab had been removed.

His heartbeat quickened and he nearly hooted a shout of triumph.

Lily gasped but said nothing.

In the ground was a gaping hole with a metal ladder leading downward into the blackness below.

Chapter 12

Mike glanced up at Lily's shadowy form, willing himself to be calm. She was leaning her shoulder against the stone wall.

"What is it?" she said. "Did you know this was here?"

"I've *never* seen this before and I have no idea what it is." His voice wavered. "You wait here a minute, Lily, and I'll check to make sure it's safe."

He sat down, wedged the handle of the flashlight between his teeth, and swung his legs into the hole, placing his heels on the top ladder rung. Pleased to find it sturdy, he descended three rungs, testing each one and holding the floor with his forearms for support—and then turned around, gripped the side poles, and lowered the rest of his upper body into the hole.

A good six meters down, continuing to test each rung as he went, he began to wonder just how deep the abyss might be when his boots scuffed against a dirt floor.

Mike removed the flashlight from his mouth and turned around, sweeping the beam through the blackness before him.

He was standing on the edge of what

appeared to be a huge room, cylindrical and high tech —his flashlight ray unable to reach the far end of the room. He moved the beam back and forth, up and down; heart drumming in his chest and hands shaking with adrenaline. Conduits ran across the floors and up the walls, disappearing into rows of stainless steel vats. Turning, he searched the cement wall behind him and found an electrical panel mounted next to the ladder.

"Mike?" Lily called down to him from above, her voice bouncing off the walls. "Are you okay? Can I come down now?"

"Just gimme a sec," he said, yanking open the metal box and flicking on an entire row of breakers.

The room came to life, its walls and ceilings completely whitewashed, and industrial lamps hanging from the high ceiling. The vats encircled the entirety of the room and he counted six in total; three on each side. A metal ladder ran up the front of each one. In the center of the room was a coroner's table, at least thrice the size of any he'd ever seen before. The air was indolent of formaldehyde.

Goosebumps tripped up his arms and down his back. What was all this? How could he have lived here for five full years without discovering it? Especially considering how thoroughly he'd searched these tunnels.

"You can come down now," he shouted up to Lily, against his better judgment. "I *think* it's safe." Ha. How should he know if it was safe? He had no clue what it even was, and by the looks of things, whoever was using this room was a force to be reckoned with.

He glanced at the examination table again and shuddered.

While waiting for Lily to descend, he wandered toward the nearest vat on his right and climbed the ladder, hoping to get a look inside. It was tightly sealed, however, with an eight-digit combination pad in the center of the lid. He climbed back down and looked at Lily. She was huddling next to the ladder like a frightened child, arms crossed over her chest.

Deciding to ignore her for the moment, he scaled each ladder and found the same locking mechanism atop each one.

"What is this place?" she said in a squeak of a voice when he came near again.

"I'm not sure . . . " No, that wouldn't do. Better to act like he had at least a small amount of inside information. "It's probably just the equipment necessary to run the aquarium," he said, feigning confidence.

"Then why is it hidden in the depths of the earth?"

"Well, that I don't know." He was agitated now. It would have been better to find this room on his own. Lily might prove to be a liability. At any rate, he would have to swear her to secrecy.

"Mike, we should go," she said in a whisper, gaze darting to and fro. Her green eyes were limpid with what was likely fear. "Something feels wrong in this room. I want to leave."

He paused his investigation of a stainless steel cabinet and looked in her direction, trying to mask his annoyance. If only she wasn't with him right now. He needed to find out what was in the vats.

She started climbing the ladder and he exhaled noisily. "All right, I'm coming." He hurried to catch up, feeling responsible for her, and shut off the breakers. He aimed the flashlight beam upward so she could see where she was going, and followed her up the ladder. It was probably better this way, come to think of it. He'd take her back to safety, make sure he wasn't being followed, and then come right back.

He took her all the way up to her bedroom and let her in through a panel to the left of the fireplace. "Lily, do you mind telling Hannah I won't be here for lunch?" he asked.

"Don't tell me you're going back down to the dungeon."

He threw on a merry smile and followed her into the bedroom. "No-no, of course not. I'll just ask Ian about it later. Like I said—it probably runs the aquarium. Regulates the growth of algae or something along those lines."

She gave him a look that said she wasn't even remotely convinced.

"Do me a favor?" he said, forcing a chummy lilt into his voice. "Don't tell anyone about this. *Please.* I'll talk to Ian first and then let you know what he says about it, all right?"

She nodded. "Sure, Mike. No problem."

They parted ways in the hallway and Lily went downstairs.

Mike opened his bedroom door and stopped short as a voice called to him from down the hall.

He cursed under his breath as Ian stepped out

of the spare bedroom. Had he seen him leaving Lily's room a moment ago?

"What are you doing?" he asked, moving toward him; a dark look in his eyes.

Mike put his thumbs through his belt loops. "If you must know, I'm about to grab some tools to tinker with that finicky pipe in the kitchen."

A slow nod.

Mike averted eye contact but tried to look casual. "Well, I'll see you around. How's that arm of yours doing?"

Ian clasped his hands together behind his back. "Quite well, thank you." A thin line creased his forehead though his expression was deadpan.

Eager to get away, Mike offered a parting nod and slipped inside his room, shutting the door.

Man that guy could be creepy sometimes. And contrary to what he'd told Lily, he had no intention of asking Ian anything about the hidden room.

After Mike had gone into his room, Ian went to the end of the hall and opened the entranceway to the attic stairwell. He shut the panel behind himself and went up the staircase to the attic.

Switching on the overhead light, which was nothing but an exposed bulb hanging from a wire, he pushed aside the stacks of boxes that Lily hadn't already moved. He then stood with hands on his hips and stared down at the ancient trunk.

It was a Pandora's box to him—a beautiful, terrible thing.

He wished to destroy it, but couldn't be so selfish. He must continue to live a life of loneliness and isolation in order to protect the secrets it housed.

Somehow he was going to have to convince Lily to move out. The risk of her staying was too great —though his heart ached to think of her leaving. He was deliberately pushing her away with his erratic behavior when all he wanted to do was hold her close and never let go.

With a heavy sigh, he looked down at the scattered footprints on the dirty floor, and kicked the nearest stack of boxes, sending them toppling to the floor in a cloud of dust. Why did she have to poke around at everything?

It was lunch time and the others would be waiting for him in the dining room now that he was making a habit of joining them. He didn't feel like eating though. His heart was weary from the burden it carried; draining his strength.

What had Mike and Lily been up to? He knew they'd been in her room together.

He'd never really trusted Mike, especially as the years had gone by. When Auguste initially hired the handyman, Ian had held to a glimmer of hope for a comrade. But it didn't pan out that way.

Mike was just as secretive as he.

All Ian wanted to do was lie down on the floorboards and never wake up.

With a final look at the mansion looming in the moonlight behind her, Lily hurried past the ebony gargoyle and into the forest.

At supper time, she'd strategically informed everyone that she was not feeling well and would be retiring early. Hannah seemed surprised and mentioned that Ian, who'd skipped dinner, had also retired early and was sleeping in the spare bedroom; and she hoped the two of them weren't coming down with something. Lily verified Ian's whereabouts by softly knocking on his door. When he mumbled his presence, she told him she was going to bed and that if he wanted to talk to her about anything, she would see him in the morning at breakfast. He'd agreed in an uncaring, groggy tone and she hoped against hope that he would truly stay put.

Lily hurried down the blackened trail, ignoring the orb lights when they flicked on and zigzagged the path.

The woods were strangely silent; not a rustle in the undergrowth, not even a breeze. She'd brought along a flashlight this time and was glad she had. The lower lights weren't on in the workshop this time and the tree looked like a massive black giant reaching spindly arms up to the starry sky.

She paused for a minute when she reached it, and listened for movement in the woods surrounding her. Absolute silence prevailed besides her own pounding heartbeat. If anyone was following her, they hadn't made a peep.

Too edgy to dawdle, she reached for the handle of the front door and tugged sharply, relieved to find it again unlocked. She switched on her flashlight and took the ladders to the top floor.

In the unnatural ray of the flashlight, the bizarre tropical bird peered at her sidelong through one emerald eye. The key was still fastened to its ankle.

She opened the cage and the bird narrowed its eye.

Her skin crawled, palms growing clammy.

Instinct suggested she turn around and leave —run, in fact.

But no. No, she mustn't. The key was too tantalizing. She *had* to know what was in that trunk.

Moving her hand toward the bird gingerly, for fear it might bite or try to escape, she untied the string with nimble fingers and removed the warm key, all the while keeping an eye on that beak. The bird made no inclination to move and watched her shrewdly, blinking once.

She tucked the key in her jean pocket and went to close the cage door.

"Out of my way."

She gasped. "I didn't know you could talk—"

"I said: get-out-of-my-way."

The bird glared at her, scowling—if that was even possible for a bird. No, she was reading too much into it. It was only the flashlight beam causing grotesque shadows and caricatures.

This was just an animal.

A pet.

Nothing to fear.

"What a pretty bird," she cooed. "Can you say

pretty bird?"

With a squawk of seeming rage, the bird surged forward and burst out of the cage, knocking her backward to the floor. She dropped the flashlight and tried to grab the bird as it flew past her. Catching only a fistful of air, she cried out in dismay as the bird dove through the hole in the floor.

Grabbing the flashlight, she scooted down the ladder—listened—and then scooted down the next ladder to the bottom floor—whipping around just as the bird flew out the gaping front door. Hadn't she closed that door? She was certain she had.

With no time to think straight, Lily tore out the door and scanned the surrounding tree branches for the bird.

Ian was going to be livid.

She turned in a full circle and halted, blinking in the moonlight. The bird was perched on a branch high above her, nearly blotted out by tree boughs. There was no way she could reach it without climbing the tree. Her only hope was to coax it down somehow.

"Here, pretty bird," she cooed.

"Take the key and then you die," said the parrot voice from above.

She glanced around. Was anyone watching from within the shelter of the trees?

"Pretty bird—" it taunted with a throaty squawk. "Pretty bird!"

It began to whistle a haunting tune.

"Please—" she said, voice strained and desperate. "Oh, please come down."

As though in obedience, the bird flew down

and landed on the low branch of a spruce overhanging the nearby trail. It continued to whistle the same tune.

Lily crept toward it and when she neared within a meter, it flew away and veered off the path, perching on another low branch. Great, he was taunting her. Leaving the trail, she pushed and crunched her way through the undergrowth and tried to grasp for the bird's long tail feathers. It merely fluttered off to another nearby branch.

This continued a while longer with Lily following the bird farther and farther away from the trail. She kept an eye on the distant lights of the orbs, figuring as long as they were in sight, she needn't fear getting lost.

Though the air was crisp, she'd worked herself into a sweat, and paused to roll up the sleeves of her sweater. Was it getting darker? She peered up through the cloistered boughs of the trees, barely able to make out the moon. The bird was two meters ahead, six feet above ground and within her reach. It was preening the feathers of one wing as though it hadn't a care in the world.

She moved closer, one step at a time, cringing when a twig snapped and the bird startled. He did not look her direction though and she held her breath until it resumed its preening.

Lily's throat tightened as she reached the base of the tree. She took a deep wavering breath. Then, in one swift motion, she snatched the bird's ankle and yanked the creature to her chest—pinning her arms around its flapping wings and hoping it wouldn't bite.

After a moment of intense struggle, the bird calmed down and stopped moving altogether.

She turned around, panting, and squinted through the tree branches, seeing only variances of darkness. The orb lights were no longer in sight.

"Well, well, well," clucked the bird. "Look who's here."

Chapter 18

A presence moved through the bushes in Lily's peripheral and ice water flooded her veins.

She clutched the bird tighter and held her breath, not daring to move.

A sudden, deep-throated cackle sounded to her right and something snorted to her left. Then all went silent.

Her only choice was to go forward, in the direction she'd come. She looked up through the leaves and branches to the sky. The moon was gone, snuffed out by pewter clouds. She willed one leg forward and then another—fully expecting to be pounced on by a bear or wolf.

Nothing happened.

The darkness was disorienting. Was she even walking in the right direction? The crunching of her footsteps echoed all around her, and the bird's heart beat calmly within her arms, out of sync with her own racing one.

Stupid, stupid, stupid. Why had she wandered so deep into the forest? She should never have opened that bird cage in the first place.

What had growled and cackled, and why had they stopped? Was she surrounded by a pack of drooling, camouflaged wolves waiting for the right moment to attack?

Something furry brushed her leg and she lurched forward in full speed panic. The bird screeched and bit her finger. She let go and its silky feathers flapped against her face as it took off into the trees above. Hands outstretched, chin tucked, she tore through bushes and tree boughs, cheeks and limbs burning with pain as branches whipped at her body. She didn't dare slow down.

All at once a deafening chorus of whoops and howls surrounded the forest around her and dozens of glowing eyes blinked at her in the murkiness ahead. She froze like a frightened rabbit and held back a scream as she pivoted in place.

White noise filled her ears and it took a moment to register that the glowing eyes had vanished and the forest had fallen silent. Her breathing was choked and raspy, heart slamming against her ribs. Her skin grew cold and she hugged her arms around her body. It was as though she'd suddenly stepped out into a bitter winter night.

Goosebumps pricked across her flesh like ripples of water and she trembled, lowering herself to the ground, dead leaves crackling beneath her. Her only plan now was to huddle on the forest floor indefinitely; hoping that whatever animal was out there would leave her alone.

A hand clamped down around her wrist: hard and thick and calloused. It jerked her to her feet and slammed her up against a furrowed tree trunk as another hand pressed hard against her jugular. She blinked rapidly, struggling to breathe—unable to make out the face of her attacker.

"What is your relation to Auguste?" a horrible voice hissed, the fingers around her neck releasing slightly.

"I'm his granddaughter," she choked out the words.

"Who is your mother?"

"She's—dead."

"*Who* was she?"

"Let me go—" she garbled, straining to breathe as the hand pressed into her throat.

"Answer me," he screamed, throwing her to the ground.

She landed hard, smacking her forehead against the root of a tree. Pain streaked through her skull like a lightning bolt.

Not a second later, her attacker was upon her, pressing his weight into her back—his scruffy cheek against her own. He let out a long exhale; breath like a dead rat. She choked on a flow of nausea and tried to claw out his eyes, but he grabbed both wrists and pressed her fisted hands into the ground; her knuckles crunching into a rock. She cried out in pain.

"Who was your mother?" he repeated, pushing his knee into her back and putting his face against hers again. A glob of spit landed on her lips.

"Screw-you."

"Wrong answer." He let go of her and she gulped for air as the pressure on her lungs released.

The relief was short lived. He grabbed her by the shirt collar and pulled her back up to her feet.

Before she could catch her breath, he clamped the back of her head in his palm and smashed her face into a tree. The skin tore from her cheek.

"Who was your mother?"

She sobbed. "Let me go, you have the wrong person—" Blood from her face trickled into the corners of her lips, filling her mouth with the taste of copper. He relaxed his grip and moved away from her. She wobbled in place and tried to look at her assailant, but couldn't see. Had he gone? Not waiting to find out, she stumbled away and broke out in a run. With one arm over her eyes for protection against branches, she ran blindly, looking at the ground only and using her other hand to feel for branches.

A shout sounded nearby, followed by a rolling growl and a screech. Moments later, heavy footsteps clopped behind her—gaining on and then reaching her side.

Something soft brushed against her throbbing cheek and she was overcome with a sense of peace. Closing her eyes, she skidded to a stop and leaned her head back against a silky snout. The animal's hot breath poured over her body like a soothing balm and the fierce pain in her hands and face subsided to a warm tingle.

She was lowered to the ground and lain across a bed of moss.

Lily opened her eyes and realized she was dead. At least, it was the only logical conclusion—for all around her the forest was suffused by white light with a greenish tint. It was as if she'd donned a pair of night vision goggles.

The animal who had nuzzled her cheek was seemingly gone; she was alone.

She sat up and examined her crushed knuckles, but there were no abrasions. She lifted tentative fingertips to what she thought was a shredded cheek, but it was as smooth as a baby's bottom.

There was no pain.

Lily pulled herself to a standing position and surmised her surroundings. There was a big boulder, a rotting log, and a row of ferns. She took a few steps through the trees and realized she wasn't far from the trail at all: A gargoyle statue was perched nearby.

Relief stampeding through her veins, she approached the statue with brisk steps, pushing aside various branches as she went and fully expecting to find the whole row of them with their zig-zagging lights.

She reached the statue and nearly cried.

There was only one gargoyle and no dirt trail: not even a clearing. An unlit, white orb lay at its feet.

"Where are your buddies?" she asked, heart sinking.

"Foraging through the forest, of course," a voice responded.

Lily jumped backward, breath catching in her throat as the gargoyle turned its solid stone head and looked at her with glowing red eyes.

No, she wasn't dead.

She was dreaming.

"You—you can't be talking to me," she said.

"Okay then, crazy lady." It stretched out its legs, one by one, and instead of marble, a very fine fur covered its entire body and face.

"How . . . how are you talking to me?" She lifted a tremulous hand to her breast and glanced all about.

"What kind of stupid question is that? With my mouth, of course. Having a tongue helps."

She blinked. "I've obviously fallen and smacked my head. But as long as you're talking—how do I get back to the mansion?"

"You want to go to the mansion? You're going the wrong way."

"Can you show me the right way?" she said, deciding to play along with her delusions. If this was only a dream, at least it was more pleasant than the nightmare she'd just endured.

The gargoyle studied her a moment with a look of mild curiosity and rubbed a paw across its heavy brow. Its face was flat with eyes the size of eggs and four tusks jutting out of its muscular jaw. "All right, I'll take ya," it said gruffly, "but don't you go telling Ian I been talkin' with ya."

"You k-know Ian?"

"Um . . . Ian? What's 'Ian'? Crazy talk!" The gargoyle shifted its gaze as though nervous. "You's lucky you came across me instead of some of the others. You're walking about the woods during hunting time, don't ya know. Not very smart. Plus, there's something sinister wandering this forest. I don't like it one bit."

"That's why I need to get back to the mansion."

"Follow me, but hurry. I don't want to be seen

with you."

With that, the gargoyle took off in the direction she'd just come and ran through the trees on all fours, breaking through the branches like a charging bull. Surprised by how fast it could run on such stubby legs, she hurried after it and tried to keep up; but soon fell behind.

"Wait," she cried, "wait—"

But the gargoyle was gone.

The greenish light in the forest was fading, shadows forming all around. Was she going blind? Quickening her pace, she followed the path of broken branches before her, and reached a clearing.

"There you are, slowpoke," a voice said to the right of her. The gargoyle was sitting on a pile of dry leaves.

"You could've slowed down," she said.

Its grin withered. "You shouldn't linger here, lady—it isn't safe. Nopey-nope-nope." The gargoyle peered into the still forest behind her with a narrowed gaze and then focused its red eyes back on her. "Why are you still standing there! I told you to get back to the mansion." There was a sense of urgency in its voice.

The forest was nearly dark again and Lily could barely make out the trail ahead.

With a snort, the gargoyle took off in the direction she'd come from, its thudding footsteps growing softer and then silent as the distance grew between them.

Still figuring it was only a dream, she wandered down the path blindly, hands stretched out, wondering if it would lead her to Ian's workshop.

Her foot snagged without warning and she tumbled down an embankment, striking the back of her head on a boulder.

Chapter 14

Lily awoke with a headache.

She blinked and squinted in the harsh slivers of sunlight beaming down on her. The twisted tangled branches high above stretched up to the sky; some of them barren, others covered in bronze and russet leaves.

She groaned and sat up, rubbing the goose egg on the back of her head. How long had she been unconscious? It was daylight now—had she lain on the forest floor the entire night long?

She climbed the embankment and found the trail again. Up ahead, visible now in the sunlight, the gargoyles were perched in their usual places with orbs in hand. She went to the first one, touching its head. It was solid and cold. Marble. She turned around. Ian's workshop was in the distance behind her, the lights off. She didn't remember reaching it, let alone passing it, but perhaps in the darkness she'd walked right by it. Had she tripped over the same blasted root again and dreamed the entire series of events? She looked at her knuckles and touched her cheek. Perfectly normal.

A man's form appeared from behind the workshop.

Ian.

"Lily! I've been searching everywhere for you —" He closed the space between them and folded her in his arms brusquely.

She stood stiffly in his engulfing embrace, half delirious and confused. His heart was racing against her chest. "I'm s-sorry," she said, fighting tears as nightmarish memories played over and over in her mind's eye.

It must have all been a dream as she'd lain there unconscious. It had to be—otherwise, how could her hands and face be free of injury?

"I must've fallen," she said. "Hit my head pretty darn good." She touched her fingers to the tender swollen area behind her ear. "I had the strangest dream, too."

He held her at arm's length then, studying her face—fine lines about his eyes. She was chilled to the bone and his warm palms fairly burned her triceps.

She shivered involuntarily and he wrapped his strong arm around her waist, providing ample support as they walked together down the trail to the backyard.

When they reached the mansion, a fretting Hannah put her to bed, insisting that she rest until the headache was gone.

When Lily's eyes fluttered open a couple of hours later, it was to find Ian sitting in a ladder-back chair next to her bed, his head hung low. Instead of being disturbed, she was pleased to see him. He seemed to sense her gaze and she greeted him cheerfully when he looked up. He was wearing an open-necked black pullover sweater and gray jeans, his short hair spiked on top.

"I brought you brunch," he said, smiling. "Oatmeal and buttered scones." He rose from the chair and retrieved a legged tray that was perched atop the chest of drawers.

"Oh, that's so kind of you," she said, letting him prop the pillows behind her so she could sit up.

He settled the tray over her lap and sat down again in the chair next to her bed. "How are you feeling?" he asked, eyes wider than usual. So this was what he looked like when he wasn't brooding.

She took a sip of tea from a China cup and smiled at him again. "I'm feeling much better. Headache's gone."

"Do you . . . " He paused and cleared his throat. "Do you remember anything about last night?" He furrowed his brow, watching her carefully.

She dabbed a cloth napkin to her lips. "I remember it, but most of my memories are just of a nightmare." She let out a laugh. Why was he was so grave anyway? She was fine. "And by the way," she said, "I think it's about time someone removed that root from the path before I kill myself on it."

He cracked a half smile. "Can you tell me about the dream?"

Frowning, she broke off a piece of scone and chewed a moment before responding. She then told him about being attacked by a hideous man who'd asked about her mother and smashed her face; how she was calmed down by what she thought was a horse; and finally, how she was led back to the trail by a walking, talking gargoyle. It struck her then that she couldn't recall whether or not she'd actually gone into Ian's workshop and lost his bird. He'd made no mention of it—and she didn't dare ask.

Ian listened in silence, the slightest twitch of a muscle in his cheek the only sign of distress. She took another sip of tea and fiddled with the spoon in her oatmeal. Recounting that nightmare had sapped her appetite, replacing it with mild nausea.

"You're certain this man was asking about your mother?"

"Yes." She met his gaze. "But as I said, it was only a dream." She pointed at her cheek. "Hello."

He straightened in the chair, hands on his thighs. "I think it's about time you left this place, Lily. You can't stay here any longer."

"But, I don't want to leave."

"How much money do you want for your half of the estate? Give me a number—any number—and it's yours."

"Ian . . . I'm not leaving."

He stood up and paced at the foot of her bed. "I want you gone by dinner time." He stopped and stared down at her, one hand gripping a canopy pole, his knuckles white with tension.

"But . . . why?" It was impossible to tell if he was angry or sad.

He let go and turned, strolling for the open

door. "Be gone by five o'clock," he said coldly. "My lawyers will be in touch."

Without a glance over his shoulder, he went out into the hall and slammed the door shut behind him.

Lily waited a while, hoping he would come back with a change of heart and tell her he wanted her to stay.

But he didn't come back and five minutes stretched into ten, then twenty.

Tears trickled down her cheeks and she hated herself for it. She knew next to nothing about him and she still didn't know what was in that trunk—so what did it matter if he wanted her gone? Was he dangerous? She thought of the room full of vats and shivered, swiping at her tears. Maybe it really was best for her to take off and never return.

She refused to cry over a man who might be some sort of mad scientist or serial killer . . . or both.

Moving aside the breakfast tray, she got out of bed and changed into clean clothes, brushing her hair back into a ponytail. She yanked her suitcases out of the wardrobe and stuffed her clothing and possessions into them, not bothering to fold or organize.

Someone rapped on the door. Was it Ian come back to apologize?

"Who is it?"

"It's Mike—can I come in?"

She hesitated. "Is it . . . important?"

"I think so."

She looked in the mirror to make sure her face wasn't puffy and red from crying. Taking a deep, steadying breath, she went to the door and pulled it open. He brushed past her and turned around a few feet away, grinning. "I got something for you while I was in town today." His brown eyes fairly sparkled as he pulled a bouquet of carnations out from behind his back.

At the sight of the flowers, she burst into fresh tears and turned away from him, cupping her face in her hands.

"What's wrong?" He approached and wrapped an arm around her shoulder. "Is it the flowers? I'm so sorry—I can throw them away. I didn't mean to upset you."

She wiped her eyes. "No, Mike. It's not you. It's just that, I've decided to leave."

He embraced her, tucking her face into the crook of his shoulder. "You can't be serious," he said. "You just got here. I thought you were moving in for good."

"It's complicated," she mumbled into his chest, letting out a shaky exhale. She considered pushing him away but his strong warm arms were comforting.

"It's not Ian, is it?" he asked, stiffening. "Is he forcing you to leave? I'll knock his face in."

She withdrew from the embrace with a jerk. "Why is giving someone a beating always the first solution to men?" She shook her head. "No, the reason I'm leaving is because I'm tired of all the secrets. How can I be a part of this family when no one will tell me a darned thing about anything?"

"I showed you the secret passages in the walls, didn't I?" He put his palms out in a don't-look-at-me gesture. "Ian is the only problem. He's the one who forces us to secrecy. Not that we know much anyway. Just ignore him and you might start enjoying yourself."

"I'm sorry, Mike, but my mind is made up. I'll be leaving this afternoon." There was no way she could make a life for herself here while ignoring Ian. He was too formidable . . . yet surprisingly tender at the same time.

A baffling disparity.

Mike reached out and took her hand in his. "Let me cheer you up," he said. "I'll drive you into town and we'll get a cappuccino."

She smiled in spite of herself. "Okay. Sure. That does sound nice." Perhaps getting away from the mansion for a little while would clear the cobwebs in her head.

Mike laid the bouquet of flowers on the dresser and led her to the door. He paused, letting go of her hand, and bent down to the floor to pick something up next to a weaved hamper.

"What is it?" She leaned in to see.

In his palm was an elongated golden key. She gasped, recognizing it as the one from the bird in Ian's workshop. Hadn't it all been a dream? Maybe she'd stolen the key first: *before* hitting her head. Had it then fallen from her pocket when she'd changed clothes a few minutes before Mike's arrival?

But, if that were the case . . . it must mean Ian's bird really had escaped.

"Oh, the key to my diary—" she said with a forced laugh, snatching it from his hand. "I've been looking for that."

An hour later, having driven into town with Mike in a silver Lamborghini and enjoying a couple of cappuccinos at a quaint little café, Mike suggested they go somewhere else; a place of interest he wanted to show her.

They left the café and climbed back into the gleaming car. It made the rest of the cars in the lot look like heaps of junk and she wondered vaguely who it belonged to, doubting a handyman could afford such a vehicle.

They drove in silence, Lily deep in thought as she watched the stores whip by. She barely noted that the sunshine and blue skies were disappearing behind fast-growing rain clouds.

Leaving the town center, they drove through winding country roads, eventually parking at the top of a rocky cliff overlooking vast forestland far below.

Oh gosh, he'd taken her to some kind of look-out spot.

She'd have to be upfront and tell him she didn't have those kinds of feelings for him.

"The view here is *amazing*," he said, cutting

the engine and climbing out of the car. "Come take a look."

She climbed out of the vehicle and hugged her jacket around her waist, following him to the cliff's edge. An old post and rail fence ran along the edge, its paint chipped and splintering. There was no one else around.

A breeze carrying the scent of decaying leaves whipped up from below, flicking her ponytail.

"Where are we?" she asked, scanning the horizon.

"Not far from the mansion." He grinned at her. "If you look closely, you can actually see it in the distance, sticking outta the treetops over there." He pointed. Sure enough, the tips of the turrets and chimneys could be seen but little more.

The overcast sky was deepening from white to gray. "I think it's going to rain," she said. He reached out and took her hand in his but she tugged slightly and he let go, taking the hint.

She gave him an apologetic smile and clasped her hands together behind her back, gazing down at the endless expanse of gloomy woodland. She hoped she hadn't hurt his feelings too much. "It's hard to believe those woods are full of man-eating wolves," she said with a chuckle, hoping to lighten the mood.

He laughed. "I personally don't believe they're as bad as Ian says. He gave me that same story about staying out of the woods years ago too, when I first started working there. I think he just wants to keep everyone away from his work shed. Who knows what all he's got stored up in there. To be frank, I've always thought it kind of juvenile for a grown man to have a tree fort."

"You've never seen inside it?"

He shook his head. "No, don't care to. And like I said, he forbids everyone to go anywhere near it." A sardonic laugh.

She thought about all the jewels and diamonds and sculptures. "You should see it," she said. "It's really beautiful. He's quite the artist."

Mike rubbed his chin, glancing at her sidelong. "Yeah?"

"Mmhm. Hey, Mike . . . " She searched his face a moment. "Did you ask Ian about those vats yet?"

He averted eye contact. "Yes,"—he cleared his throat—"and it was just like I thought. The vats are full of filtering water; keeps the aquarium clean. The table was for the sharks, in case they might ever need medical care." He met her eyes again and grinned. "See, nothing at all to worry about."

Relief warmed her and she unfolded her arms. "Thanks for this," she said, smiling.

"For what?"

She noted again how handsome he was. But then, Ian was handsome too. Why was she falling for the man with all the secrets when Mike was the one who'd been friendly and open from the get-go?

"For being a friend," she said, "for talking to me, taking me out this afternoon and trying to cheer me up. Things like that."

"Hey, no problem, sunshine. Besides, it's not like it's a chore to spend time with you. I should be thanking you for the honor of your presence." He smiled wide and took a step toward her, gazing into her eyes intimately, grin fading.

Her heartbeat picked up a notch; vat room forgotten. He took another step forward and brushed his lips across her cheek, heading for her lips.

She turned her face away from his and lifting her palms, gently pressed them into his chest, stepping back. He stuffed his hands in his pockets and moved away from her, staring down the cliff at the forest below. A frown tugged at the corner of his lips but he said nothing.

She crossed her arms over her chest again. The wind was picking up and in the distance a sheet of rain was falling, moving toward the mansion.

"We should head back," Mike said, moving away from the fence without looking at her. She followed him to the parked car and climbed into the passenger seat.

It was going to be an awkward drive home.

By the time they approached the estate driveway, it was pouring rain and the headlights reached only two meters ahead. The mansion was dark—not a single window lit.

As they drove through the open gates and up the long road leading to the front of the estate, a dark masculine figure appeared in the headlights, standing in the middle of the road with his head tilted to one side.

Chapter 15

Mike slammed on the brakes and rolled down the window.

The black figure just stood there, the contours of his face obscured by the rushing rain.

"Ian—that you?" he said. "Come on man, no games. Is the power out?"

Without a word, the man strolled off the driveway; disappearing from the scope of the head-lights.

Mike rolled up his window, his foot still on the brake pedal. "What the—"

No sooner had the words left his mouth when someone wrenched the driver's seat door wide open.

Lily yelped but was quick to regain her composure when the car's interior lights lit the face of their supposed assailant.

"Ian—" she shouted furiously, leaning over Mike's lap. "What are you trying to do?"

He was wearing a trench coat with the collar up, wet hair plastered and rivulets of water streaming down his face. "I could ask you the same question," he said. "I thought I told you to be *gone* by five o'clock."

"Just chill man," Mike interjected. "What's the

hurry?" He shot a glance at Lily. "So—it *was* Ian who told you to leave."

"I didn't ask for your opinion," Ian said, voice low and intimidating. "Cut the idle chit-chat, grab a flashlight from the glove box, and go see if any fuses are blown."

Lily climbed out of the passenger seat and stepped into the deluge. Ian came around the front of the car and took her hand. "Come on, I'll get you inside," he said. "Sorry I don't have an umbrella."

They jogged the rest of the way up the flooded driveway—Mike in tow with a flashlight beam to guide their way—and hurried up the slippery stone steps. Ian let go of her hand and yanked open the heavy oak doors.

Leaving Ian and Lily to their own devices, Mike hurried down the vaulted corridor and yanked on the warrior's axe, opening the wall panel leading to the basement.

There was a fuse box in a cellar-like room accessed through the scuba supply room. Mike had used it as a makeshift work area for three years now. He had a long work bench, a stool, some power tools, and shelving units used to store cans of paint and various household maintenance supplies.

With the aid of his flashlight, he went into the room and swept the beam across the floor to the far end—and dropped the flashlight.

Fumbling for it at his feet, he shone the light once more to the far end of the room, his breath shallow in his chest.

His worktable had been overturned, cans of paint were splattered across the floor, and his tool box was open and upside down. Instinctively, he flicked the flashlight back and forth—searching the nooks and crannies of the room for a lingering culprit. Satisfied that the room was unoccupied, he stormed to the fuse box, avoiding the paint splatters, and reached out to yank open the fuse box.

He froze.

Four jagged slash marks marred the front lid of the fuse box.

Mike darted from the room and pounded up the stone stairs. He had no idea how an animal had found a way into the mansion *and* into the scuba room, but somehow a large animal had found its way in, and he intended to shoot every last one in the forest if he had to. Probably one of them hired marine workers had come in through the basement and forgotten to shut the doors upon leaving. He'd find out who had done it and have him or her fired. This was beyond carelessness. And that animal had better be back outdoors and not wandering about inside the mansion. The last thing he wanted to do was wrestle a grizzly bear in his own bedroom.

"Where are we headed now," Lily asked as

she followed Ian down the main corridor. Her clothes were clingy and damp and she figured her mascara had trailed down her cheeks. Most of her hair was pulled back but several wet strands dangled about her face, getting in the way.

After checking to make sure Hannah, Angie and Chris were all fine, they'd taken a spare flashlight from Hannah and had gone back downstairs.

"Need to see what's taking Mike so long," Ian said, glancing at her sidelong. "He was supposed to be checking the fuse box—though if there's a tree down on the power lines, the fuse box won't help us. Still, he should be back by now."

A flashlight beam emerged from the stairwell at the end of the corridor ahead of them, followed by Mike, and they quickly closed the gap between them.

"Some wild animal got in and trashed my workroom," he said matter-of-factly, huffing. "Probably looking for food. Not sure how it got in—but whatever it is, it's big."

Ian gave Mike a nudge in Lily's direction. "Take Lily straight to Hannah's room and wait for me —I'll be right back."

Mike stood in place.

"Go!"

Lily pivoted on her heel and headed for the front entrance. "I don't need to be taken anywhere, thank you. Come on, Mike, let's go." He hurried after her, mumbling a few curses at Ian, and shined the flashlight beam ahead of them.

Satisfied they were well on their way to Hannah's, Ian slipped into the stair well and quietly made his way to Mike's workroom. When he reached the room, he stood staring at the mess before him only a moment before flicking off the flashlight; he didn't need it anyway. It was just for show when the others were around.

The sight of the shredded fuse box lid made him prickly all over, like pins and needles coursing through his veins. He had to get Lily out of this place; while she was still free to leave. That is, if it wasn't already too late for that. He wanted to wring Mike's neck for deterring her all afternoon. She should have been long gone by now.

One thing had become sickeningly clear to him in the last 24 hours.

A soulless killer was looking for her.

Ian let out a cry of rage and grabbed a wrench off the floor, pelting it at the wall with all his strength —chipping the stone. What was that lunatic up to? Why had he shut off the power?

A chill like winter's breath flitted down his back and he left the room, tearing up the stairs and hurrying down the hallway.

"Ia-a-ann . . . " an icy voice whispered somewhere behind him. "Or should I call you Zever?"

Ian froze, recognizing the wretched voice.

He turned around to face a tall shadowy figure standing in the middle of the hall.

"What do you want from her?" Ian snarled.

The figure let out a sharp laugh. "You can't protect her forever. For all you know—I've already got her."

"If you did, we wouldn't be having this conversation," he said in a gritty voice; clenching and releasing his fists. "You don't belong here. She's done you no harm."

"I want but one thing from her—and then I'll be gone."

"And what is that?"

"Her life blood pouring through my hands." He laughed.

Ian lunged toward him but the figure stepped aside and cracked him on the back of his skull with something hard—sending him straight to the floor. Lights dotted his vision as he struggled to stay conscious.

"Useless." A booted foot settled against the back of Ian's head, pushing his nose toward the marble floor. "You won't be able to stop me, just as you couldn't stop me from killing Auguste. Ha! I'd have killed you long ago if it weren't for your father."

"*You* killed Auguste?—You bastard, I'll tear your throat out—"

"Ah-ah-ah, there'll be none of that." The boot slammed down hard against Ian's head, breaking his nose.

Chapter 16

Ian awoke to throbbing pain in the center of his face.

He was slumped against a stone wall in one of the hidden passageways surrounding the pool room, dried blood on his lips and chin. His attacker must have dragged him here after knocking him out.

Lily!

He was too late.

Scooting to a seated position and then a standing one, Ian staggered a few steps, facial nerves exploding in pain. He touched his fingertips to his crooked nose and steeling himself against the pain, snapped it back in place. Eyes watering, he stumbled toward the nearest exit panel and took the stairs up to the main corridor; determined to find Lily.

The walls in the brightly lit hallway seemed to be moving—shifting and warbling—going in and out of focus. The power was back on. He gripped the railing at the front entrance and leaned into it, putting one foot before the other as though they were wooden. He reached the upper floor and squinted in the brightness of the hallway. Someone was approaching him from the opposite end, moving with swift steps. Was it Hannah, coming to tell him what had happened to Lily?

His legs gave way and he fell to his knees, shoulders shaking as he began to sob. His own self-ishness had killed her. If only he had banished her the very first day she'd come.

It was all his fault.

"Ian—" Hannah's voice broke through his sobs. "What happened!"

"Don't tell me—" he cried. "I don't want to hear it."

"Whatever's the matter, dear? You look terri-ble—what happened to your face?" She knelt down and took him into her arms as though he was a small boy, and dabbed a tissue at his cheeks. He pushed her away gently and struggled to stand up. She gripped his elbow until he'd steadied himself.

Ian blinked several times and focused on her face. She didn't seem horrified or tearful—just con-cerned.

She didn't know then.

Did anyone know yet?

"Why were you crying?" she asked, examin-ing his face, one hand on her plump hip. "That's not like you at all. Is it the pain?"

He hesitated.

"It's . . . just allergies. Mold."

"Oh, nonsense. You've got blood all over your nose, bruised eyes, and you're white as a sheet."

She reached a motherly hand toward his cheek and he stepped out of the way. He didn't want anymore coddling. He had to find Lily's body before someone else did. And then he had to figure out what to do from there. People would eventually come looking for her. The police as well.

But aside from all that, how could he endure life even one more day now that she was gone?

"Ian—answer me. What happened to your face."

Her sharp words were like hammer blows to his skull. If he didn't know any better, he'd think he was hungover. He pressed a palm to his temple. "I'm fine, Hannah. Just had a fall in the dark and bumped my nose."

"Well, goodness, Ian, what on earth were you doing wandering around in the dark? I thought you had a flashlight—I gave you one."

He closed his eyes, fighting back more weary tears. "Have you seen Lily?" he asked evenly, though his voice caught at the end.

"Of course, we all stayed together until the power came back on. She's in Angie's room right now."

"Lily's in . . . in Angie's room?" His eyes widened, skin tingling all over. How was this even possible? He gulped in a lungful of air to stop the dizziness and balance himself.

"Yes, and we'll soon be heading downstairs for a late dinner of some sort." She gave him a once over. "Your nose is swollen and purple. Is it broken?"

He blinked, relief beginning to warm his body like a soothing massage oil. "I've got to see her," he said, starting down the hall.

Hannah grabbed his bicep. "You'll do no such thing, young man. Not until you've cleaned yourself up a bit."

Lily finished off a slice of cold pumpkin pie. She dabbed her lips with a napkin and pushed back her chair. Mike and Chris were speaking in subdued tones together at the opposite end of the dining table —discussing the damage done in the fusebox room— and Hannah was sipping a cup of coffee with a far-away look in her eye. No one had spoken much with Lily over their makeshift dinners and she'd felt out of place; like a visitor.

She hadn't seen Ian since he'd ordered her and Mike up to Hannah's room, and no one had cared to look for him either; being used to his come and go nature. "He'll be back when he feels like it," Hannah had said. "He could be outside searching for the bear. If it was still inside, we'd know it—most likely went straight back out through whatever door it came in. Poor thing was probably just hungry."

Lily collected everyone's empty plates, stacked the fine China carefully, though it clinked here and there, and carried the lot into the kitchen where Angie was already washing dishes. When she went back into the dining room to collect the utensils, a disheveled Ian appeared in the open doorway—his short hair wet and tousled, shadows beneath his eyes, and a mildly bruised nose marring his handsome face.

For a moment their gazes locked and then his face lit with a brilliant smile. He hurried around the table and scooped her up in his arms, swinging her around in a full circle and nearly whacking her feet off the China cabinet. He was laughing: the foreign sound of it like heaven to her ears. Had she ever once heard him laugh before?

Ian beamed down at her, eyes alight, and set her on her feet. He gripped her shoulders in his warm palms. "You have no idea how glad I am to see you."

Mike groaned and interjected loudly: "Give up the sap man—this morning you freaking banished her—and now this?"

Lily flushed. She too was confused by his change in demeanor. Why was he so overjoyed to see her when he'd expressly told her to leave and never return? She tucked a strand of hair behind her ear and went to the table, gathering the scattered utensils.

Without a word, Ian retrieved some of the empty cups and followed her into the kitchen. She avoided eye contact with Mike as she passed him but sensed his watchful gaze on her back.

After putting the silverware in the sink, she washed her hands and dried them on a dish towel, turning to face him. "What did you do to your nose?"

He averted his gaze and Mike entered the room.

"Yeah—what happened to your face?" Mike reiterated; a look of distaste in his eyes.

"If you must know, I slipped in the mess of your workroom."

Mike seemed to consider this a moment and nodded, his features softening. "Ah yes—the paint. Sorry man."

"Paint?" Lily startled. "What are you talking

about?"

Mike shrugged. "Your guess is as good as mine, Lily. Seems an animal trashed the room." He shifted his gaze to Ian. "What's weird about it is if a bear came in here scrounging for food, why go looking downstairs instead of sniffing out the kitchen? Makes no sense." He raised an eyebrow but Ian didn't respond.

"Well—I'm heading down there now to clean up a bit," Mike said, rapping the counter top. "Care to lend a hand?"

The apparent happiness at seeing Lily was gone from Ian's face now; replaced with the brooding look she was growing to resent. And something else. Irritation.

"Lily—" he said, taking a gentle hold of her elbow and searching her face. "I'm going to go with Mike just for a few minutes. Promise me you'll stay here in the kitchen with Angie until I get back? I'll only be gone a half hour at most."

"All right. I'll help Angie finish the dishes."

"Actually, why don't you come with us?" He reached for her hand.

"No way man," Mike cut in. "She needn't trouble herself, she'll just ruin her shoes."

Lily laughed. "Yes, my poor little dainty shoes."

Ian had a wild look in his eyes now, as if he desperately wanted to say something but was holding back. "Fine," he said after a handful of seconds, "but don't leave the kitchen."

For a moment she wanted to rebel but decided

if Ian was going down to the basement with Mike for a while, this would be the perfect opportunity to see if the key in her pocket was the right one for the trunk in the attic. She would slip upstairs quickly, give it a try, and hurry back down before Ian returned.

If she was going to stay here any longer—and she fully intended to—she had to be sure he wasn't hiding something.

Ian seemed overly hesitant to leave, a fine line creasing his forehead. "*Promise* me you'll stay right here in the kitchen till I get back?"

"Sure, Ian," she said. "I'll be here."

He searched her eyes once more, looking distrustful. She turned away. To be fair, she had set his pet parrot free into the forest and had done nothing to earn his trust at all; on the contrary. Was it possible he still hadn't yet discovered the bird was missing, or did he know but hadn't said anything? Her heart contracted at the thought, fresh guilt making her nauseous. She hoped the bird was okay.

She glanced at Mike who was standing by the door, watching them carefully with a look of impatience.

Ian moved away from her and followed Mike out into the dining room.

Lily stood before the dusty old trunk and stared down at it, fingering the bow and blade of the key in her pocket.

She hunched down and examined the carvings up close. They seemed to be telling a story of some sort. On both the left end, sides and curved top of the chest, there were humans and creatures alike, dancing and feasting in a joyous party. In the center of the front side of the chest, a maiden stood with arms above her head. She held what appeared to be the sun in her hands, and in the middle of the sun was the key hole. On the right sides and top of the trunk, the carvings depicted monstrous creatures screaming in rage and pain while encircling a figure shrouded in robes.

Lily pulled the key from her pocket with trembling fingers, heart racing and a prickly heat moving through her body. This was it—if she opened the trunk to find a dead body, she would run away and never, ever return.

Inserting the key in the lock, she turned to the right until it clicked, and with a deep breath, lifted the heavy lid.

No corpse.

Just folded clothes, a disintegrating hooded cloak made from dried leaves, a handful of Polaroid photographs, and a leather-bound journal.

No riches, no skeleton, no horrible secret—just the average sort of things one might expect to find inside a trunk. Though the cloak was rather strange.

She picked up the stack of photos, frowning. There were three in total.

The first had been taken in this very attic: an old man and a young dark-haired boy standing in front of the closed trunk. Neither were smiling. The next was of the same boy whittling away at a piece of wood while the old man sat nearby watching with a pipe in his mouth. It appeared to have been taken at the maiden fountain in the backyard. The final photo was more recent—the boy in his late teens. The man had grown a curly beard. They were standing beside one of the gargoyles at the front entrance of the mansion. Lily recognized them now: It was her late grandfather, Auguste Kline, and the young man was Ian Hawke.

She shuffled to the first photo again, wondering why she hadn't recognized the young boy as Ian. She stared at the photo and squinted. With a sense of unease, she realized there was something wrong with his eyes. Maybe it had to do with the age of the photo or the lighting, but they seemed to be solid black— like two empty holes in his skull. She rubbed the photo on her sleeve in case it was still marred by dust and lifted it closer to her face. Yes, his entire eyes were black. Not even a trace of white around the irises.

Lily shuddered and placed the photos back into the trunk, picking up the journal instead. A silky, maroon-colored ribbon was tied around the leather cover and the papers were yellowed. The cover wasn't dusty like the photos. Had it been looked at more recently? She noted the time on her wristwatch and reluctantly set the journal back down. She'd been gone from the kitchen ten minutes now and had best be heading back before her absence was discovered. She'd have to take a look at the journal later when she had more time.

Before closing the trunk, she pulled the folded clothes and the cloak out and set them atop a nearby crate, wanting to see if there was anything else in the bottom.

There was nothing to see but a protrusion in the center—something flat, round and golden. She leaned in over the rim to get a closer look. It was another lock. Was there a narrow compartment in the base of the trunk? It could be no more than three inches deep, if even that.

Retrieving the key from the lid, she tried it in the second lock.

It didn't fit.

Lily sat back on her heels and sighed. Here she was momentarily relieved that Ian had nothing hidden in the trunk besides some dusty photos and a journal. But now this. What might be contained within the locked compartment? Incriminating papers of some sort? More jewels?

Straightening up, she gathered the folded clothes and cloak in her arms and put them back in the trunk as she'd found them; sneezing on the cloud of dust that billowed up out of it. She picked up a couple of dried leaves that had fluttered to the floor and tossed them into the trunk. Noting the time again, she locked the trunk, and tucked the journal beneath her shirt, securing it behind the belt of her waistband. She switched off the overhead light and crept back downstairs; listening for any sounds in the hallway.

Seeing and hearing no one around, she hurried down to the kitchen, hoping Ian hadn't returned.

Chapter 17

When Lily reached the dining room, Angie was sitting at the table drinking a coffee and reading the paper. She smiled up at Lily as she entered the room.

"I just made a fresh pot of decaf if you'd like some," she said. "It's in the kitchen."

With a pleasant smile and nod of thanks, Lily went into the kitchen and instead of pouring a coffee, went to a private corner where Angie would be unable to see her, and pulled out the journal. With an eye on the door, she untied the silk ribbon and slipped it into her pocket for safe keeping. She opened the journal to the first page, glancing at the open door again. If Ian returned, she should be able to hear him in the dining room first with enough time to hide the journal.

There was no name written in the front page, just the first entry. The handwriting was in black pen: wide loops, slightly shaky. She couldn't tell if it was a man or woman's hand.

She read quickly, fairly skimming the entries:

August 8
I do not know why I am bothering to begin a new journal when no one will ever read it, but I suppose old habits die

hard.

The summer is coming to an end and I am worried about the winter. I lost my job of twenty years, the bank took my home, and I am penniless. All of my resources are tapped and stretched thin.

I have no family and nowhere to go.

It's over for me.

September 13

There is a bitter nip in the air. Summer has packed up and gone and autumn has taken its studious watch. When his brother winter arrives in a torrent of wind and ice, my time will come to an end. I do not have the fortitude to stay in a homeless shelter. My pride will not let me. I will not be that kind of man. Despite what others may think, I still have my dignity.

I intend to spend my final days in the heart of the forest, enjoying nature and solitude, away from judgmental, uncaring civilization. When the cold inevitably comes, I refuse to huddle in a city alley under a blanket of soiled newspapers eating scraps from a dumpster. I would rather freeze or starve to death sitting against the bark of an indifferent tree.

She flipped the page.

September 15

I can not believe my good fortune.

I have discovered an abandoned hunting cabin in the woods. At least, I presume it to be abandoned. It is run down and in disrepair and looks as though it hasn't been used in a decade. Nevertheless, there are several cans of beans and soup in the cupboard, a box of matches, a wood stove, and an axe. There are also two rifles and a crate of ammo. I will be able to hunt for food! I can only hope the owners do not return until spring. It is my hope they will never return.

There is a small shed behind the cabin, but it is padlocked. This is strange considering the cabin was left wide open. I wonder what is in it.

From all I have observed, I have come to the conclusion that whoever was here before me fled in a hurry.

I hope I am not squatting in a criminal's lair.

Lily paused at the sound of footfall, back stiffening. She shut the cover, stuffed the book into her pants under her shirt and stood squarely, heart pounding.

But it was only Angie—come to refill her coffee mug.

Lily busied herself by rooting through a pen drawer, pretending to be looking for something, and as soon as Angie went back into the dining room, she reopened the journal and began reading again; overwhelmed with a voracious hunger to read every last page before Ian's return.

September 26

I finally managed to break into the shed using the axe. There is absolutely nothing inside it except a large wooden chest. It is a marvelous work of art. The carvings covering its surface are intricate and flawless. They seem to jump out at you. The chest is locked unfortunately, and though I have searched both the cabin and the shed thoroughly, I can

find no key.
I have to know what is in it!

October 7
I made a grisly discovery today.
I found a human skeleton thirty yards behind the cabin beneath some balsam firs. I'm not sure how long it has been there. It could be from the summer, or it could be fifty years old.
I would not have discovered it had I not been chopping down trees and clearing away brush in preparation for winter. There is a rusted machete between the ribs. This is most definitely a case of murder, but if I go to the police, I will lose my home for the winter. My life! I can not.
There were two golden keys lying in the tattered coat behind the spine. I suspect the victim must have swallowed them right before death. But I can only speculate.
I am going to see if one of the keys is for the chest.

Lily frowned, biting her lower lip in disappointment: The next few pages had suffered water damage and the ink had run all over the pages, making the text illegible. The next readable entry wasn't until an entire year later.

Footsteps sounded in the dining room, along with the voice of Mike greeting Angie.

Lily stuffed the diary beneath her shirt and went into the dining room with a casual air.

Mike was alone, however.

"Lily," he said, turning toward her with a customary smile, a wistful look in his eyes. "Ian asked me to bring you to the study." A humorless laugh.

"Thinks I'm his butler or something."

"Can he wait a minute or two?" she asked. "I'd like to go to my room for a second."

"Sure." He shrugged. "Don't see why not. I'll let him know you'll be there in a few."

With a grateful smile, she went out into the corridor, hurried up the staircase, and closed her bedroom door behind her with a click.

Unable to restrain her curiosity, she pulled out the journal and opened it to the next legible entry.

July 28
I am moving into the mansion this week. I still can not believe this is happening to me. I owe it all to that blessed chest, but I absolutely must make certain that no one else ever gets their hands on it. No one must know.
I need to find a safe place to hide it and guard it with my life.

September 1
I have fallen in love. In all my life, I have never seen such a beautiful woman. My heart leaps for joy in her presence. My dearest Serena, I would give all that I have for you. I would leave all this newfound wealth behind and never return, if only to have the honor of your companionship, your love.
I wonder if she realizes how much I love her. I must tell her! I can not keep this to myself a day longer.

She skimmed through the following year's worth of entries, much of them the honeyed reveries of a man in love enjoying his newfound riches and fortune.

By now she knew the journal was Auguste's.

June 4
This past year has been heaven, the best year of my life. Two years ago, I thought I would freeze to death in the forest. Today I am a rich man living in a huge mansion.
My darling Serena is with child.
We were married privately because she did not want our relationship to be known. Sometimes I wonder if she is ashamed of me, but I realize she has her reasons. Maybe in time she will change her mind and we can make our marriage public.

The next page was covered in rain drops.
Or perhaps . . . tears.

January 8
Oh, bleary, wretched day of hell. My heart is torn in a million pieces. I shall never recover. My precious Serena has died giving birth to our daughter.
I feel only resentment toward my child, for she took my angel from me. I know it's not her fault, but I can not bear to look at her. She has her mother's eyes.
Perhaps in time I will grow to love her. That is, should this heart of mine ever find within itself the ability to love again.
For now, when I look at this infant's face, I see only the cold white face of my poor dead Serena.

There was only one more entry after this and the remaining half of the journal was nothing but blank pages.

April 21
Horrible things are happening. I was such a fool! There is
too much danger for my daughter and I. The chest must be
locked and the keys hidden. My daughter must be sent
away. It is no longer safe for her to stay with me! Oh, how
I will miss her. She is the last thing I have to remember my
dear Serena by.
I have lost everything.
Everything!

Lily hid the journal as well as the key from her pocket by folding them carefully together into a sweater and tucking them into the chest of drawers with the rest of her shirts. She brushed her hair, touched up her makeup and went downstairs to the study where Ian was purportedly waiting for her.

Ian paced back and forth on the Persian rug filling the sitting area in front of Auguste's desk; waiting for Mike to show up with Lily. As long as everyone was up and about he knew the killer wouldn't make a move, but it was eleven o'clock now and they'd soon be retiring. He had so much to tell her and so little time.

Plunking down in Auguste's leather chair, he leaned against the tall back and drummed his fingers on the desktop loudly. He had decided to meet with

Lily in Auguste's study specifically because it was the only room in the mansion with soundproof walls. He hadn't decided how much he would tell her, but he wanted to be sure no one else could overhear.

The room was lined with twenty-foot bookshelves with spiraled pillars dividing them into sections, and the ceiling was painted in the Renaissance style of horses and royalty. A rolling ladder was needed to reach the uppermost books and he recalled many hours as a child sliding back and forth along the walls, much to Hannah's ongoing chagrin.

He smiled at the thought of Hannah. She'd always been special to him.

He was going to miss her.

She wouldn't understand why he had to go. It would break her heart. Nevertheless, after all these years, the time had come for him to leave and there was really no choice in the matter. He'd already written letters of dismissal for Chris and Angie, which he'd slipped under their bedroom doors a half hour ago. Each letter included a substantial cheque enabling them to live in luxury for the rest of their days, with the stipulation that they had to leave this very night. Angie had always dreamed of owning her own restaurant and Chris had talked about retiring in Europe and buying a vineyard. They would both be able to pursue their dreams.

He was going to wait until the end before talking to Mike, however.

Mike would be instructed to drain the aquarium and burn down the mansion once everyone had gone, and his payment would be all the jewels in the forest workshop. Then Mike must burn down the tree as well. When Ian had first arrived in the attic as a boy, he'd brought along the seed for a fast growing tree in his pocket. In his teen years he'd hollowed it out it and converted it into a bedroom and a workshop.

Nothing must be left of this place but a smoldering ruin. That way no one else could ever make the same mistakes as Auguste.

Ian didn't know what exactly to do about Hannah though. There was no way she'd accept any money from him; nor was she likely to leave without kicking and screaming.

The intercom buzzed on the side of the desk, interrupting his thoughts like a brass gong.

"Who's there?" he said, holding down the talk button.

"It's Lily."

He pressed the release button and the heavy oak doors swung inward.

Though the study was usually left unlocked, it could be securely sealed from the inside whenever necessary. He had a feeling they were being watched; even if only from a distance.

Lily came in through the open doors, sea-green eyes widening in a child-like way as her face lit with a smile. Her hair was loose and hung in straight lines to her shoulders.

The very sight of her soothed his aching chest while simultaneously filling him with dread. But it wasn't just her looks that drew him. It was her playfulness, her fighting spirit and strong mind, her carefree laughter. She was like a splash of color in his drab gray world.

Ian jumped to his feet and went for a glossy chair, pulling it up to the desk so they could sit facing one another. She sat down and he pushed the button under his desk to shut and lock the heavy doors.

"What's this all about, Ian?" Her look was guarded.

He let out a long exhale, sitting down in Auguste's chair with squared shoulders. "It's time I answered some of your questions."

She clasped her hands together, unable to mask the intrigue that sparked in her eyes. "Why the change of heart?"

"Because your life is in danger." His tone was grave.

She glanced over her shoulder at the closed doors and seemed to stiffen. Did she think it was *he* she had to fear?

He tugged up his shirt sleeve and began unraveling the gauze around his arm, working quickly lest he lose his resolve. He flicked her a glance and she opened her mouth to speak, but closed it again.

After unraveling the final section, he laid his bare arm over the desk.

Lily stood and leaned over it. Other than a ring of indented pink scars, the shark bites were completely healed.

"How is this possible?" she said in a whisper, meeting his gaze as though afraid.

He leaned back in his chair and she sank into

hers.

"What I'm about to tell you," he said, "will be . . . difficult for you to believe."

Chapter 18

Mike stood in front of the portrait of Auguste and gripped a pair of keys in the palm of his hand.

One was the key he'd just now foraged from Lily's dresser, and the other was a key he'd discovered weeks ago under a floorboard in the hallway where Auguste's body had been found. After the body was taken away, Mike noticed a loose one-foot section of board, and not wanting it to worsen and become a tripping hazard, he set about repairing it straight away. He retrieved his tools, removed the piece, and startled to find a golden key lying in the gap.

The first thing he'd done was tried it in the warden lock of the trunk in the attic.

But it didn't fit and he was terribly frustrated; for the entire time he'd been working for Auguste as a handy man, he'd been searching for the key to that trunk. Many nights over the years, Auguste went up to the attic and stayed there for hours at a time; or stranger still, even several days at a time. Mike had investigated only to find nothing of interest but the locked trunk. His curiosity was not to be appeased until he'd finally taken a look in the trunk himself.

He had a hunch that the key in Lily's room that morning—which she'd claimed to be for her diary—might just be the key he'd been searching for. It was physically identical to the other, but the cut was different.

When Lily had tripped over the flat stone that ended up being the lid to a manhole leading down into a vat room, Mike was certain he'd found the mother lode: Auguste's hidden treasure troves. He returned to the room this very morning, on his own, and spent two full hours trying to open them. He was experienced with reprogramming codes in gated communities and hoped he'd have the same success here. The keypads were a product by a manufacturer he'd dealt with several times before and he knew how to access and change the master codes; that is, if they hadn't been changed by Auguste. He began experimenting and found that five of the vats had indeed been changed; but the sixth vat, in the middle of a row of three, had beeped—letting him know the master code hadn't been altered. He reprogrammed the code and punched it in.

There was a moment of great anticipation as the light on the digital keypad switched from red to green. But as the lid slid open like elevator doors, he found the vat to be empty.

Aggravated to tears and running out of time, he left the vat room, determined to return later when he had more time to crack the codes of the other five vats. He then went to town to run some errands and picked up the bouquet of flowers for Lily.

He could not believe his luck when he'd found that key on her bedroom floor, and feigned indifference when she picked it up and said it was hers.

There were many delays with the rain and the power outage and having to clean up the mess in the workroom, but now that he was alone, his priority was to open the trunk.

Mike stuffed the keys into his back pocket and reached out for the painting, intending to press down on the bottom right hand corner: but something jolted within him and pecked at his insides.

He paused and waited for the indigestion to pass—but the pain intensified and radiated outward from his stomach—his face flushing with fever.

Suddenly parched and desperate for water, Mike reached for and gripped the railing and descended the staircase, rushing down the corridor toward the dining room and kitchen. The little sparks of pain had turned to red-hot flames—consuming him from within.

With a cry, he fell to his knees and rolled across the floor, clawing at his belly.

The fiery fingers in his midsection found their way to his spinal cord and climbed up to his brain. Convulsions seized him and he foamed at the mouth, eyes rolling back in his head. A numbing coldness started in his fingertips and toes and spread up his arms and legs into his back—extinguishing the fire and leaving his body devoid of any sensation at all. The cold crept into his brain and choked out the last bit of fire.

He lay flat on his back in the middle of the corridor with eyes shut, basking in the numbness as his wits returned.

What had happened? Was it a heart attack? at

his age?

Deciding he'd better call an ambulance, he tried to open his eyes.

They didn't move.

Mike swallowed down a surge of panic and mentally willed his body to obey. He tried to wiggle his fingers but they didn't budge either. His toes were equally disobedient.

Now in a full-blown panic, he urged his body to kick and scream—pictured himself doing it—but nothing happened. Not even a twitch or a whisper. How long must he lie here before someone found him? And what if they thought he was dead?

His eyes snapped open, but not of his own doing.

And through the windows of his eyes, he watched himself stand to his feet; yet he felt nothing.

Hannah emerged from the dining room and walked toward him. As she drew closer, she furrowed her brow. "Are you okay, Micheal? You look at a bit pale."

He wanted to scream for help—beg her to call an ambulance—but instead he heard himself say: "I'm fine. Just tired."

Why had he said that?

He wasn't fine at all!

"All right then, just checking." She smiled. "I'm off to bed, and you look like you could get some sleep yourself." She patted his shoulder and moved past him, continuing down the corridor and heading upstairs.

He began to walk toward the front entrance;

again not of his own doing.

As the walls went by, the various arched door-ways, paintings and statues, he sensed himself being pushed further and further back into the recesses of his mind until it seemed he was looking out at the world through a very narrow tunnel.

A prisoner in his own body.

Someway, somehow, he was at the mercy of an unknown puppeteer.

Ian rolled his sleeve back down and crossed both arms over his chest. "Do you believe that earth is the only place where life exists?" he said.

"Are you asking if I believe in alien planets?"

"No, more like, different dimensions."

She gaped at him as though he'd lost his mind. "It's not something I've given much thought to, Ian. Are you trying to change the subject? Tell me about your arm already!"

He drew in a breath and made an effort to keep the impatience from his voice. "Let's say there *were* other dimensions," he said. "What do you think would happen if there was a rift?"

"Are we talking about a portal to another world?" She raised an eyebrow and cracked a grin.

Despite the room being soundproof, he lowered his voice and leaned forward. "What if I were to tell you that there is an object—here from the beginning of time—that can take you to another dimension.

An object that has been fought over for millennium."

She made no response to that, not even the twitch of an eyebrow.

"Everyone wants its power," he said, "but no one can control it."

She pursed her lips. "What are you getting at, Ian?" she asked, frustration in her tone, the humorous glint gone from her eye. "You're talking nonsense."

"Stay with me. I'm getting there."

She sighed. "Go on then."

"That object now resides in the attic of this mansion, you see, and it's the reason Auguste became wealthy. Before he found it, he was only a homeless pauper."

She sat bolt upright, eyes widening. "The secret compartment in the trunk—I knew it! Is it stocks or something? Gold, jewels?"

"How did you—"

"—I'm sorry, Ian," she interrupted. "I took the key from your workshop. Didn't you know it was missing—? Your bird, he . . . he flew away." She gave him a timid look as though anticipating a blasting, and cleared her throat. She broke eye contact. "That's why I got lost in the forest. I'm so very sorry about your bird." She lifted contrite eyes. "I was chasing after him but just couldn't catch him, and got lost and . . . somehow bumped my head. I must have fallen . . . "

Ian had to bite his tongue to hold back his temper, but a muscle twitched in his cheek. "No," he said calmly, though it took all his strength, "the bird is still in his cage, safe and sound. I didn't notice the key was gone." Blast it. His pulse picked up its pace and beads of sweat broke out on his forehead.

"Lily—" he said slowly, dreading the answer, "where is the key now?"

She hesitated. "It's in my room, tucked away."

He let out a sharp, breathy exhale. "Fine. We'll have to go get it. It can't be left lying around, you have no idea—"

"What's in the bottom of the trunk," she asked again, sounding impatient. "Stolen jewels?"

He considered this a moment and thought of his workshop. Did she think all those jewels were stolen?—that he was a thief? No wonder she wouldn't stop snooping around.

"Suffice it to say that Auguste didn't use the object simply for financial gain," he said in a flat tone. "He did something that disturbed the natural order of things in another dimension. Think I'm crazy if you want, but it's the truth." He steepled his hands and stared her down. "In so doing, he caused a war of evil against good, and evil was quick to win out. Anyone with a shred of good left in them went into hiding, but many of them did not escape with their lives. Some of them fled into this dimension"—he cleared his throat—"and I have sheltered them within the forest and the estate for many years now."

He paused, wanting to put this delicately. "All of this happened because of your grandfather."

201

Lily could only stare at Ian.

She didn't know what to think and could hardly process anything he'd said. The only thing that made sense so far was that something in the trunk had made her grandfather rich. Auguste's journal entries admitted much the same. Everything else Ian had said was some kind of sci-fi blibble-blabble. Was he hallucinating, or high on drugs?

"What did my grandfather do to incite this, um"—she paused—"this war, in a, what did you say —other dimension?"

Ian's dark eyes were smoldering; no doubt he knew she was patronizing him.

"He is responsible for the death of Serena—a powerful enchantress who ruled over the land of Alvernia—" he explained, "the other dimension. When she died, Morack—who was imprisoned deep within the core of Alvernia—escaped. See, for many years, he and his followers were kept captive. But her death allowed them to escape and they set loose like a cloud of locusts—devouring everyone in their path." His brow was heavy as though he carried a great burden. "Alvernia is but a shadow of the world it once was." He looked away. "It is completely ruled by evil now."

Lily searched for a deranged glint in his eye when he made eye contact again, but found none. "Ian," she said, "Serena, wasn't she my grandmother? She . . . died in childbirth."

His eyes widened and he blinked. "How did you know that?"

She averted eye contact, earlobes growing hot.

"I . . . hope you won't be too mad, but . . . I read the journal that was in the trunk." She grimaced. "Auguste's diary."

He looked flabbergasted at this.

A handful of seconds passed.

"Well, let's not waste any more time then. Auguste must have gone back to Alvernia shortly before he died and let—someone—in behind him. That would explain *a lot*." A look of angst filled his face and he leaned back in the chair, frowning. "Lily, you've got to believe me. There's a killer on the loose and he's looking for you. He knows who you are!"

She gasped and raised a hand to her heart. "Why would someone want to kill me?"

"Because you're Serena's only surviving heir to the throne."

She remembered something then and stiffened, heart skipping a beat. "My—my dream. In the forest. I was attacked by someone asking about my mother—"

It hadn't been real, had it? Her hands went cold and clammy. No, it couldn't be. Her face would still be torn up from the tree bark if it was. She touched her cheek. "It was only a dream though. A . . . a coincidence, I guess." She tried to laugh but Ian was taking her quite seriously.

"That wasn't a dream, Lily, and thanks to your grandfather's greed, millions of innocent creatures have lost their lives. He never intended it to be that way, but what's done is done. I've spent the past fifteen years dealing with the filth he let in through the rift."

Lily gripped the arms of her chair. He was really starting to scare her with these fantastic stories. It was one thing for him to have delusions about another dimension—but all this talk about a killer out to get her was too much.

Was *he* the killer?

"Ian, you still haven't answered. How is it possible for your arm to be healed within days of nearly losing it to a shark?"

"I come from Alvernia," he said, a pained look in his eyes. "I was born with the ability to regenerate instantly, except for scars. But my abilities are greatly weakened on earth and healing takes up to a day or two here, depending on the injury." He pointed to his nose which was no longer bruised. "This afternoon my nose was broken and bent sideways."

Lily swallowed the lump in her throat and resisted the urge to look toward the doors. "Who is this, uh, killer, out to get me?"

"The same person who killed Auguste is now seeking you." He crossed his arms. "There's something else. The shark attack wasn't an accident. The assassin infected them with a virus that makes its host homicidal. He was hoping for a 'natural' death—that I'd be torn to shreds. And I . . . almost was."

Her chest tightened. This was all so irrational, making a tall tale out of the shark attack too? Was he paranoid or schizophrenic? Or worse—psychopathic?

"If what you're saying is true"—and she didn't believe for a second that it was—"why didn't the sharks just kill each other?"

He frowned slightly. "The virus is a dark

magic, like a spell. Whoever infects another puts an image in their mind of who they must kill. They become robots, essentially. This is why they had to be put down."

"But why would someone go to all that trouble? There are much easier ways to kill someone."

"To get to you—don't you see? I'm not that easy to kill." Impatience flashed in his eyes. "With me out of the picture, the assassin tried to attack you in the pool room during the night," he went on, "he was obviously lying in wait. I didn't know it was him at the time but it makes sense now. Someone, probably one of Serena's handmaidens, saved you. Did you seriously believe that hackneyed story the fake policeman told you?"

Her stomach turned. "Are *you* infected with the virus?" What was he going to do to her? Should she try to escape?

A pregnant pause.

If only she could read his thoughts.

"I'm immune to dark magic," he said finally. "But you aren't."

What was that supposed to mean?

She struggled to process which bits of information were credible and which should be discarded as nonsense; but everything congealed together.

He rose and came around the desk as she stood to her feet. He reached for her hand and she recoiled, ready to bolt.

"Lily . . . are you—afraid of me?"

She swallowed. Was it safer to play along?

"No-no," she said, taking a step backward,

"it's just so much to take in all at once, is all."

"It's nearly midnight," he said, glancing over his shoulder at the cuckoo clock mounted between the windows behind the desk. His eyes darkened. "The killer will be less likely to stay in hiding once the staff are all in bed sleeping."

Her back stiffened painfully. What was he saying — that his alter-ego takes over at bedtime?

Ian stared down at her. "You're the only person who can kill Morack and save Alvernia. That's why your life is at stake."

Her head was spinning with questions. If Ian was the killer, did that mean he was the one who had murdered Auguste?

"Is this all a big joke?" she said with a nervous lilt. She tried to chuckle, glancing around. "Are Hannah and Mike hiding behind the drapes waiting to jump out and laugh at me? Because if it is, I don't know how you're able to keep such a straight fa—"

A tremendous crash stopped her short and the oak doors bulged inward like rubber.

The color drained from Ian's face like sand seeping from an hourglass — and he grabbed Lily by the wrist, yanking her toward the roll ladder and pushing it down the track.

"What's happening—" she cried.

"Hush." Releasing her wrist, he darted up the rungs of the ladder, and at the halfway point from the floor to the ceiling, ran his index along the books. He grabbed the binding of a hardcover and tugged it outward.

A narrow, vertical passageway opened in the

shelves to the right of him.

"Hurry," he said, jumping down from the ladder and motioning for her to enter ahead of him.

She froze. Should she go with Ian—who was out of his mind—or stay and find out what was causing the doors to bulge inward?

Another crash sounded from the corridor and she jumped, letting out a little scream.

The door buckled further; they would soon burst open.

"Get in," Ian whispered fiercely, his entire eyes morphing into pools of black.

Seeing no alternative, she slipped through the opening in the wall, heart racing—and set off at a blind run.

Chapter 19

Mike watched in paralyzed silence as his body tore the covers from Lily's bed. He took a pocketknife from his tool belt and sliced open the mattress, yanking out the stuffing clump by clump. He then shredded the pillows; sending a spray of down-feathers fluttering to the floor like snow.

What on earth was he doing?

Apparently not finding whatever he was looking for, his body stormed over to Lily's dresser and pulled the clothes out in a crazed frenzy. He heard a thunk behind him and his body spun around, digging into the pile of scattered shirts to seek the source of the sound.

There, amidst the articles, was the same leather-bound journal he'd seen before when he took the key.

Hunkering down, his body snatched it up and rifled through it. All he saw was a blur of words.

The puppeteer seemed satisfied, however, and tucking the book under his arm, Mike left the bedroom and went downstairs, walking past the dining room toward either the TV room or Auguste's study.

Using her hands to feel the walls surrounding her, Lily rushed down the narrow passageway without sight, deathly afraid she might fall through a hole in the floor straight down to a lower level, breaking a leg or worse. But she didn't dare slow down. If Ian was in the tunnel with her, he might just grab her at any second.

Without warning, she crashed full-force into a wall, hands folding inward against her chest.

She grappled the walls about her frantically—scraping her hands over splintered wood.

There were no walls on either side of her and she realized the tunnel had divided into two different directions. Without hesitation, she took off to the left just as a hand grabbed her shoulder and yanked her backward against a firm chest. In the same instant, another hand clamped down over her mouth, stifling her scream.

She inhaled a familiar cologne.

Ian.

Scratching at his face with her hand, she sought his eyes and dug a thumb into one of them. Those ink-black eyes without the whites: she couldn't get the hellish image out of her head. What was wrong with him?

Stifling another cry, he yanked her hand away from his face and held it down at her side. "Don't fight me, Lily—please." His whisper was hoarse in her ear. "I'm not trying to hurt you."

She would have spat curses at him but his left hand was pressing her mouth.

"You've got to be quiet," he said in an undertone, "we're being hunted. The killer is here. That was him trying to burst through the study doors—I'm sure of it. I thought he would wait till midnight, but I was wrong."

He was insane, completely out of his mind.

She tried not to tremble, standing very still within his clutch. What kind of sick game was he playing? Was *he* the one who had attacked her in the pool room and then slipped back to his room while she was unconscious? And what about in the forest? Had she really tripped after stealing the key or had someone knocked her out?

"Promise me you won't scream," he said, lips brushing against her ear, "and I'll take my hand away."

She nodded; holding back a whimper.

He lowered his hand from her mouth, and took her left hand securely in his right. "Follow me." She obeyed, knowing she was no match for him in a tug of war. She would stay silent for now and wait for a chance to escape.

They moved through the narrow tunnels between the walls, turning right, then left, then right again. How he knew his way so well in the pitch black was beyond her. Perhaps he had the tunnels memorized from years of use.

After about five or ten minutes, they stopped and he explained that they were going to take a ladder down to a lower floor. She got down on her knees and felt for the square opening in the floor, lowering herself through it while gripping the wooden ladder rungs like a life line. Ian followed.

Having traveled downward a distance of about twenty feet, she whispered for him to stop, so he wouldn't collide with her head. "How much farther?" Surely they must be to the lower floor level by now—or were they going down multiple levels?

"Keep going," he said.

Great, he was probably taking her straight to the basement. Maybe he was planning to store her body in one of those creepy vats.

She thought of the giant coroner's table and almost palsied, but steadied her grip on the ladder. If she let herself panic, she'd never find a way to escape; yet what if Mike's explanation about the table being used for the medical care of marine life wasn't true?

She continued her descent, moving down yet another ten feet, the air about her growing more cold and stale with every step. The darkness was disorienting and she wondered if her calculations were completely out of sync by this time.

Her foot struck bottom.

A dirt floor.

The vat room had a dirt floor. And she'd let him lead her here like a lamb to the slaughter. Why hadn't she screamed at the top of her lungs ten minutes ago when there was still a chance of someone hearing? No one would hear her screams now.

But wait—the ladder to the vat room had been metal, not wooden.

She let go of the ladder and turned around, stretching out her hands and taking a tentative step forward. If there was enough space she could either run away or hide.

There was a palpable scent of damp earth. And instead of stainless steel, her hands came into contact with bumpy dirt walls on either side; but open space in front.

A tunnel.

If only she had a flashlight, she would make a run for it; but for all she knew, she might be standing on the edge of a chasm.

Ian's shoes scuffed against the ground as he dismounted the ladder behind her. She couldn't see him but sensed his body heat in the dank atmosphere. If only he were a friend and not a foe.

Without a word, he took her hand again, despite her flinch, and moved around in front of her, gently pulling her along behind him. His hand was burning hot over her icy fingers. The tunnel seemed to be no more than three feet wide and she followed after him without protest, tripping occasionally on small roots and stones. The tunnel inclined upward at a steady slope and soon her shins grew tired. They stopped after what seemed about thirty meters and Ian whispered to her that there was a ladder. He put her hand on it and told her to wait while he climbed up first. She listened to him ascend but could see nothing. Should she turn and run back the way they had come?

Something heavy shifted out of place over-head.

Stone grated against stone and a round open-ing appeared ten feet above them revealing a twilight sky and half moon. She drew in a deep breath of fresh air.

Ian looked down at her and silently motioned for her to follow. He climbed out of the hole and she mounted the first ladder rung, briefly considering again whether to follow or backtrack. She decided it would be easier to escape outside than in.

When she stuck her head out of the opening, it was to discover the maiden fountain statue in the backyard. It had shifted to one side and Ian was standing on a wide stone pedestal that encircled the hole. She took his outstretched hand and he helped her to her feet. He then pivoted and pressed one of the marble eyes of the maiden. With a slight shudder, it began moving back in place. Ian jumped over the small Koi pond to the ground and Lily followed suit. The statue finished assuming its center position; completely covering the hole in the ground.

Ian took both her hands in his, casting a distraught glance at the mansion which was entirely dark. "We need to get something from my tree, Lily. Can you run with me?"

She stared up at him, lips parting, speechless. His eyes were back to normal; lots of white around the irises. Had she only imagined the black demon eyes at the height of her fear?

"I, I guess so," she said.

"Listen to me carefully, Lily. If the killer finds us, run as fast as you can and don't look back—understand?"

"Why can't I just leave now? Why do I have to go with you to your tree?"

He shot another glance at the mansion, sweat glistening in the spikes of his hair. "There's no time to explain—Let's go!" Without releasing her hand, he took off running across the dewy grass toward the tree line as she struggled to keep up.

They reached the forest edge and hurried down the dirt path, gargoyle orbs blinking on one at a time as they passed. By the time they reached the tree, Lily was panting for air.

Ian yanked open the door and scooted her inside ahead of him. He stepped in and closed the door, bolting it from the inside. He switched on one lantern, and scrambled up the ladder to the floor above without waiting for her to follow.

She was beginning to think she might be relatively safe with Ian after all. If he'd truly intended to kill her, the underground tunnel would have been the perfect place to do it. No one ever would find her there.

He must be mentally ill; perhaps more of a threat to himself than to her. He really seemed to believe they were being pursued by some maniacal killer.

But the bulging oak doors in the study—how could he have staged that? It denied the law of physics.

Her fear returned full-force with the memory and she rubbed her clammy palms on her thighs, wondering what to do.

Up above, Ian was stomping about, moving things around and making noise.

Forcing thoughts of butterflies and puppies and ice cream and all sorts of happy things—anything to hold back the panic—Lily stared at the bolted door in front of her and imagined it bursting open. She shifted from foot to foot and sat down on the edge of the wingback chair. Why was she sitting down? Shouldn't she be halfway back to the mansion by now?

She got up and went to the door.

"I'm back," Ian said from behind her.

Lily jumped and turned to face him. She hadn't heard him descending the ladder, her heart-beat was so deafening. He cracked a sheepish grin. The turquoise bird with the fiery tail feathers from the diamond room was perched on his left shoulder. All that was missing was an eye patch and wooden leg.

Despite her fear, relief washed over her. So the bird hadn't escaped into the forest after all.

"Ian. What-on-earth." She motioned at the bird.

"Never mind," he said, "we still have lots to do before we go."

"Go where?"

He turned his head to look at the bird. "I need you to sing again."

"Again?" she asked.

"Not you dummy—me," said the bird.

Her throat tightened. "You can talk? I thought I'd dreamed that part."

The bird cocked its head to one side and nar-rowed an eye at her.

She lifted her hand, touched her smooth cheek.

Ian exhaled, obvious impatience snapping in his eyes. "We don't have time to discuss this. Sing,

Bogart, or I'll roast you for dinner."

Bogart glared at Ian with a look of abject hatred. "When you stole me from Morack," he hissed, "you promised me freedom—but you're a worse slave driver than he. So, if you want your pretty little wench to be eaten, that's fine by me. It might even be amusing to watch." The bird lifted his beak and puffed out his chest feathers. "I'll do what you ask for that reason only."

Ian's eyes were smoldering. "Don't ever insult her again."

"Or what? You'll ring my neck?" A snort. "We both know you need me."

Ian rubbed his temple; closing his eyes for a half second. "Just sing already."

"O-o-O-okay, Master, but when they're picking their teeth with *her* bones, don't say I didn't warn you."

After shaking his head, the bird began to whistle a slow, haunting tune—the one from Lily's dream. Her pulse quickened again.

The mournful strains seemed to have a substance to them, as though a river of music was filling the room and seeping through the walls out into the surrounding trees.

Ian unbolted and opened the front door. "Wait for me here, Lily," he said over his shoulder. "And whatever happens, do not leave the tree—stay out of sight—Got it?"

She nodded—for what else could she do?—and he took the bird outside, shutting the door behind them.

Lily ascended the ladder to the second floor. She climbed up onto the cot, sitting on her knees, and looked out through the octagonal window.

Suffused by the moonlight, Ian was standing down below with the bird perched on his shoulder.

Unable to hear anything, she examined the window for a latch and realized it could be pushed open at the bottom. It swung open. Bogart continued to sing his haunting tune—a howl joining it out of sight down the pathway that lead to the back yard.

Goosebumps trickled down her arms like invisible spiders.

Was it a wolf?

A dry crunch sounded—like a skeleton cracking its knuckles—and the gargoyle at the foot of the path sprang to life, dropping the orb and unfolding its head and limbs.

Her heart stopped.

The smooth-skinned creature stretched to full height, about six feet tall, and turned to face Ian. It had broad gorilla shoulders, a protruding spine and a tusked maw. Long muscular forearms and hands hung nearly to the ground, tipped with clawed fingers.

Had Ian knocked her out when he came down the ladder a few minutes ago? Was she draped in the wingback chair blissfully unaware of her true predicament?

She pinched herself repeatedly and painfully as Bogart flew away to a nearby tree and perched on a low branch.

The beast looked up at the window, spotting

her—its beady eyes wild with hunger.

She froze.

With a screech of rage it lunged past Ian toward the tree and dug its claws into the elaborate carvings on the side—climbing up to her at a rapid pace.

Lily screamed and the tusked beast fell to the ground.

Chapter 20

The beast shrieked as it hit the ground belly first.

Ian was up on its back, grasping it by the spinal ridge. Had he pulled the creature down somehow?

Lily strained to see through the open window, barely believing her eyes.

The gargoyle shook its head violently but Ian held on tight, pinching his knees into the beast's sides. In one deft movement, he let go of the spine and gripped its neck in a strangle hold.

Eyes wide with fury, the creature jerked its head backward; trying to thwack him.

"Enough," Ian shouted, striking the beast on the snout with a closed fist.

The beast grew so still Lily thought it had turned to marble again. But then it lowered its body to ground submissively, and Ian climbed off.

"I'm sorry, Master," it keened in a deep, sandpaper voice. "I didn't realize you were here." He lowered his tusked maw. "I lost control of myself. It won't happen again."

Ian stood over the creature, hands on his hips. "It better not. Because next time I won't be so forgiving. You are not to attack a human—ever."

From the tree branch where he sat perched, Bogart was singing his heart out again.

Another orb dropped to the ground and the next statue stretched and yawned, stepping down off its pedestal. She couldn't see down the trail—it was too dark—but she supposed they were all doing the same. Four creatures now gathered below the tree, zoning in on her open window: some with surprise and curiosity, others with hungry intent. How could they even see her from that distance?

If she hadn't so firmly believed this to be a dream, she might have been hyperventilating by now; nevertheless, her pulse drummed in her ears and her breathing was shallow.

One creature, with the toned body of a man's, approached Ian slowly, a cautious look on his face. He wore a black loincloth and his body was covered with short charcoal-gray hair; or at least, it appeared gray in the moonlight. Atop a thick neck, he had a long canine snout rimmed with serrated teeth. Furry dog ears pointed backward and scruffy brows hung part way over his eyes. He resembled the Egyptian Anubis.

Ian crossed his arms over his chest and watched as the Anubis peered up at Lily's window, meeting her gaze with shiny, shrewd irises. She held her breath. Would he lunge up the tree as the other had?

The dog-man's lips curled back from crocodile teeth as he let out an abrasive snarl. She swallowed down a wave of nausea and surprised herself by growling back at him. What on earth was she thinking? The look in his eyes became so savage she thought he'd surely go for her throat.

Then, just as quickly as it had come, the savage look faded and his features softened.

"Well, played, my dear," he said in a loud, warm voice; grinning like a jackel. "Name's Varkis and I'm pleased to meet you . . . human."

She pinched herself again. Oh, let this be a dream.

"I'm—uh, pleased to meet you too," she said through the open window, her hands on the rim.

The gargoyles, six of them, spoke amongst themselves in hushed tones and eyed her window with looks of unease. It was as if they were afraid of her; though maybe not specifically of *her* but of Ian, who stood between them and the tree with his strong arms folded over his chest.

Varkis scratched the tip of one ear with a long claw. "Ian," he said, "you must introduce us to this remarkable female human of yours and explain why you've allowed her to know of our existence."

"She's far more remarkable than you realize. Her name is Kline. Lily Kline."

The gargoyles whispered comments to each other in response to this. She couldn't make out the words. From the low evergreen boughs to the left of Ian, a creature like a Komodo dragon entered the clearing. Ian turned toward it, without unfolding his arms, and the creature paused; narrowing its red-eyed gaze and licking its lips.

"Do not come any closer," Ian warned in a low voice.

The beast inched closer as a rumbling growl rose in its breast. "You said we could eat anything non-magical in the forest," it snarled in a deep, grating tone. "We have left your humans alone within the mansion and grounds, as you requested, and have stayed within the gates—but now you've brought a tender morsel into our very domain—and expect us to walk away? I don't think so."

"Get *back*. Remember who saved you from Alvernia. I could have left you there to die."

"As if earth is any better. We are prisoners here," the lizard-like beast growled. "Forced to be statues by day and then to abide by all your silly rules at night. I'm sick of it!" He lowered his voice to a savage undertone: "I was better off serving Morack."

The creature took another step toward Ian. Though it resembled a Komodo, it had jade scales instead of tough gray skin. There were no visible ears on the sides of its head; just a black hole behind each serpentine eye. A forked tongue flicked in and out of its mouth.

In a sudden blur of motion, something lunged out of the forest behind the scaly beast. There was a wall of red and blood splattered across Ian's chest. Gasps of shock erupted from the cluster of gargoyles below as the source of blood became clear.

In front of Ian stood a black unicorn, the reptilian gargoyle impaled on its horn; wriggling and squirming in anguish.

With a powerful shake of its head, the unicorn's horn sliced through the lizard, splitting it in two, and the halves fell to the ground in a thudding splash of entrails.

In the wake of the slaughter, the unicorn took four regal steps over the body and peered up at Lily's window with scarlet eyes; its body smoking like an extinguished fire. Its horn was a double-edged sword, not the fairytale spiral she might have expected, and its lipless mouth stretched from ear-to-ear—jagged teeth protruding out over its jaw and cheekbones.

There was no flesh on its face.

The forest was deathly silent. Strangely, she was suddenly unafraid, and as the scarlet eyes bore into her own, she sensed only peace. For the moment all that existed in the world was the unicorn and herself—everything else faded to a mist and the distance between them vanished.

They stood face to face in a swirling cloud of light.

"Lily—" he said in a voice of thunder, his mouth remaining shut as he spoke. She realized his voice was inside her head. "Long have I awaited your arrival. You will do great things for Alvernia. Through you, we shall finally be rid of Morack. We shall once again be free to roam our land."

"I am only a human," she said, "and a girl." Her voice was clear and solid, but she knew she hadn't spoken the words out loud. "What can I do?"

The unicorn's harsh bony features transformed to ivory horseflesh and he dipped down, nuzzling her cheek with a velvet snout. "Do not doubt yourself, my lady. Self-doubt is the first step to failure."

"It was you who rescued me, wasn't it. In the

forest, when that vile man attacked me. Can't you see I'm of no help to anyone?"

"Hush. Remember who you are. You are Serena's heir to the throne. If the others hear you speak of failure or weakness, they will lose all hope."

"But this is too big of a burden for me to carry!"

"You do not have to carry it alone. We will all be with you—fighting for our freedom. Great power lies within you, Lily—awaiting your command. You *will* find it."

"What if I can't?"

He snorted and bared his grizzly shark teeth. "You had better or we shall all die. Now—Stop feeling sorry for yourself. I have an important message for you. The time will come when you'll be forced to make a terrible decision. And when that time comes, remember this—the value of one life must not outweigh the value of many lives. Now: Let us tarry no longer. The others are waiting."

The light around them vanished and the moonlit forest came back into sharp focus. She was once again peering down through the round window. Ian stared up at her with a questioning look. The gargoyles were watching with narrowed eyes and hackles up.

"Lily," he said, "what happened? We were all in a trance."

Before she could answer, the unicorn touched its snout to the ground and nearby undergrowth quivered. As though a giant magnet attracted it, the surrounding Autumn leaves whipped through the air and swirled about the unicorn, blocking his form from their view.

She cried out in alarm, digging her fingernails into the window trim.

"It's okay," Ian shouted up at her, "unicorns camouflage themselves to match the environment they're in. They only stay in their true form during battle."

The small cyclone dispersed as quickly as it had come and the unicorn emerged; twisted gray vines constituting his mane and tail, and bark and dried leaves clothing his sinewy body. His eyes were a lustrous cinnamon.

He bowed from the neck to Lily. "My name is Callamous and I am here to serve you, your highness."

The gargoyles gaped up at her and whispered amongst themselves as though astonished. One by one they bowed before her, all except Bogart, who scowled audibly from his nearby branch. Heat crept up her neck and into her cheeks, and she shrunk back from the window.

For a long moment no one spoke until finally Ian broke the silence.

"So, it was you who healed her in the forest," he said to Callamous. "And gave her temporary night vision."

A slight nod.

"Well, it must be undeniably true then," he said. "She *is* a descendant of Serena."

Another nod.

Ian put his hands on his hips and lowered his

voice. She strained to hear.

"Morack's assassin is still here," he said. "He's gone after Lily twice now. He might even be laying in wait as we speak." A pause. "He came after us in the mansion but we escaped through an underground tunnel. I suspect he doesn't want to be seen by Hannah, Chris, or any other human, and is consequently holding back for the time being. It's not like him to be so reserved."

"He will not risk a direct attack while our numbers are so great," the unicorn said. "For now, the girl will be safe—as long as she is never left alone and unguarded. That being said, his powers are also greatly dampened here on earth, as you know. Yet— you must find a way to destroy him. Then we can figure out what to do about Morack."

"She's nothing but a pathetic little wimp," Bogart squawked. "You don't honestly think she's a better ruler than Morack?"

Barely had the words left his mouth when Varkis leaped into the air and snatched the bird from the tree, flinging it high into the air. The bird flipped and turned, caught its bearings, and flew off. "I've wanted to do that for so long," he said, laughing. The other gargoyles nodded and cackled in fiendish agreement.

"Varkis," Ian shouted in exasperation. "You can't just slap around everyone who merely irritates you—"

"—He is still loyal to Morack," Callamous interjected solemnly, "we can't abide by that."

Ian ran his hands through his hair. "I'd always

hoped he would change . . . " He stepped up to the half-circle of gargoyles. "I need one of you to do me a favor." He hesitated. "Do I have any volunteers?"

The tusked gargoyle who had been the first to come to life, stepped forward and knelt to one leg. "I will do it, Master. I owe you for my behavior earlier."

Ian nodded. "Go to the mansion and let the others know what is going on. But first, you must discreetly make sure that my staff has obeyed my orders and cleared out. If they haven't left yet, you must keep well out of sight—as usual. Got it? Report back to me if this is the case."

The beast lowered his tusked maw in a head bow and rose to his full height. He then headed down the trail and disappeared from Lily's line of sight.

Ian glanced up at Lily's window, as if to make certain she was still there, and then faced the remaining creatures. "Varkis is going to divide you into two groups," he explained in a loud and commanding voice. "One group will take the first watch and spread into the nearby forest to keep guard. No one is to enter this tree unless I give direct permission. The other group can take a couple of hours to hunt for food. You know the rules. At four, you are to trade places. Understood?"

The gargoyles crowded around Varkis, and Lily moved away from the window. She stood up from the bed on wobbly legs and sat back down again.

Below, the front door opened and closed with a soft thump. She tensed and considered taking the ladder to the third floor.

"Lily?"

Relief flooded through her.

"I'll be right down," she said.

She descended the ladder.

Ian was sitting on the wingback, hands clasped over his knees as he hunched forward. He looked up and gave her a half-hearted smile.

She fidgeted and put her hands on her hips to still them.

"I'm so sorry about all this," he said, breaking eye contact and letting out a ragged sigh. "It's such a mess."

She decided not to say much in response.

"I should have stopped Auguste long ago," he said.

"Stopped him how? It's not like you could have killed him or locked him up somewhere." Or maybe he had killed Auguste in the end. Nothing could surprise her now.

"I was so naïve," he said, shaking his head. "I unknowingly helped him do many horrible things." His voice was heavy with what seemed to be regret.

"How are you going to stop the killer?" she asked.

He stood up and paced back and forth. "I haven't even come close to defeating him before." He met her eyes briefly. "He's the one who broke my nose, it wasn't an accident . . . "

Her breath caught in her throat. "Why didn't he kill you?"

"I guess he's playing a game. Probably has some perverted plan for my demise." He crossed his arms over his chest and stared her down with those witch-black eyes. "I have information he needs. But for now, he seems preoccupied with you." He scowled, shook his head. "Why didn't you just leave when I told you to?"

She ignored that. "What information do you have that he needs?"

"It's safer if you don't know."

"Ian . . . " She paused thoughtfully. "If you're from this alternate world like the others, why don't you turn into a statue before sunrise too?"

He flicked her a glance. "I told you before, dark magic has no effect on me." His voice was even, level; as though controlling his tone. "Nor on the assassin."

"So, both of you are immune to dark magic. Why?"

He waved his hand dismissively. "Not important." Moving in front of her, he crossed his arms over his chest and stood with a wide stance, his head nearly grazing the lantern-covered ceiling. "What's most important right now is figuring out how to defeat him."

A loud knock sounded on the door.

"Let me in. It's Varkis."

Ian looked through the peephole and unbolted the door. He opened it wide and the Anubis ducked down to fit through, and then stood bent at the shoulders—flashing Lily a wolf-like grin.

He squeezed into the wingback, which groaned beneath his weight. He smelled like sweat and swamp water.

She realized she was giving him a wide-eyed look.

"Aw, come on now," he said in a gruff baritone, "don't be scared, lass. I won't bite."

"Leave her be," Ian snapped, "she's already freaked out enough as is."

"I am not!"

Ian raised an eyebrow and Varkis let out a throaty laugh.

"I'm not some weak and helpless female," she said, flushing. "Contrary to popular opinion."

"Have a seat, Ian," Varkis said, pointing at a squat stool.

"I'm fine standing, thank you very much."

"Suit yourself," he said with a shrug. "Though in my opinion, you ought to have more chairs in this place." He looked around. "It's so cramped in here though, like an elf hut."

"And in my opinion, you should be wearing more than a loin cloth if you're going to get comfortable in my chair. I'm going to have to burn it now."

Lily studied the dog-man's face as he spoke. His eyes were like amber marbles and his canine teeth were ivory with black tartar and plaque built up around the gum line. Fine gray hairs on his cheekbones and husky ears glistened in the lamplight of the room.

"You'd think he'd be happy to have a guest for a change," Varkis said in an undertone, glancing her way as he cleared his throat.

She looked to Ian and back again.

"It's true, lass," Varkis went on. "Poor bloke

used to sit here day in and day out carving animals from wood and other wacko things like that. I started coming by at night to play cards and keep him company—tell him how pathetic he was." He laughed.

Ian closed his eyes with an exaggerated look of long-suffering. "Enough already," he said, exhaling. "Did you come here for a specific reason, or what? Why aren't you standing guard with the others?"

Varkis rubbed his furry knees. "I want to help you make some plans. We'd make a good team."

Ian leaned one shoulder into the ladder. Lily stood across from him, next to the stack of tomes, with her hand on her hip.

"The assassin is clever," the dog-man continued, "and it's only a matter of time before he gets past our defenses—if he hasn't already. We need to work together."

"No. I have to kill him by myself."

A harrumph. "You're a fool and you know it."

"I'm not going to let him kill you and Lily just to get to me."

"Honorable, but not true."

Lily took a step forward. "Why do I get the impression you're both hiding something from me?"

"There's nothing to tell, Lily." Ian shook his head and zoned in on the floor.

"Fine, I'll tell her if you won't," Varkis cut in. "When Ian was born—"

Ian lunged forward and grabbed the dog-man by the scruff of his neck, yanking him out of the chair. "Say one more word and I'll throttle you."

"When Ian was born," he choked out, a fierce glint in his eye, "he had a hideous growth on his back."

Ian let go and stepped back. "What?"

Varkis cleared his throat and rubbed his neck, turning to face Lily. He was a full foot taller than Ian, even with hunched shoulders and an inclined head. "The best surgeons in Alvernia removed it." A drawn-out pause and a conspiratorial look. "But after it was detached, it continued to grow . . . "

"Are you out of your mind?"

"Go on," she said to the Anubis.

He nodded solemnly and lowered his voice. "It grew into a deformed man . . . so awful in appearance that just to look at him might kill you. . . . That's why he hides in the cloak of darkness—so you'll never see his horrific face."

She gasped and touched a hand to her throat. "A parasitic twin . . . "

Varkis plunked back down on the wingback and roared with laughter.

A grin twitched at Ian's lips and his shoulders seemed looser than before. He ran a hand through his spiked hair.

Varkis stood up and reached for the door handle, which seemed tiny in his large furry hand. "I'll put some thought into your dilemma, Ian, but for now I'm going to check on the others." He paused, turning to give Lily a bow from the neck, and ducked outside.

Chapter 21

Mike stood in Auguste's study watching a man wearing a hooded duster cloak pacing back and forth in front of him, muttering to himself.

"Master," Mike heard himself say, "I thought the old man's diary would please you. It proves she's —"

"Please me?" The cloaked man turned toward him but his face was hidden in the shadows of his hood. He spat on the floor. "You dimwit—I already know who she is. Why do you think I waited in hiding for two endless weeks for that girl to arrive? I went after her twice to test the waters. The fact that her face is completely healed proves her identity without question. The only one who could heal her like that would never reveal himself to any human but Serena's heir." He spat again, cussed. "I shouldn't have bothered to question her—I should have killed her on the spot. Now I'm stuck here playing hide and seek with her . . . and Zever. I want to tear her to pieces! Her very breath threatens my existence." He took a step closer and lowered his voice to a growl. "That woman has the power to destroy us all."

Mike had a sudden sense of claustrophobia and the room seemed to fade all around him until the only thing he could see was the cloaked man before him, the man his voice had called, "Master." Was he some kind of grim reaper?

Nothing made sense.

After finding the diary in Lily's room, the puppeteer had run him down to Auguste's study where he had discovered this man in the corridor, feeling the locked study doors all over as though searching for a soft spot. The puppeteer had approached the stranger waving the diary in his hand in triumph, calling him Master; but the cloaked man had given him a quick once over and said nothing, returning to his examination of the doors as Mike stood nearby watching.

At first Mike figured the man was some kind of burglar. But then the stranger raised his fist and smashed it against the door with such force that it actually buckled inward as though made of rubber.

If Mike had had any control of his body, he would have hightailed it out of there, but the puppeteer didn't even flinch. He might as well have had cement legs.

The madman backed away from the door with a growl and lunged forward, ramming his shoulder into it and buckling it further this time. This he repeated over and over until the doors finally caved in.

The study was empty. Ian and Lily must have left the study before this hooded man arrived. If only the puppeteer would have the same sense.

"No, no, no—" the madman threw his head back in rage, raising fisted, black-gloved hands. "Not again! She can't have escaped from me again—" He ran to the nearest wall of shelves and tore the books down like Dominoes, one row at a time. What was he searching for? Mike had never been able to find access to the tunnels through the study, though he wouldn't be surprised if there was one.

The hooded man gave up on the books only a third of the way through, and yanked up the Persian rug, dropping to his knees and searching the floor for something—a trap door likely. There were none. He jumped to his feet and kicked over a standing Globe. It broke loose from the stand and rolled away.

Rounding the desk, he plunked down into the high-back leather chair and gripped the arms with rigid gloved fingers. Metal vambraces girded his arms and he wore leather pants with strider boots. "What are you still doing here?" he growled at Mike.

Beneath his duster cloak was a leather vest with braided ties. Who on earth was this man?

"Master," Mike heard himself say, "I may have more information that could be useful to you."

"Something other than that redundant journal?"

"Yes. Far better." Mike tried to halt his talking lips but the words continued to flow unabated. "I have *both* keys . . . to the trunk in the attic."

The madman stiffened in his seat. Though Mike couldn't see the man's eyes, he felt them boring into his face like fire; scrutinizing him from head to toe, sizing him up.

"You had better not be lying," he said slowly. Standing, he rubbed his hands together like a miser and approached. "Show me."

The puppeteer reached into Mike's pant pocket and dug out the keys he'd stolen from Lily. He held them out in the palm of his hand.

The madman snatched them with a shout of victory. "Excellent. Excellent! I can finally get some reinforcements from Alvernia."

"I'm glad I could be of service," Mike heard himself say proudly, bowing at the waist.

The madman inclined his head, face still obscured in shadow by the heavy hood. "Just who are you, anyway?"

"A gorslich. I have no physical body: without a host brain, I'm like a transparent mist, with no audible voice or powers."

"A gorslich . . . " His tone was thoughtful. "Yes, I've heard Morack speak of your kind on occasion. This could prove interesting. Tell me—how did you get here?"

"Through the trunk. But I was locked in a vat in Auguste's dungeon for nearly ten years until this here moron set me free."

The vat! Mike wanted to cry out in despair. The empty vat . . . Not so empty after all. Oh, he was such a fool . . .

"Auguste's dungeon?" The cloaked figure stepped forward and gripped Mike by the shoulders; his black eyes becoming visible at close range. His chin was stubbled with a day's worth of beard and a grisly scar covered the length of his jaw on one side; from cheekbone to chin. "You must take me there immediately," he said, his teeth yellow with decay.

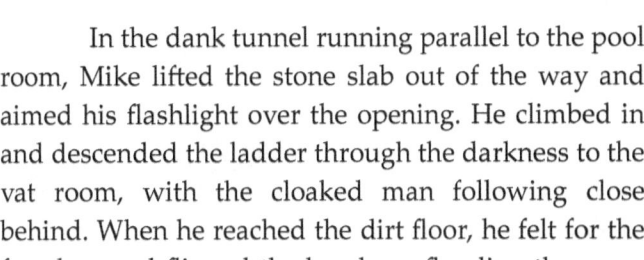

In the dank tunnel running parallel to the pool room, Mike lifted the stone slab out of the way and aimed his flashlight over the opening. He climbed in and descended the ladder through the darkness to the vat room, with the cloaked man following close behind. When he reached the dirt floor, he felt for the fuse box and flipped the breakers, flooding the room with industrial light.

"I don't know the codes for the vats," Mike heard himself say, "but I'm positive Morack isn't in any of these."

"How do you know? You were locked up for ten years—anything could have happened in that time."

"Kline used most of the vats to lock up the beasts that kept slipping through the trunk in the attic —because he didn't know how to deal with them. They go into stasis. When I came through the trunk possessing the body of one of Morack's followers, I underestimated that boy, Ian Hawke. He captured me and brought me down here."

The madman's face remained hidden beneath the shadow of his hood. He splayed his gloved hands on his hips revealing the hilt of a sword. "There must be another entrance to this room then," he said. "There's no way Auguste was carrying beasts down this ladder."

Mike nodded. "Yes—there was once a large tunnel leading in from the side yard. It's sealed behind that stainless steel wall." He pointed to the opposite end of the room. "I have no idea how to access it though." He heard, rather than felt, himself exhale. "I thought of fleeing the body when Hawke captured me, but as the saying goes, curiosity killed the cat. After he sealed me in a vat, Kline came down and gassed it, put the beast to sleep. I passed out with the body I was in and when I awoke, I was strapped to that table over there."

"Torture?" the man asked with a tone of eagerness as he headed over to the giant coroner's table to examine it thoroughly.

Mike cleared his throat. "Presumably. He said if I—well, the beast—didn't answer his questions, he'd kill me. That's how I learned Morack wasn't in any of these vats. Kline said so himself."

Mike was aghast by this information. He would never have thought Auguste to be capable of such an atrocity as torture. Had Ian known about it? Was he a willing accomplice? Sure sounded like it.

"What information could you have possibly possessed?"

"Who knows. The old man was desperate. He wanted to find out how to kill Morack. He said Morack was locked in a special, high-security vat somewhere else in the mansion, and that though he'd tried gases and poisons of various sorts, nothing had succeeded in killing him."

"If I'd known that earlier, I would have made sure the old man died a much more painful death," the cloaked man snarled. "What answer did you give him?"

"I said only Serena's heir was capable of killing Morack."

"And why didn't he kill you after that?"

"He did. The body I was in, that is. Lethal injection. I passed out and when I awoke later, I was locked in the vat again. It filled with some kind of vapor and the body completely disintegrated around me. But I was trapped. In my mist state, I went into hibernation—the years felt like mere minutes." The puppeteer paused, as though contemplating something. "Think about it," Mike's voice went on. "There's no reason why Kline would later risk transporting Morack down here when he was already safely secured elsewhere."

The cloaked man paced back and forth, halted. "We've got to find that vat," he said in a low growl. "Did Kline indicate where in the mansion it was?"

"No, why would he?"

Mike had no clue who this Morack character was but he sounded dangerous. Still, if he'd been locked in a vat for ten years, how could he possibly have survived without food and such? Was he in stasis like the others, or had Auguste and Ian secretly been feeding a prisoner all these years?

"If you don't mind my asking, Master," he heard himself say, "how was Morack captured by Kline in the first place?"

"He wasn't."

"But—"

"It was Zever."

"Zever?"

"You know him as Hawke, idiot. Zever caught him."

"But how—"

"I don't know. Morack was so enraged by Zever's betrayal that he hunted him down to seek bloody revenge. That's when he was captured."

What had Ian—or Zever, rather—done to this Morack fellow that would make him a target for revenge?

"Why didn't he just send out a minion?" the puppeteer asked. "Why risk coming himself?"

"Enough with the questions already—slaveling. I'm the one who asks questions. One more and I'll kill you on the spot. Now . . . " He splayed his gloved fingers over his hips again and tilted his chin up, revealing the edge of a scarred face. "Let's go find that hidden vat."

Lily awoke with a start. She'd fallen asleep on Ian's cot while he kept guard down below.

She sat up and listened to the sounds of the night. It was black outside, save for the half-moon; likely pre-dawn hours. If it weren't for the Victorian oil lamp burning on the floor next to the ladder leading downstairs, the room would have been dark as well.

A faint groan sounded below.

Without making any noise, she slipped to the floor and crawled toward the round opening, straining to hear. She peeked over the edge.

A single lantern burned below as well, illuminating a dark figure in the wingback chair, legs spread out in front. Ian, of course. Had he fallen asleep while on watch or was he just reclining? He let out a long, throaty moan as though in great pain.

She climbed down the ladder and touched his shoulder. "Ian—" she whispered, "you okay?"

"No," he muttered, "don't touch her."

"Ian?"

His eyes were closed, face in a grimace, brow damp with sweat.

"Ian—" she said again, "you're having a bad dream—wake up."

"Don't hurt her."

"Wake up." She shook his shoulders.

"I said, leave her alone—" He jerked forward, knocking her to the floor. She landed on her bottom.

He glared down at her in a fierce rage, eyes black pools in his head; not a speck of white to be seen. So she hadn't imagined those eyes before. They were real. In fact, she was beginning to believe this whole thing was real . . . and not merely the dream she'd at first supposed.

She backed away across the floor, bumping into the stack of tomes. They toppled over. Ian blinked and his eyes returned to normal, the savage look draining from his face; replaced with surprise.

"Are you all right?" He reached out his hand to help her up. "Did I hurt you—!"

She hesitated, not knowing if she could trust him enough to take his hand.

"I'm so sorry," he said, evidently distraught. "I didn't mean to hurt you—"

"It's okay, I'm fine," she said, taking his sweaty hand and letting him pull her to her feet. "I thought you were in pain."

"No, just a nightmare," he said, shaking his head. "I get them most nights. That's why I always told my staff not to wake me when I'm sleeping. I don't want anyone to get hurt."

"Your face is white."

He rubbed his eyes and sat back down on the chair, shoulders hunched. "Varkis is out front—he told me to get some shut-eye. As soon as the sun rises, we need to get to the mansion." He let out a ragged exhale. "I hope Hannah and the others left long ago, though Mike will still be around—I haven't talked to him yet. I highly doubt the assassin will bother them, he's no reason to, but I hate to think of them accidentally getting into trouble. I can't leave you alone right now, Lily." He met her gaze intensely. "I have to protect you."

She straightened the books and used them as a stool. "You're the one I'm worried about, Ian. What are these nightmares about?"

He stared at her for a long time before answering.

Outside the forest was deathly still. In the far distance a barn owl let out its screeching call, which echoed through the trees.

"I dream about my mother."

She waited for him to continue.

"My father was a barbarian." He broke eye

contact and stared at his clasped hands, forearms draped over his knees. "From the moment I could walk, he taught me to hate. He said love spoiled a child. Every night he locked me in a cellar—said it would make me tough." A pause. "One night my mother came to visit me and gave me a bundled cloth she had hidden under her robe. It contained a unicorn carved out of wood. I hid it in the cellar and examined it every night. It was my only connection to my mother—I almost never got to see her."

Lily's eyes watered but she blinked back the tears.

"For her birthday that year, I decided to make a similar sculpture, so we could both have one—a bond between us. I worked on it for three months knowing my father would allow me to see her that day."

He flicked Lily a glance, as though to see if she were still listening. She kept her expression neutral, not wanting to distract him. "Go on," she said softly.

"Well, she was thrilled. And when father took off for a few minutes, she told me she'd found a portal that we could escape through. She tucked a rolled up map into my hands and said she was going to fetch me later that night." He dropped his voice to an undertone. "When father returned, he snatched the sculpture from her hand, accused her of turning me into a sissy. He was enraged by it."

He stopped talking and stared at the door.

"What happened after that?" she asked, afraid of the answer.

Ian went to the door and looked through the peephole, likely checking to be sure Varkis was still standing guard. He crossed his arms over his chest. "He took her away and killed her. I never saw her again."

Lily's hands went cold, a lump in her throat.

"I unrolled the map she'd given me," Ian went on in a toneless voice, sitting back down on the wing-back. "It was directions to the portal. I made a run for it the next morning and father sent a hell hound after me. It chased me all the way there—and straight into Auguste's attic. Seconds later Auguste came bursting in with his gun and shot it dead." A shrug. He didn't make eye contact. "And there you have it. You know the rest."

The cloaked man reached down into the drain he'd opened up next to the mortuary table, and howled with glee. "There's a lever."

They had searched the vat room high and low for any sign of a hidden door or button; figuring the specialized vat was likely in the vicinity—underground, that is—and possibly adjacent. They had nearly given up when the puppeteer suggested they check inside the drain hole. The cloaked man removed the grate and stuffed his hand down into the opening.

"It's definitely a handle," he said, glancing up at Mike. He gave it a hard yank and stood up to wait, looking about.

A creak and a groan sounded.

A square panel opened up in the center of the wall on the opposite end of the room from the ladder they'd used to enter.

"Push the button."

"Which button, Master?"

The cloaked man nudged his hooded head toward it, resting a hand on the hilt of his sword as though he thought he might need it. "The one above the panel. Push it."

Mike walked past the cloaked man and the mortuary table, and stood in front of the panel, examining it carefully. Mounted above it was a round intercom-like device, with a red button and a speaker.

The cloaked man moved further back. "Push it," he said again.

"What if it shoots me or something?"

"You can leave the body and find a new one."

"I suppose," the puppeteer said. "Though I kind of like this one. Here goes . . . "

Mike watched his hand reach out and was surprised to see it trembling. The puppeteer had never shown fear before. Or was it Mike's fear making its way through? He pressed the button and jerked back his hand.

The panel opened up like a mini elevator and the smallish square space inside was illuminated with a neon green light—like a scanner.

"Please place your hand in the box and identify yourself," a female computer voice instructed.

Chapter 22

"What do I do?" Mike hissed, glancing over his shoulder at the cloaked man who was standing twenty feet back at the mortuary table.

"Exactly what it says."

"But it won't recognize my hand. This is the body of the handyman, remember? I've examined his brain and he's never seen this before."

"You're trying my patience, slaveling, but you do have a point." He opened a cabinet full of medical tools, and pulled out a pair of forceps. He tossed them to Mike and went back to the table to wait. "Stick those in the box and see what happens."

Mike put the forceps halfway into the opening. "This is Auguste Kline," he heard himself say.

The green light scanned up and down the forceps and the computer woman spoke again. "Voice . . . not recognized. Fingerprints . . . not recognized. Palm prints . . . not recognized. Pulse . . . not detected. Access denied."

Before Mike could withdraw the tool, a laser sliced the forceps in half. He jumped backward and dropped the detached handle.

The cloaked man chuckled; a low, gritty rumble. "Guess the system was designed to keep out intruders," he said. "I wonder if this was dear old Zever's idea."

Mike's face twisted in a scowl. He sensed the puppeteer was irritated or frazzled. "What do we do now?" it said.

"We go get Zever. He's the only one left who knows anything about this."

"But what if you're wrong?"

"Then Zever gets his hand cut off."

Mike wanted to shrink back farther into the recesses of his mind. "What makes you think he'll cooperate?"

"Lily, of course." The cloaked man went to the entry ladder and began to ascend.

Mike jogged across the room to catch up. "The tree house is surrounded by gargoyles," he protested.

Gargoyles?

The gargoyles lining the trail? What kind of a threat was that?

"Do you ever stop whining?" The cloaked man stopped his ascent and glared down at Mike through the shadows of his hood. "Your head would be in that scanner right now if I still didn't need you." He let out a ragged exhale. "Let me spell it out for you, since you're obviously too thick to grasp it. Lily probably trusts you—she thinks you're the handyman. As does Zever. Get it?"

Mike was horrified. He wanted to cry out in protest but he was powerless to do anything but watch and listen. He cared for Lily and would never do anything to hurt her—or any woman, for that matter.

"But she's just as dangerous to Zever as she is to us," the puppeteer said. "He'd be insane to try and rescue her."

A cackle of delight. "Yes, but he's in love with her, you see. The fool has fallen in love with his Arch-enemy." A snort. "I couldn't have planned it better myself."

In the early rays of dawn, Lily sat outside with her back against the carved tree, eating a peanut butter and jam sandwich. Varkis sat beside her and gnawed on a dead squirrel while eying her sidelong.

"You don't look like you're enjoying that sandwich," he said. "Would you like some meat?"

He thrust the carcass toward her and she jerked away from it, swallowing down a rush of nausea. "Thank you, no."

She finished her sandwich and hugged her arms around her midsection, wishing she had a coat. The late October air was crisp and chilly, saturated with the tangy scent of fallen leaves.

The door to the tree opened and Ian stepped out, shutting it behind him.

Lily stood to her feet, brushing dirt off the seat of her pants.

"We should expect him to make a move soon," Ian said, looking off into the tree-shrouded distance. None of the gargoyles were in sight. They had not returned to marble in the morning.

"If he was in the forest, we'd have found him by now," Varkis said in a low voice.

"And you're sure no one's missing?"

"I did a head count about an hour ago."

Lily peered down the dirt trail ahead. It was murky with shadows, only a dusting of muted sunlight breaking through. Something dark lumbered up the path, its features indiscernible from this distance. Goosebumps rose on her flesh and her pulse quickened. "Who's that?" she whispered, pointing.

"He's one of us," Varkis said, showing no sign of concern.

"How can you tell?"

He flicked her a glance. "I can see who it is. My eyesight is superior to humans."

The dark figure drew closer, revealing two long tusks. It was the beast that had tried to attack her the night before.

"Hello, Master," the beast said as it entered the clearing. "I bring word from the mansion." It sat back on its haunches like an obedient pet.

"Has my staff moved out?" Ian asked, stepping away from Lily.

"The quarters of the cook and gardener are empty of personal effects, their cars are gone, and there's been no sign of them all night."

"And Hannah?"

"We couldn't find her anywhere, but her clothes and belongings are still in her room."

He frowned, paling slightly. "And Mike?"

"We searched everywhere and he was nowhere to be found."

Ian rubbed his jaw, dark eyes brooding. "Hannah wouldn't leave without her things," he said. "Were their cars still there?"

A nod.

He straightened his shoulders and lifted his chin. "She's still here."

"I'll go find her," Varkis offered, heading for the path.

"No, you stay with Lily." Ian took off at a long-legged stroll. "Hannah will be terrified if she sees you." He paused at the edge of the clearing and looked back at Lily. "Varkis will protect you. He's a very capable fighter, and the others are surrounding the forest. You're much safer here than out in the greensward. I'll be back as soon as I find Hannah." He disappeared down the trail.

Mike crossed the greensward and stopped at the edge of the forest where the trail to Ian's workshop began. The ebony gargoyle was missing: only an empty pedestal left in its place and the orb lying in the grass. Had someone taken the statue?

The sun hadn't risen fully over the mansion yet and a mild fog lingered in the air. He'd seen no one since leaving the mansion through the back exit, but his pulse was pounding in his ears and the puppeteer kept looking over his shoulder. What was he looking for? He sensed the puppeteer was afraid. But afraid of what?

Mike set off down the trail with slowish steps and tremulous hands; scanning the forest left and right with a darting gaze. Ian had warned him about man-eating wolves time and time again, but why would the puppeteer care about anything like that? The cloaked man seemed much more terrifying than a mere animal—

His thoughts were cut short as something massive leaped out of the foliage ahead and came hurtling toward him like a rhinoceros.

The puppeteer cried out in surprise. He veered off the path and into the forest, breaking through branches in a frantic attempt to get away. Spiky twigs and evergreen boughs whipped his face and body as he tore through the bramble, jumping over logs; snorting and thunderous footfalls pursuing him at a decreasing distance. Whatever was chasing him was far too big to be a wolf.

He screamed as something grabbed from behind and sent him flailing to the ground—flat on his back.

The puppeteer scrambled to get on his feet again but a disfigured shape loomed above him; its hazel eyes bright and regal. The creature had muscular shoulders and resembled a female lion—or a wolf genetically altered in some kind of Frankenstein lab. Had Ian actually been telling the truth about the wolves?

The puppeteer continued to scream, shuffling Mike away on his elbows and heels. The beast swung a paw at him and grazed his chest with hooked talons, exposing his flesh through the torn fabric of his shirt. Blood seeped out, plastering his shirt to his skin.

He felt nothing; only terror.

"Don't kill me—" the puppeteer begged. "I'm Mike—one of Ian's staff!"

The beast roared and raised his talons as if to deliver the death blow—but hesitated as Mike began to blubber.

He was embarrassed in spite of himself. "Please—I'm Ian's friend."

A shout sounded close by and a similar beast with the horns of a ram broke through the clustered tree boughs.

He surveyed Mike like a salmon on a plate.

"I found him on the path," the first beast said in a low growl.

Mike was stunned. The animal could talk?

"So kill it," said the other in an equally unearthly voice.

The lion-wolf licked its bloodied talons. "It claims to be Ian's friend . . . "

"A trick, probably." The second beast slapped out a pinkish tongue and pulled back his whiskered lips, exposing sharp, blackened teeth. "I could use a snack."

"He *is* a human though. . . . so, I'm inclined to believe him." The lion-wolf reached out and trailed a talon across Mike's jugular without breaking the skin. "Are you telling me the truth?" he growled, narrowing his gold-flecked eyes into slits.

"I promise you—it's the truth."

"Take him to Varkis," said the other, tossing

back his horns and glowering down at Mike. "He'll know what to do."

Ian had been gone for thirty minutes. Lily and Varkis remained on lookout at the workshop.

"How long do you think he'll be?"

Varkis didn't respond and she turned to face him. He was leaning forward, staring intently into the forest with tensed muscles and eyes narrowed. The fur on his back stood up on end.

"What is it?" she whispered.

"I heard someone wailing," he said without glancing her way. "In the distance."

She hadn't heard anything. "Are you sure?"

A nod. "It has stopped now." He sniffed the air, one ear rigidly perked.

"What do we do?"

"We wait." He flicked her a glance and brought a clawed finger to his canine lips. "We mustn't talk anymore." A pointed look. "Just listen."

She pressed her back into the carvings of the tree and surveyed the forest. Nothing but shadows and a smattering of bronze and russet here and there where leaves had not yet fallen.

Varkis moved closer to her side, whispering. "I hear voices again. They've captured someone. He's injured."

"Do you think they've caught the assassin?"

He shook his head. "Not a chance."

She could hear something now. The crunch of footsteps breaking twigs and stepping on dead leaves.

Two upright gargoyles appeared from the trees to their left, dragging Mike between them. His face was pallid and a scarlet stain spread across his chest in a trio of slashes. She gasped.

"Mike—" She rushed forward. "Let go of him!"

The two beasts gawked at her and then looked to Varkis for approval. He nodded. "Do as Lily tells you."

They let go simultaneously and he fell forward, landing on his chest with an umph. He scrambled to his feet, arms splayed and a wild look in his eyes.

She reached out to touch his shoulder, heart hammering against her ribs. "It's okay, Mike, it's me—Lily."

"Get back." He shoved her away.

She spread her hands. "It's okay, Mike, you're safe now. They won't hurt you anymore—"

He pointed at the beasts. "All of you stay back, or I'll . . . I'll . . . "

"You'll what?" Varkis asked, approaching, lips pulled back in a canine grin.

Mike moved from foot to foot, unable to stand still, gaze darting back and forth in evident hysteria. "Where's Ian?" he demanded. "Did you kill him? Huh? Huh?"

Lily clasped her hands together at her waist, unsure of how to soothe him. She needed him to calm down so that she could examine his wounds for severity. She took a step forward and he watched her with the wide eyes of a cornered animal. Dirt smudged his face, and his lip was cracked and bleeding.

"Can you please leave?" she spoke to the two beasts.

The gargoyles nodded and with a disapproving look toward Varkis, tromped off.

She took another step toward Mike and reached out for him slowly, touching his hand.

He seemed to relax a little and didn't pull away this time. "Here," she said, taking his clammy hand into her own, "come inside and rest. I'll explain everything. This is all new to me as well."

Chapter 23

Mike decided the puppeteer was a clever actor.

After entering Ian's workshop, Lily had removed his shirt and washed his wounds with water from a bottle. She had then cut a sheet into strips and used them as a makeshift bandage tied around his chest. The dog-man stayed outside.

While she worked, Lily explained everything that had happened to her from the time she'd left Auguste's study with Ian the evening before. Through everything, the puppeteer reacted with the appropriate level of shock and horror as though all of this were news to him, and Lily had shown no signs of suspicion—only sympathy and concern for his well-being.

Mike was growing increasingly distressed and frustrated—on the verge of losing his mind from not being able to express himself. If only he could communicate with Lily somehow and warn her of the danger she was in. She was so close—so close that he could kiss her lips—yet she may as well have been all the way across the ocean. And with the puppeteer being such a good actor, how was she ever to notice that something was amiss?

The puppeteer would have no trouble baiting

her.

He could only hope that Ian would know something was wrong, and might even be able to save him.

If only he were here now.

"Did the others tell you about Ian's letter instructing them to pack up and leave?" Lily asked, moving away from him and sitting down on a stack of tomes.

"His letter?"

Mike was instantly hopeful. The puppeteer seemed confused. Maybe he would slip up after all.

"Yes, he left them a letter saying to vacate the mansion immediately. That's why he went back to the mansion this morning—because he suspected Hannah hadn't left, and no one could find you either."

Mike was horrified. This would play perfectly into the cloaked man's plan.

"Oh, the letter," the puppeteer said, posturing as though his mind had simply gone blank in the excitement of the morning's events. "Of course they told me about it. And you can imagine how devastated Hannah was. I spent a considerable amount of time consoling her." An appropriate pause for effect. "After she calmed down, I told her I'd help her pack," he continued. "But when we reached the foot of the stairs leading to our rooms, we saw a hooded man dressed in ancient leather standing on the landing, looking down at us. He had a sword in his hand."

Lily's face visibly paled. "How did you get away?" she asked in a choked voice.

"We ran like crazy to the back door and didn't

look back, but Hannah fell on the greensward and hurt her ankle real bad."

"Is she . . . all right?" Lily's sea-green eyes were wide and limpid, full of fear.

"I don't know," the puppeteer said in a regrettable tone as though he cared very deeply about Hannah's welfare. "I didn't have car keys on me," he explained, "so I carried her into the forest and covered her with evergreen boughs and leaves—told her to lay very still while I went for help. As far as I could tell, the maniac hadn't followed us outside." He paused as though to increase the suspense; Lily's attention was rapt.

"I considered running down the road to seek out a neighbor, but I didn't want to risk passing the mansion—in case the maniac had come out the front or side doors. . . . In the end, we opted to spend the night in the forest and just wait it out."

"And that's when you came looking for Ian—this morning."

"Yes." A nod. And perhaps for effect—a painful cringe. He looked down at his chest and her eyes followed his.

She grimaced and gave him a look of compassion.

Somehow Mike knew this was the response the puppeteer was hoping for. He was winning her over through her nurturing spirit; using it as an Achilles heel.

"Hannah's still hidden in the forest," he heard himself say, "but she's caught a chill and is delirious. I need to get back to her and make sure she's still safe

—especially with those-those *beasts* out there." He put on a frightened look and cast a furtive glance at the door.

"I'll inform Varkis," she said reassuringly, "and he'll instruct the others to leave Hannah alone if they find her."

"I can't stay here any longer," his voice said. He stood with a groan and leaned forward to take her little hand in his, pulling her to her feet. "I must check on Hannah and go find Ian. He's wasting his time searching for us in the mansion, and in the meantime, we're all in danger." They went to the door. "I'll tell Varkis where to find her," he said. "If you trust him, I trust him."

"I'm coming with you to find Ian," she said, hands on her hips and lips set in a firm line. "I feel like a sitting duck and I can't stand it any longer."

No! Mike screamed inwardly, soundlessly. *No! It's all lies—lies. Don't listen to this psycho!*

Mike's hands reached out and took Lily by the shoulders, rubbing them with his thumbs in a gesture of affection. "You must stay here, where it's safe," his voice said to her in a soothing, caring tone. "I don't want that maniac to have any chance at getting his hands on you. That canine creature out there can protect you far better than I can."

She shook her head. "No, Mike. I don't want your death on my conscience. I'm coming with you whether you like it or not."

He let go of her shoulders and moved closer, searching her eyes. "Is there nothing I can say to convince you to stay here?"

He's playing you—Mike shouted in vain. *He's making you think it's your own idea. It's exactly what he wants you to do!*

She stepped back and folded her arms over her chest. "I'm coming," she said, "but I'm bringing Varkis with us for protection."

"Out of the question." He spoke too sharply and her eyes registered confusion. "Hannah hasn't seen any of the creatures," he explained in a softer tone, redeeming himself. "In her current state, a fright like that could put her over the edge. What if she has a heart attack?"

Her eyes were downcast. She sighed. "You're right, of course." She met his eyes again. "Varkis will never allow me to leave without him, but I have an idea." She spoke in a whisper. "You act like you've gone mad with fear and run down the path back to the mansion. They'll leave you be. I'll catch up with you after I figure out a way to get past Varkis."

He frowned. "There's too much that could go wrong."

"Do you want to save Hannah or not?"

Mike's hand reached for the door handle and he took a deep breath. "Don't keep me waiting too long, okay?" He kissed her forehead. "Here goes nothing . . . "

Lily followed Mike out of the tree with a gesture of helplessness as his Oscar-winning performance unfolded.

He ran forward, picked up a stick and waved it at Varkis, who was surveying the scene with aloof superiority and a vague look of amusement in his amber eyes.

"I want out of here," he said, eyes wild as he waved the stick. "You're all a bunch of freaks . . . monsters . . . vermin. Look what you've done to me—" He pointed to his chest with a tremulous hand. "I'm leaving this mansion for good and don't any of you try to stop me."

Lily put out her hands. "Mike—please. Calm down." She met eyes with Varkis and frowned apologetically before turning back to Mike. "I told you—no one is going to hurt you again. You're safe now."

"Lies! They ate Ian, didn't they?"

The dog-man's lips curled back over his teeth but he said nothing.

"I told you," Lily said in a tender voice, "Ian's at the mansion searching for you and Hannah."

His eyes widened with feigned panic. "Shut up—you're in on it. I bet you helped cook him up—"

"You're losing it, Mike. You're talking crazy." She approached him with tentative steps, hands raised in surrender.

"Stay away from me—" he screeched, throwing the stick at her and racing off down the trail toward the mansion, kicking up dirt and leaves in his frenzied wake.

Varkis let out a low growl. "Want me to go break his neck?" he said.

"Of course not." She gave Varkis an exasperated look. "He's just terrified, and rightly so. Didn't you see the wound on his chest? He needs stitches."

"I'll send someone to follow him," he said, peering down the trail. "He might be a foolish coward, but Ian will expect us to keep him safe. Great job we've done so far, I might add." A wink.

Lily looked upwards. The sky was overcast and the air damp with the anticipation of rain. She hugged her waist, considering how to make her escape from Varkis.

The dog-man whistled through his furry fingers and a crunching sounded nearby. Soon a gargoyle entered the clearing. Varkis gave instructions for the creature to pursue Mike from a distance and to help him out should danger befall him.

After the gargoyle had taken off, Varkis turned to look down on Lily. "Let's just hope the fool can find his way off the property without running into the assassin."

She nodded. "Varkis, um, I hope you don't mind, but . . . I really need to use the washroom." She avoided eye contact and cleared her throat, as though embarrassed.

"No problem," he said. "You pick a spot in the forest and I'll turn my back."

"I don't want company. Sorry."

"Fine," he said. "But don't let me out of your line of sight. You have two minutes and then I'm coming after you. If you hear so much as the wind rustling in the leaves, you give me a shout."

She agreed and slipped into the forest to the right of the trail. As soon as she was masked by the foliage, she took off at a run. Varkis would hear her do so; there was no time to lose. When she reached the greensward, Mike stepped out from behind the maiden statue and motioned for her to hurry. She closed the space between them at full speed and Mike took her hand in his, pulling her after him toward the mansion.

Mike despaired as the puppeteer led Lily closer and closer toward the cloaked man who was waiting for them behind a tree next to the wrought-iron gates at the front entrance to the estate; as had been previously planned.

Initially, Mike had felt abject loathing toward the puppeteer, struggling and fighting mentally against his captor in a futile attempt to force him out. But his rage had had no effect on the puppeteer—if anything, it seemed to spur him on, like fueling a fire. Now he was just too tired to kindle the loathing any longer; could feel only an overwhelming agony which stripped him of every last ounce of strength.

If any harm came to Lily through his own hands then it didn't matter if he should ever be set free. He wouldn't want to live anymore. If only he could disassociate somehow and not have to watch the wretchedness unfold; but he had no control over his eyelids and was forced to observe everything.

"I hope Hannah's all right," Lily said breath-lessly as she hurried to keep up step with him.

"You're so kind to have stayed behind to look for help —instead of abandoning her."

Stop saying nice things to me! If you only knew . . .

"You've comforted me so many times since I've arrived here," she said as they skidded around the side of the estate, ducking beneath the dangling bronze pendant leaves of the willows. "I'm so glad I got to see you once more."

It was more than he could bear; especially when the puppeteer smiled down at her and she met his eyes with a girl-like trust. Lily was like an angel to him—beautiful and radiant and innocent. He would never willingly hurt her.

A fierce, aching love for her welled up in his heart and he would've wept if he could.

That's when it happened.

He felt his heart thud in his chest: his first physical sensation since the puppeteer had taken over.

Mike flinched and nearly lost his footing. He slowed to a stop and let go of Lily's hand.

"What is it?" she asked, glancing behind and before them with a look of fear. "Did you hear something?" Feathery willow leaves surrounded them, shielding them from the view of any of the lancet windows; and obscuring their profiles from the road as well. Lily's face was cast in shadow and another wave of love for her surged in his heart—painfully.

The puppeteer lifted a shaky hand to his throat, heartbeat pounding in his chest like a jackhammer now. Why could he feel it now?

Was the puppeteer so corrupt that an altruistic emotion might act as a poison to him?

Summoning up all the love he could muster, Mike deliberately brought to mind everyone he had ever cared for; his family, his sister, his first car, and Lily—oh, wonderful Lily.

Mike fell to his knees and let out a choked gasp as pain filled his body.

Lily dropped to his side, hand on his shoulder. "Mike, what's wrong? Is it your chest?"

A cold breeze moved over them and goosebumps prickled his skin.

He could actually feel it.

"Mike? Talk to me—"

Her sweet, musical voice was soothing—like a warming balm. The puppeteer refused to look at her now. Mike filled his thoughts with heaven and eternal peace; anything he could think of to torment his captor.

His body spasmed and a slight cry slipped from his lips.

Mike flooded his mind with every happy memory he could recall, and a tingling filled his hands and feet; like pins and needles. He continued to focus his thoughts and the tingling moved up through his legs and arms, warming them. More gasps escaped his lips and he caught a glance at Lily, who was recoiling in fear.

Somehow, he had to warn her—before the cloaked man accosted them.

Chapter 24

Lily dropped to her knees on the walkway as Mike convulsed on the ground. He clutched his head in his hands, writhing.

"You're scaring me," she said, heart racing, "how can I help? Please answer me!"

Fresh blood seeped through the bandaging wrapping his chest as he tried to sit up. She reached out to touch him and he turned toward her. His eyes widened with a sudden look of clarity. "Run," he gasped. "Run, Lily—run to Varkis—"

A shiver rippled down her back and she glanced about wildly as though the world was closing in on her from all sides.

"Run," he cried again, in a strangely disembodied voice. "You can't save me—you have to go." He began to choke and gripped his throat: falling to one side and not letting go. He either couldn't breathe or was trying to strangle himself.

Lily jumped to her feet—and rejecting Mike's command to go to Varkis—ran to the nearby scullery entrance of the mansion instead. She yanked open the door and plunged inside. Her only hope of escape was by vehicle and she must retrieve her car keys. There was no way she was going back into the forest.

The scullery was empty; dull light from the windows barely suffusing the cupboards. Lily peered into the dining room, hurried through, and paused to surmise the corridor. There were several open doors and the assassin could be in any of the rooms, or none. But Ian was here somewhere too, and she could only hope that if the killer were still here, Ian had already captured him: and not the other way around.

She scurried down the hallway toward the front entrance, trying to keep her footfall light, and went up the staircase, avoiding the creaky steps.

The upper level seemed devoid of persons. All the doors were closed, and like the scullery, only a dull light entered through the leaded glass windows at the end of the hall. For all she knew, the assassin could be waiting for her inside her bedroom, behind a drape or settee; or even inside one of the wall passageways, watching through a peephole.

She opened the door slowly and looked inside, breath catching in her throat at the sight.

The room had been torn apart, furniture overturned, drawers dumped, and mattress feathers coating everything.

She went in, keeping an eye on every shadowy corner, and looked for her purse. She found it emptied on the bed, her car keys beside it. Whoever had ransacked her room evidently had no interest in her car.

Stuffing the keys in her pocket, she left the room and hurried downstairs, pausing on the landing to check for any intruders—and seeing no one, slipped out the front entrance and hurried down the steps. It had begun to rain.

She ran down the walkway until she reached the six car garage built of stone, and though she scanned the area under the willows, she couldn't spot Mike where she'd left him. Was he masked by dangling leaves or had he gone?—or worse, had he been taken? She hated to leave him like that but the only possible way she could get help was to leave this place.

Her sedan was parked in front of the garage where she'd left it, and not waiting to catch her breath, she fumbled with the lock and the door swung open with a familiar creak. She climbed in and slammed the door, locking it fast—heart slamming against her chest.

She dared not look back.

Ahead of her, through the trees, the tall wrought iron gates stood wide open, and she exhaled in relief. But why were they open? Had Ian taken a car and abandoned them all or had Chris and Angie left them open upon their departures the night before?

Rain drops spattered the windshield as she turned her key in the ignition with shaky fingers. The vehicle revved to life. She switched the car into reverse and cranked her neck to see out the rear view window as she positioned the nose of the car away from a tree. All was clear. She faced forward, switching on the front and back wipers, and pushed the gas pedal to the floor.

The engine roared and strained but the car didn't move.

She cranked her neck over her shoulder again and yelped.

A hooded man stood behind her vehicle with his hands on the trunk of the car, vambraces on his forearms.

She blinked at him, lifting her foot from the pedal.

He raised a fist above his head and smashed it down on the trunk of car, crumpling it like tinfoil.

Her airbag exploded open. She tried to push the puffy bag out of her face but froze as the man approached in her side view mirror. The rain continued to beat down on the windshield and roof of the car.

Beneath his cloak was an archaic vest. The hilt of a sword showed at his waist.

She waited helplessly as he tore open the driver's side door, ripping it from its frame and tossing it to the ground. She screamed as he ripped off her seatbelt and pulled her from the car like a rag doll.

"We meet again," he snarled, dropping her to the ground next to the door. She landed painfully on her back, scuffing her palms on the wet pavement.

"W-who are you?" she choked out, blinking up at him through the rain. His face was black beneath the hood of his cloak.

He laughed.

"Who I am doesn't matter," he said in a low, gravelly voice. "Now tell me where Ian is. We're going to pay him a little visit together." He reached for her and she covered her face with her forearms.

An unworldly screech sounded behind her.

She lowered her arms just as the hooded man took a quick step backward, bracing himself for an attack.

Callamous appeared out of the rain, galloping, and lowered his deadly horn to chest-level; ready to charge.

Lily scooted out of the way and scrambled to her feet. Without looking back, she raced down the driveway, through the open gates and down the dirt road, the soles of her shoes thudding against the soaked ground.

A piercing screech stopped her in her tracks and she whipped around.

Visible through the trees, the cloaked man had lodged his sword in the fleshy area between the unicorn's ribs and hip. Callamous reared, trying to trample him with his hooves, but the cloaked man dove out of the way, somersaulted and jumped to his feet again. He reached out and yanked his sword from the unicorn's flank, swinging it at his throat. Callamous blocked it with his double-edged horn.

Lily wanted to keep running, wanted to flee, but she couldn't. This was the third time the unicorn had intervened to save her life.

She owed him.

A fire welled within; fierce anger and hatred toward the killer. And without stopping to reconsider, she grabbed a fallen branch from the side of the road and ran back to the gates. With a holler to get his attention, she raced after him, adrenaline coursing through her veins as the rain beat down on her face.

"Get away—" Callamous shouted in his thunderous voice as she came upon them.

The cloaked man flicked her a glance.

She knew the tree branch was a mere twig up against a sword, but it might at least provide the distraction Callamous needed to run the assassin through with his horn.

She swung with all her might as he turned his attention back to the unicorn.

The branch broke in half as it hit the side of his head, falling to the ground.

Undeterred, he took another swipe at Callamous with the sword. The unicorn caught it between his shark-like teeth and yanked it from his grasp; sending it spinning across the pavement. In one deft movement, the cloaked man ducked around the unicorn and kicked the oozing wound in his side. Legs buckling and an airy cry escaping his lips, Callamous crashed to the ground.

Lily took off running as the killer pulled a dagger from his belt and charged after her with a shout.

She shot a glance over her shoulder and forced her legs to pick up speed on the slippery, mushy grass. He was less than twenty feet behind; Callamous struggling to his feet. She tore up the walkway and fairly threw herself up the stone steps.

The heavy oak doors were shut and she plunged full-force into their hardness as the killer ascended the stairs two at a time. She turned around, screaming from the depths of her belly and pressed her back into the wood; bracing herself for the impaling.

The hooded man slid to a stop in front of her and let out a belt of guttural laughter. "You can never escape me," he snarled.

His slight pause was all the time Callamous needed.

The unicorn leaped up the steps and threw himself between Lily and the assailant—just as the killer drove his dagger deep into the unicorn's neck.

With a strangled intake of breath, Callamous eyed Lily sidelong with one scarlet eye, and the light within went dim.

He crumpled to the ground, already looking like a corpse with his skinless battle face.

Before she could react, the hooded man jumped over the body and lunged for her. Within the same second, one arm was wrapped around her chest and the other held the dagger to her throat—its cold tip piercing her skin.

Chapter 25

"Lily—" a muffled male voice shouted from behind the closed doors.

The killer turned her around as the doors opened inward.

Ian stared back at them.

"I'm sorry, Ian," she sputtered.

"They're over there—" a voice shouted from the front yard, drawing their attention.

It was Varkis.

"Get down the stairs," the killer ordered Ian, his breath moist and foul against her cheek. "And close the doors behind you."

Ian stepped out, closed the doors and moved past them slowly, his hands raised and eyes never leaving the assailant.

A dozen gargoyles charged towards them across the front greensward, Varkis in the lead, sending up great splashes of water from the soaked turf.

"Stay back—all of you," the killer shouted, pressing the blade tighter against Lily's throat. A trickle of blood fell down her neck like a drop of warm water.

She winced from the sting and pushed her head further back against the man's chest to relieve some of the pressure; but he merely tightened his grip.

"Do as he says," Ian yelled, motioning for the gargoyles to cease their approach.

Varkis came to a halt, palm raised to the creatures behind him. "Is that Callamous?" he snarled through barred teeth, staring at the heaped form of the unicorn atop the stairs.

Ian nodded.

The assassin pointed his gloved index finger at Ian. "You—Come with me. The rest of you beasts—make yourselves scarce. If anyone follows me, the girl dies."

"I'll be coming with you," a human voice sounded from behind the wall of gargoyles.

Mike stepped out from behind the group, his pants and bandages soaked with rain and clinging to his body, and a pistol in hand. He mounted the steps to where Callamous lay.

"Ahh, now there you are," the killer said with a note of satisfaction. "I was beginning to think they'd killed you, but you delivered the goods nonetheless."

Ian narrowed his gaze at Mike. "You traitor."

Mike's expression was impassive, his eyes seemingly vacant.

"Yes," the assassin interrupted, "he delivered the girl right to me, in fact. The only thing missing was some gift wrap and a pretty bow."

Mike opened the door and gestured for them to enter.

With Mike in tow, the gun pointed at Ian, the assassin dragged Lily along in front, and they went into a sitting room. At Mike's instruction, Ian retrieved a flashlight and opened up a wall panel. They entered the darkness between the walls. Ian went first, though unwillingly, and was followed by Mike. The killer released his grip on Lily and turned her around so that she stood in front of him—with the blade of the dagger in the small of her back.

"Where are you taking us?" she asked.

"Ian's torture chamber."

"His—what?"

"The vat room," Mike interjected with impatience.

The vat room? A shudder coursed through her body. There was no possible way of escape now.

"Why did you call it a torture chamber?" she dared to ask the killer.

"Just shut up and you'll soon find out." The tip of the dagger pressed deeper into her shirt and she straightened her back.

They climbed down a ladder to the basement and after a few more turns, came to the spot where Lily had tripped over the slab of stone in the floor. Only now it was lifted away from the hole and light was shining out of it from the room below.

When they reached the bottom of the ladder, the cloaked man pushed her in front of him again and held the blade to her neck.

Ian's jaw was set and his eyes fixed on a square opening in the wall on the opposite side of the room. The interior of the box glowed a fluorescent green.

He swallowed hard, Adam's apple bobbing

with the motion. "Don't make me do it," he said.

"You will. Or the girl dies."

Casting a grieved glance at Lily, Ian went to the far wall and stood in front of the opening. The killer followed behind, dragging Lily with him.

Ian turned to face him but made no other moves.

"Hurry up," the cloaked man snapped. "I haven't got all day."

After a long exhale, Ian pressed the button over the opening.

"Please put your hand in the box and identify yourself," a female computerized voice said.

Ian placed his hand in the glowing opening and said, "This is Ian Hawke."

The green light scanned up and down his hand.

"Identity confirmed," the computer said. "Access granted."

"There." Ian turned again. "It's done. Let her go."

The killer backed Lily away from Ian and scanned the room. "What exactly is done? I see nothing."

"It opened a room in the west wing of the mansion." Ian's voice was subdued and low. He let out an impatient exhale. "If you follow me, I'll take you to it."

"Not yet. First, you need to delete your clearance and give it to me instead."

An exasperated look. "Why?"

He tightened his grip on Lily. "Do I have to

remind you again that I'm holding a dagger to the throat of your beloved?"

Ian narrowed his eyes, lip curling downward, but said nothing. He turned back to the box and put his hand inside, identifying himself. "Delete my clearance and input a new one."

"Acknowledged. Remove hand and your clearance will be deleted," the computer responded. "Clearance of Ian Hawke deleted. Standing by for a new input and voice command."

Ian nodded at the assassin. "Go ahead."

"If this is a trick, I will not hesitate to kill her."

"It's not a trick. You watched me do it—you heard the computer."

Hesitating a moment longer, the hooded man removed a glove, while still holding Lily against his chest, and reached his hand into the glowing box.

"Kurik," he said, loud and clear. The green light scanned his hand.

"New identity and clearance confirmed," the computer said.

"Excellent," he said slowly, withdrawing his hand. He moved himself and Lily to the side. "Tie Ian to the table," he said to Mike.

Mike approached from across the room.

"What?" Ian protested. "I told you the room is in the west wing of the mansion. Don't you want me to take you there?"

"It's time Lily dear learned the truth about you . . . *Ian*." He lowered his lips to her ear, foul breath making her eyes water. She tried not to inhale. "His real name is Zever," he said in a growl, "and you'll soon see the monster he really is. It's best he be tied down for it."

Lily blinked but didn't breathe a word.

Mike held the pistol to Ian's head and tied him down to the table with buckled restraints around his wrists and ankles. Kurik moved Lily away from his body so that she was facing him; while keeping the dagger in place. He pulled back his hood with his free hand.

She let out a cry, eyes widening.

Though not a twin, he was clearly Ian's brother. His hair was shaved close to his head and his jaw was thicker than Ian's. He couldn't be much older but his face was weathered and a gruesome scar stretched from the corner of his upper lip over his right cheekbone and ended somewhere above his ear.

He grinned, exposing blackened teeth, like a dog's. "That's right, you've guessed it. I'm Zever's brother and our father is Morack. Your precious Zever is just as much a monster as I." He moved closer to Lily until their faces were only inches apart. He examined her face, her lips. She tensed up, holding back a scream. "You realize," he growled, "that if you kill Morack, it will result not only in the death of all his followers, but of Zever and myself as well." His lips were a mere inch from her own. She couldn't breathe.

This must have been what Callamous was talking about when he said she'd have to make a choice between the life of one or the lives of many.

Her heart sank to the pit of her stomach and tears trickled down her cheeks.

"Now, Zever," Kurik went on, jerking Lily's

head back by the hair and running the dagger lightly across her throat, "why don't you show us who you really are?" He looked down at Ian and grinned.

"Let her go—" Ian's eyes had turned to pools of black. He strained against the buckles, trying to break them.

"I can't let her destroy us, brother." Kurik yanked on her hair, pulling her even further back. She could barely maintain her balance and clenched her jaw against the pain. "How should I kill her? Fast or slow? Slow might be more fun. Should I carve up her face just like you did to mine?"

"Let . . . her . . . go," Ian said, voice growing deeper and rougher. His lower jaw seemed to dislocate as his mouth stretched open unnaturally. He let out a cry of rage and frustration as a pair of fangs shot out of his gums above his canines, like a cobra about to strike its prey."

"You see," said Kurik, laughing, "he's nothing but a freak."

Ian struggled against his restraints again, the corded straps beginning to tear. "You tied me down because you're nothing but a coward."

The pressure of the knife against her throat began to slacken.

"I cut you the night you tried to prevent me from escaping through the portal," Ian shouted, "and you ran off. So, unless you want to spend the rest of your life reminded of that, be a man and fight me now. You've had far more training than I—" His voice was feral now. He tore one of his legs free from the table, busting the strap with brute strength.

Kurik seethed with evident fury, his body quivering, but he maintained his grip on Lily.

Mike continued to aim the pistol at Ian but kept his distance. His face was stoic.

"Don't make excuses," Ian said, ripping off the restraint on his right wrist. "Fight me and prove it—"

"Make one more move and she dies." Kurik's voice had a twinge of something like fear in it now, and his brow glistened with sweat.

Ian busted the final restraints, but rather than leaping from the table, he merely sat up. His fangs retracted and his jaw snapped back into place. Only his black eyes remained. "You're a coward," he said calmly.

"I am not a coward," Kurik screeched. "You think putting a scar on my face makes you a tough guy?" He threw Lily to the ground and she landed hard against her shoulder, momentarily stunned. "Watch her, slaveling," he shouted at Mike. "He makes any move, you shoot her."

Kurik charged Ian then, who was standing now, and made a slicing motion at his face with the dagger. Blood dripped to the floor at Ian's feet, but Lily couldn't see him through Kurik's back. He made no moves to defend himself.

"There." Kurik grinned. "Every time you look in the mirror, you'll see me and remember who your real family is." He stepped to the side with a sweep of his hand, as though to say "ta-da!".

A gaping cut ran from Ian's lip, up over his cheek, and to his ear.

Lily swallowed down the nausea that rose in

her throat. She was still on the ground. "You're wrong," she said with a tone more bold than she felt. "Ian's real family was his mother, Auguste, Hannah, and all his friends here on earth."

Kurik let out a belt of laughter. "Do you really think Auguste was a better father than Morack? He used to torture creatures down here! What did you think this table here was for—and that?" He pointed to one of the drains. "That's where he washed away all the blood." A smoldering pause. "And Ian was the one who brought him all his victims."

A beat passed.

"Is that . . . true, Ian?"

"They were evil creatures that Auguste accidentally let through the trunk," he said, his tone sombre. "I locked them up down here in the vats, it's true, but I didn't know what he was doing with them. He told me the table was for autopsies. It was stupid of me to believe him."

"Yes, of course," Kurik sneered, "because dead creatures need restraints, right?"

"Look, I loved Auguste. I didn't want to believe he was capable of such things."

"Blah, blah, blah—lovey-dovey trash. You knew exactly what was going on down here and you enjoyed it—because your blood is just as black as mine." Kurik came forward then and grabbed Lily by the wrist, yanking her to her feet. "Now show me where the room is."

Chapter 26

Ian wiped the blood from his face with his sleeve. The cut had stopped bleeding but still burned. It wouldn't be long before the pain subsided though and the wound healed.

Lily's face was pallid as she watched him, her eyes haunted. Did she believe him? He longed to pick her up in his arms, to cradle her against him. If he didn't fear for her life, he would've killed Kurik by now. But he had to figure out how to get Mike and his pistol out of the picture first.

Kurik motioned toward the ladder with a flick of his hand. "Get a move on, brother. Slaveling, follow. Anyone tries anything, you shoot."

Ian led the troop to the west wing in silence, his feet like lead. If his brother got what he wanted, he'd kill Lily. There was no doubt about that. And Ian's own death wouldn't be so quick. His father would first make him pay for all those years of imprisonment.

The west wing hallway was dark, despite the drape-less windows. Beads of rain on the glass further marred the bit of daylight coming in. The floor was coated in dust for the most part but a scuffle of footprints scattered it in trails from one room to the next. He frowned. Had Lily been up here recently? Or Mike? The thought of Lily accidentally stumbling upon Morack's prison sent a shiver up his spine.

"Almost there," he mumbled reluctantly, running his fingers along the length of his cheek. The edges of the cut were pulling together and the bleeding had ceased. He didn't want to admit defeat, but was losing hope by the second. He was confident he could kill Kurik—but if Morack was set free, the whole earth would be destroyed.

He led them into a room at the end of the hall and pushed a sheet-covered wardrobe away from an inner wall, revealing a pair of doors hidden behind it with a molded design of golden leaves; the beauty of which was dulled and marred by dust and cobwebs.

Placing a hand on each door, he gave a firm push and they swung open, revealing a room swathed in shadows.

Two windows with closed drapes were on the exterior wall of a long and narrow room. Rain smattered against the glass with a forceful gust of wind. The contents of the room were indiscernible.

Ian stepped inside and turned a dimmer to full power and the room came to life. The walls were covered in Cordova leather, dozens of candlelights from a crystal chandelier reflecting off the sahara-gold carpeting. He blinked, eyes adjusting to the light. Mike stepped in behind him, followed by Kurik and Lily. No one spoke.

All the furniture was covered in sheets but Ian couldn't help remembering the way it used to be as a young boy and teen. The days when he sat on a loveseat across from Auguste in his favorite armchair, slippered feet on a footstool as he smoked a pipe. In front of the lancet windows was a grand piano, and nearby an antique billiard table. Hannah often played show tunes on the piano when they had a game. If only those days hadn't come to a screeching halt: when Morack crossed over and was locked away. Just like that, the room had been sequestered permanently.

Ian stood staring beyond the sheeted billiard table. The wall behind it was covered in a tapestry. He went to it and pulled the tapestry up and out of the way. Behind it was a hidden archway revealing a short hallway beyond with a plain wooden door at the end of it.

"Is that it?" Kurik asked.

"Yes," he said, refusing to look at his brother. "He's in there."

A weight settled on his shoulders, so heavy it threatened to push him down through the floor. The breath left his lungs as Kurik stepped around him, dragging Lily with him like a ragdoll as she struggled to keep her footing.

"I can't believe I've finally found him—" Kurik cried, his body fairly shaking with excitement.

A click sounded behind Ian and the cold muzzle of a pistol touched his neck. "Go on then, get going," Mike said in a flat tone.

He exhaled slowly. "Why are you doing this, Mike?" he whispered. "Kurik is insane. He's just using you—once he has what he wants, he'll kill you, too."

"Shut-up and mov—"

Kurik interrupted with an exclamation. "—
What is this!"

Lily wasn't sure what she was looking at.

A six-foot tall vat stood in the center of the
closet-like room. It was stainless steel like the ones in
the basement but was completely entangled in thick,
black, ropey vines.

Ian entered the room, followed by Mike.

Dark circles rimmed Ian's eyes and his hair
was askew. Lily reached for him but a sharp pain in
her neck brought her to a halt as Kurik turned to face
his brother and tightened his grip on the dagger.

"Where is it?" he said through clenched teeth,
body quivering.

"Where's what?"

"Don't play stupid with me—you're killing
time. Where is the skeech that wove this web?"

"Behind the vat."

Kurik lowered the dagger but his arm around
her chest tightened and she struggled to take in a full
breath of air.

He pushed her forward and halfway around
the vat where a giant spider came into view. Dozens
of glassy eyes protruded from a wide, flat head; a pair
of pincers above and below a fanged mouth. Lily stifled a scream, then exhaled in relief.

It was on its side with eight legs tucked
against its belly.

It was dead.

"No—" Kurik wailed in an otherworldly voice. "What have you done!"

Ian crossed his arms over his chest. "I killed it."

Kurik dug his fingers into Lily's tricep until she grimaced. She jabbed her elbow into his side but he didn't flinch. She might as well have poked him with a feather.

"Why don't you just cut through it?" Mike suggested. "I have an ax in the workroom."

"Are you daft? A skeech's web is indestructible. The only way through is to dissolve it with the acid stored in the sacs in its head. Why of course!" Kurik jerked Lily to the insect's side and pushed the head over with his boot, revealing the back of the skull.

Someone had cut a hole out of it, leaving nothing but an empty cavity.

"You fool—" Kurik screamed at Ian. "If there's no way for me to get into this vat, then I no longer have any reason to keep you or Lily alive." He yanked her head back and poked the dagger into her neck, breath hot against her throat.

"Wait-wait,"—Ian held his palms out in front of himself in a calming motion—"there's another way to do it."

Kurik grunted in response.

"There's a plant that contains an acid that can dissolve the web."

"Let me guess, back in Alvernia? Not going to happen. I don't believe you."

"No, there's one here. I brought a variety of seeds with me from father's palace when I left. A seed for the Jubaka plant was one of them."

A long pause. The room was suffocating and dark.

"Where is this Jubaka plant."

"North-east of my workshop, in the center of the swamp."

"You're lying . . . "

"I swear, I am not. I wouldn't risk Lily's life like that." His eyes were wide; and she thought, sincere. "If you just follow me," he said, "I'll show you."

"It's a trap. I wouldn't even make it to your tree without being ambushed. Or if I did get to the Jubaka, no doubt some new and equally absurd task will await me there before I can extract the acid. It's a wild goose chase—"

"No, the acid is easy to remove. I promise." His voice was strained.

"I don't believe you—Lily dies."

"No—" he cried, rushing toward them.

A shot rang out as warm blood splattered Lily's face.

She screamed, expecting Ian to fall to the ground. Instead, the dagger slipped from her throat as Kurik staggered away, clutching his hand in agony.

Ian was there in an instant, wrenching her to his side. She searched the room, wildly, heart pounding, expecting Mike to shoot again. Hadn't he aimed at Ian and missed?

But it wasn't Mike.

Hannah stood in the door frame with a rifle

aimed at Kurik.

Mike ducked past her and vanished in the room beyond.

Ian pulled Lily with him to Hannah's side. "We have to get out of here—now."

Kurik lunged toward them then, his face contorted. She fired again but he darted to the side. Ian grabbed Hannah's arm and pulled both her and Lily out of the room and down the short hallway. "Run for it," he shouted when they reached the archway. "I'll slow him down."

Kurik rushed toward them. "Now—ladies—now," Hannah shouted.

The sheet draped over the piano pulled off as a trio of angels leaped out from beneath it.

"*Orealas*," Kurik said with a gasp. He darted to the closest window, throwing himself through the curtains and the glass. Hundreds of glimmering pieces crashed to the floor as his boots disappeared from view.

Ian went to the window, peering out as rain splattered him and the room.

Lily hurried to his side. "Is he dead?" she asked, looking down through the opening. Bits of glass shimmered on the ground below, two stories down.

"He's heading for the forest, for the Jubaka plant."

"It's real?"

"Yes." He took her hand and moved them away from the window.

"Who cares if he's after some silly plant,"

Hannah said hotly, her braid hanging over her shoulder, apron untied. "I'm just glad he's out of our house." She clucked her tongue and approached Ian. "Oh, my poor boy—what have they done to your face?"

"I'm all right, Hannah. It's just a scar." He wrapped the little old woman in his arms, kissing the top of her head.

"I'm so glad to see you again," she said. "I thought I'd lost you forever." She stepped back and gave him a once over, balancing the rifle on her shoulder. "But I wasn't going to walk away without a fight."

He chuckled and rubbed his forehead. "You sure saved our a—"

"—mind your language," she scolded, waggling a finger.

"How'd you learn to shoot like that?" he asked, nodding at the rifle. "I'm impressed."

"Auguste used to take me out back to shoot targets, don't you remember? Said I needed to learn to defend myself against the wolves." She looked toward the broken window, frowning.

"Oh yes, the wolves . . . right."

Lily stared at the trio of angels who were standing back demurely, recognizing them instantly as the angel statues from the pool room. Their skin, hair and robes were golden; plumy wings folded neatly behind their backs. The one in the middle had an ethereal beauty distinct from the others. She noticed Lily's glance and smiled.

"I'm so glad you made it out of the baths

alive," the angel said with a voice like a dove. "Kurik nearly got you, but he didn't fight back when I intervened. I didn't know it was Kurik, unfortunately, or I would have informed Ian."

Lily's breath caught in her throat. "You're the angel who rescued me?" Her cheeks warmed. "I'm so sorry for jabbing you with my elbow. I . . . I thought you were attacking me."

The angel smiled in response and Lily's tense, aching muscles relaxed ever-so-slightly.

"I'm not an angel as you call me, however. We're known as Orealas. Our mothers were Serena's handmaidens."

"Speaking of which," Ian cut in, "did anyone see where Mike went? For all we know, he could be lying in wait in the next room, though my guess is he's hightailed it out of here." He reached for Hannah's rifle, saying, "May I?" and she passed it to him. "I've got to go after Kurik—the sooner the better."

Lily went to him and touched his forearm, searching his dark eyes with earnest. "I'm coming with you."

He agreed. "Hannah, stay with the Orealas—they'll protect you from Mike and anything else."

Chapter 27

Ian opened the back door of the mansion a crack and peered out into the yard. The sky was slate and the rain showed no sign of letting up. A low fog was spreading across the greensward, obscuring the outline of the forest.

Taking Lily by the hand, he pushed his way through the door and they moved across the lawn, staying low to the ground. When they reached the trail, the heavy-duty gnarled branches served as an umbrella, reducing the rain to a drizzle. It was icy cold and Lily began to shiver; she was wearing a zippered jacket and jeans, her hair wet and flat against her cheeks.

"Where's the swamp?" she whispered.

"About a fifteen-minute jaunt from the workshop." He stopped, turning to face her and pulling her closer to his side. "But there's something I have to warn you about—"

"—did you hear that?" She interrupted, eyes widening.

"What?" He shot a glance to his right, where she was gesturing.

"I heard something moving." Her voice was barely a whisper now.

He glanced in the direction again, scanning the thicket. "Can't be Kurik," he said in a hushed tone. "He's way ahead of us."

A branch snapped in the foggy distance.

Ian's back went rigid. Putting a finger to his lips, he motioned for Lily to follow him. Keeping down, he went to a thick log on the opposite side of the trail and ducked in behind it, pulling Lily all the way down beside him, their cheeks to the wet forest bed. They looked out at the trail from a gap beneath the log.

More twigs snapped, closer now, and a creature appeared in the gloom before them, fog swirling around multiple insect-like legs. From the middle of a bulbous torso rose a head with an elongated skull. Its six eyes were ablaze like fireflies.

Ian kept a protective arm over Lily's back.

The creature moved closer to their side of the trail, flicking its eyes in the direction of their hiding place. Had it seen them? Caught their scent?

Seconds passed, an entire minute, rain dampening their backs, and the creature started off again, disappearing into the fog. They waited until the footsteps had faded to nothing and until several minutes of silence had passed after that.

"What was that?" Lily whispered, her face only inches away from his own. He fought the urge to move a strand of hair away from her cheek.

"A Leerk," he said with an exhale. "One of Morack's mindless soldiers." He stood up and Lily followed suit, brushing wet leaves and muck from her jeans. "I don't know what it's doing here though," he said in an undertone, senses on high alert. "I thought I'd captured all the creatures Auguste let through . . . unless—" His pulse quickened, sudden dread constricting his throat. "Lily, where is the key to the trunk, the one you took from Bogart's cage—do you still have it?"

"I . . . I hid it in my dresser but—" She frowned. "When I went for my car keys, the bedroom was ransacked . . . "

"Mike," they said in tandem.

"The trunk has been opened then," he said gravely, moving around the log and back onto the path. "The inner key has been missing since Auguste's death—Kurik must have taken it. We'll have to be extra cautious. There's no way of knowing how many Leerks have been released—and who knows what else."

They hurried toward Ian's tree, keeping an eye on all directions.

"I hope I never see Alvernia," Lily said in a whisper. "It sounds like a horrid place."

"It was beautiful before Morack took over."

"Do you have any good memories there?"

"No."

"Then why do you want to save it? Why didn't you just destroy the trunk and be done with it?"

He considered this a moment, but didn't slow his pace. "My mother used to tell me stories whenever she had a chance to talk to me. Of a great ocean filled with sea people who lived in an underwater city. There were also spectral creatures of all colors, that drifted on the winds, and humanoids on land. Unicorn populations covered the hillside like sand. Then there was the singing forest. The trees lit up indigo at night, making a humming sound that was the most wonderful melody you've ever heard . . . "

The fog was growing denser but the rain was letting off. The air was chill and piquant with decaying leaves.

"Tell me more, Ian."

He glanced her way, gaze lingering on her eyes, her face. He looked away.

They reached the workshop and went around it. "She also told me about great chambers of precious jewels, tended to by thousands of fairies. I've never seen them myself but it's probably where Auguste acquired his fortune and the ones he gave me for the tree." He lowered his voice from an undertone to a whisper, tucking his head down to speak into Lily's ear as they trudged through the forest. "Once Morack is defeated, the creatures of Alvernia will be free again and Alvernia can return to its original state of beauty—"

Ian froze in his tracks, grabbing Lily securely by the wrist and pushing her behind him, shielding her.

Someone or something was approaching through the gloom ahead and it was too late to hide.

A silhouette appeared.

Lily's legs were like Jello. She let out a rush of breath. "Varkis, thank goodness."

Varkis approached nonchalant. He'd likely caught their scent long before they saw him, and already knew they were coming.

"Man, am I glad to see you," Ian said, letting go of Lily. "We've got trouble."

"Tell me about it—" Varkis lowered his voice. "Had a near brush with a Leerk a couple hours ago." His gray fur glistened and dried blood formed a trail down one forearm. "I've informed the others."

"Either Kurik or Mike have the trunk keys. I'm afraid this place'll be crawling in no time, if it isn't already."

Varkis narrowed his amber eyes, lips rolling back in a growl. "Speaking of which . . . where *is* Kurik?"

"Heading to the swamp. He's after the Jubaka tree. We have to stop him."

"Count me in. I'd love a chance to sink my claws into him."

Ian was visibly relieved. His cheek was smeared with mud and his shirt wet and clinging. "Great," he said, smacking Varkis' upper arm and moving around him, heading in the direction the Anubis had just come from.

"Once again," gruffed the dog man, puffing out his chest, "I come to your rescue."

Ian laughed and shook his head.

Lily fell into step beside Varkis.

"How're you holding up?" he asked.

"I'm surviving," she said, moving a tree

branch away from her face. "Trying to keep my sanity. Might need a straight jacket if things keep up." She crooked a smile.

"I'm sure Ian's strong loving arms are the only straight jacket you need." He let out a bark of a laugh.

"Shut-it," Ian said, glaring over his shoulder at them. "Want the whole forest to know we're here? Keep it down, man."

They walked in silence for a while, keeping a vigilant watch on all sides.

"Do you look like your father, Ian?" she whispered impulsively, quickening her stride until she was beside him.

"Not really." He flicked her a distracted glance, maneuvering around tree trunks and pushing aside branches. "I suppress those features. There's a darkness in me." His voice was low and gruff. "If I give in to it, I begin to change, to look more like him —like you saw in the vat room. It takes a lot of self-control to stay this way."

"It must be challenging to fight an inner battle like that . . . "

He gave her a contemplative look. "Everyone does really. For me it just happens to be physically obvious."

She nodded. "So, tell me about my grandmother then. Serena. How'd she acquire magical powers?"

"She wasn't human."

Lily's breath caught in her throat and she nearly tripped over a log. "Then what am I?"

"Oh, you're part human," he said. "Auguste

was human."

Lily's heartbeat drummed in her ears and she began to sweat, despite the dampness and cold. "But what else am I."

"If you take after your grandmother then . . . well, then you'd be . . . you'd be part shape shifter."

She gasped.

"But she only ever took human form, as far as I know. Nobody knows what her true form was."

"If my bloodline is diluted, do I even have the power to kill Morack?"

"As long as her blood runs through your veins, I have no doubt of it."

His voice wavered slightly in the middle, as though he lacked conviction. Her throat tightened.

Varkis pushed his way in-between them. "Lighten up on the heavy talk," he grumbled. "We're nearly to the swamp and can't be distracted. It's time to get stealthy."

Lily and Ian nodded their agreement and took the next half mile at a quick and cautious pace, finally coming to a dead stop at the edge of swamp land.

The rain had ceased and a mist swirled around them.

The swamp stretched out ahead of them. Dead trees reached upward from the murk at odd angles, casting spindly shadows over the oily surface. Floating weeds shifted positions as gaseous bubbles rose to the surface and burst around them.

Ian turned to Varkis who was standing with hairy arms crossed over his chest, feet spread wide.

"What do you think?" he asked. The last thing he wanted to do was enter the swamp, but Kurik had given him no other choice.

"I think it wasn't a smart idea to come with you after all," the dog man responded.

"Come on. Seriously."

"Who said I wasn't being serious?"

Lily was standing between them, one hand on her hip as she squinted up at the sky. Dusk was fast approaching.

Ian ran a hand down his face and took a deep breath, nearly choking on the stench of the water. "Well. . . . Let's get this over with then." He stepped into the cold goop, weed-muck sucking at his foot.

He took another step forward and sunk down, slimy vegetation and dank water swirling about his knees.

"Come on guys," he glanced over his shoulder. "We have to get to the Jubaka and get out of this swamp before nightfall or we won't live to see morning!"

Varkis harrumphed. "This swamp gets deep fast, you do realize. We're going to have to swim a lot of the way and it's going to be freezing."

"I know." He met eyes with Lily in an apologetic glance. She looked frightened. "We'll take breaks as needed and warm up afterwards."

She frowned. "Does anything, uh, dangerous, live in this swamp?"

"Not that I know of."

It was a lie.

There *was* something lurking in the swamp; something that had started out quite small but had been growing for many years since.

When Ian left Alvernia as a boy, he'd taken some kind of tadpole from his father's collection of species, thinking it a frog. He'd then released the little creature into the swamp. Later, when he realized his mistake (that it was no tadpole), a year had already passed. Of course it was possible the creature had died right off the bat, for he'd seen no sign of it in the few times he'd been at the swamp—but he wasn't about to assume this. Better to err on the side of caution.

The three of them trudged forward in a row, every step threatening to suck off their boots.

He looked at Lily. Her face was ashen and taut, but she was at least keeping up.

Varkis, on the other hand, would not stop voicing his complaints.

"I'm never gonna get this guck out of my fur. Couldn't we fashion a boat so we don't have to swim through this slime?"

"We don't have time."

"I'm going to itch for weeks. Look at this—" He raised his arms from the goop, revealing half a dozen leeches.

"You're also going to smell like rotten eggs," Lily cut in. She grinned as she said it but her eyes remained clouded.

The sludgy waters had nearly reached their shoulders.

"It's not the swamp that smells like rotten eggs," the dog-man responded. "The mushrooms I had for lunch made me gaseous."

Ian took another step forward and the water bed gave way beneath him, forcing him to tread water. "Here we go," he said, swimming with wide frontward strokes, arms getting tangled in the weeds.

Their progress was slow-going as they swam around protruding tree branches, logs, and patches of reeds. He tried not to think about what might lurk beneath but his heart drummed in his chest. What if something sucked Lily down before he could do anything to stop it? The water was opaque: even if he dived after her it would be impossible to see anything.

Brown bubbles broke the surface around him and he choked on the smell. Slime splattered his face as a large one burst in front of him. He wiped away the goo, gagging.

"Ian," Varkis barked, laughing, "hold it in, man."

"What are you talking about?" He shot a glare over his shoulder.

"The bubbles, what else? You ate more mushrooms than I did."

"Ha." He paused, treading water, and peeled a leech off his neck. Lily wrapped an arm around a log, propping herself up. Varkis followed suit.

"Is that a child—!" she gasped, pointing toward the fog ahead.

"Where?" He grabbed onto the log and peered over it, straining to see through the mist.

Some forty feet ahead, something or someone lay slumped over a tree branch—the lower three-quarters of its body submerged in the swamp.

"Hey, kid," Varkis shouted, "you okay?"

The child didn't move.

"Oh, he must be unconscious—" Lily cried, eyes wide.

Or dead.

"We've got to save him. If he slides off the branch, he'll drown!"

"Lily—" He grabbed her arm, restraining her. "Why would a child even be out here? We're miles from civilization." He looked about in all directions. Varkis was sniffing the air.

"I don't know how he got here," she said, blinking rapidly, a tear running down her cheek. "But we can't just leave him!"

Ian frowned, straining to get a better look at the unmoving, powder-white back of the child.

Black weeds clung to its skin like tangled overalls.

"Ian, I can smell you and Lily," Varkis said in a low voice, eyes narrowed, "but I can't smell that kid."

"What are you saying?"

"I'm saying—"

"—Ian, look," Lily interrupted, her voice high-pitched with fright.

As if in slow motion, the child's body raised itself to an upright position, rivulets of water trailing down his back. His head was completely bald and weeds swirled around his waist as his body twitched, increasing in momentum.

Like someone waving a rag doll on a stick.

"He's alive—" Lily yanked her arm free and hiked a leg over the log. She dropped into the water on the other side and took off toward it.

"Wait," he shouted, climbing over the log and plunging after her as she swam with wide strokes toward the child, pushing vegetation out of her way as she went.

"Lily, stop," he cried out, "it's a trap—"

"—I'm almost there." She reached the child and spun him around.

A pallid face without a nose stared back at them with unblinking eyes and a fish-like mouth.

Lily screamed.

Ian's boots struck something soft and squishy as he tried to pull her away. He steadied his balance only to be raised two feet above the water—his feet squarely planted on the head of a giant eel.

The doll face and torso rose higher, revealing a tentacle rather than legs. Useless arms hung at its side like rubber.

It was an appendage, not a child. A "finger puppet" lure.

Varkis reached them and yanked Lily into his arms. They took off as Ian struggled to keep his balance.

He looked down.

The lower jaw of the inky eel jutted out beneath him in a grotesque underbite with dozens of needle-thin teeth.

Attempting to toss Ian aside, the slick body

thrashed to and fro, sending waves of swamp water in every direction.

Ian dropped down and wrapped his legs around the throat. He pulled a knife from his belt and thrust it into the gills. The eel let out a screech as yellow blood oozed from the wound.

Hissing, it dove under the water and took him with it. With no chance to grab a breath of air, he got a mouthful of rancid water instead and lost his grip. He tried in vain to grab hold again as he slid down the eel's back and slipped off the end of the doll-face tail.

Ian thrashed his arms and legs, opening his eyes to look about, but it was too murky. The eel could be anywhere by now—behind him, about to attack, or gaining ground on Lily and Varkis.

He kicked hard and propelled himself upward, breaking the surface with a gasp of air, and grabbing onto the first branch he could find.

The eel's giant head rose above the surface of the water in his peripheral vision, some fifteen feet away, and charged toward him—sending up great arcs of water on either side.

Chapter 28

A bullet whizzed past Ian, piercing the eel in the jaw.

Shaking its head left and right, the eel dove back underwater and with a great whip of its tail, shot out of the swamp and hurtled through the air toward Ian—its mouth agape.

Another shot rang out, then another and another. Bullets zipped overhead embedding themselves in a row up the backside of the airborne creature until one hit it right between the eyes. It let out a roar and belly-flopped to the water as Ian dove out of the way.

Within seconds, the lifeless body had sunk out of sight in the murk, bubbles breaking the surface in its wake.

For a moment all was still.

Then the sleek black body bobbed up again and floated on the surface.

Ian half expected to see Hannah to the rescue again as he scanned the swamp for the source of the shots. Instead he found Mike clinging to the trunk of a nearby tree, a gun in hand and weeds tangled about his waist.

"Don't kill me, Ian," he said gruffly, wiping swamp water and mud from his brow with the side of the hand that held the pistol. "I can explain every-thing—"

"First, give me the gun."

"It's empty," he said, tossing it over anyway.

Ian caught it and checked the cartridge. "All right," he said, catching sight of Lily and Varkis returning through the distant fog, likely drawn by the sound of gunfire. "You'd better have one good expla-nation for all this. Have you been following us all this time?"

"Yes."

Ian narrowed his eyes.

For some reason Mike had saved his life in direct rebellion of Kurik's orders. It didn't add up. "Let's get out of the swamp," he said, "then we'll talk." He let go of the branch and swam. "Don't try anything either," he said over his shoulder, "or you'll never set foot on dry land again."

After about ten minutes, they reached an isle covered in bronzed willow trees. Varkis and Lily caught up with them as Ian and Mike stood on the shore, peeling weeds and leeches off, and shaking out some of the water clogging their clothes. Mike explained to him about the puppeteer.

Varkis climbed onto shore on all fours and barred his teeth, growling, but Ian raised a hand. "Leave him be. He saved my life."

Lily gave Mike a wary look. "Can we trust him?"

"He was possessed by one of Morack's crea-tures. It used him like a puppet. But it seems to be gone now." Ian let out a long exhale, relieved beyond measure to have Lily by his side again. "We haven't time to discuss it. It'll be dark soon and I don't want to spend the night in this swamp." He was beginning to doubt Kurik was ahead of them. There'd been no sign of him.

"Are there any more of those eels out there?" Mike asked.

"Don't think so. He's the only one I brought here years back and they can't reproduce without a mate." Ian ran both hands through his wet hair. "Let's get to the Jubaka tree, and then get the heck out of here."

In the center of the tiny island, cloaked by the willows, was a grouping of six trees which formed a perimeter around a clearing. The trunks were transparent and fireworks of all colors exploded continuously within them. The coniferous boughs blotted out the colors from any plane that might fly overhead.

It was like a mini carnival in the middle of a shrouded swamp.

There was no sign that anyone had been here either. No tracks leading up to the trees, no scent of Kurik.

How was it possible that they'd beaten him to it? Was he lost?

Or was he trailing close behind, waiting for them to do the work for him?

"Are those trees from the singing forest?" Lily's whispered.

He nodded, holding her close to his side. "You stay here with Varkis and I'll go in alone to extract the acid sacs."

She grabbed his arm. "I want to come with you."

"You can't. They'll kill you."

"Who will?"

"The trees."

Her face paled and she nodded. Mike stood further back beside the waving pendant leaves of a willow, arms crossed over his chest as he kept an uncertain eye on Varkis. It was dusk now and the sky was turning blacker by the minute. Shadows filled the spaces between bushes and the fog was closing in on them, threatening to suffocate. The air was cold and damp. Ian didn't want to leave Lily alone but knew Varkis would protect her.

He left them and approached the brilliant trees, hesitating at the edge. Death lurked in the intertwining branches fifty feet above the clearing in the form of the gaping maw of the Jubaka plant. Should anyone enter the clearing, the great mouth would shoot down and shallow them whole. It was what he'd hoped would happen to Kurik.

Ian stood between two trees and looked up.

The Jubaka's mouth resembled a Venus Fly Trap: wide, flat, and rimmed with hundreds of spiky teeth.

He considered climbing one of the trees to reach it but discarded the idea. It would be too easy for the Jubaka to pluck him off the trunk. There was only one option.

Ian lunged into the clearing.

The maw came shooting out of the treetops, its long neck a mass of plaited vines. The jaws snapped shut inches from Ian's head as he dove out of the way and rolled across the dirt. Jumping to his feet, he leaped onto the Jubaka's neck, wrapping his arms and legs around it. The creature let out a cry of rage and recoiled like a spring, raising Ian high up into the treetops above.

Desperate to rid itself of him, the Jubaka thrashed about, smashing him against jutting tree branches. He struggled to hang on, clenching his teeth against the pain. And just when he thought the Jubaka was beginning to tire, it slammed him into a tree trunk. Pain coursed through his spine. Not wanting to risk a broken back, he let go.

The Jubaka opened its mouth and snatched him up in its powerful jaws.

Ian grit his teeth together, waiting to be impaled. Instead, the plant flipped up its head like a heron with a fish, and he tumbled into the throat.

The esophagus constricted, pulling him in head first.

He could barely move but struggled to reach the hunting knife in his belt. He could no longer breathe. Any minute now his ribs would be crushed.

He wrapped his fingers around the handle and withdrew the blade. With all the strength he had left, he tore at the esophagus wall, slashing it up and down, left and right. The beast roared and tried to regurgitate him, but he dug the blade in deeper, slashing repeatedly. Warm blood spurted about him, soaking his clothes and skin. He continued to cut.

The Jubaka's roar turned to a choked gurgle as the knife finally split through the throat. Ian pushed himself into the wound until it ripped open—and he fell through, plummeting to the ground.

His shoulder popped out of its socket as he collided with a hefty branch. Pain coursed through his body and he was unable to grab hold of the branch. Slipping from it, he dropped another five feet before colliding with another branch—blue blood from the Jubaka spraying down around him.

He then fell ten feet to the clearing floor, the earthy ground like cement upon impact. His knife landed a second later, the blade penetrating the ground inches from his face.

Ian lay sprawled on his back, his dislocated arm twisted beneath him, his ribs cracked. It was all he could do to breathe through the pain but he knew it wouldn't last long.

Blue blood continued to splatter the dead leaves and earth around him. He closed his eyes, imagining a warm summer rain.

"Ian!" Lily's voice pierced his drifting consciousness and he opened one eye.

Lily, Mike and Varkis were hurrying towards him.

Already the pain was decreasing as his body grew numb mending itself.

"I'm fine," he said, bright lights flickering before his eyes as he struggled to his feet, brushing leaves and blue goop from his clothing with his good arm. "Varkis, can you give me a hand popping this arm back in place?"

Varkis probed Ian's shoulder with his fingers, bent his elbow, and rotated his arm and shoulder in towards his chest. Then, keeping Ian's upper arm against his side, he rotated his shoulder and forearm outwards. Ian's brow beaded with sweat and he grit his teeth against the pain.

Varkis' long, dog-like tongue slid over his lips as he focused on the most difficult part of the task. Gripping Ian's wrist, he pushed slowly, forcing the shoulder back into its socket with a sickening pop.

Ian relaxed. "Thanks," he said gratefully, rotating his arm to see that it was working right. He retrieved his knife and put it into his belt. "You must have done this before, Varkis."

"Many times."

"Are you hurt anywhere else?" Lily asked, touching his shoulder and searching his gaze.

He shook his head and looked up into the tree branches. "Not anymore."

"Is it dead?" Lily asked.

"Almost." He pointed at the nearby tree trunks. "Take a look."

Lily's eyes widened, face falling into shadow as the multicolored lights of the tree trunks faded to gray and flickered white. As the Jubaka bled to death, it was sucking the life out of the trees. Far out of sight above them, it groaned like the distant howling of a wolf.

Ian nudged them to the side. "We'd better move out of the way—"

No sooner had he spoken then the Jubaka's head slid from the branches above and fell towards them, stopping inches from the forest floor as the long neck reached its limit and went taut; looking like a pendulum in the clearing.

The Jubaka was dead.

All around them, the clear tree trunks were a greenish white, like skeletal X-rays. Soon the lights would be out completely and they'd be surrounded by darkness. Time was running out to retrieve the acid sacs.

Ian stepped up to the head, pulled the knife from his belt, and dug it into the base of the skull. He pulled back a flap of skin large enough to expose the bone just as a splash sounded in the nearby swamp.

Pausing, he went to the edge of the circular clearing, motioning for Varkis to follow, who was already on the alert.

"Can you see what's out there?" he whispered. Though Ian could see exceptionally well in the dark, Varkis' vision was nearly twice as good.

Varkis peered intently at the swamp and his lips curled back over his canine teeth. "It's your brother," he snarled, "about one hundred feet away. And he's not alone." Varkis lowered his voice so the others couldn't hear. "There appears to be two ogres surrounding him like bodyguards. Lorgans."

Ian's chest tightened.

Lorgans used to guard his father's palace. They were creatures the same height as men with muscular shoulders, protruding bellies, and mottled gray skin. Moles, warts and bumps covered their bodies and they had multiple misshapen eyes as though their faces were made of melting wax.

Ian motioned for Varkis to follow and then hurried to Lily who stood next to the Jubaka, her eyes wide. "Is it . . . him?" Her voice was the faintest of whispers.

He nodded. "We're out of time, they're too close. By the time I cut through the bone to get to the sacs, they'll have reached the clearing. We've no choice but to leave it."

What a fool—he'd played right into Kurik's hands—had nearly killed himself in vain.

Ian led Lily out of the clearing on the opposite side, with Mike and Varkis next to them. "We'll circle wide around," he instructed.

"What about Morack?" Varkis whispered fiercely. "If he's released, we'll all be doomed."

"There's no time to argue—we've got to get out of here."

Chapter 29

Lily's heart was like a rock in her chest as they made their way across the opposite side of the ever-darkening isle.

Behind them, the last of the light in the transparent trees had gone out and the night sky was settling over them like a smothering drape. Kurik surely would have seen them in its midst if the multicolored trees had remained lit.

She couldn't believe how far they'd traveled for nothing.

Ian had nearly died in his struggle against the Jubaka, and now all that effort was completely to Kurik's aide: they'd left the dead Jubaka waiting for him like a pig on a platter.

They swam across the swamp to the other side, which unlike the direction they'd come was only a short distance, and climbed out of the muck onto the solid ground of the forest floor.

When the swamp was well out of sight, Varkis spoke for the first time: "Where to now?"

Lily could only make out contours and the whites of eyes. It was a moonless night due to the clouds, and they would soon be unable to see.

"We need to find the others," Ian said. "Who

knows what Alvernian creatures are on the loose by now."

"But how will we find them?" she asked, standing stiffly, bone-chilled in her soaked clothing. She shivered. "Everything will be completely black in few minutes."

"I have pretty decent night vision," Varkis spoke decidedly. "Ian as well."

"How's that possible?" Mike's voice was low and hollow, and if Lily wasn't mistaken, deeply afraid. "Ian is human, isn't he?"

"Mike—you saw me in the vat room." There was a hint of irritation in Ian's voice, but something else as well. Embarrassment?

"Right! That ghastly face. Can you change your features completely?"

A pause.

"Yes . . . but I choose not to."

A mournful howl sounded somewhere far off —echoing in the distance. Lily grabbed for Ian's muddy hand. He held hers tightly.

"Let's keep silent," he spoke in hushed tones to the group. "Varkis will lead the way."

They moved through the forest, occasionally taking cover whenever the Anubis caught scent of something dangerous. But the time was mostly spent with Ian and Varkis helping Lily and Mike over fallen logs like helpless children, and maneuvering them around branches, boulders, shrubs, and roots.

After a half hour of this, Varkis grabbed her shoulders without warning and pushed her down.

Twigs scraped her arms as she hit the ground.

She stifled a cry. In the next second, Mike winced also as Varkis shoved him to the ground next to her with more force than necessary.

She didn't dare speak.

Ian crouched in front of them on one knee and Varkis stood with legs spread and shoulders girdled. The darkness was closed around them like a sepulcher. All she could hear was her own shallow breathing. She tried not to tremble from the cold.

A pair of glowing red orbs pierced the blackness in the distance and a chill shot down her spine.

She nearly jumped from her skin when Varkis spoke aloud: "You sure gave us a fright. Glad to see you are well."

Ian lifted her to her feet and relief coursed through her body. "Who is it?" she whispered.

"Callamous."

She gasped. "But I thought he was dead!"

The unicorn approached and became visible; his contours at least. He lay his soft muzzle against her forehead and instantly the forest lit up with indigo overtures; as though she'd donned a pair of night-goggles. It was the second time he'd done this for her; only now she knew his identity.

"There you are, my dear Lily," he said. "You can see in the dark while your enemies remain blinded." He backed away from her. "But it is only temporary."

"Thank you," she breathed. "But how—how are you alive?"

"Unless I am given an instantly fatal blow, I can heal myself. I was up and running only minutes after Kurik took you into the mansion."

She looked at Ian and where the deep slash had been across his cheek. The sides of the wound had pulled together and healed hours ago. All that remained was a jagged scar.

In contrast, the unicorn's body was sleek and unmarred, not a single scar to be found.

"Why don't you heal as fully as Callamous?" she asked Ian. "I mean, why do you scar?"

He met her eyes and held her gaze.

"Because of you, Lily," he said finally. "That's why my father, brother and all his minions have limited powers on earth. Callamous is not one of my father's followers. All good creatures can perform their magic in its fullness in *your* presence, but evil can not—or at least, is greatly diminished in power."

She protested: "But you're not evil!"

"I am Morack's son. He put a curse on Kurik and I. Even though I can heal myself, the scars are to remind me of my failures. He said if I didn't learn to protect myself and become a skilled fighter, I'd eventually become horribly disfigured."

"—Morack is of the purest evil, if those two words can even be used in conjunction," Callamous cut in with his thunderous voice. "Lily—have you thought about what I said to you earlier?"

She glanced around the forest. Not a creature in sight. Mike was busying himself trying to look like he wasn't listening, but he wasn't fooling anyone. His eyes continually darted in her direction, as though he'd forgotten she had night vision.

"Do you mean whether I could sacrifice one to

save the lives of many?" she asked, wrapping her arms around herself for warmth, trying not to tremble with mild hypothermia. The unicorn nodded.

Her throat tightened. "I don't know if I'm capable of making such a decision. Especially if it's—" She willed herself not to look at Ian. "If it's . . . someone I care for." She focused on the ground and blinked back tears. She knew it then.

It was Ian.

Callamous expected her to kill Ian.

"What are you talking about, Lily?" Varkis snapped. "The lives of thousands, even hundreds of thousands, depend on you. If you don't kill Morack and anyone that stands in the way of that—we *all* die."

Her cheeks grew hot and her heart heaved within her chest. She could barely breathe. "Who's to say I'm even capable of killing? I'm no fighter, I have no training. This whole thing is just—insane!"

"You're the only one who can do it," Varkis said gravely. "Morack will be stripped of some of his magic in your presence, not ours. I'm not sure how you'll do it, but you're our only hope."

She was angry now. "You ask too much of me, all of you. There's no way I could kill an innocent person—"

Ian stepped forward and cupped her cheeks in his warm hands, wiping her tears with his thumbs. "Lily, you're so much stronger than you realize."

She buried her face in the crook of his shoulder and he held her tight.

Varkis cleared his throat and she broke the

embrace, skirting a circular glance through the forest to make sure they were still alone.

She took a deep breath but stumbled with sudden vertigo. She staggered a few steps backward as the trees swirled around her. What was happening? White noise filled her ears. Mike fell to the ground next to her and Varkis gripped his head in his hands. Then, just when she thought she was going to lose consciousness, she caught her footing again, and the dizziness vanished almost as fast as it had come.

Ian and Callamous stood stolidly nearby as though neither had been affected.

"What was that?" She lifted her fingertips to her temples and blinked several times.

"What was what?" Ian's eyes were wide.

Mike scrambled to his feet and groped around in the dark.

"Sudden dizziness," Varkis said, knitting his brow. "Like a passing cloud. It was here one second, gone the next."

Callamous flared his nostrils and scanned the area. "We need to keep moving. Three of our supporters have been killed already."

"What did you say?" Ian faced the unicorn squarely.

"I said three of our supporters have been killed already. More and more of Morack's followers are pouring out of the trunk as we speak, and there's no way to stop it. We've been fighting a bloody battle in the cover of the forest all day long and so far there are more casualties on their side—but as their numbers increase, our losses will too. We have no reinforcements."

Ian rubbed the back of his neck, exhaled. "We need to get the keys back from Kurik."

The unicorn nodded. "If it isn't already too late." His nostrils flared again. "I suggest Varkis take Lily back to the mansion, and you and I will hunt down your brother. Keep them separated as long as possible. He'll be making his way back from the island."

Ian shook his head. "No, we need to rest first. I'm so done." He rubbed his eyes, muddy swamp water dried and caked on his hands. He sat down on a boulder.

"I really don't think that's wise. We shouldn't waste another second." The unicorn's voice had dropped to a low growl.

"Especially considering Kurik has the acid necessary to free your father now—" Mike cut in, a pointed look on his face, though he faced a tree rather than Ian.

"Shut-up, Mike." Ian's patience was clearly wearing thin; anger flashed in his eyes. "Maybe I'd like a little nap before my inevitable death." He sounded exhausted and bitter.

Deflated.

Did he know?

"Look," Varkis growled, "as much as we'd all like a nap, if we just sit around, Kurik will find us and kill us in our sleep. Is that what you want?"

Ian dropped his hands to his side and began to walk away from them. "Suit yourself," he said over his shoulder. "I'll catch ya later."

"This makes no sense, you're being completely unreasonable," Varkis snarled, the skin pulling back over his canine incisors. "This isn't like you. What—are you a coward now?"

Ian paused and looked back at the dog-man.

"There's no time to rest—" Varkis continued. "You of all people should know that."

"Look, I don't see your hide on the sacrificial altar. I nearly killed myself wrestling a giant eel and fighting the Jubaka tree, and all I did was make it easy for Kurik. I'm an idiot. I've been to hell and back for you guys more times than I count and it's obviously not enough—"

The hair rose on the back of Varkis' shoulders, a growl in his throat. "What are you talking about? Any of us could die. We're all willing to lay down our lives for the cause—" His eyes were blazing now. "Are you hiding something from us?"

Lily took several steps back as they argued, her limbs stiff like ice. Nausea filled her throat.

Callamous stamped his hoof and threw his shoulders back, eyes fierce and voice booming: "If you want to cower under a bush for the night, so be it. I'll go after Kurik myself."

Ian's mouth quivered and contorted as two long fangs emerged from his top jaw. Lily stifled a scream. "Don't make me fight you, Callamous," he hissed.

"The man I know would never stop to sleep on the job. There is too much at stake. You do not want to *die* to save earth, is that it? What are you planning—to slip off and return to Alvernia, leaving us all behind?"

"Ian," Lily interrupted, trying to soothe him. "We're just confused by your sudden change of heart. If you would help us understand . . ." She walked forward and touched his shoulder, hoping to soothe him —but his eyes turned to black pools. She recoiled. "Please," she said. "You're losing control of yourself! Please calm down."

His lips curled back over the fangs. "Why am I going to all this trouble to help some wench who's just going to kill me in the end?" His voice was hard and cold now, drained of all passion.

Varkis stepped in front of her in a protective stance. "Think this through, Ian," he said. "This isn't you. What about your mother? I thought you wanted to avenge her death and save everyone else from harm."

"Don't ever talk of my mother again." The flesh on his face began rippling as though hundreds of bugs crawled beneath it.

Lily stood frozen in place, unable to breathe.

"You don't want us mentioning your mother?" Callamous pawed the ground, nostrils flaring. "Well —I'm not afraid to. Now that the time has come to show what you're made of, you've chosen to be a selfish coward. You spit on your mother's grave."

"I said not-to-talk-about-my-mother."

"Why? Because it hurts your conscience?"

Ian lunged at Callamous.

"Run you three," the unicorn warned. "Get out of here!"

Before she could stop to think, Varkis had

thrown Lily over his shoulder and was racing through the forest with Mike chasing after them blindly, one hand clinging to Lily's shirt. She pounded on the dog-man's shoulder, begging him to set her free but he ignored her, whipping through tree boughs as Mike struggled to hang on.

The last thing she saw, craning her neck, was Callamous rearing on his hind legs as Ian withdrew a dagger from his belt.

Chapter 30

Ian stepped away from Callamous as his fangs retracted and his eyes returned to normal. He exhaled loudly and rubbed his aching jaw. "Do you think it worked?" he asked.

The unicorn nodded solemnly. "Yes. I looked into her eyes as Varkis ran off. Her heart was most certainly broken."

Ian looked away, pretending to stretch his shoulders and shake out his arms. He didn't want Callamous to read his eyes too. Deceiving Lily was the last thing he wanted to do, but he and Callamous had agreed to it telepathically while she, Mike, and Varkis underwent a dizzy spell. They decided that the only way Lily would be willing to kill him was to make her think him a traitor—or at least deranged. She must believe that he had abandoned them and lost all self-control. Otherwise they ran the risk that she would try to protect him and be unwilling to defeat Morack.

"So, I guess it's best if you go back and join the others now," Ian said, scanning the forest around them. "Make sure they're safe for the night."

Callamous nodded. "I'll tell them I barely escaped death at your hands and that you've gone to join forces with Kurik."

"Yeah, say whatever you need to convince her. I don't want her to be half-hearted about it—she needs to really believe that I've turned. I don't want her to feel any regret about what she has to do. A broken heart is better than guilt."

"Take care of yourself," Callamous said softly.

Ian squared his shoulders and took a deep breath. "It's about time I faced Kurik once and for all."

"And what about the Lorgans?"

"If Kurik wants to prove he's a better fighter than me—which I've no doubt he will—then he won't call on the Lorgans to aid him."

"Is he a better fighter?"

Ian laughed bitterly. "Not a chance." He turned away from the unicorn.

"Good-bye, Ian."

Ian retraced his steps back to the swamp.

With his limited night vision, he followed the fringe of the swamp, looking for tracks in the mud. Too much time had passed for Kurik to still be within the swamp—by now he was probably well on his way back to the mansion if not already there. If Kurik had been by himself, tracing him in the dark would be next to impossible, but not with two heavy-footed Lorgans at his side.

Ian found the tracks he was looking for within

minutes and traced them through the trampled forest. He heard nothing but hoped he was gaining on them quickly.

He reached his workshop tree and took the trail to the greensward.

No sight or sound of the Lorgans nearby.

Was he too late?

He rounded the final bend in the forest trail.

"Why hello, Ian," came a voice like a bogy.

Kurik stood next to the first empty gargoyle pedestal at the edge of the forest, his face masked by the hood of his duster cloak. Like the Grim Reaper.

He gripped something in his gloved hand at his side.

A large rock.

"Father always liked you better," he snarled. "No matter what I did he was quick to remind me that you, five years my younger, were more powerful." With a cry of fury, he whipped the rock at Ian with incredible strength.

Ian dove to the ground, rolling, as the earth where he'd stood exploded with the impact of the rock, leaving behind a muddy crater.

"You don't have to do this," he said, scrambling back to his feet. "We can fight our father together—we can destroy him."

"And then die with him? No thanks."

Kurik snatched a dagger from beneath his cloak and threw it at Ian within the same second.

Ian dove to the right as the dagger grazed his shoulder. He leaped to his feet and charged toward Kurik, intending to plow him down, but Kurik turned and planted his elbow squarely in Ian's stomach, thrusting him over his shoulder. Ian somersaulted in the air and landed on his back with a loud crack.

He struggled to catch his breath as Kurik ran to a nearby tree and tore a thick branch from the trunk with supernatural strength. Ian winced and clutched his chest. His ribs were cracked again.

Kurik approached slowly this time, his face hidden in the shadow of his hood. With both hands, he lifted the branch high above his head, ready to strike.

Clenching his teeth against the pain, Ian rolled to the side as the branch hit the earth and splintered in half.

"Wait—" he said, jumping up. "Let's end this madness. I don't want to kill you."

Kurik roared with laughter, eyes glinting through the shadows. "You think you're going to kill *me*?" A slight pause. "Well, you'll have to catch me first . . . " He turned on his heel and darted into the forest, out of sight.

"This isn't a game—" Ian shouted after him; without following.

He stood in the sudden silence, waiting, muscles taut. There was no way he would follow Kurik into the trees. He took a deep breath and winced. Come on ribs, hurry it up.

Sweat beaded his brow and his spine prickled. He dare not let his guard down for a second.

A rush at his side, like a gust of wind, and Kurik raced out from the trees, pelting two large stones at him.

Ian dove to the side but one rock made impact with his thigh, cracking the femur. He cried out and fell to ground.

Kurik had vanished again.

He was like a cat, circling the injured mouse, batting at it with his claws; drawing out the kill to add to his pleasure.

Ian pulled himself up, favoring his good leg. "Stop hiding," he growled. "Show yourself and fight me like a man."

Silence answered him and he struggled to focus, blinking, head swimming. He ran the back of his hand over his forehead and took several panting gulps of air. His ribs were healed but his thigh was burning like fire.

A rustle at his right side and a fist came at his face.

With a jerk, he managed to sidestep the blow, and chopped Kurik on the back of his neck.

Kurik staggered a few feet away, gripping his neck. "You'll pay for that," he hissed, charging afresh.

Ian braced himself, unable to run on his wounded leg, and tried to dodge the blows with dips and dives. Outright blocking them wasn't an option, unless he wanted shattered forearms.

The first blow to make impact flooded his body with so much pain, he wasn't even sure where he'd been hit. White light filled his vision and he staggered backward, crying out from the pain in his thigh. A second blow sent him flying backward, slamming into the grass and grinding to a halt two meters away.

Momentarily paralyzed, Ian lay sprawled on

his back, watching helplessly as his brother approached.

Kurik knelt down beside him, leaned down and whispered in his ear: "I wonder if Auguste thought it was you who tried to kill him that night. He was old and his vision was poor. Can you imagine if he died thinking the boy he raised as his own son had scared him to death in cold blood?" A laugh, his breath hot against Ian's ear. "I want to watch your face as you die, knowing that you failed both Auguste and your precious Lily."

Rage surged through Ian's body like an electric shock of adrenaline, numbing the pain and revitalizing his limbs. He narrowed his eyes but made no move.

Kurik stood to his full height and drew his sword. "This was way too easy," he said with tone of regret. "I'll make sure I take more time killing Ms. Kline."

He lifted the sword and would have driven it through Ian's heart, but Ian rolled to the side and jumped to his feet just as the blade plunged deep into the earth. The brief time on his back had enabled the crack in his femur to finish mending, though his right shoulder felt disjointed. Kurik cried out, letting go of the sword—and in one swift movement, Ian wrenched the sword from the ground and swung it at his brother's neck.

Kurik ducked his head and raised his arm high in defense, causing the blade to slice into his side between his ribs. If not for Ian's damaged shoulder, which reduced his strength and precision, Kurik would have been sliced in half.

Kurik twisted away from the sword, the blade wrenching free, and clutched the wound in his hands, blood spurting between his gloved fingers. He wheezed for air with a punctured lung, knees buckling.

"Please brother," he gasped, "don't kill me—"

Ian stepped forward, lifting the crimson blade to Kurik's throat.

"I have not the strength left to fight," Kurik said, bowing his cloaked head forward in defeat. "You've won . . . "

The heavy sword trembled in Ian's grip, pain screaming in his shoulder, his grip slackening.

He wavered.

Evidently sensing the hesitation, Kurik dropped down and grabbed Ian's ankles, flipping him off his feet. The sword dislodged from his grasp and hit the ground. Ian tried to grab it but his fingers closed over air as Kurik snatched it with a screech of triumph.

"You're such a fool," he howled, swinging the sword toward Ian's neck. "Time to die!"

Lily's face flashed before his eyes and he ducked, swinging his leg out at the same time. Kurik fell backward, his feet swept out from beneath him, but didn't drop the sword—instead he held it out in front like a shield.

With his last ounce of strength, Ian pounced onto his brother, pinning him to the ground as the blade went through his own abdomen and out the back. He let out an involuntary scream but forced himself to remain focused as stars blotted his vision.

He opened his mouth wide as his fangs appeared. Before the stunned Kurik could make another move, he embedded his fangs deep in his brother's throat—injecting venom into the carotid artery.

Kurik's face twisted in agony and surprise, eyes wide with horror as he let out a silent cry. There was no way his body could heal itself fast enough now. The acid-like venom ate through his veins and arteries, dissolving flesh and bones in a matter of seconds. He gagged and spit out blood as his skin turned purple, then gray; his body withering. With a final gasp, the light went out in his eyes as they shrunk and shriveled into his skull.

Ian pushed himself up and over, falling onto his side. He tore the sword from his abdomen, fangs retracting and vanishing.

Trembling all over from the mortal wound, he crawled away from his brother's deflated, mummified body, and soon lost all consciousness.

Chapter 31

Lily sat with her back against a furrowed log, huddled in silence with Mike, Varkis, Callamous, and six gargoyles. They sat resting in a circle under the cover of the forest, waiting for the next command from Callamous, who had joined them a little while ago, much to their relief. Another six gargoyles stood watch nearby. They had no torches but continued to see with the night vision provided by the unicorn.

It was raining lightly now, helping to wash some of the stench of the swamp from their skin, and they were able to cup their hands and drink from the gathering puddles of rainwater.

All she could think about was Ian.

How could he have turned on them like that? Her whole body ached with the memory of his betrayal. Would she ever see him again?

A terrible cry sounded far in the distance.

Callamous lifted his head in the direction of the sound.

"One of Morack's creatures?" she whispered.

"I don't think so," Varkis snarled. "Sounded human."

"Hush—" said Callamous, eyes darkening with an emotion more like grief than anger. "Stay right where you are. I will go."

"Hannah, we must leave this place at once." The Orealas huddled together, begging the housekeeper to listen.

"But—how can I leave when Ian and Lily are still out there?" She paced back and forth in the narrow secret passageway at the back of the mansion where they'd been hiding for several hours. Its cobwebbed interior was suffused by faint light radiating from the three Orealas.

Minutes ago they'd heard a monstrous whoop of triumph from the direction of the web-covered vat on the floor above them.

"We still have no idea what made that sound," Hannah whispered fiercely. "It might be nothing at all."

"It's him," the Orealas cried together in the faintest of whispers.

"I told you—it's *Morack*," explained the head Oreala, Miriam, for the second time, her voice calmer than the rest. "They have failed in their mission and he is free. We can not protect you from him. We must leave at once."

"I can't leave without Ian," Hannah said, crossing her arms over her chest.

"Ian would want us to get you out of here safely, Hannah—you must know that."

"At least let me look out back one more time,

just to make sure they aren't trying to get in. They should be here by now."

"There are many secret entrances to the mansion—Ian knows all of them."

"Just humor me—please. You're asking me to leave behind the man I love as my own son. At least let me have one last look."

"It's too dangerous."

Hannah stamped her foot. "I will have one last look at the backyard or I will fight you every step of the way. You'll have to carry me out!"

"Keep your voice down," Miriam hissed, her patience clearly waning. "I'll allow you one peek, then we must go."

They headed down the passageway with a muffled tread and stopped behind the back of a portrait painting to wait and listen. After a few minutes, Hannah let the painting swing out an inch, and peered into the hall to make sure the way was clear. If anyone saw her there'd be no escape.

But the corridor was empty.

They climbed out into the hall one by one and shut the painting behind them, scurrying as a group past Auguste's study, and went to the back entrance doors.

Callamous burst out of the forest onto the greensward, knowing the scream had come from Ian.

He came to a halt next to the maiden fountain;

the one statue on the property that was truly a statue. The grass and earth around it were scuffed up, and blood polluted the rain puddles—looking like an oil spill with his night vision.

But there were no bodies.

Callamous surveyed the shadowy yard for any lurking intruders.

He sniffed the chill autumn air. Ian was nearby. There seemed to be a dark mound of something lying on the ground near the corner of the mansion on the right-hand side. He perked his ears and strutted forward, hooves slurping in the muddy grass. The coppery smell of blood temporarily overtook all other scents and his nostrils flared with disgust.

He drew close enough to see the mound clearly.

On the ground before him lay a skeletal corpse that looked like it had been dead for many weeks. Its whole face was shriveled up, there were no eyes in the sockets, and its mouth was open in a silent scream.

I'm too late—

Something else caught his eye, around the corner of the building.

He stepped around the corpse and approached a second body.

All hopes of saving Ian left him fully.

Ian lay on his back in the waterlogged grass, lips slightly parted and eyes half open staring blankly into the night sky. His face was gray.

Callamous dipped his nose down to investigate further. There was a gaping hole in his gut and a bloodied sword lay on the ground a few feet away.

"Your suffering is over now, Ian," he whispered, flicking his damp mane and letting out a snort of sorrow. "Rest in peace, dear friend. You did what you came to do and now Kurik is dead. I applaud you. I will take care of Lily now."

Ian's bottom lip quivered.

Callamous stiffened. Was it . . . possible?

He lowered his muzzle to Ian's neck, checking for a pulse. Ian's skin was like ice but a faint pulse beat against his snout—so weak it could have been the kiss of a butterfly. Ian was probably within seconds of death. There was no way his healing abilities could repair such advanced damage within enough time to save him.

Without a second thought, Callamous lay down next to Ian and draped his snout over Ian's impaled midsection. He closed his eyes, breathing steadily in and out.

The outer flesh of Ian's gouged abdomen crawled back together like fingers—interlocking, sealing, shutting. Color began to seep into his hands and up his neck.

Weakness engulfed Callamous' body and he broke contact with Ian.

The healing wasn't complete but it was all the life energy he could spare without killing himself in the process.

Ian would have to do the rest.

The unicorn rose on unsteady hooves and staggered a few steps as though drunk, looking down at Ian to survey the remaining damage. His lips were no longer gray and there was breath in his lungs now, though he hadn't yet regained consciousness. There were probably extensive internal injuries but Callamous was confident Ian could now finish healing on his own.

A movement caught his eye.

The back door to the mansion opened a crack.

Hannah peeked out.

The greensward was black, the moon hidden behind an overcast night sky. She opened the door a little further. There was a form, a body, lying on the ground a couple of meters away from her.

A crash sounded in the mansion from an upper level.

Two of the Orealas squealed in fright and barreled out of the mansion, pushing the door open all the way and nearly knocking Hannah to the ground. She hurried after them.

"Quick, close the door," Miriam hissed to the others, "but do it quietly—don't draw attention to us. We'll circle around the estate and make a run for the road!"

Hannah didn't wait to see if the Orealas closed the door or not—she was certain she'd seen something looming nearby.

Two red orbs hovered far above the ground.

If those were eyes, the owner must be massive.

"What—is that?"

Miriam grabbed Hannah's wrist. "Run," she whispered hoarsely.

"No." Hannah jerked her hand free and withdrew a gun from the waistband of her skirt. "What if that's Ian or Lily lying on the ground over there?"

Miriam put a hand out to stop Hannah. "Stop. Let me."

The Head Oreala stepped forward in the direction of the glowing orbs. "Show yourself, creature of the night," she said loud and clear. "Are you a friend or foe?"

"I'm neither your friend nor your foe," came a deep, gravelly voice. "But I recognize you as Ian's comrades. Therefore, I will not kill you."

"Oh, for goodness sake," Hannah said with a huff, stepping forward. "If you don't want to be a friend, that's fine with me—I have plenty. All I care about is whether that is Ian or Lily over there." She pointed at the shadowy mound on the grass, too far for her to see clearly.

"You would do well to shut your trap, woman, before you draw all of Morack's creatures to your side," the gravelly voice continued. "They have the hearing ability of wolves."

"Woman!" she gasped, ignoring his warning. "I have never been treated with such disrespect—"

"Hannah, shush," Miriam whispered, putting a hand on her shoulder. "He's right—we're being much too noisy."

Hannah snorted. "All this talk of monsters and I've yet to see a single one."

"Then what am I?" the creature said, stepping forward out of the darkness.

Hannah's hands went limp at her side and she nearly dropped the handgun.

It was like an otherworldly Black Beauty, its jaws open from ear-to-ear exposing jagged thorn-like teeth, and no flesh at all on its skull. It stared down at her like a Gytrash steed, ready to cart her off to hell.

Miriam clamped a hand over Hannah's mouth, stifling her scream, and wrapped her other arm around her, pinning her in place. Hannah struggled to break free. Her elderly heart pounded against the prison walls of her chest and she struggled to breathe.

"It's a unicorn, "Miriam whispered, "one of the most dangerous and respected creatures in Alvernia." She didn't let go but turned to address the creature. "So, what are you doing here, Great Unicorn? And whose body is that over yonder? Is it dead or alive?"

"My name is Callamous," it said, "and I'm here to help the girl, Lily, destroy Morack." His eyes flashed. "Forget about the body. The one you care about is over there, around the side." He gestured to the right side of the mansion. "Ian."

Hannah squealed behind Miriam's soft hand and struggled once more. *Ian, no, not Ian!*

"I'll let you go," Miriam said gently, "but you have to promise to stay still and be quiet."

She nodded her head, acquiescing, and Miriam let go.

The terror Hannah had felt at the sight of the

338

unicorn was long gone with the overwhelming fear that Ian was dead. Every bone in her body ached to rush forward but she stood stock still, looking at the unicorn; waiting for a cue to proceed.

"His brother did this," said the unicorn, gesturing from them to follow with a toss of his snout. "Kurik."

"I'll kill him," she growled, plunging forward and slipping on the wet grass. She windmilled her arms to keep upright.

"Already done," said Callamous calmly. "That's Kurik's dead body back there."

Hannah continued her advance, this time with cautious steps; squishy in the grass. She reached the unconscious form of Ian and dropped to her knees, oblivious to the icy rainwater soaking her skirt. She took his hand in her own and held it to her cheek. It was warm. His eyes were closed, breathing labored.

"Ian? It's me, Hannah." She could barely make out his features in the dark. "Are you with me?" she asked, running a loving hand over his cheek. Her fingers touched something rough and bumpy. She recoiled, gasping. "What happened?"

"A knife wound," the unicorn answered. "It happened many hours ago and is healed. But the scarring is extensive."

Him being alive was all that mattered. And with his fortune he could easily hire the best plastic surgeons to repair his face if need be. If he'd let them of course. But if not, she'd get used to his new face and love him just the same.

"We need to get going," said the unicorn. "We

need to get him out of the open."

"Yes," said Miriam in a hushed tone, looking up at the mansion. "Morack may soon be upon us."

The unicorn's body went rigid. "What do you mean."

"I'm almost certain I heard him in the mansion just a couple of minutes ago."

"But that's impossible—Ian stopped Kurik just in time. Unless . . . Quick—check the body for the keys to the trunk, and the Jubaka's venom."

Miriam went to the shriveled corpse and rifled through the pockets. She let out a squeal of delight. "The keys! I've got the keys."

The unicorn snorted in apparent relief. "Great. And the venom sacs?"

She continued her search and then stood, wiping her hands on the side of her gown. "There is nothing else."

Callamous stamped his hoof in evident frustration, splashing rainwater on their skirts. "Curses!" His eyes flared an even brighter red. "Morack is indeed free." He clenched his thorny teeth together and narrowed his eyes into slits.

"What can we do?" asked Miriam.

"Go lock the trunk—but be very careful." He glared up at the mansion, his voice low and murderous. "Try not to be seen or heard by anyone or anything. Use the secret passageways and keep your tread as soft as silk. I must get back to Lily immediately now that Morack is free."

"Wait—don't leave us," Hannah cut in, breathless, chest heaving. "We need your help to protect Ian. I can't lift him myself."

He shook his mane regretfully. "Would that I could. Ian's survival is up to you now, I've done all that I can. Ms. Kline is the priority." With that he turned and galloped.

Chapter 82

Hannah wrung her hands, startling at every little sound. The mansion loomed high and dark behind her. Every shadow seemed to move. If Morack was on the loose in there, what on earth was he doing? Was he standing at one of the upper windows, peering down at them? She dared not return indoors.

"Come, ladies," she whispered, afraid to raise her voice now that the knightly unicorn had left. "If we get Ian out of the open and warmed up, his body will heal faster. We need to take him to his tree house, it's the only place I can think of." She dared not think of what would happen if the tree was occupied when they got there. But by what? As yet, the only so-called creature she'd seen was the unicorn. Were there many more such things out and about, or were they all contained within the mansion? And as to who or what Morack was, she hadn't the first clue.

"No," Miriam said firmly. "We'd never make it there in one piece. The trail is probably heavily guarded by now by Morack's troops. I say we take the young man into the side forest over there and shelter him under our wings until the rain stops. Once I am assured of his health and safety, I will find a way to get to the trunk."

With quiet and painstaking efforts, they dragged Ian into the neighboring forest, away from the back yard, and nowhere near the trail that led to his workshop.

Hannah and the Orealas huddled in the cover of low tree branches just out of sight of the mansion, Ian lying between them. It was nearly dawn and the sky was beginning to lighten. Soon they'd be able to see again. Ian was as pale as ever but his chest was rising and falling steadily as he breathed.

Hannah held his hand in her own and gave it a gentle squeeze, gasping when he squeezed it back.

"Ian!"

His eyes flickered open and focused on her face.

"Where am I?" He winced.

"In the forest on the west side of the mansion."

He groaned and struggled to sit up. She pressed down on his shoulders. "Don't move, you've been severely injured," she said.

"No kidding. I feel like I swallowed a grenade." His voice was garbled but gaining strength. "What happened? How did I get here?"

"We found you in the backyard, nearly dead, with a unicorn named Callamous. He said your brother did this to you."

Understanding lit his eyes. "My brother . . .

yes, I remember now. I must get to him—"

"Ian, I don't think you realize how badly wounded you are," said the head Oreala. "You need to rest longer. If you're worried about the keys to the trunk, I already have them. I'm sorry to say, however, that Morack has been freed."

He groaned and closed his eyes, resting his head back on a pile of dead leaves. "I was too late. I have failed."

"It's okay, Ian," Hannah soothed. "Callamous is going to take care of it."

"No. You need to go with the Orealas and get as far away from the mansion as you can. Now that it's dawn, you aren't safe hiding here anymore. They'll see you through the trees, if they haven't already."

"I'm not leaving you."

"For crying out loud, Hannah, why do you always have to be so stubborn?" He tried to sit up but was too weak.

"You would do the same for me."

He let out a ragged exhale and rubbed his face.

Miriam and the other two Orealas withdrew their overarching wings and folded them behind them. Miriam made moves to leave. "I must get to the trunk now," she said gravely. "Moya," she said to one of the Orealas, "you stay and take care of Hannah and pray I'll be successful in my mission." She turned to the other: "Mae, come with me."

Lily glanced from the dog-man, the unicorn, and Mike, to the group of misfit gargoyles. A sudden affection filled her breast and temporarily eclipsed her grief; though it swelled back as quickly as it had ebbed.

Callamous had returned to the group to inform them that while Kurik was dead, Morack had already been released. They pressed him for details on Kurik's death and who had done it, and whether there was any sign of Ian, but he was evasive on all fronts. There was no time for her to reflect on this either, however, because soon after his arrival, a gargoyle ran up to them on all fours and spoke in hushed tones with Varkis.

"Lily," Varkis approached her. "One of our messengers has just returned with word from the mansion."

"Is it too much to hope that Morack has decided to surrender?" Her voice trembled, the chill from her damp clothes and bewildered heart threatening to take over. She didn't know how much longer she could continue.

His amber eyes flashed. "I wish it were that simple. We've received a challenge from Morack. It is to be a fight to the death."

"Do you mean to tell me he's just sitting at the mansion waiting for us, twiddling his thumbs?"

He nodded. "Yes. That about sums it up."

She willed her heart to be numb and lifted her chin. "What are our chances of winning?"

"Next to nil. If any of us knew how to kill Morack, we would've done it long ago. It's up to you,

I'm afraid. The best we can do is try to fight off his followers for you, so you'll have a chance to go straight for him."

She said nothing.

"Just remember that Serena was your grandmother," he went on, evidently trying to bolster her courage. "I know you never met her, but you must have some of her power. Neither Morack or his followers can practice their magic fully while you are here—they're hindered, weakened. That's huge. There must be some sort of power emanating from you."

"I don't feel any," she said. "I've never been lucky in life and nothing strange has ever happened until I came to this mansion. I don't feel any different from anyone else."

"But how would you know? You've never lived in anyone else's shoes. You could feel completely different from them and never know it."

"I don't even have a weapon," she added feebly.

"If you had one, he'd just take it from you and use it on you."

"But what if I approach him and he just kills me on the spot. Then what?"

"Then he'll take over the earth, just as he did Alvernia. This is our one chance to get him while his numbers on earth are still relatively low. Even by tomorrow, it will probably be hopeless. We must act now."

She sighed, shook her head. "It just feels hopeless. A suicide mission."

He said nothing but his eyes seemed to agree.

"Well, let's get this over with," she said in a monotone. "It's time for me to fight the most dangerous warlord ever known—without a single weapon or plan. Genius."

Chapter 33

Miriam and Mae scanned the stone walkway between the shelter of the willow trees and the west side of the mansion, before taking gingerly steps toward it.

They reached the walkway and crossed it, glancing from side to side. Some birds flitted to and fro but there appeared to be no one around; at least, no one who was making their presence known. Miriam hoped against hope they wouldn't be spotted or followed.

She tried the knob of the scullery door and finding it unlocked, cracked the door open two inches; peering inside. A cold, stagnant breeze wafted out and goosebumps rose on her skin. Seeing nothing but a shadowy kitchen, she stepped in and shut the door once Mae had followed her in. Together, they passed through the room with feathery steps and peeked out into the dining room. Confident nothing of any great size could be hidden under the great table without being visible, she went past it and straight for a life-size gilded painting next to the China cabinet.

Something dark moved in her periphery and she spun around, heart pounding. But it was only Mae's shadow. Mae raised an eyebrow but said nothing. With a deep breath, Miriam pushed on the bottom corner of the painting, moving aside as it swung open. They dipped inside and pulled the frame shut behind them, blinking at one another in the darkness.

They then moved down the musty passageway, one in front of the other, palms outward and wings folded behind them. They turned right, went straight a distance; and stopped at what Miriam knew was the front entrance of the mansion.

A thump and growl sounded on the other side of the wall, and for a second, a pin-stripe of light from a minuscule hole in the wall vanished as something moved in front of it. When the stripe returned, she put an eye to the hole.

A gargoyle was rolling across the floor biting and clawing at a giant beetle that had jaws like a lamprey and was latched to his shoulder. She wished she could help the gargoyle, but couldn't risk drawing attention to herself.

She watched a moment longer as he managed to break free and bolt down the corridor on all fours with the beetle chasing after him. Feeling for a wooden ladder, she climbed to the next level, which was the bedroom of the handyman, Mike. Mae followed closely behind.

There was no way to access the attic except through Auguste's painting and they had no choice but to leave the passageway they were in and enter the hallway. After looking through a peephole and seeing no sign of life, the two Orealas stepped out from behind a tapestry and braced themselves for attack.

Mae let out a gasp.

Many of the paintings in the hall were shredded by claws and the wooden banisters were split and gnawed on as if by beavers. Trestle tables and potted plants were overturned, and blood and soil soaked the rug here and there, as well as clumps of fur. The hidden entrance to the attic was already open.

Without further delay, they scooted toward it —just as a crash sounded from below.

Stale air emanated from the dark opening. For all they knew, they'd be meeting their deaths on the winding staircase as some newly escaped beast descended, but it was the only possible way to reach the trunk.

They hurried inside, darting glances behind them lest anything should be on its way up to the second floor, and Miriam pressed the button to slide the door shut behind them; gambling there'd be nothing hiding in the darkness surrounding them.

The only sound in the stuffy room was their heavy breathing. Miriam took a deep breath to steady her nerves. If a creature was there behind the wooden stairs, surely they'd at least be able to smell it.

Miriam moved forward to the first stair and stepped onto it lightly, wincing as it let out a creak. She stiffened but forced herself to ascend. Mae followed two steps behind. At the bend in the stairs a full step was missing, leaving a gaping hole in its splintered wake. If not for the checkered light from the lattice window above, Miriam would have fallen through.

She reached the top and exhaled with relief to

find the landing bare.

But what if someone stood guard behind the attic door, or what if something was even now emerging from the trunk?

They moved to the door on tiptoes and Miriam tried the handle.

It opened slowly, stiffly, with a groan.

The trunk lid lay wide open, a bright light shining forth and illuminating even the darkest corners of the long room.

But other than storage, the room was empty.

Warmth flooded her body but her back remained rigid. She didn't dare let down her guard. Mae stood guard by the door as Miriam went forward and leaned over the trunk.

A mouth rimmed with hundreds of needle-like teeth snapped shut on air as she jerked backward.

The creature tried to wiggle its way through the opening, snarling and slobbering, but its hairy shoulders were too wide.

Miriam darted to the opposite wall, legs shaking and palms sweating as she gripped her skirt in her hands, wondering what to do. The beast thrashed back and forth, braying, and managed to pull its right forelimb through. It paused to stare at her with hungry yellow eyes and then resumed its task. The muscles in his arms bulged severely as he tossed his head back, and he pulled his left forelimb free. He let out a screech, struggling to free his other arm.

Miriam broke free of her horrified stupor, motioned to Mae, whose eyes were wide with fright, and put her hands together in a steeple. She hummed softly and slowly pulled her hands apart, keeping her fingers connected at the tips. A ball of light formed in the cage of her fingers. In her periphery, Mae was doing the same. It was a struggle to produce a sufficient ball of energy; spending so much time on earth had weakened her.

The beast continued to screech and strain, his second arm nearly free.

Sweat dripped down Miriam's brow and stung her eyes. Suppressing the overwhelming urge to run, she focused on the ball of energy, willing it to grow bigger and stronger.

The beast pulled himself free with a sickening shlurp, and leaped into the attic. A chunk of skin flapped from each shoulder, blood oozing down his triceps.

Miriam sung louder, heart pounding against her ribs, and the ball expanded to the size of a cantaloupe.

Come on, come on, come on.

The creature was a good five feet tall, four limbs planted on the ground firmly like a gorilla. The hind legs were underdeveloped while the forearms were corded with muscle. Its digits had talons and there was no neck. Two beady eyes glinted above reptilian nostrils.

He grinned.

Miriam pelted the half-formed energy ball at him.

He darted to the side and the orb whizzed past, slamming into the wall behind the trunk with a loud explosion. Dust rained down on them from the rafters as the room shook from the impact. She sneezed.

With a screech of triumph, the beast leaped into the air with its talons extended.

Miriam turned to run but he rammed into her back and pinned her to the floor. She couldn't breathe. She tried to wriggle out from beneath but to no avail. The creature let out a guttural sound like a bullfrog and a searing pain shot through her wing as he embedded his teeth into her flesh, breaking the bones.

Mae threw an orb of light at the beast and it jumped backward off Miriam to avoid it. The orb whizzed passed and smashed through the lattice window, leaving a gaping hole in the wall, rising sunlight pouring through.

Licking Miriam's blood from its lips, the beast rolled its beady eyes in Mae's direction, narrowing them. Miriam struggled to get up but the searing pain in her wing was like a dead weight. "Mae, run—" she cried. "Get out of here!"

The monster clawed at the ground like a bull getting ready to charge and lunged toward Mae—wrapping her in a deadly embrace of powerful limbs, talons and teeth.

Miriam pulled herself up frantically—desperate to save Mae. But the Oreala's cries had come to a sudden stop. The room was silent save for the hideous scraping of talons through flesh and the heavy breathing of the beast.

"Get off her—" Miriam howled, leaping onto its back with no thought of her own safety.

The creature bucked but she wrapped her

arms and legs around its chest like a vice. As she dug her fingers into its hairy flesh, she realized the trunk keys were no longer in her hand. She shot a desperate glance around the room and spotted them ten feet away on the floor. The beast twisted and her fingers slipped. It scratched at her with its hind legs like a dog, digging its claws into her thigh. She let go and dropped back to the floorboards, scooting towards the keys in the split second it would take for the creature to turn around.

She closed her fingers around the two keys and grabbed at the rim of the trunk. The beast roared in her periphery as it turned around awkwardly; its body hunching over. He licked his lips, eyes gleaming.

Miriam locked the inner door of the trunk, yanked down the lid, and fumbled to put the second key in the lock. Her hands were trembling and slippery with sweat.

She locked the outer lid as the beast plunged.

He grabbed her leg in his teeth and jerked her to the ground like a plaything, shaking her back and forth. Black dots formed in her eyes and nausea swelled in her throat. The beast released her and she crashed into a wooden ladder, snapping the rungs.

She couldn't move. The beast was looming above her now, drool dripping from his lower lip, talons outstretched.

A magnificent flash of blue filled the shadowy room as a fully-formed ball of energy blasted into the side of the beast, blowing it to pieces.

Chunks of roasting flesh splattered all over

Miriam and she wiped the gore from her face, gasping for breath.

She blinked.

In the middle of the room stood a great male Oreala.

Chapter 34

Miriam was certain she must be dead or dreaming.

The male Oreala was more handsome than any creature she'd ever seen. His skin was a shimmering silver and his wings were black and partly folded behind him.

She'd never seen a real male Oreala before and believed them extinct; especially after Morack's tyranny over Alvernia.

"How bad are you hurt?" he asked with a strong timbre voice.

She gawked up at him. "How . . . where . . . who—"

"My name is Targolan. I arrived through the trunk last night."

She blinked twice. "You mean there are still Orealas alive in Alvernia?"

"There are many survivors in hiding."

"But how-how did you know we were in trouble—?"

"All of us that came through the trunk last night fled to the forest, for this mansion is overrun with ghouls. We found others out there who are planning to attack at any time now. Your friend Lily is among them—Serena's last heir, I'm told." He paused.

"From the fringe of the forest we saw a chunk of the attic wall get blown away. I'd been informed that an Oreala had been sent to lock the trunk and was probably in grave danger. Since I could get here quickest, I was sent to investigate."

He reached down and helped her to her feet with a firm hand. Her bloodied skirts were plastered to her legs and she self-consciously tucked a wet strand of hair behind her ear, and put all her weight on her good leg.

"How bad are you hurt?" he asked again, motioning to her mangled wing. "We need to get you out of here before Morack's lemmings come to investigate. I'm surprised they aren't already here. If we saw the explosion, no doubt they heard it." He surveyed the room.

"I'm afraid I won't be able to fly out of here," she said with great difficulty, the pain suffocating her voice and reducing it to a rasp. "My wing is broken and I've torn the ligaments in my leg, so I can only hobble at best. You're going to have to leave me here. Please. It's okay. Go. And take these—" She handed him the trunk keys.

"No one else needs to die in this room," he said gravely, looking down at the mutilated body of poor Mae. Miriam stifled a sob and closed her eyes against the unbearable sight.

"I'll fly you out of here."

"There's no way you'll be able to stay airborne carrying me." She opened her eyes. He was looking down at her tenderly.

"I'll manage," he said, squatting to put one

sturdy arm under her knees and the other around her back, beneath her wings. He then straightened as though she weighed nothing at all, and turned and headed to the gaping hole in the wall. Her heart was pounding; surely they would plummet to their deaths. There was no way his wings were strong enough to carry her as well. But she was too weak to protest further.

They stood in the opening and she looked down at the stone walkway far below. They'd never survive a drop to the ground from this height.

"Here we go," he said, leaping through the gap in the wall without further delay, keeping his wings tucked until he'd cleared the opening. Then he whipped them out to full breadth. But instead of flapping to remain airborne, as she'd anticipated, he held them straight and glided to the ground below on a steady angle.

They landed hard at the edge of the driveway, having cleared the entire front walkway with the glide. He let out a grunt as he struggled to keep his footing while still cradling her in his arms. Coming to a full stop, he folded his wings behind him—but instead of putting her down, he continued to hold her as Moya appeared from the foliage to meet them. Miriam exchanged a look with Moya and the sudden tears that sprang up in the Oreala's eyes confirmed she had received the tacit message that Mae had perished. The three of them entered the cloak of the forest together. Overwhelmed with pain and exhaustion, Miriam rested her head on Targolan's chest and slipped out of consciousness.

Lily approached the mansion and went around the side to the front, Callamous and Varkis on either side of her. Mike and the others held back, remaining under the veil of the willow trees until the time was right to emerge. Their numbers were few; Morack mustn't find out.

Rainwater stains remained on the driveway, but the sun had broken through the clouds and the sky was a radiant blue. On a normal day, the sun would be a welcomed sight, a friend in the sky. But today it was somehow malevolent, glaring down on Lily as though hungry to see her blood spilled.

She swallowed hard and looked around in relief to find the front lawn deserted of all signs of life. Granted, creatures could be hiding anywhere; perhaps waiting behind every door and window.

"Where is he?" she whispered to Varkis.

As if summoned by her thoughts, beasts began to appear over the crest of the mansion roof and turrets.

Others climbed out broken windows and scurried down the vine-covered walls.

It was like goo bursting free from a container and oozing out of every crevice.

Lily stood stock still; Callamous and Varkis equally still beside her.

Within seconds at least thirty abominations had gathered on the lawn before them, some fifty feet away, ready to plunge at the first order.

"I can't do this, I can't do this—" she whispered through closed lips, clenching and releasing trembling fingers.

Varkis placed his scruffy hand on her shoulder and gave it a squeeze, but said nothing.

How could it have come to this? She was nothing, a nobody. All this talk of her inherited powers seemed nothing but wishful thinking. She had yet to experience even the slightest amount of supernatural inkling, let alone power. To say nothing of skill. And what of Ian? She recalled his kiss in the tree house. It seemed like ages ago now. Yet how her heart still throbbed at the thought of him. How could he have betrayed her, betrayed them all? He'd been raised to hate, it was true, taught to be evil by a father who was the very epitome of that word—and yet— hadn't Hannah and Auguste's unconditional love for him changed all of that?

"Where's Morack?" she asked again, banishing all thoughts of Ian; lifting her chin and squaring her shoulders. She would soon be dead and it would no longer matter whether Ian cared for her, or she him.

The mass of creatures ahead of them were like a great mound of squirming insects—whining and twitching and drooling—but staying obediently in place—waiting for some unforeseen cue to attack.

Without warning, the great entrance doors of the estate flung open—rent from their hinges—and slithering, creeping, leaping critters poured forth like the bursting of a dam.

Lily gasped and started to reach instinctively

for Varkis—but withdrew just as quickly to avoid any sign of weakness to the crowd before them. She squared her shoulders afresh though her limbs felt like jelly.

"He's here," Callamous snorted in her ear. "I can feel his presence. *Morack*. You must order him to stop hiding, and come out and face you."

She took a deep breath. "Morack—" she squeaked.

"You can't show any fear," the unicorn warned in a sharp undertone.

She cleared her throat. "Morack—" She said it louder this time but hardly above a whimper.

Callamous stamped his hoof and glared at her, eyes glowing red. "You're going to get us all killed!"

Lily could barely breathe but she forced herself to stand taller. She fisted her hands and in the most commanding voice she could summon, shouted: "Morack—get your pathetic backside out here already. I'm tired of your silly games. Face me like a man."

At this word, the monsters parted like the red sea, revealing a tall and strikingly handsome young man.

He wore black armor pieced together by thousands of reptilian scales. Yet unlike the stiff metal armor of knights, this suit moved and flexed organically with his every step, like a second skin—so much so that as he began to approach, she wondered if it were not his real skin after all.

The corner of his lips lifted in a half grin. "Ms.

Lily Kline," he said eloquently, "how long I have been waiting to meet you."

Who was this? Surely not Morack?

"That's close enough," she said, putting out a palm with feigned command.

He paused and held out his arms as if beckoning her for an embrace, eyes lifting in a warm smile. "Come now, my dear, there is no need to be on the defensive. Can we not begin with a civil conversation and get to know one another?"

She stared at him, studying his features, uncertain how to proceed. She dared not ask who he was, though she could only conclude he must be Morack. But he neither looked like someone capable of mass murder and evil with no equal, nor old enough to be the father of two grown sons. A heartbreaker perhaps, but an arch villain?

Yet now that he was up close with the sun beaming down on him, she had to admit there were traces of Ian in his expressions, though the lines of his face were sharper and more square.

All this time she'd envisioned an aging tyrant with sunken eyes and wrinkled jowls.

"I can't imagine what we would possibly discuss with one another—" she said in a strong, clear tone that surprised her. "Unless you wish to surrender."

Callamous let out a snort of approval.

Morack laughed.

It was neither unpleasant nor dark. In fact, it was warm and inviting, much like Ian's laughter.

Morack dropped his hands to his side and

tilted his head like a bird, eyes narrowing in the bright sunlight. "I think it would be wise for you to listen to what I have to say and to take the time to consider my offer before you make any further responses."

She stared at him, waiting, heart thudding in her chest. She willed her face to remain neutral.

"Look around you," he said, gesturing to the beasts on either side and behind him. "You are vastly outnumbered. Any attempt to fight me will lead to your instant death. Your friends will be wiped out simultaneously and nothing will be accomplished—at least by you. Is that what you want?"

She said nothing.

"Don't be a fool, Lily." The honey was gone from his voice now. He took a step closer. "Surrender yourself to me and I will spare all of your friends. None of them need die today."

"Liar!" Varkis barked. "You'll kill us all regardless."

"Do you always let your slaves do your talk-ing for you?" Morack asked. "Do they really have so little respect for you?" He tilted his head and searched her face.

Varkis let out a low growl but she put a hand on his arm and he quieted.

"So—" she said. "You're asking me to sacrifice myself to save them."

"I think it's a fair enough trade," he said light-heartedly, smiling.

She took a step forward and Varkis grabbed her arm forcibly. She looked at him and shook her head. He hesitated, amber eyes lit from behind as though with a fire, and lips curled back over his canine teeth—but he let go.

Morack watched her with hungry eyes. They were the only thing about his current demeanor that indicated his true nature. If eyes were the window to the soul then his was a dark and eternal void.

"Why take my life though?" she asked coquettishly, stopping a foot from him and looking up into his eyes, smoothing her fingertips over his right shoulder. "A man as powerful as you ought to have a woman by his side." She moved closer, placing both hands flat against his scaly chest and giving him a little smile.

It was the oldest trick in the book, but he eyed her; seeming to consider.

"I'll go with you right now if you'll give me your word that you'll spare the others," she said, "and I'll serve you hand and foot till the end of my days. Your every wish and desire will be my command."

He grinned and moved in as though to kiss her.

As he did so, she reached into her sleeve, pulled out a dagger, and went for the jugular. But before the knife could even knick his skin, he'd latched onto her wrist so tightly she thought the bones would snap. The dagger dropped from her fingers and fell to the ground as he spun her around and twisted her arm up behind her back.

"Do you take me for a fool," he snarled into her ear with breath as rank as Kurik's.

She gritted her teeth together as he lifted her

onto her toes by her arm.

"You can't be all that smart," she said, "since your own son managed to keep you locked in a vat all these years as though it were the easiest thing in the world. I figured it was worth a try." She sounded ten times more confident than she felt.

With a cry of unrestrained rage, he threw her to the grass.

Chapter 85

Lily rolled over onto her back and moved to get up, but he planted his boot on her abdomen, pinning her in place.

With an inhuman howl he began to grow—his body shifting and distorting until he towered above her at a height of eight or nine feet. Then his skin began to melt, dripping off him like candle wax.

She held back a cry and fought the urge to vomit as the last bit of flesh dribbled down his chin. His skull was covered in a gray web-work of muscle, making his jaw thick and powerful. His nose was a pair of slits in his face, and instead of ears, he had a hole in either side. He had six eyes: two in the regular place and two on each side of his head. Scarlet and yellow striations surrounded his pupils. He grinned revealing dozens of serrated teeth.

The pressure on Lily's stomach increased, making breathing difficult, and she looked down at his boot, fearing he might crush her. She gasped. His feet had transformed as well: The boots had broken away to reveal elongated feet with talon-like toes. He flexed the fingers on his clawed hands.

So, this was it.

She had no hope in hell.

Ian hurried through the woods toward the west side of the mansion.

Targolan, the male Oreala, and Miriam, had met up with him in the cover of the forest after the explosion in the attic, and had explained the situation with the trunk and the enemy occupied mansion. They made plans and parted ways, the keys safely in Ian's pocket. Hannah had been ordered to stay put with the injured Miriam.

He picked his way through tree boughs, bushes, and boulders as quickly as possible without making much noise, and within a minute had reached the willow tree across from the scullery. He took cover under its dangling branches as a pair of scarab creatures scuttled about—and decided to push through them. They made no attempt to attack, stopping short at what seemed to be the sight of his face.

"It's me, Kurik," he said in a low voice, taking advantage of their hesitation. "Get out of my way." He sported the same scar as his brother now and could easily be confused for him. And if they had any doubts (he knew his jaw was much narrower), their fear of making a mistake would prevent them from challenging him.

Ian rounded the corner of the building to find a clog of beasts. They were silent and staring in the direction of the mansion's front entrance stairs.

His spine tingled, hands going clammy. Was he too late?

Filling his lungs with crisp autumn air, he pushed his way through the mob, and barged into the opening upon which they all stared.

There was Lily.

She was on her back with Morack looming over her and transforming into his true self.

Without a second thought, he began running toward his father, shouting, "Callamous—attack!"

Immediately the few faithful beasts around Callamous and Varkis started screeching and howling and stomping their feet. Varkis let out a war cry and charged toward Morack, teeth and claws flashing.

Morack looked down in surprise as Ian rammed into his side, knocking him off Lily. He grabbed at Ian with his talons, but something slammed against Ian at the same time, sending him flying backward into the crowd where he lost sight of Lily and Morack as the hoards of beasts closed in on them.

The sound of roaring and screaming flooded his ears like white noise.

Looming above him was a creature like a plucked turkey with the neck of an ostrich. He could not tell where the neck ended and the head began for the top of it was nothing but a gaping maw with hooked teeth and a pair of black eyes on either side.

He leaped to his feet and transformed into his more lethal form—barring his fangs at the goose monster—and attacking.

It had all happened so fast, Lily wasn't quite sure what was going on. Someone had shouted and then chaos erupted around her as the battle for earth began. One second Morack was pinning her down—the next she was free.

Sweat and blood splattered around her as beasts clashed. She scrambled to her feet but talons clamped down on her shoulder—piercing her skin like hooks. Her heart lurched in her chest and she tried to pull away, but Morack only dug his talons in deeper, laughing.

She kicked at his legs but it was like kicking stone. He was too tall for her to make any attempt at gouging out his eyes, so she clawed at his hands on her shoulders instead until her own nails tore.

"Pathetic," he shouted to be heard over the deafening roar, lifting her off the ground with just one hand. With the other he grabbed her by the hair and wrenched her around to face him. Holding her within inches of his ever-grinning face, he stuck out a forked tongue and licked her cheek. She jerked her head to the side and he laughed.

"Maybe I'll roast you once I'm done killing you," he said. "You'll be the main course of my victory dinner."

She continued to kick but he didn't flinch; there was no evident kink in his armor, and no sign of her having any supernatural powers whatsoever. She could never win this.

"I'm going to enjoy killing you," he went on, grinning and licking his teeth with the forked tongue. "Be prepared to feel pain like you've never felt before."

His six eyes flared and he threw her onto the flagstone, knocking the air out of her. Bright lights exploded before her eyes as her head cracked backward against the ground. She groaned and staggered back up to her feet while he watched her with evident delight. She had barely straightened when he kicked her in the stomach—sending her flying ten feet through the air and colliding with the armored backside of a fighting beast. She slid to the ground, pain ricocheting through her body like forked lightning.

Morack stormed toward her and reached for her again, talons outspread—but Varkis appeared and interceded, lunging at his throat.

As if he were nothing but a mosquito to be swatted, Morack grabbed the dog-man by the jaw and wrenched it open, snapping the joints, and then tossed him into the crowd.

"Where were we," he hissed, closing his talons around her ankles as she struggled to get away.

She kicked frantically at his hands as he dragged her toward him.

Hideous beasts pressed against Ian at all sides, pinning him in place. Claws sliced his back and teeth grazed his legs.

Something lunged from behind and he thrust a dagger into its gut. The beast crashed to the ground. Another attacked from the right but he grabbed it by the throat and crushed its windpipe.

Out of the corner of his eye he spotted Mike backing up against the ivy-clad wall of the mansion, swinging a sword back and forth like a gimp. For a split second he considered going to his aid but in that very moment of distraction a burning warmth covered his ear as a beast prepared to close its jaws around his throat. Before he could react, a loud thwhack sounded and the beast fell away to the ground.

There stood Hannah, wielding a shovel with a crazed look in her eye.

"Hannah—"

"No time to talk," she said. "Keep going!" She took off, ducking and side-stepping her way toward Mike.

He glanced quickly in every direction, still unable to catch sight of Lily. He had to find her before it was too late—yet already the beasts were closing in on him again.

Morack grabbed Lily by the back collar of her jacket and lifted her to her feet. "Come on and fight princess," he snarled, "you're making this way too easy."

She twisted and turned in vain, trying to wrench herself free, and stumbled forward when he let go of her unexpectedly.

He was toying with her.

"Show me what you've got," he taunted. "Surely you must have *some* of Serena's power."

She turned to face him and winced as she inhaled. Were her ribs cracked?

"Too slow," he said, back-handing her across the face, his knobby knuckles cutting into the flesh of her cheek. She let out a cry and stumbled backward several steps.

It was hopeless. She hadn't the slightest chance against him. Her whole body pulsated with pain. He was simply holding back his strength for his own amusement.

Deciding she would die regardless, she lunged at him and grabbed his shoulders, pulling herself up and biting into his neck as hard as she could, twisting and grinding her teeth in an attempt to sever an artery. But her teeth couldn't even break the corded skin.

He laughed and pulled her from him, throwing her back to the ground. Something cracked in her left leg this time and a crushing pain shot up her thigh.

"This is comical," he said. "Now get up and try again."

She tried to sit up but collapsed on her back instead, spots before her eyes.

"Get up!" He kicked her in the ribs.

Lily's breathing grew shallow and whistle-like. He'd collapsed her lung.

Her entire body went numb.

She was going into shock.

"Get up—" he roared, kicking her so hard

across the flagstone that she slid, landing face down.

"Pathetic." He grabbed her by the hair, lifting her face up. "I win."

Her eyes closed as everything went black.

Chapter 36

Morack stood to his full height and stared down at the girl's crumpled body. He couldn't believe his luck. It had been easy *and* entertaining. Like a wolf sparring with a rabbit.

A warm tingling started in his hands and spread up his arms.

What was this?

He turned his hands over in surprise, examining them.

The warmth grew hotter still and was instantly painful, like hundreds of fire ants marching up his arms, biting his flesh each step of the way, and spreading out over his entire body within a matter of seconds. He had no time to think, it was happening so fast. He opened his mouth to howl as the searing pain engulfed his limbs like invisible flames and a mounting pressure in his chest cavity burst like an internal grenade.

All around him the beasts continued to wage war oblivious to his crisis but his screeching voice permeated the throngs until they finally took notice and stopped to stare. His cries were so deafening they clutched their ears and squeezed their eyes shut.

Above him the sun vanished and the sky

darkened instantly as though a slated blanket had been tossed across the heavens. Thunder clapped, eclipsing his wails.

Then, as quickly as it had started, the burning pain vanished and a cool, tingling sensation replaced it—as though a bucket of ice water had doused his body.

His mouth hung open a moment and then he let out a shout of sudden triumph as renewed strength and power flooded his body.

The world seemed to freeze around Ian as he heard the first blood-curdling scream.

He had just downed another beast. His whole body ached and blood flowed freely from numerous slashes and bite wounds.

None of the creatures he'd faced thus far had induced any terror in him like this sound had. It was like thousands of nails dragging down a chalkboard all at once.

As if on cue, everyone stopped fighting and turned toward the source of the noise. He knew without a doubt it was Morack, though there were too many creatures in front of him to see through.

Ian pushed his way through the beasts, trying to catch a glimpse of what was going on, but suddenly collapsed to the ground as waves of pain washed over his body; as severe as if a hose of acid had been turned on him. He writhed back and forth, clawing at his skin and wildly scanning the crowd to see who or what had done this to him.

A spreading chorus of distressed wailing surrounded him. Thunder crashed. Then, just as the agony peaked, it left as quickly as it had come, leaving him with an all-consuming sense of power.

The slashes and gouges and bite marks on his skin and muscles closed up and scarred over within a mere half second. Physically, he felt better than he had in years, as though nothing could ever stand in his way again.

Yet his heart sank to his feet.

The reason his ability to heal had been suppressed and sluggish lately was because of Lily. And the only possible reason for its returning strength was . . . her death.

The sky above him had turned to slate as his father's cries of pain became shouts of triumph.

The thunder ceased.

Ian jumped to his feet and lunged through the crowd, bumping beasts out of his way like bowling pins. He broke through the cluster encircling Morack and there stood his father—looming over Lily's lifeless body. Morack's face was upturned to the sky, hands raised palms up, energy surging up and down his arms like static.

Ian hesitated and stopped short, catching sight of Callamous and Varkis nearby. The look of despair in their eyes confirmed his worst fears. They were bloodied, broken, and defeated. Mike stood near them, tears making trails in the dirt on his cheeks.

Morack stopped gloating and lowered his

head, scanning the crowd until his vermilion eyes locked onto Ian's.

Utter fury filled Ian's body and his face distorted as he thrust his hands out in front of him—casting streaks of fluorescent green at his father with a deafening crack.

Morack blocked the lightning bolts with his palms and they dissipated against an invisible shield emanating from his hands. Then, holding his arms out straight at his sides, the energy that had been building in them acted like a giant magnet drawing creatures toward him. As the first beast made contact, Morack's arm went into its body as though it were liquid and instantly absorbed the creature into him.

Morack's body grew taller.

Callamous, Varkis and Mike were far enough back to take instant cover, running in the opposite direction, but many of the beasts did not clue in soon enough, and though they dug their claws into the ground, they were dragged to Morack's side and absorbed one by one until he towered above them all: losing all recognizable features as his body twisted in and out of grotesque shapes.

Ian too was jerked toward his father along with the others, digging his heals into the ground to no avail.

Morack's magnetic power was like a collapsed star.

Forming balls of energy in his palms, Ian blasted them into the ground ahead of him and the explosions sent him flying backward, released from the pull. He hit the ground hard, rolling a few feet before coming to a stop. He scrambled back to his feet just as Callamous galloped up to his side in battle form; smoking black with blazing eyes.

"What's happening?" he asked, skidding to a stop and stamping a hoof.

"I'm not sure," Ian said. "I've never seen him do anything like this before!"

"Is Lily—?"

"Don't say it."

"Do you have a plan?"

"Yes—I'm going to kill him."

"But without Lily—"

"Ssh—something's happening."

Morack stood two stories tall now and would soon dwarf the mansion. Appendages grew and disappeared as he struggled to take a notable shape.

"We should attack now while he's still transitioning," Callamous growled.

"No—we're no match. If you touch him while he's like this, you'll just be sucked in like all the others."

Morack's body completed its transformation as they spoke. It became long and segmented, each section covered with a tough shell, and sprouting dozens upon dozens of centipede legs. He dropped down to the ground with a thwumph, showing himself to be ten feet tall and the length of three school buses end-to-end. His face was a giant maw, lined with the teeth of a lamprey. A pair of jade eyes gleamed on either side of his head.

"It has been an honor fighting with you," Callamous said.

THE ATTIC

Ian nodded. "For Lily," he said, voice catching on her name.

"For Lily."

Callamous charged forward.

Ian followed suit, grabbing a fallen sword from the ground.

The world seemed to slow around him as he ran, the cries of dying beasts fading away as he focused solely on his target. In his periphery, a gargoyle charged from the forest with an axe aimed at one of the centipede legs, but Morack lifted the limb and stabbed it through the gargoyle's back.

Like a blade through a fly.

Chapter 87

Callamous reached Morack first and dodged his swinging jaws, galloping beneath him and ramming his horn up into the underbelly over and over again, but Morack's armor-like plating was tightly-knit and there was no time for precision in aim. He galloped out the other end but just as he thought he'd cleared the beast, searing pain tore through his hindquarters as Morack's maw clamped down on him. He hadn't realized the beast would be so fast and flexible.

In the next second he was flying through the air a hundred feet above the battle-gored ground.

He began to fall.

Morack's jaws were wide open below, waiting to swallow him whole. There was no escape. He closed his eyes as the jaws clamped down, impaling him. The beast shook him to and fro and spat him out.

Callamous crashed into the trunk of a tree and slid to the ground.

With a final glimpse of Ian taking a swing with his sword at one of the centipede legs, darkness closed in on him.

Enraged by the mauling of his friend, Ian swung his sword with all his might, severing the leg in one fell swoop.

Morack snarled and turned to face him.

Knowing he had mere seconds, Ian focused his energy on his palm and a sparking ball of light formed in front of his outstretched fingers. When it reached the size of a basketball he pulled his arm back and thrust it forward, sending the glowing ball of energy hurtling toward Morack's open jaws.

The beast had no time to react and the orb hit him square in the face with an explosion of energy and light, tearing his head clean off.

Morack's body twitched spasmodically and his dozens of legs tried to walk in every direction at once before he finally collapsed.

Ian fell to his knees and let out a lung-full of air. He inhaled deeply, staring ahead at the unmoving, headless body.

Morack was dead.

He stood to his feet and a chill ran up his spine.

The shreds of skin hanging where Morack's face had been began jiggling and knitting themselves back together. The nearby severed leg twitched and then skittered across the ground, reattaching itself to the stub.

Ian's heart faltered.

He'd always believed Morack could be killed if a death blow was received too quickly for healing to occur. But evidently even decapitation was no match for his father.

Morack stood up on his dozens of centipede legs and roared. He then bristled and quivered all over like a wet dog shaking off water, and focused his jade eyes on Ian.

He lunged.

Ian dove to the side and grabbed onto one of the legs—clinging to it.

The beast howled in rage, twisting his body around and snapping at him with the lamprey teeth. Ian scrambled up the leg and went underneath, grabbing hold of an armored plate and hanging upside down from Morack's belly. Sweat dripped from his forehead and his muscles bulged as he dug his fingers and boot tips under the plates to keep from falling.

Morack curled his head in and under his belly to try and swallow up Ian, but he couldn't reach.

Supporting himself with only one hand, Ian pulled his sword from his belt and drove it into the soft flesh between the plates.

He cut and slashed everywhere he could, digging deep, hoping to perforate an organ. Morack writhed and squirmed. Ian let go and dropped to the ground, rolling out of the way as the beast tried to impale him with his many legs. Rancid heat bathed his neck and he spun around to meet Morack's wide open maw coming toward him. It let out a roar, sending globs of spittle all over him; and would have swallowed him whole if Varkis hadn't appeared and rammed the jade eye with a sharp stick.

Ian yanked Varkis away from the beast as it shook its head to dislodge the stick. The Anubis' ear was half torn and his bottom jaw hung at an odd angle, clearly broken. Blood dripped from between his canine teeth and his eyes were glazed and dim, but he gave a nod and indicated a plan.

Catching the cue instantly, Ian ran to Morack's side while Varkis started jumping up and down, distracting the beast who couldn't seem to decide who to attack first. Deftly grabbing a leg, Ian scooted up to Morack's back and crawled on his hands and knees, gripping the armor to keep from sliding off. He reached the neck and withdrew his sword, preparing to drive it into the back of the beast's skull between the plates and into his brain. If he could effectively leave the sword in place, Morack would be prevented from healing.

As if sensing his plan, Morack tucked in all the legs on his left side and rolled over. Ian was dislodged and flew through the air, flailing his arms and legs, sword slipping from his fingers.

With a thwack and a crunch his body collided with stone wall of a turret, snapping his back. He fell to the ground paralyzed.

Morack was only thirty feet away and quickly approaching.

Ian lay watching; helpless.

Varkis yelled and jumped and beat the ground to no avail: Morack was ignoring him now.

A prickling sensation engulfed Ian's legs and the bones in his back crackled as they fitted themselves back together. The sword lay only a meter away.

He snatched it just as the beast lunged, and turned and jumped up, grabbing hold of Morack's lower jaw with his left hand and swinging from it—just barely missing being impaled by the row of teeth. The beast tossed its head to shake him off and Ian let go deliberately, dropping down on Morack's back and gripping the plates with one hand to steady himself, while tucking in his sword with the other. He then scurried up to the head, withdrew the sword afresh, and rammed it between the plates—skewering Morack's brain.

Morack gasped and collapsed to the ground.

But there was no time to rejoice.

The jade eyes snapped open again and the beast rose to its feet, lifting Ian into the air with him.

Chapter 38

Lily could see nothing but darkness all around her—yet it wasn't the darkness of being blind or unconscious—it was more like being in a windowless room with all the lights shut off.

Though come to think of it, she couldn't feel her body even remotely. She was neither hot nor cold. Just . . . there.

And she sensed a presence in the room with her, too, in the darkness. But good or bad, she couldn't say.

Where am I?

Lily had only thought the words, but an angelic feminine voice responded from nearby: "The in-between."

I don't understand.

"You are neither dead nor alive, just in-between."

How is that possible?

"Morack defeated you and now you are faced with the most important decision of your life."

What is it?

"To live or to die."

I'd like to liv—

"Stop. You must think this over very carefully.

Your whole life has been a test. All the past guardians of Alvernia have been keeping an eye on you from our place of rest. We have been waiting to see if you are worthy of our power. Today you have finally proven that you are. You fought valiantly against Morack even though you knew you had no chance. And now, you are ready to receive our gift. That is, if you want it."

Is there any reason why I wouldn't?

"The life of a guardian can be long and hard. You will be in control of an entire planet, responsible for keeping the peace and rebuilding it from the ground up after the destruction of Morack's reign. It is in shambles—war-torn. You will have to prevent others like him from rising up. It is no easy task and once you've chosen it, you can not go back on your word. You will not be immortal, however; but you will outlive many."

Was my mother given this choice?

"No. She died before she was ready. She had no knowledge of Alvernia and she had not shown the will or stamina needed for so much power. It was not her calling. Since she had an heir and we knew the line would not die out with her, we allowed her to pass straight on to the next life at her death. We have watched *you* ever since."

If I choose not to live, what will happen?

"I will take you with me to rest with the other guardians in a place of unimaginable beauty and peace, where you will never suffer again."

But what will happen to Earth and to Alvernia?

"They will fall under Morack's supreme reign.

His insatiable hunger for blood and power will be his eventual undoing, but not until both worlds are utterly barren and he is the only living creature left. Unlike you, he *is* immortal, but with one vital exception: He can be killed by a guardian—permanently. No one else, no matter how powerful, can ever do so."

If I . . . decide to live . . . how can I ever defeat Morack? I already made a pathetic attempt and was nothing but a fly to him. And even if you gave me powers now, I have no training in how to use them.

"You will not need training. With the gift of powers comes all the wisdom and memories of the past guardians. . . . "

A pause.

"And there is one more thing, child."

Yes?

"Do you realize what will happened if you kill Ian's father?"

Yes . . . I kill Ian too. But are you certain?

"Lily, you must not let Ian distort your longterm vision. If you choose to live, destroying Morack must be your first and foremost responsibility, despite the cost. His death is the only way to save both of these planets."

I choose to . . . to live.

"A wise and self-less decision. Now . . . this will feel strange—"

The darkness around Lily burst into explosions of color and light.

Images spun through her at the speed of light yet her mind retained them all—a millennia of memories flooding her brain, weaving their way through, and settling themselves in as if they were her very own. And though she retained all of her original memories they were different now somehow, as though she had been sleepwalking all these years. She could recall them but they seemed a faint shadow, antiquated and detached. Like another life. In contrast, her memories at Auguste's estate were as vivid and solid as ever.

She felt as though she was made solely of energy—full of power beyond imagination—power that in an instant she understood thoroughly and could manipulate according to her will without the slightest effort.

She was ready.

With a feeling of utter dismay, Ian jumped off Morack's back, rolled across the grass, and watched as the beast finished rising to his full height on its dozens of centipede legs.

How could this be? The sword remained skewered in its brain, sticking out the back like a single porcupine quill—a mere toothpick.

Ian's worst fears had been confirmed: Morack was truly invincible.

Without warning, the ground beneath him rumbled and shook as a bright light exploded all around.

Ian covered his eyes and ducked down. The beast screeched and hissed as the light passed over and through both of them like a tsunami.

Then, as quickly as it had come, it vanished, and the earth stopped shaking.

Ian opened his eyes and straightened, blinking rapidly. He followed the turning gaze of Morack, whose giant green eyes were bulging with evident shock.

Across the lawn ahead of them, on the flagstone path leading up to the entrance of Auguste's estate—where Lily's crumpled body had been lying slain—was a woman standing upright and glowing bright like the sun.

Ian squinted and shielded his eyes against the searing light but could not look away. The woman's hair stood out all around her as though floating in water and lightning bolts coiled around her body like a brood of vipers. Her eyes were completely white and shining even brighter than her body.

"It can't be—" the beast hissed in an otherworldly voice. "Serena is dead!" He scrambled backward in retreat and Ian took quick shelter in the woods next to Varkis who was peering out through the bronzed pendant leaves of a willow.

The glowing angelic woman stepped toward Morack and lightning shot out from her body, engulfing him like a python constricting its prey.

Morack squealed as cracks splintered all over his protective plates, the kinks glowing orange like furnace-hot coals. The lightning cords tightened more and more around his body until finally, with a sickening crunch, his insect bodice sliced into a dozen strips, all the pieces tumbling to the ground with a thump and a splat.

The light around his deli-meat remains did not leave but continued to glow brighter until all the chunks were nothing but ashes—and even the ashes themselves disappeared, leaving nothing behind but an enormous black char which crossed the expanse of the front property.

Like a vacuum, the glowing woman sucked all of the light and energy back into her body and the light faded away until she had fully returned to her human form.

Ian gasped. "Lily—"

She looked exactly as she had when Ian had first met her; except without a single blemish. Her skin was porcelain and her hair silk.

He came out from beneath the willow and stopped short when her eyes locked on his. There was recognition in them, but also what seemed a terrible sadness. How could she be so sad when Morack was finally destroyed for good?

Then he remembered.

One by one across the yard, Morack's remaining followers, who had not been absorbed, were turning to dust and ash. He was suddenly dizzy and looked down at his own figure. Smoke was rising from his body and twisting upward as though it was emanating from his very pores. The pain that suddenly followed was so intense, he nearly vomited, but he didn't want Lily to see how much he was about to suffer.

Sweat trickled down his face but he refused to scream in agony, though his body felt like it was going to explode.

He dropped to his knees without breaking eye contact with Lily. Though it took every last drop of strength and resolution, he smiled at her with resignation and a real sense of peace, relieved beyond measure that she was safe and alive, and that Morack was gone forever.

His strength sapped, Ian collapsed onto his side.

With a cry, Lily rushed up and knelt beside him as dark spots filled the corners of his vision. Her sea-green eyes shimmered with tears. She put her arms around him and held him against her as his life drained away. He was too weak to hold her back and his arms hung limply at his sides.

If he could have any wish, it would be to tell her the truth—that he hadn't betrayed her. But his parched lips could not open to speak.

Lily's heart constricted as Ian's eyes dimmed and his body sagged against her. She gently rolled him onto his back and his eyes sought hers again, trying to lock gaze. She ran her fingers lovingly across the side of his face and leaned down to kiss his lips one last time. She had the power to heal but knew it would do him no good: she could not help someone with the darkness inside.

The smoke rising from his body had turned from gray to pitch and she waved it away so she could still see his face. The smoke had an acrid scent of metal, of charred blood.

He grimaced. "I love you, Lily, I'm so sorry," he said in a nearly inaudible voice, eyelids twitching then sliding shut. She waited for them to open again, longing to see those dear eyes one last time.

But they didn't.

He was gone.

The burden of her responsibility as a guardian now settled heavily upon her as she imagined living a long life ahead without Ian Hawke, the man she had grown to love. The thought was too much to bear and she laid her head upon his chest and sobbed freely. She knew within a few minutes his body would turn to ash and he'd be gone forever.

Something crackled and she clutched him even tighter, knowing he was about to disintegrate.

She pulled him up into her arms and kissed his dry, cracked forehead. "Rest in peace, darling. They will tell your story in Alvernia for centuries to come! I will never, ever forget you."

A crunch and his face shifted.

"No!" She couldn't bear to watch but couldn't bear to look away either.

But instead of turning to dust, the skin of his face was moistening, cracks vanishing and a rosy blush warming the baby-like skin from beneath. As new blood flowed through his veins, like an opening of a dam upon a desert, his lips and nose and brow returned to original fullness and luster: he was as handsome as ever.

His brown eyes opened fully, clearly, and he

clasped her hand in his own warm palm against his chest.

"How—how is this possible?" Goosebumps raced up her arms and down her back. Not a single piece of information in her millennium of memories provided any explanation for it.

A smile touched the corners of his lips. "My mother had a pure heart," he said in a husky voice, "there was no darkness in her. By killing Morack you have purged my body of all the inherited evil that came from him." His voice was full and strong now. "For the first time in my life I feel . . . " He began to sit up. "I feel clean."

"Morack's curse has been broken—" she cried out in awe.

"Lily." He searched her face. "I need to tell you—I need you to know that . . . that I—"

"I know," she said softly, squeezing his hand. "I know you didn't really betray me. I can see that now." She thought back to the scene in the forest when Varkis had carted her off and she'd turned back just in time to see Ian about to ram a dagger into the unicorn's breast. Callamous was in on it, she realized now. They had staged it together.

Obvious relief washed over his features and he exhaled roughly. Then he stood and pulled her to himself, lifting her up to her feet and embracing her fully, nuzzling his nose into her hair. She laid her cheek against the crook of his shoulder as joy surged in her heart.

Eventually Ian broke the embrace and held her at arms length, his strong hands warming her shoulders and sending tingles down her arms. They stared at one another for a long moment and then burst out laughing.

The dog-man limped up to them then, a smile twinkling in his eyes though his broken jaw still hung at an odd angle. He slapped Ian on the back with a big hairy palm.

Lily reached out and touched his jaw with the tips of her fingers and it immediately snapped back in place. He rubbed it and moved it around a bit, and then his lips rolled back, exposing his teeth in a wolfish grin. With a smile she stepped away from the two of them to survey the surrounding area.

Others who had survived the battle were now approaching and gathering around, cheers on their tongues and the very air full of celebration. The sky had cleared and the sun was shining down on them all, warming their backs.

The sound of a door slamming grabbed her attention and she looked toward the mansion as Hannah came charging down the front steps with a shovel in hand. Blood and animal hair stuck to the edge of the blade but Hannah appeared completely unharmed; her disheveled hair and sullied dress the only signs that she'd been in any sort of fight.

She reached them panting. "One of those little buggers had me cornered in the dining room," she said breathlessly. "I thought I was done for but he suddenly turned to dust—just like that. Dust!" She held the shovel at her side like a pitchfork and threw her shoulders back with confidence. Then her eyes widened as her gaze moved from Lily to Ian. "Well, upon my word—" she said. "Ian, your scars are gone!"

Everyone laughed and Hannah looked bewildered.

Lily spent the next few minutes healing the wounded and dying. She came upon Callamous lying in a heap beneath a willow tree, too severely injured to heal himself and nearly dead. She laid her hands upon him; instantly mending his wounds. He clambered up to his hooved feet and let out an exuberant whinny.

A crowd had gathered around.

"Long live Lily—guardian of Alvernia!" they shouted.

She smiled gently, moved and humbled by their gratitude.

Sirens sounded ever so faintly in the far distance and the cheers came to an abrupt halt, everyone on sudden alert.

The smoking disaster area must have been spotted by an airplane.

"It is time for us all to go home," she said in a voice that lifted on the breeze and reached every ear. "Gather all our fallen comrades and do so quickly— we must bring them back to Alvernia with us to give them a proper burial at the palace. We will build a memorial so that their sacrifice will never be forgotten."

Miriam stepped forward through the crowd and approached Lily, her wings whole once more and a smile on her face, a tall male Oreala at her side. Ian approached as well and handed Lily the keys to the trunk. There was no need to speak. Then, one by one the creatures, at least thirty in total, began to respectfully gather up the bodies of their fallen friends and filed after Lily into the mansion through the arched oak doors, heading up the stairs to the attic as fast as their legs would carry them. There was no time to waste.

Varkis picked up Mae's crumpled body from beside the trunk and was the first to pass through into Alvernia.

Within five minutes, the final creature had passed through, leaving only Ian, Hannah, Mike and herself.

The sirens were loud now—they were entering the driveway. Soon the mansion would be swarming with police and firefighters. Sunlight filled the attic through the gaping hole in the wall.

"Here we are," she said, "at the end of one journey and at the beginning of another. Once we go through I will close the portal forever. Who wants to stay and who wants to leave?"

"I'm coming," said Hannah without hesitation.

Mike rubbed the back of his neck and looked at the open door leading out of the attic to the staircase. "You know, those cops will just arrest me if I'm the only person they find here," he said. "And how would I explain it? Besides, there's nothing keeping me here. I want to see this place called Alvernia. There are ladies there, right?"

She laughed. "Of course there are. Get going."

Mike took Hannah's hand and helped her through first, following after her.

Ian took her hand. "You ready?"

"Yes."

The cops would find lots of blood and ashes and a decimated mansion, but there wasn't a single body left behind and any lab tests performed would reveal next to nothing as most of the creatures were from another world. Any traces of human blood they found would likely be written up as an unsolved murder mystery. Hannah, Mike, Ian, and Lily would all be presumed dead. And as for the trunk, once Lily and Ian were through and the portal closed, it would be locked forever; nothing but a wooden base inside. The only thing left of value was Ian's tree full of jewels. Perhaps this would all go down in history as the case of the missing jewel thieves.

"Good-bye," she whispered to the room; to planet Earth.

Voices sounded below in the front entrance corridor.

They climbed into the trunk and Lily pulled the lid shut above them.

Chapter 39

Passing through the portal was like stepping through a door.

There was no swirling whirlwind of a tunnel, no colors. Just one moment they were climbing into the trunk, the next they were climbing out in Alvernia.

They stood on a plateau of a mountain overlooking the land.

The ground was parched and dry. The great forest should have filled the expanse as far as the eye could see, but was nothing but dead tree trunks sticking up out of a foul-smelling wamp.

The sky above was overcast and everything was cast in a gray hue.

The others around her who had not been to Alvernia in many years looked around them with sorrow. Mike was pale, a look of grave indecision on his face, probably wondering if he'd made the right choice after all. Varkis stood with furrowed brow and slumped shoulders.

Ian put his arm around Lily's waist and gave it a gentle squeeze. "We mustn't despair. One day it will be restored to its former glory. It just needs time to heal and be replenished."

"But even if the land heals, we're all that's left," Varkis cut in gruffly, his voice thick with emotion. "We can't repopulate the planet."

"Take heart," Lily said, both to Varkis and everyone else huddling on the platform with them. "We've come too far to give up now. Appearances can be deceiving." With that, she stepped away from them all and walked to the edge of the plateau. Lifting her arms up in the air, she closed her eyes and began to sing.

The notes at first sounded like a flute but they morphed and changed into a full-bodied instrument entirely her own. The music of her vocal chords wafted down into the valley below. It was as if she'd bottled joy, peace and hope and transformed them into a melody. As she sang her body transformed, glowing so bright it was soon only an outline. The song hit a high note and the light burst forth from her, expanding and filling the entire landscape as far as the eye could see.

The ground beneath their feet moved and the parched soil grew moist. Cracks sealed and like a time-lapse video, grass and sprouts burst through the dirt and flowers blossomed, releasing their fragrance. Down the mountain it spread, turning the swamp land into a shimmering lake surrounded by mature forest; the gray sky at first mottled with blue and then fully blue; clouds dissipating like rapidly melting snow.

When she finally put her arms down, the light faded from her body, leaving her tremulous in its wake. Ian approached and took her into his arms. She turned to look up at him, smiling peacefully.

He kissed her temple.

A cheer erupted around them and they laughed, breaking the embrace.

"Hey, listen everyone—" Mike cut in. "Do you hear that?"

Somewhere off in the forest was the sweet trill of a song bird.

Callamous stamped a hoof, snorting. "Look over there," he said, nodding in the direction of a distant meadow. "Unicorns!"

Sure enough, a group of unicorns appeared from behind boulders and trees; many other creatures and humans gathering with them as well.

There *were* survivors after all—hundreds, perhaps thousands of them, of all shapes and sizes, heading their way—coming out of their hiding.

Lily rested her head against Ian's shoulder.

Morack's reign had come to an end.

Forever.

It was time to begin a new life, with her true love, as a guardian of the beautiful planet of Alvernia.

Short Story Collection
By Bekah Ferguson

I See You
Finding a strange item locked in a shed, a young woman grows
preoccupied with the cold case disappearance of a child.

The Jaguar
A spotted cub fights starvation when he's banished from his
family of black panthers.

These and more available free on the author's web site
bekahferguson.com